Transcendent

Transcendent

Katelyn Detweiler

VIKING

VIKING
An imprint of Penguin Random House LLC
375 Hudson Street
New York, New York 10014

First published in the United States of America by Viking,
an imprint of Penguin Random House LLC, 2016

LIBRARY OF CONGRESS CATALOGING-IN-PUBLICATION DATA IS AVAILABLE
ISBN: 9780451469632

Printed in the USA

10   9   8   7   6   5   4   3   2   1

Set in ITC Baskerville Std and Sympathique Pro

To Carebear and Denny,
again and always—you transcend every day.

Transcendent

Turning and turning in the widening gyre
The falcon cannot hear the falconer;
Things fall apart; the centre cannot hold;
Mere anarchy is loosed upon the world,
The blood-dimmed tide is loosed, and everywhere
The ceremony of innocence is drowned;
The best lack all conviction, while the worst
Are full of passionate intensity.

—WILLIAM BUTLER YEATS, "THE SECOND COMING"

Descent

WHERE WERE YOU the day Disney World was bombed?

This is the question that will haunt my generation for the rest of our lives. The twenty-fourth of August. An awful ghoul now, still so fresh in our memories, fading into a hazier shadow that will walk beside us until the very end. Our skin will prickle as we drive by a summer carnival or see pictures of an old castle and its arching, majestic towers; when we tuck our own children into bed someday, and they ask us to read them a story filled with princes and princesses. Because our fairy tale ended that day. Our castles were covered in blood.

This type of question is not new, of course. Each generation has its own markers, its own moments that were so devastating, so beyond comprehension, that the world stopped spinning when they first heard the news. The fundamental truths of their existence, their everyday certainties, stripped away and shredded into a million incongruous little pieces. Where were you when JFK was shot? When the planes crashed into the Twin Towers?

We come together in the wake of these epic tragedies, find a bittersweet new unity that bridges any former divides. We hope for change; we promise ourselves and each other that this won't happen again, can't possibly happen again. That this time, our world will be different.

Then it does happen, somehow worse than the last time, despite our intentions. Our world—it is not so different after all. Humanity is predictable in its restlessness and its frustration, its ability to cause destruction, and its ability to so soon forget.

But we cannot forget this.

If there is a next time—if there is a grander, more terrifying next time—the world will end. It must. Because how could there be worse? How could there possibly be anything worse, without our whole broken, beautiful world going up in flames?

My simple answer to this question is that I was lying on a bench in Brooklyn overlooking the East River, holding an iced-coffee cup to my forehead to cool my burning skin. It was a scorching August afternoon, the kind of hot that made New York feel like a city inside of a big, tightly sealed box, no holes to let in any fresh air—or to let any of the stale, putrid air out. But I always felt better being near the river, a wide open space with no delis or apartments or stoplights—just peaceful, flowing water. Water that had been there long before me, and would hopefully be there long after me, too.

I had gone to the riverside specifically that day because I was stressing about dumb boy problems—or more like my lack of dumb boy problems, since I had been flying completely, absolutely, not-a-single-kiss solo for every single one of my seventeen years. This summer I had hoped it was my turn, working myself up to flirt with Gabe Goodman, the sweet, soft-spoken golden blond violinist who had the seat next to me in Summer Strings Camp. Gabe had been flirting, too, I'd thought. Until I'd found him by the concession stands on our camp night out to the Yankees game the weekend before, his lips, tongue, hands making music with the absurdly gorgeous redheaded cellist.

It was fine; I would be fine. Summer and camp were almost over anyway. I only had senior year to get through before I'd be off to Juilliard or Berklee or Oberlin. Only a year before high school would be in the past, and I could find my real place.

My eyes had just started to close, surrendering to the heat, when I heard a woman's scream. I jerked up, knocking the coffee cup from my head, ice spilling over the ground. The woman was a few benches down, her face an ashy white, mouth gaping with disbelief as she stared down at her phone. Her other hand gripped the stroller at her side, pulling it in closer.

"Disney World! What kind of monster bombs *Disney World*?"

I grabbed for my phone, along with a handful of other people scattered along our path.

"What's happening?" asked one man who had stopped midrun, hunched over as he gasped for breath. We all looked back toward the woman, who was just now realizing that she had an audience. She stood up and plucked her little boy from the stroller before turning to face us.

"A series of bombs just exploded all around Disney World. Magic Kingdom. They don't know much yet, but they think thousands could be dead. Thousands of . . ." Her voice broke as she buried her face in her baby's checkered blue blanket. "Thousands of children."

I stood there frozen with the others, trying to make sense of those words. No one would bomb Disney World. No one was that evil.

The baby started crying, his tiny face scrunched in agony. I leapt onto my bike and pedaled, as quickly as I could—toward Park Place and my brownstone, my parents, my ten-year-old brother, Caleb—those wails following me the whole way home. No matter how hard I pumped my legs, how fast and frenzied, sweat pouring down my face, my back, the ride felt like it was happening in a vacuum of slow motion. The people walking, biking, driving in cars around me seemed warped and choppy, the noises distorted, nonsensical. All I could hear were the same words looping inside my head: *Magic Kingdom . . . bombs . . . thousands of children.*

I needed to see my family. I needed to know that my life—my bubble—was still the same as it had been that morning, the same as I had left it when I'd strolled out of the living room and hopped on my bike. I felt selfish, desperate, entirely alone.

I pulled into the entrance of our brownstone and threw my bike down on the stoop, flew up the front steps. My mom and Caleb were hunched on the floor in front of the TV when I pushed through the door, Caleb's head tucked against her shoulder as she stared straight ahead, unblinking. I collapsed on the sofa as my dad, home from work in the middle of the afternoon, walked in from the kitchen with two mugs of steaming coffee. He put the mugs down and wrapped his arms around me, but I couldn't look up. I couldn't look away.

The scene playing out on the television screen was utterly unreal. It looked like something from a gruesome apocalyptic action movie—fiction, with actors and fake explosives and carefully choreographed pretend destruction. But this was the news. This was live. This was happening. Masses of people screaming and running in a chaotic crush, smudges of black and red across their faces and clothes. Smoking heaps of rubble, bits of metal and cement and paper and a thousand other things I couldn't identify and didn't want to identify, destroyed beyond any kind of recognition. Sirens, flashing lights, stretchers, and bags, big, black, human-sized bags. The reporter was turning to interview a woman in a torn, bloodstained Snow White costume, her stage makeup smeared in bright clumps all down her face, and strands of blonde hair falling out from beneath her matted black wig. And in the background, past the carnage littered along what had once been the famed Main Street, U.S.A., I could see the crumbling remains of Cinderella Castle.

The kingdom, the fairy tale, was destroyed. And in its place, there was hell on earth.

Chapter One

"I CAN'T BELIEVE you convinced me to do this, Iris," Ethan said, eyeing the crowds all around us warily as he unrolled his yoga mat next to mine. "It's nine o'clock on a *Saturday* morning. And besides that, I can barely even reach my knees when I bend over, let alone do any downside dogs."

"It's down*ward* dog," Ari corrected him, already stretching, head pressed against her shins as she latched her fingers around her toes. Her long, strawberry blonde braid dangled, grazing the mat as she swayed side to side. "And a little yoga would be good for you. A little of any physical activity besides lugging around textbooks and comic books would be good for you."

Ethan flushed, pushing his thick, horn-rimmed glasses farther up the bridge of his nose as he plunked down on his mat. He closed his eyes, like a little Buddha with his plumpish belly and crossed legs, searching for some sliver of Zen to rise above Ari's abuses.

"I'm glad you came," I said, squeezing Ethan's shoulder. "I'm glad we all did." I craned my neck, checking Ethan's other side. "Are you good, Delia? Do you have room?"

She nodded as she pulled her thin black braids into a bun. Her light brown eyes, almost golden against her dark skin, scanned the long rows of mats behind us and in front of us. "This is pretty awesome," she said quietly. Delia was an artist, a painter mostly, and I could see her etching the scene into her mind, the faces and the colors, the tiniest details my eyes would always miss.

It *was* awesome. It was Times Square as we'd never seen it before—packed with human bodies as per usual, but today the bodies were barefooted and dressed in yoga pants, lined up in neat rows, mats side by side, so close they were nearly touching.

I had known the event would be popular—September was National Yoga Month to begin with, but more important, this was the one-month anniversary of the Disney attack. In honor of the victims and the survivors, the city had planned a massive open yoga class right in the middle of Times Square. It was supposed to be a morning for New Yorkers to come together and at least try to think positive thoughts, to breathe out a little of the crushing anxiety that had, in one way or another, affected us all.

I would have done yoga regardless that day—I tried to do it every day, even if it was only ten minutes of stretching and breathing on the mat—but today was special. Today I had dragged along my three best friends to do it with me, even Ethan, despite his worries about causing any humiliating public displays.

I settled on my mat, lying back so that I could see everything above me. The famed Times Square signs blinking, flashing down at all of us. But the signs, they were very different today. Businesses had replaced their ads with the faces of Disney. I watched a particularly massive sign high up on the Times Tower, one face fading out as the next appeared, a string of heartbreaking eyes and smiles. Little kids, teenagers, adults. There were victims of all ages that day, though it was always the faces of the children that stung the most.

The bombs may have erupted in Florida, but New York City had not gone unscathed. No place anywhere in America had gone unscathed. Countless families from our city had been down at Disney World that day, several from my own neighborhood in Brooklyn. I hadn't known any of them personally, but now, staring up into the flat blue eyes of the faces posted right in front of me—a brother and sister, both no older than four or five, their identical dark curls shining in the white lights of a small Christmas tree—whether I had ever met them or not didn't matter at all.

Ten thousand three hundred and eighty-nine.

Ten thousand three hundred and eighty-nine lives destroyed, and countless thousands of others injured—scarred inside and out, shells of who they once were *before*. Ten thousand three hundred and eighty-nine people who had, by random chance, by destiny, by some kind of fate I could never comprehend, simply walked into Disney World that morning. People who had expected dreams and were handed nightmares instead.

A new photograph filled the screen, and I gasped. This boy looked to be about ten or so, with wild, dark curls, deep golden brown eyes, and a big, gap-toothed grin. He could have been my brother Caleb's twin, a miniature version of my father. Had this boy had a big sister, too? A big sister like me, who had maybe survived, and who would never for the rest of her life fall asleep without first seeing this precious face burning behind her eyelids?

I shuddered, squeezing my eyes shut as I rested one hand on my heart, the other on my stomach, breathing deep to steady my pulsing nerves.

It had been a month, and we still had so few answers. The wondering made it worse. Most people were pointing their desperate fingers squarely at the Middle East—but there was no solid proof. All we knew for sure—or at least all the public knew at this point—was that a message had rained down over the destruction, small sheets of paper dropped from a single plane that no one could seem to locate.

> *Woe to you who are rich, for you have received your*
>   *consolation.*
> *Woe to you who are full now, for you will be hungry.*
> *Woe to you who are laughing now, for you will mourn*
>   *and weep.*

I couldn't get those lines out of my head. None of us could, I don't think.

And we couldn't stop worrying, either—what next? What more? The terror alert for New York City was especially high, given what an attractive target we made. There were uniformed security guards all along the perimeter of Times Square today, hovering, buzzing, their massive guns waiting at their fingertips—reminding us all that even here on our yoga mats, we weren't necessarily safe. There were no guarantees.

"Do you feel guilty sometimes?" Ethan asked, his soft voice almost lost in the murmurs of the crowd around us.

I opened my eyes, tilting my head to see him staring up at the signs.

"Guilty about what?" I asked.

"Guilty because none of us lost someone that day. Everywhere we look, there's so much grief and pain. But the four of us at least . . . the four of us escaped it. It doesn't seem fair, really."

"None of this is *fair*," Ari cut in from my other side. "This whole thing shows how completely freaking messed up our world is. We're all screwed."

"Ari." I sighed. "Don't say that. It's not *all* messed up. Look at everyone here today. Lots of people still want to do good."

"Aren't we really just here to help ourselves, though?" Ari asked. "We're here to feel better, feel like we're a part of something."

I frowned. I wasn't a religious person—I didn't pray or believe in the rules or traditions of any kind of church. But I did believe that there was something divine about this, all of these people together, honoring the victims of that horrific day—putting aside work, errands, brunch dates, normal routines to be *here*. I turned to Ari, meeting her piercing amethyst eyes, her contact color of choice since she'd moved to my neighborhood during our freshman year. Those eyes scared most of our classmates away, but that was probably Ari's intention.

She'd never scared me, though. I had spotted her in the music room on her first morning, and then again later that day in the cafeteria, all alone, looking miserable and stranded with her tofu dog and tater tots, and I'd invited her to sit at our lunch table. She'd shrugged and acted indifferent, but she'd sat there the next day, and the day after that, and then every day since. We had orchestra to talk about, the four of us—the one passion we all had in common, the obsession that kept us together no matter how different the rest of our personalities could be. Music. Me on the violin, Ethan the clarinet, Delia the flute, and Ari with her drums, beating and crashing and speaking with so much more than just her words. I'd loved her edge from the beginning—her daily uniform of black T-shirts promoting all her many eclectic causes. Today's shirt said *Straight Against Hate,* a regular in the rotation. Because no matter how tough she seemed on the outside, I knew it was mostly surface—deep down she cared about everything. She cared too much, maybe.

Ari and her mom had moved to Brooklyn to live with her grandparents after her dad was killed serving in Afghanistan. I always wondered what the old Ari had been like before all of that, if she'd smiled more, fought less. I would never know for sure.

"Iris?"

I snapped back to the moment, Ari's eyes squinting at me with curiosity—two sparkling jewels set against her pale, freckled face. But before I could reply, a voice rose out from the speakers, calling all of us to attention. I stood with the thousands of other bodies around me, lifting my hands high to the sky as we began our salute to the sun.

For the next hour, I would focus on all the positives in the world.

Because after Disney, it wasn't always easy to remember the good.

The bad was what we saw, what we heard, what we felt.

The bad was what slowly, alarmingly . . . was beginning to feel like normal.

After yoga, Ethan suggested a trip to Asia Palace, our go-to spot for bubble tea and dumplings after school. I passed, though, saying I had violin practicing to do. I had new pieces to start learning for the school's fall recital, and I still had college auditions to master. Ethan offered to rehearse together, but I needed to work through the new music on my own. That was how I always learned best; it was how the song became mine. I was glad to have spent the morning with my friends, but now I felt the pull to be alone, just me and the violin, my jaw nestled against the chin rest, bow in my hands.

"Mom? Dad? Caleb?" I called out, throwing my mat down as I stepped inside the foyer of our brownstone. No response. I started up the stairs, pausing after the first flight outside of my mother's office door. "Mom?" I tried again.

"Oh! Come in, sweetie," her voice called out. "I didn't realize anybody was home."

I pushed the door open, stepping into her cozy lair of books—everywhere I looked, the floor, the walls, the love seat behind her desk. Books and more books, printed manuscripts, mock-up covers, fan letters. This tiny room was my mother's kingdom.

Or not quite my *mother's* kingdom—it was Clemence Verity who reigned in here. Clemence Verity, her pen name for every single book she'd ever written—a total of fourteen, the last time I'd counted, all dark and enchanting historical fiction. I'd been allowed to start reading them after my twelfth birthday, and I'd devoured every story—the more recent ones in multiple drafts. Her words were magical, transformative. She had a gift. A powerful gift.

When my mom was here, in this room, she became someone else. Distant and mysterious, untouchable almost. She spent most of her days locked away, with no one but her colorful, crazy characters to keep her company.

Clemence Verity was an enigma, an idol. But as soon as she stepped outside these walls, into the hallway, down the stairs, she became my mom again. She became Noel Spero.

"Where is everyone else?" I asked.

She looked up at me, her eyes still blinking away the hazy stardust of her imaginary world. "Who? Where's who?"

"The rest of your family, as in . . . the people who live here? Dad? Caleb?"

"Oh, yes, *them*, of course." She smiled. "Dad's still on deadline for the Brooklyn Bridge documentary. They're doing some of the underwater reshooting today. He took Caleb to hang around the set so I could get some work done. Can I get your opinion on something?" she asked, motioning toward her computer screen. I nodded and moved toward her, hugging my arms around her shoulders as I leaned in close.

"You know I hate getting new author photos done, but my editor kept insisting. Apparently the last one was a decade old, and she thought I could use something new. Which do you like better?"

I squinted at the photos. They looked nearly identical to me, both black-and-white and shadowy, showing my mom's profile as she gazed off to her left at something or someone only she could see. The only difference I could pinpoint was the shape of her lips—in the first one, they were straight across, somber; in the next, they tilted upward, though just barely. But even with her face obscured, I could see why strangers sometimes assumed that she was my older sister. We had the same thick brown wavy hair, the same petite frame and rosy, dimpled cheeks. But my green eyes, bright and piercing, were nothing like her more subtle blue ones. She was young for a mom—she'd had me when she was still a teenager, a fact that she rarely discussed and probably never would have divulged at all if I hadn't done the math on my own when I was younger. *We were high school sweethearts, your dad and I. We loved each other very much, and I don't regret a thing.* That was all she'd say, the full story.

"The second one," I said. "The itty-bitty smile. Though why not take another one where you actually look happy? In color maybe, too?"

"Oh no," she said, grinning up at me. "Why would I do that? Authors are supposed to be brooding and mysterious. Noel smiles, yes, but Clemence is too serious for that kind of fluff."

"Ha," I said, letting go of her as I stepped back toward the door. "Anyway, I think I'm going to head to the park for a little while. I'll be back for dinner, okay?"

She nodded, her eyes already hurrying back to the screen. She clicked the photos away, leaving just a document, half filled with letters, some in red, some highlighted in bright yellow. "Okay, love you, sweetie. I'm just going to write for a little bit more. Then I'll start in the kitchen . . ." Her voice faded out as she crinkled her brow, focused on some word or thought that wasn't quite pleasing her.

I smiled. "I love you, too," I said, closing the door behind me. I walked the last flight up, to the third floor, where Caleb and I both had our bedrooms. My violin was propped against the old claw-foot blue wing chair by my window, sheets of music spilled on the floor around it. My mother had her words, and I had my notes. That had been hard for her when I was younger; hard to accept that I didn't love books the way she did, that I didn't study more, didn't need to get an A+ on the top of every paper. But the more she watched me play, the more she had understood. We weren't so different after all.

I plucked the violin from the chair so that I could pack it in its case to take it with me to the park. I paused, admiring the way the sun sparkled against the engraving on the tailpiece—*Dum Spiro Spero*. While I breathe, I hope. *Spero*, "I hope," in Italian and Latin. It was an important saying in our family; my dad was born a Spero, and I was a Spero, too.

Iris Spero.

While I breathe, I hope.

Looking at the words now, I was more appreciative than ever that my dad had surprised me with this engraved violin four years ago, a gift for my thirteenth birthday. I needed hope. We all did.

I threw on his old, perfectly holey New York University sweatshirt over my yoga clothes, grabbed my case and my purse, and started for the stairs. I walked quietly past my mom's door on my way down to the foyer.

It was a short walk to the park from our brownstone in Prospect Heights, a walk I'd made hundreds, probably thousands, of times in my life. I'd always liked to think of the park as if it were my own special backyard. A magical spot of green right in the middle of a huge, bustling city. You could get lost in it, just as easily as you could get lost navigating the gridlock of streets running up and down the boroughs of New York City. It was wild but orderly, sprawling but contained. It was my oasis.

I stepped through the entrance and breathed in the crisp air, so much earthier and more alive than the air along the sidewalks. I meandered along the runners' loop that circled the park until I reached my favorite spot, a bench overlooking the whole of Long Meadow—nearly a mile long, it was the longest stretch of unbroken meadow in any U.S. urban park. This much green had seemed impossible when I was a little kid.

The meadow was crowded with people this afternoon. Blankets stretched wide for picnics, fruit and cheese and barely concealed bottles of wine and beer; couples, legs intertwined as they read from their tattered-looking novels; kids throwing footballs and flying kites. This bench was my favorite because I could see the whole scene playing out, soak in all the different kinds of people, the movements, the conversations.

I sat down, watching the picnic closest to me—two families, the adults openly drinking Brooklyn Brewery beers and cooking skewers over a little charcoal grill, watching their adorable, waddling toddlers chase around a tired-looking dachshund. The littlest child, a girl with bright white-blonde pigtails and a sparkly pink jacket, plunked down on her bottom and tilted her head as she smiled up at me, giggling.

I waved at her, and then I popped open the case and pulled out my violin. I wrapped my hand around the bow, moving the violin into position. Holding it in my arms felt as natural to me as walking, as breathing. I paused for a few beats, closing my eyes as I let my fingers decide the next move on their own.

Before I'd made any kind of conscious decision, the first notes hit my ears. "Amazing Grace." I felt the music, slower and more somber than usual, the weight of the day pouring through me as I drew out each note. It wasn't until the last, lingering vibration fell away that I opened my eyes again. The girl was still sitting there, eyes wide as she watched me. She'd been joined by the rest of her playmates, too, another girl and two boys, all of them rapt in front of me.

"More, more!" one of the boys called out.

"More, more!" the other kids joined in, their little palms clapping, banging against their knees with determination.

I smiled and started up again, this time playing a Vivaldi piece that I'd used for a recital during my junior year. I couldn't remember Latin vocabulary or geometric equations or physics theorems from the month before— the week before, even—but I could remember every note of every song I'd ever learned to play. One song melded into the next, and I forgot my audience, forgot everything but the music, the breeze against my face, the smell of barbecue and grass and dirt. By the time I came back to myself, the kids had returned to the picnic blanket, their parents glancing at me appreciatively here and there between their conversations.

Evening was settling in, the daylight more golden, subtle shadows creeping in along the edges of the meadow. The picnics were dwindling, people folding their blankets, packing up their spreads of food. I wasn't ready yet, though, and I was certain my mother would still be too preoccupied with her writing for any thoughts of dinner. I started another song, "Ashokan Farewell," upbeat but still mournful in its way, hopeful but bittersweet.

On the final note, my eyes closed as I floated in the sensation of longing, of love and loss, that vibrated through me every single time I played it.

"That was nice," hissed a quiet, scratchy voice close to me—too close. My eyes snapped open as I startled, turning my head to see a stranger on the bench next to me. "You play here a lot, yes? I think I've seen you before."

I nodded, my heartbeat slowing as the initial alarm

subsided. I studied her as she studied me back, with her catlike eyes, gold flecked and so green—greener and more vibrant than all the grass and all the leaves surrounding us. She had on a ratty red flannel shirt that was a few sizes too big for her gaunt frame, and old corduroys that were smudged and torn around her knees. In contrast, her hair was perfection, pulled up in tight braids, the intricate patterns weaving flawlessly from front to back. She looked old to me, but I didn't know how much of that was the quantity of her years, or the quality of them.

The woman was still striking, despite the shabby clothes and the tired face, like the rare pigeon that made you stop and stare on the sidewalk, its midnight-drenched feathers speckled with deep purples and greens that shimmered like gems under the sun. Warm brown skin, arching cheekbones that made her big eyes seem even wider and more pronounced, regal.

"I'm Iris," I said.

She smiled, a tiny smile that showed just a peek of her surprisingly white teeth.

"Mikki." The word was whispery, almost lost in the breeze.

"Nice to meet you, Mikki. I'm glad you liked my playing. I always worry that I annoy people when I play here on the bench, but there's just something about playing outside . . . I get money thrown at me once in a while, too. If I forget to close my case, anyway. That's not why I do it. I just like to play, and I like when anyone wants to listen."

I stopped myself. I was rambling. It was those eyes, the way she watched me. Friendly, but intense. Unhappy, maybe. But of course she was unhappy. I looked down at the bags she'd dropped at her feet: a backpack nearly exploding at the zipper, a second canvas sack filled with bottles and cans and a woolly old blanket—it was probably everything she owned, her entire world in two bags.

"Anytime you want to play for me, I'm gonna come and listen." She reached out, her hand hovering above my knee, as if she were about to touch me—but then she stopped, reconsidered. Her small, bony fingers fell back toward her own lap, and she looked away.

"Definitely," I said, extending my hand, squeezing her shoulder. *It's fine*, I wanted to say. *I'm not scared of you.*

"I'll play for you again soon, I promise. But I should be heading back now. I told my mom I'd be home for dinner." *Dinner*. I flinched. What would Mikki be eating tonight? Would she be eating at all? I slowly pulled my hand away, reaching for the violin on my lap and putting it back in its case.

"How will I find you again?" I asked.

"You come here and play, girl. You come and play if

you want me. I'll keep a-listenin' for you wherever I go."

"I'll be like the Pied Piper, then." I smiled.

She looked at me, confused, a slight tilt to her head.

"Oh, nothing, just a joke." I stood up, cradling the case in my arms like a baby. "But I will be back, okay? With my violin. Bye for now, Mikki."

She nodded, and I started off toward the gate.

Her eyes, her beautiful green eyes, they stayed with me, though. Beautiful but tired.

Beautiful but sad.

Chapter Two

MIKKI WAS STILL on my mind the next afternoon as I scanned the long line of people filtering into the basement-level dining hall of Blessed Mercy Church. I'd started volunteering at their soup kitchen for an eighth grade community service project, and then I'd kept coming in, nearly every Sunday for the past four years. But I'd never seen Mikki here before. Or maybe I had, but she'd blended in—just one of many in the crowd of two hundred or so people being served each week.

No. Those eyes. I would have remembered her, I was sure of it.

"That's a lot of people," Caleb said, gripping my hand as we stood behind the kitchen counter, waiting for our serving jobs to start up. I squeezed back as I smiled and waved at a few of the regulars.

"You're right, buddy," my dad said from behind, leaning in to wrap both of us in a hug. "There are a lot of folks who need a little extra help. Especially now. That's why we're here."

It was Caleb's first time at the soup kitchen—he'd asked me after dinner the previous night if he could come and help out, too. We'd been watching a live Disney tribute on TV, a candlelit service being held in an area of the park that had been leveled and cleared. I said yes, of course, and my dad had insisted on coming with us. Dad had volunteered with me a few times before, though not recently. He'd been so busy with work that Sundays were usually his one and only day to sleep in. But Mom had needed the morning for writing, and they'd both wanted Caleb to have a solid enough support system this first time. Growing up in Brooklyn, he'd seen a lot of hard things at an early age—it was unavoidable. Still, though, it didn't get easier.

"Hey, Cal, can you help me with the rolls?" I asked, hoping to keep him too busy to just stand there and stare. Most people who came here were quietly appreciative, though there'd been more than a few outbursts over the years. Staring was enough to set it off—enough to make them feel like they were different, outsider, other. Like they were on display.

We started stacking baskets of potato rolls alongside the two big vats of hot, steaming soup. Caleb was silent as he lined up the rolls in perfect, orderly rows, squinting in concentration. I looked back at my dad, occupied with setting up little bowls of creamers and sugar packets by the coffeepots, feeling glad all over again that they were both here with me. It was a big volunteer staff today, nearly double the people we had most Sundays. But it had been that way every week since Disney. People wanted to feel useful. Even if there was no direct line connecting these people here to the families of victims and survivors, it was still something. It was community.

The first visitors stepped up to the counter, and I moved to ladle from one of the soup pots. Caleb stood close to my side, holding the basket of rolls out with stiff arms.

I smiled at the faces, many familiar, some strangers.

"Is that chicken noodle?" asked a young girl, maybe about nine or ten, somewhere right around Caleb's age.

"It is," I said, filling up the ladle, smiling down at her. "I hope that's okay."

She nodded, tight-lipped, but her bright eyes gave away her excitement.

I had started spooning the soup into her bowl, two heaping pours, when my eyes landed on a strange mark dotting the side of her face—tiny dark music notes, I realized, trailing from just behind her ear to the spot where her jaw met her neck. My hand faltered, a few splashes of soup landing on her tray. She seemed far too young for a tattoo, too immature to be marked by something so permanent. I caught myself staring and looked away.

"I'm sorry," I said, blushing. "I spilled a little. I'm too klutzy for this job."

"It's fine," she mumbled, already moving on to grab a roll from Caleb, and I shifted my eyes to the next person in line.

"Zane," I said, the name out of my mouth before I could stop myself.

It wasn't as if he knew me, after all, or as if I really knew him.

His slumped shoulders jerked upright as he shook back the hood of his ratty red sweatshirt. Deep honey-brown eyes stared out at me, sharp as blades against the smooth darkness of his skin.

Zane Davis. We'd never spoken, but I'd seen him in the school hallways often enough, and I knew what everyone said. I knew the rumors that had swirled around him like shadows since he'd first appeared at the beginning of our junior year. I didn't believe most of them—the biggest being that he'd used a pair of school-issued scissors to kill a kid who'd somehow disrespected his younger sister a few years back. That he'd gone to juvie and been released early, though he'd been part of a gang ever since and it was only a matter of time before he'd be locked up again. For real this time, now that he wasn't a baby anymore. Now that he was perfectly capable of making more rational decisions and following rules, but still chose not to.

Even I had always tried to avoid him—I walked a little faster when I passed him in the hallway, stepped a little farther to get out of his path. There was something unpredictable in the way he stomped around, in his rough, jagged movements.

"Hey, Zane," I started again, the words coming out a few octaves too high. "I'm Iris. I don't think we've ever . . ."

His hand jerked up in front of my face, halting me midsentence. "Stop. Seriously. You don't know me. And I don't want to know you." His anger was almost a physical thing, as present in that kitchen with us as his old sweatshirt, his scuffed brown boots, his dark jeans with rips and frays and covered in what looked like scrawled words and outlines in black marker.

This was the first time I'd studied him up close. I saw now the deep scar that ran against his jaw—and, just below that, a vinelike tattoo along his neck, ending just under his right ear. Scar and tattoo, so close they were nearly part of the same solid line.

The tattoo . . . My eyes shot back to the little girl, who was hesitating by the end of the counter, unsure if she should stay or find a seat.

Zane's sister, I realized, though at first glance they looked nothing alike. Her pale brown skin was much lighter than his, and she was slight and bony, her scrawny arms and scrawny legs poking out from a massive black T-shirt that hung down over her knees. Zane's shirt, maybe. But then I saw her cool gaze, barbed and birdlike, sizing me up. She had his eyes. A dark, molten gold.

"I'm hungry," the man behind Zane snapped, bumping his tray up against Zane's with an angry thump. "Keep it moving, man."

Zane shot him a withering glare, stalking off without soup or rolls. His sister trailed after him, nearly running to keep up, as they headed for the table farthest from the counter.

Rattled from the confrontation, my hand shook as I ladled soup into the next man's outstretched bowl, ignoring his eyes. He grunted when his bowl was full enough, moving on toward the coffee stand.

"Are you okay?" my dad asked, stepping up beside me. His eyes were fixed on Zane, across the dining hall.

"I'm fine," I said. "It was just a guy from school. I was trying to be friendly, but it didn't go over so well."

"Don't take it personally," my dad said, lowering his voice. "He's probably just not happy that you recognized him. People . . . like to be anonymous sometimes. It's easier that way."

I nodded. It was true—Zane didn't seem like the type to want anyone knowing his business, especially if his business involved relying on a soup kitchen to keep himself and his little sister fed.

The rest of the line was a blur, polite nods and tight smiles and strangers shuffling to get their soup and roll and dessert and coffee before there was no more left to be had.

"I'll be right back," I said to my dad and Caleb, handing my dad the ladle in case any last stragglers came up for more. "Just need a quick bathroom break." Zane had thrown me off balance, and it took all the strength I had to stay positive here. To stay useful.

I took a turn through a side hallway from the dining room, but stopped midstep at the sound of anxious voices just beyond the next corner.

"But where? Where are we going to stay tonight?" A girl, trying her best not to cry, judging from the sound of it.

"I'm not sure yet, Zoey, but we'll figure it out, okay? Trust me."

It was Zane and his little sister. *Zoey.* The little girl with music note tattoos.

"Can't we go back to that place where the people were all so nice? United City Mission? I liked it there."

"No," Zane said, sighing. "We can't. They only open it up for emergencies, bad weather, things like that. I just need a few hours to figure it out, okay? We'll be fine. I promise."

"I'm scared, Z," she said, her voice much quieter now.

I pressed my back against the wall behind me, squeezing my eyes shut to fight off the tears. I thought I was helping, but all I could do was spoon out soup once a week. And then I left and went on with my happy, normal life, and they left and . . . ? Went where? Did what? My family would probably get takeout tonight, like we did most Sundays. Curl up together on the sofa and watch an old black-and-white movie.

"What's wrong, Iris?"

My eyes flipped open to see Caleb in front of me, biting his lip as he watched me closely.

At the sound of his voice, I heard loud footsteps moving closer, saw Zane storming up next to us. Our eyes met, his stare accusing, hostile—defensive.

"Come on, Zo," he barked, clapping his hands as he started back for the dining room. "We're leaving. Too many snoops around here."

She followed behind him, her eyes averted to the chipped tile floor beneath us. Caleb and I turned, watching them go, before we looked back at each other.

"I'm okay," I said finally. "I just feel sad sometimes when I'm here. It makes me realize how lucky we are, though."

He nodded, his face looking very solemn. "I'm glad I came with you. But . . . but can we go home now?"

I put my arm around his shoulder, his shoulder that—I realized now, with a start—was only a few inches below mine. He was growing up, literally. He wasn't a little kid anymore, even if he'd always be my little brother.

"Yeah, buddy. Time to go home." I squeezed his arm as we started walking out, tracing Zane and Zoey's footsteps.

We were going home, me and Caleb and Dad. But where would they be going?

Where would be *their* home?

"You're lucky you came with me today," I said to Caleb, ruffling his dark curls as we made our way down our block. "It's the only reason I agreed to get Chinese instead of sushi. I was thinking about sushi ever since I woke up this morning."

"Sushi wouldn't smell nearly this awesome right now," Caleb said, grinning as he waved the big plastic bag of dumplings and fried noodles in front of my face.

My dad was trailing behind us, deep in a work call that had engaged him for the entire half-hour wait for our dinner. "But we can't possibly finish it all before Tuesday. Let's get Brian on the line and . . ."

I tuned him out, the film jargon, the deadlines, the names of seemingly very important people. "Whoever gets inside first wins all the fortune cookies," I yelled, breaking out into a run. Caleb screamed and bolted after me, his long, skinny legs pumping hard as his sneakers pounded the sidewalk. We pushed through the wrought-iron gate side by side, our hands reaching the knob at the exact same moment.

"Fine," I said, gasping for breath. "We both win. But Dad doesn't get any."

"I heard that," Dad said, shoving his phone into his back pocket as he started up the front stoop. "It doesn't count if you get more than one fortune at a time, anyway. It renders them all inaccurate." He grinned at me, his bright, gap-toothed smile instantly making me forgive him for being so distracted.

"Mom!" I shouted as we stepped into the foyer. "Food's here! Come down from your lair!"

"I'm in here," she said, her voice too close, startling me. I followed the sound into the living room, where my mom sat perched on the edge of the couch.

I instantly felt the wrongness in the way she was frozen, staring at the TV screen, a sense of déjà vu that made my arms prickle with goose bumps. It was like that afternoon in August, I realized. As if Disney was being bombed all over again.

"What's happening?" my dad asked, brushing past Caleb and me as he went to sit next to my mom, folding her in his arms.

She turned to us with dazed eyes. "They found the people who are responsible. They found the people who bombed Disney World."

I froze, my heartbeat slowing, pausing. There was something about the way she was staring back at us, her lips open but not moving, that terrified me. It was something worse than what any of us had expected. But what could be worse? What was *worst*? No matter who had done it, the result was the same.

"Americans," my mom said, the word slicing right through me, cold and clean. "It was a group of very angry, very radical Americans. They apparently have at least the leader in custody now."

"I don't get it," my dad said, his face bright red and twisted as if he'd been physically slapped. "Why—how—could people do this to their own? How could anyone be *that* ruthless?"

My dad had, like all of us—whether we would say it out loud or not—expected the culprit to be discovered in hiding somewhere across the ocean, on the other side of the world. Someone who had been raised from the bottle to believe that America was immoral and that scourging our specific breed of evil was worth dying for. That kind of hatred somehow made *sense* to us, in its own warped, terrible way. That hatred was founded on centuries of violence and conflict. But this—Americans having such extreme hatred for other Americans?

This turned the whole world upside down.

"They're reporting," my mom said, her voice flat and lifeless, "that the group is a community of disenfranchised, disillusioned citizens. People with no money, no say, and no power to change their circumstances for the better. A community founded on their shared outrage over the divide between the 'haves' and the 'have-nots' in this country." She sighed, wiping at the glistening edges of her eyes. "Disney, to them, I think, was the quintessential symbol of privilege and money. A symbol of a fairy tale that wasn't meant for them, a dream, a kind of life that they could never have. That their *children* could never have. It was, in their minds, a corrupt kingdom that needed to be destroyed."

I blinked, trying to absorb the weight of everything I was hearing. My mom sounded so composed, so eloquent and controlled, especially given that the news had only just barely begun to sink in. But she was a writer—processing the world in words came naturally to her.

"'Woe to you who are full now, for you will be hungry.'" The quote spilled from my lips, the pieces clicking into place as I heard them out loud.

"'Woe to you who are laughing now, for you will mourn

and weep,'" my mom whispered back, squeezing Dad even closer against her side.

The Bible verse that had rained down over the destruction—these terrorists had punished the selfish and the proud, all of us who had shut our eyes to their suffering.

But they weren't silent anymore.

And they had proven to all of us that they were now far from powerless.

GREED IS THE ROOT OF ALL EVIL flashed below the reporters on the TV screen. It was one of their slogans, the reporter was saying, a line from the terrorist group who referred to themselves as "the Judges." I shivered, and the hairs on the back of my neck stood on end. The name was so fitting. They *had* taken it upon themselves to be judges—they had pointed their fingers and slaughtered those whom they had deemed evil. They had acted as if they were God's messengers here on earth, silencing the sinners.

The caption SECOND COMING? appeared on the screen, bright white letters juxtaposed over a picture of Disney taken soon after the bombs had gone off. Mass destruction, bloodbath, toppled kingdom. I didn't know that much about the Second Coming—we hadn't been raised with Sunday school or Bible studies—but I knew the basics from a World Religions unit I'd had in school the year before. Christians believed that Jesus would come down again to earth, based on old biblical prophecies, and that he would judge the living and the dead. Salvation for the righteous, punishment for the sinners.

Just as the Judges had done now, creating their own version of the Bible's predictions.

Caleb stepped closer to the TV, his eyebrows furrowed in confusion. I wanted to erase all of these words and images from his mind. He was too young for this, too pure. He deserved to still have hope.

"If this is really a Second Coming, does that mean that Jesus was real? And now he's coming back?" he asked. I wondered how he knew so much about the Second Coming.

My dad gasped and my mom—my mom jumped up from the sofa and grabbed Caleb and me both by the hand.

"Of course not," she said, her eyes round, unblinking. "Don't say such a thing. Don't even *think* such a thing."

And then, without another word, she dropped our hands and ran toward the foyer, up the stairs. The door to the office closed with a loud bang.

I looked at Caleb, his eyes meeting mine, both of us equally bewildered.

"Well, that was weird," he said.

I turned to look at Dad, about to ask him what in the world had just happened.

There was a tear, though, just one. Rolling slowly, so slowly, down his cheek.

Chapter Three

IT WAS THE START of first period that next Thursday, four days after the news of the Judges had come out, and it was still all everyone could talk about, louder and angrier each day. My eyes were glued to my geometry notes for a quiz I'd have that afternoon, but my brain couldn't seem to make sense of line segments, coordinates, and theorems. I leaned my forehead down against the cool wood of the desktop and closed my eyes, trying and failing to tune out the voices around me.

I hope each and every one of them burns for what they did. Here first, and then in hell forever.

Can't we line them all up and blow their heads open execution-style? Or bomb them like they bombed all those kids? See how they like feeling their bodies ripped to shreds.

Maybe someone should kill their *kids, make those guilty bastards watch while it happens. Eye for an eye, tooth for a tooth, however that shit goes.*

Listening to it all made me feel nauseated—scared by how easily hate could fuel more hate. I was furious, devastated, sick over what the *American* terrorists had done. But did I want them to be tortured? Mutilated? Sentenced to grisly, exacting deaths? No, I didn't want any of those things. I wanted them to be punished, certainly. I wanted them to pay for their heinous crimes for the remainder of their awful, twisted lives. But I didn't want the rest of our country to stoop to their level. I didn't want us to pay back evil with more evil.

I didn't know the solution—but I was only seventeen. This problem, it was far too big for me, for any of us, really.

Friday, tomorrow's Friday, I reminded myself. I was so ready for a weekend, time away from school and from so many angry people. I needed my favorite Saturday morning hot yoga class, violin, the park. I wanted to find Mikki again, follow through on my promise to come back.

I was worried about my mom, too, who had been even more reclusive than usual after her strange outburst on Sunday. I still didn't get it, what had set her off so suddenly.

"Ethan, seriously? You're still freaking out about that calc test today?" Ari's voice cut through the room as she entered, but I kept my head down. "You could ace that stupid test in your sleep. I don't know why you actually insist on studying and stressing about these things. It's a waste of your time. And it's a waste of my time because I have to listen to you stress, when there are thousands of more interesting things we could be discussing. Like, for example, how ridiculously awesome my new cymbal is going to sound in rehearsal today. Much better topic." To an outsider, maybe this sounded harsh, but this was how Ari played. This was how she loved. Usually I was amused by her and Ethan's scathing back-and-forth, but not today.

"I'm so sorry that I care about my grades and getting into an awesome college," Ethan snapped back, though I could hear the smirk on his face without looking up. "I wish that you could bring yourself to care, too, friend, because I'm not going to support your broke ass when you can't find a job someday. Protesting doesn't pay the bills, you know."

"Ha. Protesting's just my hobby. And besides, I thought the four of us were going to become a famous indie rock quartet, so who needs a degree? Ari and the Misfits, that has a nice ring to it, doesn't it?"

A hand latched on to my shoulder, shaking me.

"You okay?"

I tilted my head, catching a glimpse of Ari's long braid hanging over my desk. "What's up with you, Iris? Who stole my radiant beam of sunshine?"

Ethan and Delia stood behind her, Ethan squinting at me from behind his thick plastic frames—one lens smudged, I noticed, with what looked like a fingerprint of doughnut frosting—and Delia standing on tiptoes, peering at me from behind him. Delia carried herself like a ballerina, smooth and subtle, but strong. She looked like one, too, with her braids typically twisted up tight in a high bun, her clothes plain and solid colored, unremarkable. Her face, her eyes were all the expression she needed.

"I'm fine," I said, looking up to meet Ari's intense amethyst gaze. "I just need the weekend. Some time outside these walls."

"You're so not fine," Ari said, tapping a chipped sparkly blue nail against my desk.

"I concur with Ari's assessment," Ethan chimed in. "You haven't seemed *fine* all week, Iris. I know everyone's been off with the news about the Judges and everything. But . . . you seem particularly low. Is there more to it?" He flopped down heavily in the seat next to mine, his overstuffed bag of comics and binders and textbooks ramming hard against our classmate Noah Kennedy's back. Ethan was too preoccupied with me to notice. But Noah, a big burly guy in a Giants football jersey who generally just ignored our existence—as most of the senior class did—jerked his head around to shoot a death glare. I caught his eye first, though, before he could say anything to Ethan, and smiled at him. He looked momentarily confused, but then he smiled back, just for an instant, before turning back toward the front, as if he'd entirely forgotten what had made him annoyed in the first place.

It's amazing what a smile can do.

"Of course it's the news about the bombing . . ." I started, looking over at Ethan. "It's what the Judges did, and it's what everyone," I said, waving my arms around the room, "has to say about it now. I think it's a normal reaction to be feeling a little troubled."

"They're total fucking lunatics, the Judges," Ari said, sliding into the desk in front of me, her legs straddling the chair back so she could still stare me down. "But you have to agree, they had a point, didn't they? Even if they went about proving it in a totally unacceptable and horrific kind of way. Disney is the symbol of so many things that are wrong with this country. I'm personally glad that they're not sure yet if they're rebuilding the park."

"There's still Disneyland, though," Ethan said. "And Disney in Paris, Tokyo, Hong Kong, Shanghai . . . It's not going anywhere, Disney. If they don't rebuild this one park, it's because it seems too insensitive—most people have enough of a conscience to not properly enjoy a theme park directly on the spot where so many people died. But people hate the Judges; they don't hate Disney. If anything, Disney sales are through the roof right now. People see the mouse ears as solidarity. As if wearing a Mickey shirt somehow supports the victims."

"Ugh, that is so shitty and twisted," Ari said, "and

so exactly against the point of all this. I hope to God that people at least start thinking about what motivated the Judges. Maybe start doing a bit more to deal with all the blatant economic disparity going on. Because it's not right—it's not *fair*—that some kids get everything, and some kids are lucky to have one decent meal each day. I mean, come on. All four of us live in gorgeous brownstones, but we're right up against people who can barely afford the rent of their tiny, roach-infested shitholes each month. And we didn't do a thing to deserve that."

It was true, to some extent, but I still didn't feel comfortable with this idea that the Judges had a point, no matter how warped and terrible it had become along the way.

"How else," Ari continued, "do you suggest these people should have gotten attention? You think protests would change anything? A crowd of *peasants* with posters screaming outside the castle gates?"

A few classmates in front of us turned in their chairs, their deep frowns and eyes like knives directed straight at Ari.

"*God.* Just stop talking, you crazy hippie freak. Do you even hear yourself?" The words came out in a snarl from a few rows over. I glanced up to see Carolina Matthews's perfect pink lips pursed in disgust as she rolled her eyes at Ari. A few classmates snickered. *Crazy hippie freak.* Carolina flipped her golden curls and turned away from Ari with a dramatic sigh.

"Hey. Ignore her. Let it go for now," Ethan said, batting at Ari with his calculus textbook before she had a chance to bite back at Carolina. But Ari's usual scowl had slipped, her blank face showing a rare trace of vulnerability. My heart ached for her, this real Ari. The Ari I knew was always there, just below the surface. "I know you wouldn't advocate killing thousands of innocent people for a cause, but you're sounding scarily zealous right now. Maybe just scale it down a bit. In public, at least."

"Whatever, Ethan." Ari sighed, staring off toward the whiteboard at the front of the room. Ethan opened his mouth to say more, but then flipped through his calculus book instead, his eyes squinted as he seemed to study the page he'd landed on.

Only Delia's attention was still focused on me. She reached out slowly and gripped my hand. *I know. I'm scared, too,* her eyes told me. I squeezed back. I'd seen the sketches and paintings she'd been working on in the past month; there was a new darkness there, a new gritty depth. Her art told me things she didn't always say out loud.

"Okay, guys," Mrs. Valentine said, rising from the chair behind her desk. "Less chitchat, more *Handmaid's Tale*. I asked you to think about whether this is a *feminist* work of literature or more a critique of feminism. Any volunteers?

Hm? No? Okay, then, Ari, how about you? I know you had a lot to say about feminism and *The Scarlet Letter* . . ."

I exhaled and slumped in my seat, letting Mrs. Valentine's and Ari's voices blur into a soft, calming hum in the background. I kept my head up, my eyes open and seemingly alert. But in my mind, I was doing what I always did to calm myself, to escape into my own beautiful bubble.

I played the violin. Brahms, Hungarian Dance No. 5. A loud, fast, unstoppable song. I could see the bow, feel the smooth wood even, so perfectly in my mind. The notes sang out, vibrating inside my skull, weaving a spell that made the rest of the class disappear.

Caleb and I sat at the kitchen table later that afternoon, piles of textbooks and folders sprawled out in front of us. I had to start brainstorming essay ideas for *The Handmaid's Tale,* and study for a physics quiz, too, but the thought of doing either was entirely unappealing. I considered giving up and taking my yoga mat outside to our tiny backyard, but I wanted to at least pretend to be studious, for Caleb's sake.

"What are you working on, kiddo?" I asked, tossing a balled-up Post-it Note across the table. It hit Caleb on the lips, then bounced off to the floor.

"Hey!" He squirmed, grabbing for the paper and grinning as he threw it back at me. Perfect shot, squarely between my eyes. "I'm looking up words that could be in the big fifth grade spelling bee next month. They pick a lot of local stuff, so I'm doing weird Brooklyn words right now."

I slid the paper he was studying across the table and read down the list.

Gowanus, Bedford-Stuyvesant, Ditmas, Canarsie, Livingston, Hoyt . . .

"*Schermerhorn?*" I asked, my mouth gaping open. "Seriously? They expect a ten-year-old to spell that?"

"It's not *that* hard, Iris. S-c-h-e-r—"

The loud trill of the door buzzer cut him off.

"I'll get it," I said to Caleb, though before the words were even out, the buzzer blared again. "*Jeez*, I heard you. I'm coming—stop jabbing that awful thing." I stood up and moved toward the kitchen counter, pressing down the SPEAK button on the wall panel.

"Hello?" I called out, leaning in close to the speaker. "Who is this?"

"I'm looking for Mina." A man's voice crackled into the kitchen. "Does she live here?"

"No, no Mina here. Wrong address," I said, pulling my hand back.

"Mina Dietrich? Are you sure? Or Mina Spero now, is it?"

I looked over at Caleb, who had put down his pencil

and was staring back at me with a dramatically raised eyebrow. "Mina?" he mouthed, his forehead crinkling.

Strange. My mom's last name *had* been Dietrich, before she'd married my dad and become a Spero. But her name was Noel, and I'd never heard of a Mina in our family. "We're the Speros, yes, but there's no Mina here. So I think maybe you got the names mixed up. Sorry." I let go of the button and stepped back. But he buzzed again, one, two, three times, and without saying anything to each other, Caleb and I both ran up the first flight of stairs and knocked on Mom's office door.

There were very few causes that would have warranted interrupting her right now; she was deep inside the first chapters of her newest book, a literary thriller set in early seventeenth-century Manhattan. She was especially impossible to penetrate when she was in the process of first building a new world, constructing each detail—each name, each costume, each piece of furniture, and each bite of food—with painstaking historical research.

But this overly desperate stranger—he seemed like more than enough cause.

"Mom?" I said softly, opening the door a crack and poking my head inside. "There's a man who keeps buzzing from downstairs, and he said he's looking for a Mina Dietrich. I told him that he must have gotten the wrong address, but he's being pretty persistent."

My mom's cloudy writing eyes snapped into focus, the content rosiness of her cheeks fading to stark white in just seconds.

"Mom?" Caleb asked, leaning in from behind me. "Are you okay? Do you know who Mina is?"

She pressed her shaking hands against the desk and pushed herself up to stand. "Did he tell you his name?" she asked, her whispery voice trembling as she turned to face me straight on.

I shook my head slowly, numbed by the shock of what I saw inside her cool blue eyes. Fear, anxiety, regret. Guilt. All of this from a random man asking about Mina Dietrich?

The buzzer was still going off in the kitchen, my mom flinching with each frantic jab from the stoop below. She balled her fists at her sides as she pushed past me and Caleb and onto the landing. But then she turned back toward us, her fear replaced by a stony resoluteness that was at odds with her usually soft, contemplative face. "Please let me go handle this. I need the two of you to stay right here. Okay?"

"But, Mom," I said, reaching out and protectively grabbing her elbow, "you don't even know who it is. I don't want you going outside all by yourself. Let me come, too. Please."

"No, Iris," she snapped, pulling away. Her eyes widened and she puckered her lips, glancing down the steps and toward the front door. "I'm sorry, I'm just a little shook up. But I need to do this by myself." She squeezed my shoulder and started down the stairs, giving us one last glance as she reached the foyer. "I love you two more than anything. And I'll be fine."

She lingered in front of the first door before the vestibule, one palm resting on the ornate carved wood. I turned toward my little brother. "Caleb, go to your room."

He shook his head and frowned. "No, I'm staying out here with you. I'm not a little kid anymore, Iris. I want to help."

I wanted to remind him that he had only just turned ten, still technically "little" in my book, but I stopped myself. "I'm going to try to see what's happening from Mom and Dad's window, okay? I want you to stay here for now. I'm sure everything will be fine, though," I added hastily, realizing how red rimmed and misty his eyes looked. "Mom wouldn't have gone down like that if she didn't think she could handle it. But still, I'm just going to quick check to make sure the talk is going okay." I gave him a fast hug and headed toward my parents' bedroom, with windows overlooking the street, and closed and locked the door behind me.

Caleb could run up to my room, I realized, or downstairs to the living room, though that view was more obstructed by bushes—but if I knew him, he'd wait outside my parents' door. He'd wait for me. I opened the window and leaned in close to the screen, which gave me a clear view of at least a small sliver of the stoop. A large, muscular-looking man in a faded leather jacket, dark jeans, and black work boots was pacing by the buzzer. I was certain that I'd never seen him before, and it was hard for me to fathom who in my mom's life I wouldn't already know. Could he be a fan? Most of my mom's readers were middle-aged women, though, so it seemed unlikely, unless he was there on business for his wife.

I heard the front door pull open, and the man halted, spinning around to face the entrance.

"Mina Dietrich," he said, his deep, booming voice carrying so well to our second-story window that I might as well have been on the steps alongside him. "I can't believe I've actually finally found you."

Who was this Mina? And why did he still think that he'd found her?

My mom slammed the door and stepped out next to him, pulling her light cardigan tighter against the late September chill. "Kyle?" she asked, her pale face drawn in disbelief. I cupped my ear closer to the screen, straining to hear her much quieter voice. "Kyle Bennett? What the hell are you doing here?"

Why had she answered to *Mina*? Why didn't she say that she was *Noel*, that he somehow had the wrong person?

"It's not like that," he said, raising his hands up in surrender. "I'm not here to start trouble. Trust me, if there's one thing I regret in my life, it's the trouble I've already caused you. That's the last thing I want right now."

"So what *do* you want? I haven't been back to Green Hill or seen your face in nearly eighteen years, and now you've somehow found me and are pounding the buzzer at my front door. Why? What could you possibly want from me now?"

Green Hill. He was from Green Hill? It was where my mom and dad had both grown up, a small town somewhere on the Philadelphia side of Pennsylvania. I didn't know much about it; my parents didn't talk about Green Hill often, and we'd never visited. My mom's parents lived in Jersey now, my dad's in Florida, so there wasn't much cause. Mom's sister, my aunt Gracie, was in Texas for grad school, and her only two friends from the Green Hill days—her only friends at all, really, other than the characters who filled her head—my "aunts" Izzy and Hannah, had moved away, too, after college. Green Hill had always sounded like a quaint, rustic old country village to me, like something from a folktale. Not a place that still existed for my parents, or for me.

But it did still exist, clearly. This man was proof.

"Oh, Mina," he said, his voice breaking as he clawed his hands through his hair. "Mina . . . My babies. We were at Disney. When it happened. Parker, though, he . . ." Kyle sobbed, sagging forward until he fell down onto his knees. "We lost Parker right away. But Ella is still hanging on. Just barely at times, it seems, but my little angel isn't giving up easy. My wife had some burns, too, but nothing life threatening. And I—I came out of it without a scratch. Not a single goddamn scratch. It's not fair. Why couldn't it have been me at least?" He lost it completely then, slamming his fists against the cement steps, a broken strand of *why, why, why* spilling out with his tears.

My mom ducked her head down, concealing her face from me. There was a long pause before she spoke again. "I'm so sorry, Kyle. I can't imagine what you must be going through right now." She took a few tentative steps forward, slowly reaching one arm out to rest on his hunched shoulder. "I will keep Ella in my prayers." She paused, waiting as his sobs slowed. "I don't mean to be insensitive, but . . . I still don't understand why you came to New York. I don't understand why you came to *me*."

"Because I know, Mina," he said calmly, wiping at his tears as he raised his eyes to face her. "I know that you never lost the baby. I know that you came here to protect her."

My mom said nothing to this, made no movement. He lifted her hand from his shoulder and clasped it between his palms, shifting himself until he was bowed down before her. "God is punishing me, Mina. He's punishing all of us, using the Judges to do the work. And I feel like these horrible things have happened to me because . . . because of how I treated you. Because I refused to believe in you. But I'm sorry now, Mina, I'm so sorry. I need you and your child. Don't you see? You're my only chance at the miracle I need to save my little Ella."

"I don't . . ." my mom started, backing away. He clung to her hand, dragging his knees along the cement to follow her. "Kyle, this is insane. I don't know what you're talking about. I lost my child that day. Everybody knows that."

My mom had lost a child? A *baby*? My heart was pounding in my chest. Nothing either of them was saying made any sense.

"No, Mina. You didn't."

"I did!" My mom successfully ripped her hand away this time, disappearing from my view as she pushed herself up against the door. Her voice was too insistent, though. Too forceful.

"That was *her*, wasn't it?" Kyle asked, his face lighting up as he jumped to his feet. "She's the one who answered when I first buzzed?"

"Kyle, no, it's all a mistake. We—I can't help you. You need to leave." My mom sounded terrified by his question, which only seemed to excite him more.

"It was! I can feel it." He squinted up to the second story and I jumped back, gasping. Had he seen me?

"I swear, Mina, all I want is for her to meet Ella. And for your forgiveness. No matter what happens after that, I'll leave you both alone for good. I promise."

"I'm not listening to any of this," my mom screeched, opening and closing the door before Kyle could stop her. I leaned forward again to see him standing there frozen, staring at the empty stoop in front of him with a dazed look on his face. Just as I was about to run out of the bedroom, he glanced back up at me. My entire spine erupted in a frenzy of cool, tingling goose bumps as our eyes met. I shuddered, folding my arms across my chest to warm myself.

He smiled—and that smile, it looked so hopeful. So *desperate*.

Achingly, frighteningly desperate.

I didn't say a word to my mother when she came back inside. Partly because I didn't know where to start, and partly because she waved Caleb and me off and shut the door to her writing room before we could ask a single question.

Caleb was—reasonably so—upset with me for locking him out of the bedroom, but his curiosity was stronger. He followed me in circles as I paced around the kitchen, clinging to my waist as he tried to get the story out of me.

"Tell me what you saw, Iris," he said for the fifth time. "Please? Why won't either of you talk about it?"

"It was nothing, Caleb. Just an old friend who was in the neighborhood. I could barely hear the conversation, anyway," I lied. He gave me a pouty look that made it clear he didn't believe me and sat back down to do more homework. After a few minutes he seemed completely absorbed by his spelling list again, as if the whole bizarre encounter had never happened. Life was so much easier when you were ten.

I couldn't think about homework. I couldn't think about anything but the conversation I'd just overheard. I replayed every detail, every word, but I couldn't make the fragments fit. Only my mom could give me any answers. I sat at the kitchen table staring off toward the staircase, trying to will myself to walk up the steps and confront her. *Stand up, Iris.* Move your right leg, your left leg, repeat fifty times, twist the knob. Easy enough. But then what? How would I start?

Mom, why did that man call you Mina? Why did he say that you lied about losing a baby? And why did he think that you— that we—would be able to help his daughter? How could anyone besides doctors help his daughter now?

Before I could make myself follow through on the necessary motions, though, the front door flew open. My dad exploded into the living room, tossing his bag and coat on the sofa. Just as he started to turn back toward the staircase, my mom's office, he seemed to remember us, looking over his shoulder to the kitchen for the first time. His eyes fixed directly on mine, and my heart skipped. He looked scared and anxious and guilty. He looked exactly like my mom had just an hour earlier. Whatever she knew, he knew, too. Whatever she was hiding . . . they were hiding it together. And they were hiding it from *me*.

He started to say something, his mouth open in a silent O. But then he shook his head and turned away from us.

"I wanted to check in with your mom about . . . something. Didn't mean to scare you guys, banging in here so early. I'll, uh . . . be back down. Soon. Stay here, though? Okay." With that he started back for the foyer, not giving us a backward glance.

"Now this is getting really weird," Caleb said. He looked over at me, his face scrunched up with worry as my dad's footsteps pounded up the stairs. I reached across the table and tousled his already messy black curls. He looked painfully adorable whenever he was upset, an exact smaller duplicate of our dad—with identical big brown eyes and dark lashes that seemed to frame a mind much wiser than its ten years.

"I'm sure it's all going to be okay," I almost said. But I stopped myself. Because I didn't really know that, and

Caleb didn't deserve to be lied to. He had every right to be as scared and confused as I was. I grabbed his hand and squeezed, catching his eye before we both turned back to watch the staircase together.

After what felt like an hour but had probably been less than ten minutes, my dad came slowly down the stairs, his footsteps much less urgent this time, more subdued.

"Iris," he started, not able to look up at either of us as he walked into the kitchen. "Iris, your mom and I need to talk to you about something."

"I want to know, too," Caleb said, still holding tight to my hand. "I'm old enough."

My dad sighed. "You're right, bud. And we'll tell you. I promise. Just not right now. Not yet. We need to talk to your sister first."

I could tell that Caleb wanted to protest, but my dad looked so weary—so upset and so unlike himself—that both of us numbly obeyed. Caleb dropped my hand and stayed in his seat as I stood and moved toward my dad.

When I got to him, he leaned down, resting his head briefly on top of mine. "I love you, Iris," he whispered. "Please just remember that through everything we're about to tell you. I love you so much."

We made our way to my mom's office, my dad closing the door behind us. He moved toward my mom, hunched in her desk chair, and gripped his hands around her trembling shoulders. I sat just a few steps away, on the edge of the small love seat crammed along the wall next to her desk.

"Iris." My name cracked on my mom's lips as she tilted her tear-filled eyes up to face me. "It's time for me to tell you. It's time for you to know . . . to know *everything.*"

Chapter Four

"THIS IS GOING to sound completely absurd," my mom started. "Completely, utterly ridiculous. It's not going to be easy for you to believe any of it, but I . . ."

"*Mom.*" I leaned forward, grabbing her hand. "Stop. Just tell me."

She nodded, swiping at her dripping cheeks with the dark leafy-green scarf that was more often than not draped around her neck.

"When I was seventeen, just your age, fresh out of my junior year, I waitressed at the big local pizza place in Green Hill. Frankie and Friends'. I was alone in the front one night, cleaning up after my shift, getting ready to leave, when a woman walked in. An old woman, very old—the oldest I'd ever seen—in a crazy getup, this old patchwork jacket, a big black cane. And these green eyes, the greenest . . ." Her voice broke again, and she clapped her hand over her mouth, muffling a sob.

My dad leaned in closer, whispering something in her ear that I couldn't quite make out. But whatever it was, it made her smile—a tiny smile, but still, a smile. And she was able to keep talking.

"I sat down with her, this woman, and we chatted for a little. I'd never seen her there before, which was a little remarkable for Green Hill. It's nothing like Brooklyn, of course—in Green Hill, everyone knows everything about each other. There aren't secrets there, not many anyway. This woman, she seemed lonely and harmless, at least at first. But then the conversation . . . the conversation became strange. She said that she *knew* me somehow, knew all about me. And that I was the reason she was there at all, in Green Hill."

She shifted in her chair, pulling her knees in toward her chest and hugging them close with her free hand. Her other was still tightly clasped in mine, dangling in the space between us.

"I started freaking out then, of course. The idea of this stranger coming for me, *stalking* me even . . . She told me that they were ready for me, *everyone* was ready for me. 'The longer we wait, the more trouble we'll see, and I think that the world has seen enough trouble, don't you?' That's what she said to me. I'll never forget it. And then she . . . she said that keeping me and the child safe was all that mattered, that we were so valuable. I thought she meant my little sister, your aunt Gracie, but when I asked, she said no, it was *my* child. *My* child who had to be kept safe."

She laughed—a sad, broken sound. It was garbled in my ears. None of this made any sense. Who was this woman? What did she have to do with me? With anything?

But then Kyle Bennett's words came back to me, all of them crashing down at once. He'd mentioned a baby, too. My *mom's* baby.

Before I could ask, confess to her that I'd heard their entire conversation, she started talking again. Her voice was low and heavy, determined to push through to the end, whatever the end could possibly be.

"Your dad walked in then," she said, that same little smile creeping back onto her lips. "He worked in the back of Frankie's, in the kitchen, but we hadn't met yet. He swept in just when I needed him, like my own personal superhero." She glanced up at my dad, and he bent down, pecking her gently on the forehead. Their gazes lingered on each other for a moment before she broke away, turning back to me. "I ran off and left him to deal with her, but not before she asked me to accept, to approve of, whatever crazy nonsense she was trying to sell me. And I said *yes*. I said yes because it was easiest, because it was the first thing that came out. And that was it. I put the whole encounter behind me. But I had the most memorable dream of my life that night." She closed her eyes and took in a long, shaky breath. "Bursts of light, the most intense colors. Colors I could never have imagined myself, colors I'd never seen before then. It was like fireworks, I remember thinking the next morning. But so much better." She paused, expectant maybe. Like she was waiting for me to put together the pieces, to make sense of what she was saying without her having to spell it out altogether.

I stared at her, my face likely as blank as my mind.

"Iris, this woman, she was talking about *you*," she said quietly. "*You* were the child."

My head was suddenly so cloudy, so light. I pulled my hand from hers and gripped the edge of the love seat.

"I don't understand what you're telling me," I said. "At all. You were pregnant? Is that what you're saying? With Dad, or with . . . ?" I couldn't finish the question. My stomach was now swirling as wildly as my brain, and I swallowed hard, fighting down the bile creeping up the back of my throat.

"No! Well, yes. But *no*, not like that, sweetie . . ." My mom slipped out of the chair, crawling until she was kneeling right in front of me, our faces now only inches apart. "I didn't realize until a few months after that night what it all meant. That I—that I was actually pregnant. The symptoms were all there, but I didn't see them. Of course I didn't see them, because I was a *virgin*, Iris. I had a boyfriend at the time, not your dad, but we'd never had sex.

Nothing even close. So there was no chance, none at all, that he could have been the father. I didn't believe that I was pregnant until the tests were staring me in the face. The doctor confirmed it, too, and then . . . then there really was no denying it. No denying that something strange had happened that night at Frankie's. Something *miraculous*, even. Because of Iris."

"Iris?" I asked, stunned. There were so many other things to ask, but—*Iris*?

"Yes." My mom sighed. "Iris. That was her name, the old woman. She's the whole reason you're here, sweetie. She's the one who brought you to me. And her eyes, those green eyes—they were exactly like yours. When you were born, I just knew. I knew that you were my Iris, too, that no other name could ever possibly fit."

"But how . . . how could anyone ever believe this? Anyone back then? How could I believe this now? What you're telling me, it's . . . it's not real. It can't possibly be *real*."

"Most people didn't. Not at first. Your grandmother, though—she was amazing to me. Unquestioning. Aunt Hannah was great, too. Your grandfather and Aunt Izzy . . . they took much longer to come around, though eventually, of course, they did. Surprisingly, there were some wonderful strangers out there, too; people from all over, who believed and supported me, came to my defense.

But not my old boyfriend, and not most of the people in my town, either, or around the world when the story spread."

The whole *world* knew her story? And her daughter—her own daughter knew nothing?

"They called me Virgin Mina. And some people got angry, Iris. I was . . . very controversial, to say the least. I was claiming to be a pregnant virgin, after all, and a lot of people couldn't accept that. It got bad, so bad that during one particularly violent protest, I got knocked down by some of the people in the crowd. So we decided to tell the public that I'd miscarried after that. That you were gone. Your dad and I, we ran away then. We came to New York. Changed our names. And here we've been ever since. Keeping you safe, just as Iris had wanted us to do. Your dad"—she reached out and pressed her cool palm against my cheek—"your dad believed me from the very beginning. He barely knew me, and he believed."

I squinted, staring at my mom's face as all of the odd bits and pieces of her story floated in the air between us, shimmering, weighted flecks of impossibility. I blinked, hoping that they would blow away, scatter beyond the reach of my memory. This conversation had been a dream, maybe, or some type of hallucination. Had Kyle even knocked on our door, or had I invented him, too? Where did reality end and this ridiculous dream begin?

A soft, high-pitched laugh bubbled from my lips. Of course my mom hadn't really said all those things! And my dad hadn't sat there nodding his head, so somber, scared to look at me as my mom explained that he'd actually had nothing to do with her pregnancy. No. He *was* my dad, half of my genes, my blood.

"Iris?" she asked, her eyebrows twisting up at the sound of my laugh. "I know this all sounds so wildly impossible. I know. I might as well be telling you that your father is Santa and that you're in line to take over the North Pole when he goes. Trust me, this was all incredibly hard for me to believe at first, too, even though I could see it happening to my own body. Even though I saw Iris with my own eyes. And not just that one time, either. I want to tell you more about her, more about all of it, but . . ." She sighed, pinching her eyes shut. "I think this is about all you can probably take for right now. You've always been different, Iris—maybe even you realized that? You've always been so special. The way you treat others, people that everyone else ignores. Remember Johnson? Even then you were so fearless, I was proud, but—"

"Stop!" I scrambled farther back against the love seat, farther away from my mom. "Just stop!" I was saying it more to myself than to them, trying to snap myself out of whatever bizarre enchanted fog I'd been trapped inside of. I wanted to get out. I wanted real life back. "This isn't happening," I said, grinding my palms against my eyes. "None of this is happening."

"Iris." It was my dad this time. Or, not my *dad*, according to this dream, anyway. My stepdad? My earth father? I laughed again before I could stop myself.

He stepped around my mom and crouched on the floor in front of me, resting his hand on my shoulder. "You need time to let these ideas all settle. Okay?" He pulled my head in to his chest, hugging me tight. "You can ask us anything you need to. You can talk to your grandparents, your aunt Gracie, Izzy and Hannah. We're all here for you, sweetie. And we have a video we can show you, too, a video I made of all of us back then, that we sent out to be aired on the news . . ." He paused, rocking me gently from side to side. "We were going to tell you, you know. Soon. I swear we were. But now that Kyle knows—the stranger who showed up to see your mom earlier—"

"I know," I said, cutting him off, my words muted against his soft flannel shirt. I pulled back, separating myself. "I was listening from your window. I heard what he said. That he thought Mom could help his kid somehow, that *I* could help . . ." The words trailed off, the bitter truth of it sinking in. Kyle had come here because he wanted *me*. He thought that I could make a difference—that I could actually save his daughter somehow. That I was some kind of solution.

"I'm so sorry that you heard that, sweetie," my mom said. "Because we certainly never wanted you to find out from anyone but us. I learned eighteen years ago how quickly stories spread, and how far they can go. I didn't want that to ever happen. Not again. Not with you." She shook her head, any last remaining color in her cheeks completely drained out. She was pure white, almost glowing in her translucence.

"Kyle Bennett," she continued, "he was a bully at my high school. He was never nice to me, called me Menius— for 'Mina the Genius'—because I was the Goody Two-shoes, the overachiever, and he held a permanent grudge after I'd gotten him in trouble for cheating once. And when I . . . when I was pregnant, he told the whole school the news. In the nastiest way possible, in front of the entire cafeteria. He blared 'We Three Kings' on a stereo and threw things at me, with his friends—condoms and baby oil . . ." She was shaking now, her thin wrists trembling against her knees. "And now he regrets that. He regrets how he treated me. And he's so determined to make up for it—because of Disney. He blames himself now, for the bad that's happened to him."

"You can't," I started, pushing myself up to stand, "you can't expect me to believe any of this. I'm some kind of miracle? I have no real dad?" I saw my father flinch, and I almost regretted saying it. But wasn't that what they were telling me? Wasn't that what they wanted me to believe?

"I'm still your father, Iris," he said, his voice low and rasping. I could tell that he was fighting to sound strong, to keep the tears from spilling down his cheeks. "I will always, always be your father."

"Well, you can't have it both ways," I said, balling my hands into fists at my sides. The words came out angrier than I'd intended, but suddenly all I felt was angry. Not confused, not disoriented, not numb. Just furious. "I don't even know your real name, do I? If Mom used to be Mina instead of Noel, then you're not really Joey, are you?"

Joey Spero. Joseph Spero. *Joseph*. The name clicked with a hollow thud in my mind.

They must have seen from the look in my eyes that I'd made the connection, gotten to the punch line of their cruel joke.

"The name Joseph started with a little teasing from your mom soon after you were born," my dad said, the words nearly a whisper. "But my name was Jesse back then. Jesse Spero. We decided it was safe enough to keep my last name—we were just two people in millions here in New York, after all."

I shook my head slowly, all my thoughts colliding at dangerous speeds. "Okay. So now you've told me this . . . this *story*. And what do you expect? You tell me that I'm some half human, half . . . half—what, God? Angel?

Messiah? Do I have a mission? A job to do? Can I fly off of buildings or bring people back from the dead? Tell me, please, what the hell am I supposed to do with any of this information?"

They froze at the words, their lips paused in gaping round circles. I shook my head and started toward the door, not knowing anything except that I needed to be outside of this house. Away from both of them.

"I don't know, Iris," my mom whispered. I turned back to face her, but her head was down, her face buried in her hands. "I don't know the answers. Iris—the other Iris— she said she'd be back when the time came. So I tried to be the best mom I could be for you in the meantime. But I don't know what comes next. I wish I did, sweetie. I really, really wish I did."

Somehow her looking so sad and weak just enraged me even more. "Who *are* you?" I asked. "Do I even know either of you at all?" The words burned my lips on their way out, but I couldn't stop the fire, red-hot and blazing through every last inch of me.

Before either of them could answer, I flung the door open and ran out of the room. I ran away from them before I let myself ask the real question, the question that was too scorching, too combustible to let out.

Who am I?

I didn't think to take a jacket with me when I left. Or my phone. Or my keys. I regretted the jacket mostly, now that the sun was setting and the cool early autumn air was cutting through my flimsy cardigan. But getting out of the house had been first priority, any kind of planning a distant second. My feet traced their usual path to Prospect Park, and the rest of me followed.

My mind kept looping through my mom's story. This couldn't be real—none of this could be real. But my parents had never been good at telling even the littlest of white lies. Or so I'd thought, at least. How could I tell anymore? They'd kept this secret, after all. For more than *seventeen years*. Still, the dread on their faces, the agony—it had all felt so real. They'd meant what they said, I felt eerily certain of that much, and that thought alone made my stomach clench in fear. Were they insane? How could my predictable, stable, rational parents disappear so quickly? Disappear and leave me with *this*.

I passed through the park entrance, and my feet kept moving, making my decisions for me, until I came around a bend in the path. My lungs heaved for breath. I stood at the entrance of the playground, paralyzed. No matter how many times I'd walked here in the past month and seen the signs and the flowers and the teddy bears—and the photos, those devastating photos—I wanted to sob all over again.

I stared straight into the light green eyes of the faces hanging up right in front of me—a boy and a girl, maybe even twins, they looked so similar, with their bright red hair and their freckled, dimpled cheeks as they posed in swimsuits by the ocean. There was an article taped to the poster. An obituary. Molly and Matty Michelson. Both of them gone. And the parents—the parents had both survived, somehow. Though, like Kyle Bennett, I'm sure they felt more punished than blessed to have escaped their children's fate.

I rested my palm against the cool gloss of the next poster over, a fiercely grinning little blond boy. There were small handwritten messages scrawled on every free space of the poster, prayers and wishes that he would recover. He was in a coma now, a sign explained, and he'd lost an arm, possibly his eyesight—possibly everything, since there was no way of knowing whether he'd ever wake up. Most of the words and pictures and offerings left at the playground—at playgrounds all around the city and all around the country—were about love. Love for the survivors and for the victims. Love for those who were still fighting and would probably always be fighting, never able to escape that day. But there was hate everywhere now, too. Hate for the Judges.

I closed my eyes and stepped back from the memorial, swallowing the nausea rising up from the pit of my stomach. I realized that I'd somehow managed to forget about my own problems in that moment, and for a second I was grateful. Then a pang of guilt flared through me. I was still alive. I had my family and my friends, all safe and healthy.

But I was no miracle baby, no daughter of any kind of god. I'd never believed in God; my parents had never taken Caleb and me to church, except for funerals and baptisms and choir recitals. They didn't identify as Christians—they'd always just said they believed in a greater power. A higher purpose. I believed in people, though. I believed we created our own destiny, our own happiness, and our own sadness, too.

And really, after this kind of tragedy, how could *any* of us believe in a god? How could any supreme being sit back and watch so many children be slaughtered—for what? For political power, for some sort of statement, a reminder of how egotistical and despicable America could be? We didn't deserve this. No one would ever, could ever, deserve this kind of suffering.

But of course, Disney World was related to what was happening to me now, wasn't it? Disney World was the reason Kyle Bennett had come to find my mother. Disney World was the reason he was so desperate for the kind of miracle that even doctors couldn't give him.

What if Kyle told other people? What if suddenly

everyone was frantic for something *more*, something bigger and better? If at least some people had believed my mom eighteen years ago, what was to stop them from believing now? From believing even more powerfully, maybe, because there was nothing else left. Hope was all we had now—the only thing left besides fear and hate.

It was all too much. I dragged myself toward my usual bench and curled into a tight ball along the worn wooden planks. But even when I squeezed my eyes shut, I could still see my mom's face. I could see the belief in her eyes.

There was something she had said that suddenly struck me now, like ribbons of smoke curling and coiling up from some deep, dark place inside of me. I was *different, special*, she had said, and I always had been. She had mentioned Johnson—a stranger I'd met at this same park when I was four years old: my very first memory. I remembered it partly, I think, because it was the first time my dad had *really* yelled at me—though I understood later it was more out of fear than anger. And it was also the first time that I realized there were bad things in our world, bad people even—but that I wasn't scared of them in the way other people were. I wasn't afraid.

I had been sitting with my dad on a bench by Prospect Park Lake, coloring a picture of the sunny, sparkling water while he read the newspaper. He must have dozed at some point, and I had gotten tired of coloring, so I'd wandered off toward a beautiful patch of wildflowers. There was an older man there, dressed in just a stained, too-small T-shirt and ripped jeans that were tied at the waist with a piece of rope. He was sitting on a ratty blanket with a cup of deli coffee, staring across the park, at nothing or everything, I couldn't be sure. I said "hi" to him like I would say to anyone, and when he didn't answer me back, instead of walking away I sat down next to him on the grass. I remembered that he didn't smell good, but that I didn't really care, and I tried my best not to crinkle my nose because I didn't want to hurt his feelings. I told him my name, and he turned to me, seeing me for the first time, and said that he was Johnson. I asked him if he lived outside, and when he said yes, I asked why. He started telling me about his life, mostly things that, at four, I didn't understand, and then all of a sudden my dad was sweeping me up in his arms, yelling at me for running off and yelling at Johnson—for what, I'm not sure, because he hadn't done anything. He hadn't done anything but talk to me when I had asked him to talk.

I saw Johnson a few more times after that, always in the same spot near the lake, though I was always with my parents, who kept a much tighter lock on me from then on. I would wave, though, and he would always wave back. Sometimes he would even smile. And then one day he wasn't there anymore, and I never saw him again. I would never know if he had died alone in a dark alley or if he'd decided to make a different park his home or if maybe, just maybe, he had found a job, a friend, a piece of hope. A better way.

But did wanting to be nice to people who happened to be homeless mean that my mom's story was any more believable? I was friendly; I was compassionate. I liked listening to other people's life stories. All of that was true, sure. But that didn't make me something more than or better than human. It just made me Iris Spero, the same Iris I was yesterday and the same Iris I would be tomorrow. Why couldn't that be all there was to it? Why couldn't that be enough?

As if I'd been thinking these questions out loud, I felt a soft tap on my shoulder in response. My eyes flew open to see Mikki looking down at me, those bright eyes filled with worry.

"Are you okay, Iris?" She remembered my name.

"I'm okay," I said, knowing that neither of us probably believed it. "How are you?" I asked, noticing how thin her patched denim jacket looked over the baggy flannel shirt and the same old corduroys from before. "It's getting cold so fast this year. Will you . . . do you go somewhere else? With winter coming?"

She shook her head, then turned her eyes up toward the sky. "I'll figure things out. I always do. Don't you worry about me."

"Mikki," I started, not sure what I was asking or what I wanted to hear. I'd only just met her the previous weekend, after all. I barely knew the woman. But I couldn't stop myself. "Have you ever . . . do you ever wonder if maybe, somehow, miracles are possible? Or that things happen sometimes that no one can explain? Not necessarily because of a god or anything like that. Just more that maybe our world isn't as black and white as we think. Things that seem impossible aren't impossible after all. Or maybe there's a different way of looking at impossible that suddenly makes it become possible. In some small way."

As soon as it was out, I realized how ridiculous, how insensitive it was to ask something like that of someone like Mikki. Someone who had maybe never had a single stroke of good luck, let alone some kind of full-blown miracle. I could feel my cheeks burning, and I turned to her, my mind racing for the best way to apologize.

But she was staring straight at me with a small smile on her lips that quieted me. "Now, I don't know for sure," she said softly, almost in a whisper, "but I think I'd want to believe, if I ever had the chance. Because if I knew one miracle had happened, any miracle, then I could hope for my own someday, right? Maybe it's just the believing that's important. You know?"

I nodded, but I didn't know. Her words were so eloquent, so simple and well articulated; I wondered how long she'd been on the streets, what had happened to drive her there.

We sat in silence for a little after that, until the lamps above us flicked on and I realized how long it had been since I'd run out the front door. No matter what I was feeling about my parents, I didn't want to scare them too much. I said bye to Mikki and gave her my address on a gum wrapper from my pocket, just in case she needed food, blankets, a warmer coat.

And then, one step at a time, I walked home.

I walked back to a family, a life—an entire identity— that suddenly no longer felt like my own.

Chapter Five

AFTER MY BRIEF escape to Prospect Park, my mom immediately came up to my room, asking where I'd gone, if I'd told anyone, anyone at all. I said no, I'd just been at the park, and her face lit up with unmistakable relief. "Thank God," she said, exhaling. "Please don't talk to anyone else about this. Not even Ari or Delia or Ethan. I want this to be our secret for now—as much as it can be, at least, with Kyle Bennett knowing—until we wrap our heads around what to do next. I know you're angry with me right now, sweetie, but *please*. Please do this for me."

I said okay, and she left me alone after that. I didn't like to keep secrets, not from my best friends, but I wouldn't have known how to tell them even if I hadn't made that promise. I needed to sort it out for myself before I could talk about it with anyone else.

Our family spent the next few days moving in quiet circles around each other, but my mom and I didn't have to be speaking for me to know that she was a complete wreck. She wasn't writing; she was barely eating. She sent Caleb to school with an empty soup thermos in his lunch bag two mornings in a row, and she was wearing the same old ratty *Les Mis* sweatshirt every day, not bothering to shower, judging by the look of the greasy knot on the top of her head. She unplugged our landline phone from the wall and let her cell phone battery drain to nothing. And on the fourth night in, she forgot that she'd left a teakettle on the stove at full blast until the screeching woke the rest of us up in a panic. We found her in her office, staring out the window into the darkness.

I didn't have any clearer reactions or explanations after a few days of thinking about everything. If anything, I believed it all less, now that it was starting to feel like a more distant memory. I went to school; I talked to my friends; I did my homework. I showed up for my orchestra rehearsal and my weekly Wednesday night private lesson. But I still couldn't fake normal, not really. Delia and Ari and Ethan all picked up on my weird mood, asked why I was being so quiet and withdrawn. And I lied. I said that a distant relative had passed away suddenly, one whom they'd conveniently never met.

But my family couldn't go on like this, and we all knew it. Caleb was suffering just as much as the rest of us, but was even more frustrated because he was entirely in the dark. After over a full week of pretending that we could still go through the motions of normalcy, I came home from school on Friday afternoon to find Aunt Hannah on her way out the front door. She grabbed me and squeezed me before I could even say hello, her lavender-scented blonde curls crushing against my cheek.

"Trust her, Iris," she whispered into my ear. "Your mom is the best person I've ever known." She let go of me and stepped back, her usually impeccable makeup smudged and her big blue eyes red around the edges. "I have to get going for an editorial meeting, but please call me any hour of any day if you want to talk. Okay, sweetie?"

I knew she meant it, even though she was one of the busiest people I'd ever met—the editor-in-chief of a wildly successful women's living magazine. She was too busy to have a husband or a family of her own, maybe—not that she'd ever had a shortage of admirers—but she was never too busy for us. She'd always been a second mom to Caleb and me.

"Oh, and tell your mother to plug the damn phone back in. Izzy is going crazy with worry, but she's traveling with the team right now and can't make it to the city for a few weeks." Aunt Izzy was an athletic trainer for a pro football team out in San Francisco, and she and her wife, Ellen, and their newly adopted baby, Micah, didn't make it across the country for visits much these days.

Hannah gave me one last tight hug before rushing off. I made my way up the front stairs, one slow step at a time, and opened our door to find my mom perched on the sofa in the living room, waiting. Caleb had tae kwon do after school on Fridays—so it would be just the two of us.

"I saw Aunt Hannah," I said, skipping the hello.

"I'm sorry." Her brow crinkled as she gazed up at me. "I hope she didn't bully you. I know how protective she can be of me. I haven't told anyone else yet . . . I didn't even mean to tell Hannah. She stopped by to drop off some magazines, and she knew right away something was wrong. I broke. But I wanted to give you time to process on your own before anyone else would start harassing you."

"Okay." I stared back at her, waiting for her to lead.

"I need to give you something," Mom said simply. She motioned to the thick yellow envelope resting on her knees, and I sat beside her, wary but curious. "I wrote this all during the year after I had you, before I started school. Your dad was always out trying to get whatever work he could scrape up to save money for college, and I was always alone, with you. Trying to decide how I would ever be able to explain what had happened. So I did the only thing I could think of—I wrote it all down while it was still fresh, every last piece of what I was thinking and feeling and seeing in those first nine months. I wrote a book, my first book, but I only ever wanted you to read it. When you were old enough. And once I finished this book, I just kept writing, and . . . well, here I am today. But I knew from the start that this would be the only book about *my* life. *My* heart. Everything since has been Clemence Verity's make-believe. My escape. Building worlds of my very own that could make more sense than this one that we're in right now." She took a long, shaky breath and dropped the envelope onto my lap. "Before you say anything else or decide anything else, I need you to read this. I need you to see the world the way I saw it, to experience it all as I did. Every single word of this is true, Iris. Every last one."

"I'll read," I said. "But I can't promise anything more than that."

"That's all I can ask of you right now, sweetie. Trust me—I know how hard all of this is to wrap your head around. You're not the first person I've had to ask to take a massive leap of faith with me. But you are definitely the most important. Your leap is the one that matters most."

I pushed up to stand, my head dizzy with colliding waves of anger and excitement. I wanted to just be angry, angry that this ridiculous lie was still unraveling, still seemingly nowhere close to its end. But the weight of the pages in my hand, the idea that I was about to read my mom's first book, a book that no one else in the world would see—I wanted to tear open every little crack that would give me a better view inside my mother's stunning, complex mind.

I went to my room and locked the door, threw myself on the bed, and then slowly, carefully peeled back the envelope. The top page was mostly blank, just a single quote attributed to Albert Einstein: *"There are only two ways to live your life. One is as though nothing is a miracle. The other is as though everything is a miracle."*

I closed my eyes and let the words drip through me, each one so solid and heavy that I could almost hear them echoing from deep inside my veins. What *if?* What if life was one constant stream of miracles? From the moment we first opened our eyes every morning to a world with sunlight and friendship and love, a world where machines flew through the skies and doctors took out old hearts and put new hearts back in, repurposed and re-created life with their own hands? What if I was looking at miracles the wrong way? What if we all were?

I looked back down and flipped to the second page, the page where my mom's story began. And then I started reading.

This is the end, but this is also the beginning.
    This is the story that I'll wait to tell you until life—
inevitably, I suspect—forces the truth to the surface. A

secret that I hope to keep buried until you are old enough to ask and understand your own questions. Old enough to know that life is not always what you expect, that re-ality is not always as neat and orderly as it may seem—and that there aren't always answers, as much as we want them, as hard as we may try to seek them out.

This is the story of how you came to be, of falling in love, of starting down new paths.

This is the story of a miracle.

I reread the last page so many times I could squeeze my eyes shut and say the words out loud verbatim. So I did, letting each word burn me, scar me so that I was permanently marked by this moment. This feeling that was coursing through me right now.

Belief.

Because as crazy as it all so obviously was—so totally nonsensical and preposterous, physically and scientifically impossible—somehow I believed that my mom was telling the truth.

I could hear my mom's voice take over my own, feel every last shape and sound of the words that had been sitting, waiting for me since I was just a baby.

Maybe I was delirious—the belief felt so strong be-cause it was after midnight, and I hadn't gotten out of bed once since I'd opened up the envelope eight hours before.

Maybe in the morning I'd laugh at myself for being so silly and gullible. My eyes felt fuzzy and out of focus. I needed food and water and the bathroom, all so urgently that I suddenly couldn't decide what needed to come first.

I sat up and flinched as tingles ran up and down my arms and shoulders, realizing just how stiff my body was from lying tense and still for so long. I stood and stretched, catching a glimpse of myself in the mirror as I arched my hands up toward the ceiling. The same messy brown hair, the same wide green eyes. The same easy smile with the same small chip in the front tooth from falling off my scooter and landing face-first on the sidewalk when I was eight.

I was still *me*.

No matter what I had read, no matter what I believed now, I was still *me*.

I left my room and walked down the first flight of steps, the second-floor hallway dark except for a bright sliver of light spilling out from beneath my mom's office door. I tiptoed past, creeping down to the ground floor. I used the bathroom first, and then quietly moved around the kitchen, chugging a glass of water from one hand while I spooned heaping globs of peanut butter into my mouth with the other.

Before I could talk myself down, make myself wait until the morning when everything might look different, I walked back up the stairs and toward the office. I tapped on the door once, softly. It swung open so quickly, I wondered if my mom had been crouched in front of it, waiting for me to come. She had known, of course, that I wouldn't be able to stop until I had finished, and that I wouldn't be able to stay away once I had. She was my mother. She knew me inside and out.

We both stood there in silence, taking each other in. And then, without a word, I hugged her. I hugged her harder than I ever had in my life, and she hugged me back just as fiercely. Because we shared more than just our blood and our memories now—we belonged to each other in a different, stronger kind of way.

"I believe you," I said, pulling away from her. "I don't know how or why, but I do. I just do. I still don't believe in *the* God or any other god, or Jesus and the Bible—I don't believe in any of that stuff. But I believe that something happened to you, Mom. Something special. Something totally crazy and unexplainable. I can't understand how or why, or who that Iris lady really was, but I don't think that you're lying. Not then, and not now." I took a deep breath, forcing a big gulp of fresh air deep into my lungs, before I kept going. "But I'm scared, Mom. I'm terrified because I don't know what any of this means. And I'm still furious with you, too. I'm furious that you hid this from me for so long, that you and Dad could keep such a massive secret.

How can I completely trust either of you again? Ever?"

"I'm sorry. I'm sorry that you had to find out the way you did," she said, reaching out to tuck my tangled hair behind my ears. "Please believe me, Iris, that I'd always planned for you to know everything. I knew deep down that we couldn't hide forever." She let out a small laugh, but it wasn't a happy one. It was tired, defeated. After all, she had already experienced the consequences of this story firsthand. She had been through all of this before.

"Do you think Kyle Bennett will tell anyone?" I asked, the question that had been buzzing around my head like an angry, blood-sucking hornet for the last week. My mom had already told me how he'd mistreated her, but now after reading for myself—after learning about the nasty things he'd done to my mom in detail—I was even more scared, even *more* angry. Kyle Bennett as a teenager had been a bully—the narcissistic star of the football team, with an adoring parade of followers trailing his every step—a bully who hadn't seemed to care who he hurt or why, as long as it had entertained him and made him seem cooler, more impenetrable. Kyle Bennett got his way. If he wanted some-thing, I had no doubt he'd fight until it was his.

"He kept calling before I turned off the phones," she said, her eyes still staring straight into mine. She didn't want to be saying this, I could tell, but she was. She had no choice. "And he came again, twice, while you were at school this week. I threatened to report him and he seems to have backed off, at least for now. But do I think we've seen the last of him? No. No, I don't, Iris. And Dr. Keller— Dr. Keller, my doctor while I was pregnant with you—she lied to protect me, told the world you had been miscarried after that awful protest. She retired soon after everything happened, moved with her family to Hawaii. But Kyle managed to trace her, too. Called asking her all sorts of questions, threatening to prove that she'd faked medical records . . . He's angry, Iris. And he's very desperate. Angry and desperate . . . that's a dangerous combination."

I squeezed my eyes shut, pushing back the cold nausea that rippled through my stomach. My mom put her palms to my cheeks and pulled me in closer. "I'm sorry, Iris, but I want to be honest with you. I need to be. And I have a feeling that this—him coming here—was just the beginning. I have a feeling that there's more to come."

The words struck hard, burrowing deep inside me where they'd be impossible to shake.

There was another question, though, that I needed to ask, a question that I should have asked before now. "Mom . . . do you believe in God? Because of this?"

"I've never known what to believe exactly, honey. Because there isn't a neat label for it. I just know that I believed in Iris, and I always will. She gave me you. And I pray to her still, your dad and I both. We ask her to keep you safe."

"Will I get to meet her, too?" I asked, the words tiny and frail, so paper thin.

"I don't know, Iris. But I certainly hope so."

I was up the next morning before six and knew that there was no hope of falling back to sleep. I'd been awake for most of the night anyway, my mom's words about Kyle Bennett looping through my mind. The radiators hadn't kicked on yet, so I gathered my quilt around my shoulders and started down the stairs to make a cup of tea.

The lights were already on in the kitchen. I hesitated for a moment by the door, but it was too late to turn back. My dad looked up from the table at the sound of my footsteps, a small mountain of *New York Times* sections sprawled in front of him and a mug of coffee in his hand.

"Hey, Dad," I said. *Dad.* My throat hitched around the word. A word that had felt so guaranteed, so obvious just the week before. Would it ever feel normal again? Could it? *How?* The idea that I didn't have a biological father hit me again, a full-force body slam, and I wished I'd stayed in bed. I hadn't felt the real weight of it the night before, too caught up in the strange power of my mom's words.

But I was gutted now, an entire and essential piece of my identity stamped out with one big question mark. I wanted to run over to him, jump on his lap, and wrap my arms around his neck. I wanted to never let go. But I didn't. I stayed where I was.

"You're up early, sweetie," he said, gently putting his mug down.

I opened my mouth, preparing to tell him about mom's book, about my late-night reading, but then I noticed the purplish-gray circles under his eyes. The way he was looking over but not quite *at* me. He already knew all about it, even if he hadn't actually read the pages for himself.

"I know," he said, shaking his head. "It's all seriously fucking bizarre, isn't it? The more you learn, the crazier it gets. But just like I told your mom back when it first started, we all need a little crazy in our life sometimes. Life would be so boring otherwise." He smiled. I tried to smile back, but my lips wouldn't let me. It felt okay to talk about it, though. It felt better than not talking about it, at least.

"How about this," he said, pushing the newspaper pages together in a messy pile. "Let's get out of here for a little, grab some food and some highly caffeinated beverages somewhere. This cup of coffee won't cut it. Let's just have some breathing time. The two of us."

"You're not working?" I asked, surprised. "It's Saturday. You always work Saturdays."

He shook his head. "Not today. I've been spending way too much time away. I want to be here more. For you. For Cal and Mom. Work can wait until Monday morning. So breakfast?"

I looked away, down at the floor.

"Please?" he said. "Just a quick meal. You don't even have to talk to me if that's still too much."

I nodded finally and turned back toward the stairs to my room, where I pulled a chunky green sweater on over the T-shirt and yoga pants I'd slept in and grabbed my jacket. There was a tingling in my stomach, an uneasy churning. I was nervous, I realized. Nervous to sit down for breakfast with someone I'd known and loved for my entire life.

Mostly known, I thought, cutting myself off. I hadn't completely known him—or my mom. Not until now.

We walked the dark sidewalks in silence, both knowing without saying where we were headed. Mueller's had been our place for as long as I could remember, a tiny mom-and-pop diner tucked away on a quiet little side street, too far from either surrounding avenue for anyone but locals to take much notice. It wasn't anything special, really, but their sunny-side-up eggs were always fried to perfection, not too hard on top, not too runny either, and we could both leave full for under twenty-five dollars—with a generous tip—which was phenomenal in New York City. Caleb

and my mom could sleep well into the afternoon on weekends, so these breakfasts had always been just us. Me and
Dad. Or they'd used to be, I realized, as I stepped inside
the jangling front door and breathed in the hot, heavy
cloud of coffee and butter and bacon. I couldn't remember the last time we'd been here. I missed this. I missed
him. Most of all, though, I already missed how things had
been and how things would maybe never be again.

We both ordered without looking at the menu,
waving our hellos at Mr. and Mrs. Mueller, who never
seemed to take a day off from their posts behind the
front counter. And then we sat, waiting, unfolding and
fidgeting with our napkin-bundled silverware, staring
down at the advertisement-covered paper place mats as if
we were suddenly both in dire need of a new chiropractor
or an accident lawyer.

"This," my dad finally said, pointing to the table,
pointing at each of us, "this doesn't have to change. It's
not going to change. None of this. I just need you to know
that." He paused, sighing, as he ran his fingers through
his gray-flecked black curls. "I need to hear you say it, too,
Iris. I'm terrified right now. I'm terrified of everything
that you're thinking about us. About what I am to you.
About what you are to *me*." His voice broke on those last
words, and I could see the tears he was blinking back from
his red-rimmed, tired eyes. "You have to know that I have

always felt like your father. Before your mom and I fell in love. Before you were even born. I always, always felt like your dad."

"I believe you," I said, partly because I knew it was what he needed me to say. But I also said it because he *had* been my dad for over seventeen years, had potty trained me and given me piggyback rides up and down the streets of Brooklyn. He'd taught me how to color inside the lines and, a few years later, how to hold a paintbrush. He'd held my hand the first time I tried to scooter on my own, down Vanderbilt Avenue, and swept me up when I fell and howled for the whole neighborhood to hear.

But biologically—biologically I was my mom and . . . I closed my eyes for a moment, the shock and the absurdity hammering down on me all over again. I could ask to get a DNA test, couldn't I? See who I was at a chemical level. But . . . then what? What if something *was* off about the results, what if doctors wanted to study me? No. I wouldn't be any one's specimen.

"I believe you," I repeated, pushing away the image of sterile laboratories and scientists and needles from my mind, "but that doesn't mean that things can instantly go back to normal. This is all still hugely weird to me. You and Mom kept an enormous secret. I can't just forget that."

"I know. And I'll give you all the time and space you

need." He reached across the table and squeezed my hand. "I have faith, though. We'll be okay. You and me."

I nodded, even if I wasn't sure it was really that simple. Maybe this was progress, but still—I couldn't help but think we had a long way to go.

"What about Caleb?" I asked. "When do we tell him? He's being tough about it, but he's smart enough to know that something very strange is going on. It's not fair to him."

He was quiet for a moment, but then he nodded, slowly. "You're absolutely right. How about we tell him today? It's Saturday, so we'll have the weekend together, all four of us. He'll have some time to process before jumping back into the routine."

"Okay," I said. "I like that idea."

We both fell silent again, until the waitress came over with our plates, our perfect bright yellow eggs.

"Can we please have some mustard?" I asked, just as my dad chimed in with a "mustard, please" of his own. We both wanted the mustard to drizzle with some ketchup over our runny yolks, our shared passion that made Mom and Caleb gag every time.

As the waitress turned away, we both reached at the same time for the ketchup already on the table. Our hands knocked over the glass bottle, and we lost it after that. He cracked up first, a loud, barking laugh that must have made everyone in the restaurant turn and stare, but I was too doubled over to notice, tears pricking at my eyes, my stomach aching.

"*Ketchup and mustard, please!*" I screamed, as if they were the funniest words and the funniest coincidence in the entire history of the world.

I was desperate to believe that this was some kind of proof. Evidence that we still fit, and that my dad was right. Someday, maybe we really would be okay.

It was hard to believe now, the cuts so fresh, raw and stinging.

But I hoped. Someday.

Chapter Six

MY MOM WAS hesitant about telling Caleb, but my dad insisted.

"Iris is right," he said, sitting next to her on the office love seat as I watched them from the door. Caleb was still sleeping, just above us. "We're a family, and we have to deal with this together. We can't keep leaving Caleb in the dark."

"I don't like it," Mom said, the words clipped coming out of her tight, frowning lips. "He's too young. He's not ready for all of this."

"We might not have a choice." Dad sighed. His voice was low, but still firm and assertive. "Listen, sweetie, you know as well as I do that this might not be our secret for much longer. We've always said both of them would hear it from us. So if that's what we still want, then I say we tell him. Sooner rather than later."

Mom shuddered at that, and he put his arms around her.

"Okay," she whispered. "You're right."

We let Caleb wake up on his own, and then eat his usual bowl of Honey Nut O's as we all tried not to hover around the kitchen, waiting for him to finish up. Now that we knew what was coming, none of us seemed capable of doing anything else while we waited.

"Hey, buddy," Dad said as Caleb rinsed his bowl in the sink, "can you come to the living room? We all need to have a little talk."

Caleb's eyes grew wide and worried as he dropped the bowl with a clatter onto the rack.

"It's okay," I said, rushing over to hug him. "It's not scary. Not really."

He nodded and let me lead him to the sofa.

My mom sat across from us on the old rocking chair, and Dad pulled over a footstool to sit next to her. She looked at him; he looked at her. They both looked at me. I shook my head. *No way* was this story coming from me. Caleb had to hear it straight from my mom's mouth, just as I had.

Mom blinked her eyes a few times, and then turned to face Caleb.

"Sweetie, this is going to sound ridiculous . . . completely ridiculous," she started. "But back when I was your sister's age, living in Pennsylvania . . ." I tried to listen to most of it, the same story, more or less, that she'd told me the week before. But now that I'd read the book, this version felt so empty, so bare-bones. It was all so much harder to believe without the intricate details, the sights, the smells, the feelings that had made the story come to life for me.

My mom finished explaining. The room fell silent, all eyes on me.

"Cal?" I asked, forcing myself to look at him straight on. "Tell me what you're thinking, buddy. I know it sounds pretty impossible, right? But the crazy thing is that Mom, she wrote a book about all of this. Right after it happened. I read it last night, and—I don't know, but I actually believe it. I believe it's all true. I don't know what any of it means, really, or what's going to happen next. But no matter what, I'm still just me. Same old Iris. I need you to believe that, more than anything else."

Caleb nodded, but he didn't say anything for a moment. He just stared up at me, his eyes oddly dark and unreadable.

"I need to think," he said quietly. "I'm going to go up to my room now. Is that okay?"

"Sure," my mom said, forcing a smile onto her face.

Caleb stood and, without looking once at any of us, made his way out of the room, up the stairs. We heard the door close from two flights away, and then there was nothing but stillness.

Caleb didn't say much for the rest of the day, just a mumbled "Yes, please," or "Can you pass the salad?" while we all ate dinner. I could see a thousand questions whizzing around behind his eyes, though. Even at ten, Caleb had a way of talking only when he was ready, and then saying only what was most important. He was oddly efficient like that, always going straight to the heart of the matter. I supposed that was what he was doing now, but the effect was unnerving.

I skipped the soup kitchen the next day to be at home with Caleb. He wasn't speaking to me still, but as the day went on, I started to notice that he was following me around the house, sitting at the kitchen table when I sat at the kitchen table, watching TV when I watched TV—even when I was playing old episodes of *Downton Abbey*, a show he usually couldn't stand.

It wasn't until I caught him refilling my glass of water on the table that I pieced together all the tiny little favors he'd been doing so subtly in the last twenty-four hours: pushing all the pillows to my side of the sofa when we watched TV, insisting on mushroom and black olive pizza the night before—my favorite, definitely not his—and doing all the dishes, including my own, before I'd even left the table.

The realization dropped in my stomach with a sickening blow. Was he that scared of me now? Scared that if I *was* some kind of Messiah, I had the power to determine his whole future, to send him off to heaven or hell?

Or, just as unsettling, was he *worshipping* me, bringing me water and scraping my dishes, like a beggar bowing down to Jesus in the Bible?

Both options were equally uncomfortable to think about. I didn't want to be anything or anyone but his big sister. Just Iris. Just the same old me I'd always been. The big sister who was a pretty decent role model, I hoped, except for when she left her wet towel on the bathroom floor or forgot to pick him up on time after school.

I couldn't take it, the wondering and the analyzing. It was worse than the truth of whatever he was actually thinking—or at least I hoped so.

"Cal," I said, patting the sofa next to me. He was perched at the other end, pressed up tightly against the armrest—as far from me as he could be, I realized, while still being on the same couch. "Come over here, buddy."

He nodded, scooting over until our shoulders were nearly touching.

"I know you're still thinking everything over, and I get that. It's how you work. But you need to stop treating me like I'm someone different. Because I'm *not*. I promise you, I'm not. Even though I believe what Mom told us, it doesn't mean that I'm actually special. I don't have any actual powers or anything crazy like that. Whatever happened back then, I'm still just like anybody else. Look," I said, tearing at a hangnail so that a bead of blood popped to the surface of my skin. "Okay, disgusting example. But still. I bleed. Just like you."

"Ew," he said, his face crinkling up in disgust. But under that, I could see a little smile. "You're nasty, Iris. You better not put that on me."

I pretended to lurch for him, just to see his flash of horror, and then I wiped the blood off on a tissue. "Gross, but point proven, right?"

"Maybe." He nodded, refusing to look at me. "But what about . . . what about what I asked last week? They said *Second Coming* on the news. Doesn't that mean Jesus would come back? So what if it means *you*?"

I froze, a ripple of doubt seizing me. *No.* None of this had anything to do with me. The Judges had created this destruction—there was nothing divine about it.

"No, Cal," I said slowly, breathing in deep to force some kind of calm, at least while I was facing my little brother. "Trust me. I'm not here to change the world. Because if that was the case, we'd all be in trouble."

Our eyes met, and I could tell he almost believed

me—that he *wanted* to believe me at least.

"I'm tired," he said quickly, standing up. "I'm going to bed. Good night, Iris."

He disappeared into the foyer, leaving me without my usual hug.

I sagged back against the sofa cushions, closing my eyes. So I hadn't quite convinced Cal yet, but I'd keep trying. I was still glad that he knew the truth—it was like ripping off the Band-Aid. Things had to get worse before they could get better.

Maybe it was time to tell Ari and Delia and Ethan, too, no matter what my mom had told me to do. After all, it wouldn't be my secret forever. That much was clear. And I didn't want them to hear it from anyone else but me.

I woke up that Monday morning determined. I'd tell my friends. Today.

Luckily I was on my own for the last two classes of the afternoon—geometry and physics—no Ari or Ethan or Delia. I waited until then to slip my phone from my locker and text them, asking to meet at four o'clock at Asia Palace. It was easier than saying it to their faces, at least to start. You guys were right, I typed, committing myself to telling them the truth. There is something I've been hiding. But no more secrets. Not after today. I had debated telling my mom that morning—I knew I could trust my friends with any secret, and deep down Mom probably knew it, too. But she was too scared. It'd be easier to confess to her once I'd already gone ahead with it. I'd apologize, and she'd forgive me. I hoped. It was already too late to go back.

Ari chimed in almost instantly. I fucking knew it! You suck at lying.

I love you. I just hope you're okay, from Delia.

Do you need me to pick up any of your homework assignments? Ethan.

The last ninety minutes of the day were excruciating—I couldn't have repeated a single thing either of my teachers said. When the final bell chimed, I raced to my locker, grabbed my bag, and then plowed through the crowded halls toward the front door. I wanted to bike to Asia Palace on my own, to clear my head. I had a little time to kill, pedaling around quiet Brooklyn side streets and rehearsing the conversation in my head, perfecting my opening monologue.

I stepped inside Asia Palace at four o'clock exactly, a trickle of cool sweat sliding down the back of my neck. The restaurant was cramped and dark and half underground, and rows of hanging wooden beads surrounded tiny round tables with cushy, low-seated chairs. There were no other customers; there never were at this time of day, which was why I had picked it for this afternoon. We'd be practically invisible there.

The three of them were already tucked into a back corner, sipping on bubble teas, and I saw a fourth cup waiting in front of my empty chair. Cocoa bubble tea, my favorite.

"Hey," Ari said, reaching out to swat at my hand. Ethan gave a little wave, and Delia smiled. "Glad you showed up."

"Of course." I peeled my jacket off, pretending that six eyes weren't boring into me as I took my time hanging it very precisely over the back of my chair. "And thanks for this," I said, holding up my cup once I could no longer busy my hands with the jacket. I forced a big gulp down, even though I had no appetite.

"So this is going to sound crazy," I said, my eyes focused on the dark bubbles of tapioca swirling around my straw. "I mean, really, *really* crazy. But hear me out, okay?"

"You know you can tell us anything," Delia said. "We're here for you."

I took a deep breath, put down the tea, and made myself look up, face them head-on. "All right. So. It started when a man showed up at our front door, almost two weeks ago now. He asked for my mom, but he called her by a different name. *Mina.* Mina Dietrich."

"But why . . ." Ethan started, but I held my hand up, waving his question off for now.

"I tried telling him he had the wrong address, but he was persistent, and when I got my mom . . . she was instantly upset. She recognized the name. I've never seen her so scared about anything in my life. So I eavesdropped from the window when she went out front to talk to him, and it was all super strange and confusing. He was from her old town in Pennsylvania, and he talked about the baby that she'd supposedly lost, and how he'd tracked her down here in Brooklyn because one of his kids had been killed at Disney, and he has another who . . . Anyway, he said he needed her help, and he thought she and this baby could somehow be the answer."

I could see hundreds of questions in their squinting eyes and their furrowed brows, but to their credit, they stayed silent—even Ari, which was its own special kind of miracle.

"So, very long story short, my mom and dad called me into her office later that day. And they told me the most outrageously ridiculous story I've ever heard, and I know already that you'll think it's equally outrageously ridiculous—maybe even more so because they're not your parents—but the most ridiculous part about it is that I actually believe it's true. They told me . . . they told me that when my mom was seventeen, she got pregnant. And I don't mean she had an accident with a boyfriend or had a crazy night at a party. She was a virgin. As in—*had never had sex*. At all. With anyone." I paused, sucking in a big gulp of air. "But a strange old lady came to her one night, or descended unto her, or whatever she did exactly, I don't know—but she asked my mom if she would carry this baby. Told her that the world needed it. My mom freaked out, said *yes*, ran away. A few months later . . . she realized she was pregnant. Her boyfriend dumped her; my grandfather stopped speaking to her. Aunt Izzy abandoned her. Word got out eventually, and it became this whole big thing with the media—"

"Holy. Shit." Ethan cut me off. "Holy, holy shit."

I started to quiet him again, wanting to finish now that I'd started and managed to get most of it out. But his next question made me freeze. "That was your *mom*? *Virgin Mina* was your *mom*?"

I felt my breath hitch, my heart skip a beat. "You've . . . you've heard about this?"

"Yeah . . ." he said, nodding his head slowly up and down, never taking his eyes off of me. "*Virgin Mina*. I read articles about her a few years ago when my parents were trying out their Buddhist phase, then their Kabbalah phase, et cetera, et cetera. I never could bring myself to care that much, except for when they got briefly into this one particularly creepy cultlike group and I was kind of horrified for them. The crackpot who headed it up claimed to be a god on earth, more or less. A modern-day deity. So I started researching other people who had made crazy claims like that, and . . . there's a lot on the Internet, Iris. About Mina. About your *mom*."

Somehow, in the last week and a half, the idea to research "Mina Dietrich" hadn't occurred to me. I hadn't felt the need to, I guess, not with my mom's book in my hand and more eyewitnesses than I was ready to face just waiting for their chance to chime in. But that seemed silly now, that I hadn't thought to dig in deeper, find out what people had not only said then, but had been saying in all the years in between.

"But if that's your mom, then . . ." His beady eyes widened behind his thick lenses. "Shit, Iris, *you're* the baby. All the people who suspected the miscarriage was fabricated were right this whole time. She went into hiding and she never came back out. Neither of you did. You've been in New York all along. And your *dad* . . ." He looked too stunned to go on now, one realization after another dropping down on him like bricks, shattering through everything he'd ever known about me.

"I'm still confused as hell," Ari said, her head spinning as she turned back and forth between us. Her purple eyes landed on me. "Let me try and get this straight. Iris, you're saying you're some miracle baby? Like your mom was some wild, modern-day Virgin Mary?" She looked over at Ethan, not waiting for me to respond. "And you're saying people believed this back in the day? Do *you* believe it?"

"No," he said, his cheeks flushing a deep red. "Or *yes*. Maybe. I don't know. *Damn*. It's crazy, Ari, but a lot of people ended up believing Mina. And when she was knocked down in a big protest that happened on her own front lawn, everyone thought that the baby died. Mina disappeared after that, fell off the grid entirely . . . and a lot of people ended up regretting the way they'd treated her. Regretted that they'd been so closed-minded about the impossible being possible—about actual, real-life miracles happening, here and now, in this world."

"That's why he showed up at our door," I said, finding courage—and maybe even a little pride—in Ethan's knowledge of my mom's history. She'd been important. Enough so that nearly eighteen years hadn't been enough to wash her away. "Kyle Bennett. He was an ass to my mom when everything happened in high school, and he claims he regrets it all now. He blames his . . . his losses on the way he treated her. His children's pain is his punishment. So he tracked my mom down and came up here thinking that she could help him and his family somehow. That *I* could help them somehow. Because I'm her baby. Because I must be . . . *special* in some way." I blushed when I said it, because I could never believe that part of the story. I could never believe that I was different from anyone else. I was no more likely to lay my hand on a Disney victim and magically cure them than anyone else on this planet.

"So you really believe this, Iris?" Ari asked, her volume cranking up with her increasing disbelief. "You believe that your mom got knocked up by some—by some divine force, and now . . . and now *what*? What are you supposed to do now?"

"I don't know," I whispered. "None of us do. The woman who came to my mom . . . she said that she'd know more when the time came. My mom has no clue, which is why she kept this from me for so long. She claims that they were eventually going to tell me, but I think she was hoping she'd be able to keep it locked away forever. She's terrified for me."

"Well, I don't know what to even say about any of it," Ari huffed, scowling at her empty cup.

"It certainly seems like you have *plenty* to say about it already," Delia said, the first words out of her mouth this entire time. Her voice was calm and steady, but there was a criticism in it, her narrowed eyes frowning at Ari.

This was Delia's role—the wise-beyond-her-years mediator that kept the rest of us in balance. I'm not sure we could have survived without her.

Ari pursed her lips as Delia turned to me and said, "I think you're brave, Iris, for telling us this. But I think we all need time to let it settle in. Before we say anything *rash* or hurtful. It's a lot to take in, even for your best friends.

Especially for your best friends, maybe."

"Exactly," Ethan said. "Very eloquent, Delia."

I nodded. "Of course. You guys need time." *But not too much time*, I wanted to say. *I need you right now. More than ever.*

Ari crossed her arms over her *Meat Is Murder* shirt and let out a long sigh. "Fine. I'll reserve immediate judgment. Only because you've always been a little crazy, and that's part of why I love you so damn much, Iris Spero. But this is pretty out there, even for you."

I gave her a weak smile, and then we finished our bubble teas in silence. They hugged me good-bye as we went our separate ways, but there was something off about it. Their touch was too light, too quick. They couldn't quite look me in the eye.

I climbed back onto my bike, my legs shaking.

Please. Please let the worst be over. Let us all move on from here.

I closed my eyes for a second and I wished. Not to a god, not to Iris, not to anyone.

I just wished.

Chapter Seven

"So I WATCHED the video last night," Ethan said that Friday, his eyes meeting mine from across the round cafeteria table. "I watched the video that your dad made— that, er, Jesse made? Joey? Mr. Spero . . . ?"

"Ethan," I said, cutting him off. I put my fork down, my appetite for the leftover tofu pad thai in front of me suddenly nonexistent. "He's still my dad. It's okay to call him that."

"Right." He nodded, his head jerking up and down harder and more enthusiastically than necessary. "Of course. Of course he is." He stumbled on, muttering a stream of extended apologies under his breath.

For the last four days, in the aftermath of my epic reveal, Ethan had sweated and stuttered, Ari had snarled and snapped at everyone even more than usual, and Delia—Delia was quieter than ever, which was no easy accomplishment. They were all still there at least, sitting next to me. I should have just been grateful for that. But they looked at me differently, talked to me differently. There was an uncertainty, a new awkwardness that had never been there before.

It was hard enough at home. Caleb had stopped acting like my personal servant, which was nice, but now he seemed to be avoiding me as much as possible—doing homework in his bedroom instead of at the kitchen table, going up to bed right after dinner. And my parents were mostly tiptoeing around me, trying, I supposed, to give me some space. But as much as I wanted to move on, I couldn't forget how long they'd kept this secret. I couldn't forget how long they'd lied.

I needed one place where I could feel normal again. One place where I could still just be me.

"Your *dad* did a good job on the film," Ethan said, adding extra emphasis to the word, letting me know I'd gotten my point effectively across. I fought the urge to clench my teeth. He was trying. "Have you watched it yet?"

I shook my head, looking away. My dad had pulled it out for me a few nights back, an archaic-looking disc that was now resting conspicuously on the coffee table, waiting. I'd confessed to him and my mom that I'd told my friends the truth—that I'd known I could trust them to keep the secret—and while Mom just nodded silently, Dad had said it was the right decision. That the one thing they'd learned for sure all those years ago was that you needed to be willing to trust the people you loved most. You had to take the chance. This video, he said, proved it.

But I wasn't ready yet to see it all so clearly with my own eyes. My parents' and grandparents' tears, the awful things people had said and done, evidence in living color that this had actually happened almost eighteen long years ago. I would, though, soon. I had to. I had to see what I could potentially be up against—now, again, present day—if Kyle didn't keep the news to himself. It was making me uneasy, his silence. Could he really have just given up so easily?

"It was pretty impressive," Ethan said excitedly, taking a huge bite of his mom's blueberry pie—she owned a bakery here in Brooklyn, and Ethan had some delicious pie or pastry in his lunch bag every day—and continuing on, talking as he chewed. "I mean, obviously, any film your dad made would be good, seeing as he's a fancy director and all now. But they were so young then. It's so raw. You just feel it all. You feel Mina, her family, her friends, their world. You just get it—you get what they're really going through. And you . . . I don't know, Iris. You *believe*. You seriously fucking believe. You can't not when you see the truth on their faces like that."

"Oh, please, *enough*. You're sounding like a crazy sycophant now," Ari said, tossing a crumpled napkin that hit Ethan dead center on his chest. "Take a breath before you pass out."

Ethan and Delia both glared, but I ignored her and this latest jab in the nonstop barrage she'd been hurling since the news had dropped. No one was safe from her lashing, not even inanimate objects. I'd seen her stomping on a sparkly Homecoming poster that very morning, for no other reason than that school dances "promoted and proliferated archaic assumptions about gender norms." She was frustrated, I assumed, because for once she wasn't sure what she believed. Ari was used to having a set opinion—she was used to being firmly pro or con. This strange middle ground, though . . . it seemed to be throwing her off entirely.

"Maybe both of you could just talk a little more quietly?" I said, peering out around both sides of our table. "I don't exactly want this spreading around the school."

"Since when do you care what these people think?" Ari asked. "Remember the time Carolina Matthews made sure the whole entire class knew that she'd seen you playing Monopoly at the park with some homeless women? She warned everyone to stay away from you for weeks, said you'd probably caught some crazy bird flu. And you just gave her that damn magic smile of yours and said, 'I'd choose sweet homeless women over cruel rich girls any day.' That shut her up."

"Oh, man, did I love that moment," Ethan said, grinning as he rolled up his blueberry-goo-covered tinfoil. "I am dying for some milk. I need to grab some before the bell and—" He stood up too quickly and lost his balance as his foot slid against the shiny linoleum floor. He grabbed at his chair with one hand, the dirty pie wrapper flying from his other as he toppled down to the ground. The foil ball, unfortunately, crashed directly into the forehead of a very unhappy-looking Bryce Peters, the reigning king at the end of the basketball team's table. The wrapper stuck there for a second, fused by the blueberry goo, until it slowly peeled back and dropped to the table. At Bryce's right was Noah Kennedy from our English class, who looked torn between laughing at Bryce's misfortune and kicking Ethan's ass.

Delia immediately jumped up, grabbing Ethan's hands and pulling him back into his seat.

"Are you okay?" I asked, leaning in closer. Ethan nodded, but his head was down, so low it was nearly resting on the table. The tips of his ears were flaming, and one side of his glasses dangled to his chin.

"God, that fat kid is always such a damn klutz," Noah said, loudly enough to make sure we heard it. "Do we teach him a lesson?"

"He's a total loser," Bryce said, wiping the dots of blueberry jam from his face. He picked up the wrapper and whipped it at Ethan, hitting him straight on the lips. "Not even sure it's worth my time to show him what's up. Besides, sitting with those three weird bitches is punishment enough . . ."

Ari's face turned instantly, shockingly red. She pushed back from the table to face Bryce, the legs of her chair making a hideous screech as they skidded against the floor. "Listen. I couldn't care less that you called *me* a bitch. Because you're right, I am. But my friends are the best people I know, and they'll be ruling this world after high school. You'll be lucky to get a job mopping the floors at your dad's coffee shop, and I highly doubt even he would want to spend that much quality time with you. So maybe you should focus the rest of your senior year on, I don't know, actually trying to be a *decent* human being before your whole life goes to shit."

"Ari," I said, reaching out to pull her back. Bryce and Noah and the rest of the kids at their table were laughing hysterically now, knocking their fists together and ranting about "that crazy bitch."

Ari shook me off as she sat down in her chair, those purple eyes dulled. Furious, I looked over at Bryce and Noah, shooting them what I hoped was my most disapproving glare. They caught my eye, the laughter sputtering out into silence. They looked disoriented for a few seconds, and then went back to their food and their previous conversations.

I turned to see Delia watching us, her brows twisted together as she glanced from me to Bryce and Noah.

"Sorry," Ari said quietly behind me. "I know you hate when I go off on people like that, but I can't stand to hear anyone talking shit about Ethan or—"

The buzz of the school intercom speakers interrupted her.

"Iris Spero to the main office, please. Iris Spero to the main office." I froze, waiting for more. But the speaker just hummed and then clicked off into silence.

Had something happened? Was someone in my family hurt? Had Kyle . . . ?

No. Please no.

"What do you think that's about?" Ethan looked up at me, frowning as he pushed his glasses back into place. "Do you think it has to do with . . . ?"

He let the question dangle.

"No," I lied, packing the rest of my food back into my lunch bag. "I'm sure it's nothing."

I stood up, my legs wobbling, shaking at the knees, and I gripped the back of my chair for a moment to steady myself. "I'll keep you posted, okay?" I turned my back to them, unable to last another second under the scrutiny of their anxious eyes.

The walk to the front office was a blur, the rows of lockers, the faces of students passing by, the feel of my feet hitting the tile floors all hazy and distant.

As I turned into the office entrance, I bumped hard into another student on his way out. I backed away, embarrassed that I'd plowed into someone in my daze. "I'm so sorry, I wasn't looking . . ."

I realized then just who the student was. Zane Davis, staring down at me from under the same big red hood he had been wearing at the soup kitchen.

"Hood down when you're in school, Mr. Davis," a loud, grating voice trilled from the office. He smirked, shaking it back.

"Iris, right?" he asked, his eyes not moving from my face.

"Good memory." I jammed my hands in my back pockets to calm my racing pulse. I was too nervous to deal with any more of his jabs, not right now.

"What's a girl like you getting called to the office for? Fancy award or something like that, I bet?"

"No," I said, looking down at the floor. "I don't know why, actually. But there's a lot of stuff going on at home. So I don't know, but . . . I don't think it's good. I'm sorry I bumped into you, but I kind of need to get into the office now."

For a second, that smirk of his slipped—replaced by a wrinkle in his brow that I'd swear was *concern*. But then, just as quickly, the condescending little grin was back. He didn't say anything else, just stepped to the side and then swaggered off down the hallway.

I watched him for a few seconds before stepping into the office. I gave my name to the receptionist, whose severely browed, sharp eyes and tight-lipped fuchsia scowl seemed intentionally crafted to make any student, no matter how guilty or how innocent, squirm with paranoia.

"I've been notified that a parent will be picking you up here in a few minutes. For an eye doctor appointment. Last-minute scheduling." She crooked one of those severe brows, as if she was suspicious about the nature of the pickup. I was suspicious, too, because I knew perfectly well that I'd just gone to the eye doctor two months before and, as always, was twenty-twenty. "You can be seated while you wait, Ms. Spero." She pointed one long, red-tipped nail at the row of plastic orange chairs along the wall.

"Iris!"

My mom stepped into the office behind me, a fake smile plastered on her face.

"Mom, what's—"

"So sorry about that," she said, cutting me off and

giving me a quick hug as she turned to the receptionist. "Completely forgot about this appointment. We're already running late, so let me just sign whatever you need, and we'll be on our way."

My alarm rose as I watched Mom at the desk, my brain running through all the worst-case scenarios. She latched her arm around mine as we swept into the hallway.

I opened my mouth to ask, but she shook her head.

"Everyone's safe. I promise. Let's get home. Dad's there, and Nanny and Pop came in from Jersey, too."

"But what . . . ?" I tried again.

"Not now, Iris. Home. And then . . . and then we'll tell you the plan."

I pushed open the front door, and within seconds, Nanny and Pop were hovering on both sides of me, my dad standing just off behind them.

"Sweetheart," Nanny whispered, squeezing the air out of me as she wrapped her arms tight around my chest. "It is so good to see you." I smiled into her soft curly gray hair, which tickled my nose as she leaned into me closer. I was a good head taller than her now, but she felt so steady, so solid, I was certain she could still pick me up and cradle me, protect me from anything and anyone.

Pop was less physically effusive, but just as sturdy,

towering above both of us as he rested his palm gently on the top of my head. "My special girl," he said, leaning down to kiss my forehead.

He'd always called me that, and I'd never, before now, wondered why. But now I knew. Now I knew why I was so *special*.

"Let's sit down," Pop said, guiding me toward the sofa.

"Did your mom tell you . . . ?" Nanny asked, sitting next to me as Pop settled on my other side. My mom sat on the sofa arm next to Nanny, and my dad plunked down on the floor right in front of us. I was completely surrounded.

I looked up, meeting Nanny's worried brown eyes for the first time. They were dry now, but the redness and the puffiness lingered from what had clearly been a morning filled with tears.

"No. She wanted to wait. Somebody . . . somebody *please* tell me what's going on."

All eyes turned to my mom.

"Sweetie," she started, her brow furrowing as she frowned. "I wanted to protect you from knowing, stupid as that sounds—but I can't hide anything, not anymore. I told you that Kyle had tried buzzing again, and calling, but . . . I've seen him outside now a few times. Just leaning against the tree across the street, looking up at the house. Watching us. Waiting."

Waiting. I felt the word tear through me like icy, clawed fingers.

"I saw him this morning, and . . . I couldn't help myself," she continued, shaking her head. "I just lost it. I had to go out there. I started yelling and screaming, asking him what he could possibly achieve by stalking us like this. And Kyle, he looked at me dead-on, said as calmly as I've ever heard him talk, that all he wanted was for you to meet his daughter, Ella. To spend some time with her. He said, 'Maybe I'm wrong, maybe it won't do a thing, but I need her to try. It's her *duty.*'" She shuddered as she said it, her thin shoulders trembling, making her look more fragile than I'd ever imagined possible. She was my mom. She was invincible.

"I said no, of course, and how dare he say it was your *duty*, and I moved to go back inside. But he stopped me. He said that if you wouldn't meet his Ella, he had no choice but to tell everyone the truth about you. That he'd tried to be patient, calling, waiting around outside, and that he'd respected your distance as a minor by going through me. But if we wouldn't do him this favor, he'd make sure the whole world found out you were here. That you were alive."

The room fell silent.

Pop wrapped his arm around me, pulling me in close.

"Your mom called us as soon as she came back in the

house," my grandmother said. "Asked us if we'd heard anything from our old Green Hill friends. I don't talk to any
of them, though. I used to keep in touch a little, but it got
too hard. I'd always change the subject when they asked
about your mom, and I could never talk about you. I hated
denying you like that. So I just cut all ties instead."

I nodded, numb.

"Your mom told us why she called . . . she told us that
you knew. Everything."

"I just don't get it. How did he find us in the first
place?" I asked, blinking back the hot tears threatening to
spill down my cheeks. "If it had been a secret for so long?"

I realized now, thinking about it for the first time, just
how discreet my family had always been. My mom had the
stock author photo on her website and her book jackets,
but always black-and-white, dark and mysterious, so it
didn't give everything away. She didn't do readings,
rarely appeared anywhere publicly as Clemence Verity
other than a few award ceremonies over the years. She
didn't blog, she loathed all forms of social media—now
I knew why—and she'd never been one to keep family al-
bums. My dad was on IMDb and other film sites—his job
made at least some Internet presence mandatory—but he
refused to post anything personal, and Caleb and I had
been banned from Facebook, Twitter, all of it, until we

were thirteen. Even then, I hadn't cared all that much. I hated being at the computer more than I had to for school.

"Oh, sweetie, it seems like anyone who wants something bad enough can find it on the Internet these days," Nanny said, hugging me against her chest. I shut my eyes and inhaled, burrowing deeper into her knobby knit cardigan. She smelled like cinnamon cookies and chamomile tea, cream and molasses and just a little bit of warm, cozy spice. "He'd probably had his suspicions for a while, about what had really happened to your mom. A lot of people speculated. Maybe he searched every Spero he could find in the country . . . And really, the how doesn't matter much, not anymore."

She was right. It wasn't the past that mattered now—it was the present. The future.

"So is that really everything?" I asked, turning to my mom. I felt a new anger rising up, resentment and distrust. "Was that all Kyle said? You need to stop keeping secrets to protect me. You should have told me he's been outside watching."

"You're right," my mom said, leaning in closer behind Nanny. "You should know everything. And there's just one more thing, really . . . The last words Kyle said to me, before I ran away and slammed the door . . . was that we'd 'robbed the world of a miracle.' He said it was selfish, doing what we did. That in protecting ourselves, protecting you, we took away something that God had meant to share with everyone."

"I'm . . . I'm m-meant to be *shared with everyone?*" I stuttered, the question so bizarre, unnerving on my lips. I pulled back and stared, baffled, at my mom. "Why? Does he really think I can bless people somehow? That I can heal with my touch? Make cancer disappear, undo brain damage, raise the dead? I can't wave my hands and make anything or anyone better. I'm not magic. I'm not *special.* Kyle has to know that—he has to, Mom." The words were tumbling out faster, louder, because they needed to understand, *everyone* needed to understand.

I wasn't a savior. I couldn't be.

Maybe I was a scientific anomaly, a slip of nature, a sign that there could be mysteries in this world. But if there had been some larger intention, some big grand plan—then it had broken down somewhere in the execution. Iris—the first Iris, the Iris who had started this all—had failed to achieve her goal, whatever that goal may have been.

Because I was as normal, as *human,* as anyone else in this world. There was nothing electric in my blood, nothing otherworldly radiating from my skin. I didn't shimmer, I didn't soar, I didn't walk on water or make myself useful at parties by turning water into wine or cheap beer. I wasn't stuffed with light and love and fairy dust.

"How do we prove it to him, to everyone?" I asked, desperate for a way to turn this around, to make all of it disappear. For good this time. When my mom ran away, she had simply hit pause. We were back in play now, but there had to be a way to stop—to put an end to all of the speculation.

To put an end to all of the *hope*.

"Do I go to Kyle, to Green Hill? Meet Ella and show them how nothing happens? Make a sick old lady poke and prod me just so they'll shut up about it when she doesn't suddenly rise out of her wheelchair?"

"Iris . . ." my dad started, talking for the first time since we'd sat down. "I don't think that's the answer. I think that sometimes people, when they're desperate . . . they can find a way to see what they want to see, no matter what."

"He's absolutely right," Mom said. "I had people begging me for pieces of my clothing, my hair, anything I had touched. I didn't give those people what they wanted—just once, to a little girl who'd needed something for her mom, and I . . . I couldn't say no. But I suspect that if I had sent my belongings, meaningless scraps of junk from my bedroom, they would have found a way to create their own miracles. Found a little shred of good that happened in their life afterward, and pinned it to the artifact. Pinned it to *me*." She sighed, her blue eyes cloudy and distant, like she was suddenly seeing too many memories, too many pieces of her past all flooding back in at once. "So no," she said, more quietly now, "I don't think just going back and showing them that you look normal, *seem* normal, will solve the problem."

"I don't just *seem* normal, Mom," I said, my voice trembling, with fear or anger I wasn't sure. "I *am* normal. You know that, right? You all know that?"

I spun around, my eyes skipping from Nanny to Mom, Dad, Pop. They were all staring back at me, their eyes so *full*, so full of something I couldn't quite place. Didn't want to place, didn't want to put into words. No one spoke, their mouths gaping, at a loss for how to answer this clearly very easy, very obvious question.

Pop let out a long sigh next to me, and I turned, grateful that he was finally going to put my question to rest, so that we could all move on. Start working on a strategy to dig our way out of this mess.

"Oh, Iris, sweetie." He smiled at me, a small, sad twitch of his lips. His blue eyes seared into mine, freezing me in their intensity. "Do you really not see, Iris? Do you not see what all of us here in this room see when we look at you? What we hear when we talk to you? Feel when we're hugging you, when we're even just standing near you?"

I stared at him.

Pop shook his head. "You really don't see it, do you? In that case, you'll have to trust me. When they meet you, they will know. They will know just how right they are."

Chapter Eight

"I DON'T UNDERSTAND," I said, when I finally found the air necessary to make words. "You're making no sense to me, Pop."

"You made me a believer, Iris. You read, I've heard, an account your mother wrote of the whole time?"

I nodded, my skin still burning, hot and itchy and a few sizes too small to contain everything happening inside of me.

"Then you know what a—excuse my language— jackass I was at the time. Even at the bitter end, right up until you were born, I didn't actually *believe* her. I loved her. I supported her, yes, in the end. But that was still very different from actually believing her story, believing that an honest-to-God miracle had happened in our very own family. Anywhere, anyone, and it happened to us. To my little girl." He sniffed, pulling out a faded, checkered blue hankie from his chest pocket and dabbing at his eyes. "But then you were born, and when I held you . . . Iris, I swear to God, the whole world spun into nothing all around me and it was just you and me and light, so much light."

"Pop . . . I'm your grandbaby. Your first grandbaby. Of course it was special. That doesn't mean it was a supernatural experience."

"Now, sweetie, understand that I've held other newborn babies whom I loved very much. I held your mom and Gracie, and I held my little Caleb just as soon as he was born, too. And they were special—they were all special. Every damn baby on this earth is special. But they weren't *you*. The world didn't shake itself all up the way it did when you were first put in my arms. I'm a practical man. A reasonable man. But even I couldn't explain how you made me feel from that very first second you breathed the same air I was breathing. And I still can't."

My world was spinning, too. Now, here, this very damned second in this very damned room. "No, you're wrong," I said, jumping up from the couch, breaking my grandmother's hold around me. "You're all wrong. You see something special because you want to see something special, because you *expected* to see something special. It would have been anticlimactic after everything you went through to be stuck with a normal baby after all. But that's what you got. A *normal* baby. And now I'm just a normal seventeen-year-old, who only wants to do normal things like go to school and hang out with friends and maybe even have a boyfriend one of these days."

"It's a lot to take in, I know," Dad said, his voice low, shaky. "This is *huge*, Iris. Gargantuan. You have to process it bit by bit."

"It's only huge because you guys are making it huge. You and Kyle, but he doesn't know any better. He doesn't know any better because he hasn't met me, so he can still pin his crazy hopes on me somehow curing his kid, curing the *world*, of whatever ailments need curing. So please, why can't I just go there now, at least try to make them believe that I'm normal?"

When no one answered, a new and terrifying question occurred to me.

"Mom," I started, focusing all my energy on keeping my voice steady. I stared into her worried eyes, needing to see her answer, not just hear it. "Mom, please tell me that you know that what Kyle Bennett was asking for—it's not possible. That I can't, in any way, on any level, help his little girl, as much as I would love for her to get better. That I can't help any of the kids who were hurt at Disney, or anyone at all. Tell me. Tell me that you know that. Please, Mom. *Tell me.*"

I saw the answer instantly—I saw the truth, the hope, and the fear that she didn't want to voice—and every last bit of me crumbled on the inside.

"I can't say that, Iris," she said, the words hitting my brain one at a time, as if they were floating out of her mouth in slow motion. "I don't really know, not for sure. But I can't lie to you. I can't pretend there's not a chance."

"So why?" I asked, barely able to suck in enough air to speak. "Why are you all here? What is the *plan*? What do you want me to do next, now that Kyle threatened to tell everyone the truth?"

"I'm scared for you, Iris," my mom said, "so scared. I think we should leave. Leave Brooklyn, leave New York City, until we can figure out how best to keep you safe. We'll find somewhere for you and me to go, as soon as tomorrow morning maybe, and Nanny and Pop will stay here for now with Dad and Caleb—"

"I'm confused," I interrupted, raising my hands up in front of me. My head was throbbing, splintering straight down the middle. "You're saying you think maybe I can *actually* help. But you don't want me to? You want me to hide? Is that what you're saying?"

"I'm terrified, Iris," she whimpered, like a child, a helpless child. "I just don't think you're ready for this yet, the chaos it would start. I think that first we need to get you away from here, far away, we need . . ."

I stopped listening then. It was as if every organ, every vein, every bone and blood cell, were suddenly in free fall, spiraling and plummeting with no net, no support system, no foundation to keep everything where it belonged.

Run away, just like my mom had? Leave everything? My friends and family, school, my violin classes, my college auditions, the fall recital? *No.* I wouldn't do it.

I turned and, with every last ounce of power I had left, ran up both flights of stairs, slamming and locking the bedroom door behind me.

They couldn't—they couldn't make me leave. I didn't know what I would do, how we would keep people away. But this was my home.

This was my life.

The hours right after were blurry, uncountable. I kept my door locked, despite everyone's frequent attempts to get me out. My mom was the most persistent, coming up every twenty minutes or so to plead her case through the door.

Ignoring the voices, I grabbed my laptop from the desk and settled back into my bed to search for something I should have watched days before. My dad's video on Virgin Mina. I needed to see it now for myself, see what Ethan had so passionately described to me.

I typed in "Mina Dietrich," and my heart thudded and went still. There were thousands of pages—*hundreds of thousands of pages*—with information about my mom. I added "documentary" to the search and narrowed the hits. I opened the top listing, a virtual shrine to my mother, though it looked outdated. Untouched because the creator had lost hope, maybe, or moved on to a new cause. And there, just below a long note about what my mom had meant to her, the role she'd played in this stranger's life— there was the video, a play button in the center of the box just waiting to be clicked.

So I did. I clicked.

I held my breath as I saw a beautiful old farmhouse in a sprawling green field, all lit up and golden in the morning sun. I held my breath as I saw my mom's much younger, much smoother, fuller face, as I listened to her read hate notes from the Virgin Mina website. I still didn't breathe as I saw Aunt Gracie and my grandparents, Aunt Hannah, my *dad*.

My mom's old pastor came on next, which I'd expected, since I'd read about this exact moment in her pages. But reading wasn't the same as seeing, as hearing. His words had seemed beautiful a week before, eloquent, when I was still naive enough—romantic enough, maybe—to feel enchanted by the mystery surrounding me. Now, though . . . now the words felt like a challenge, a dare.

We can only hope and pray and open ourselves to the possibilities that God can still reach down—can touch our everyday lives in ways that we've maybe never dreamed possible. We believe in the ideas that we read in the Bible. We believe in Jesus, in his mother, Mary. Why is it so hard to believe that miracles can still happen today, in our modern world? Ask yourself that, if nothing else. Why? Or, more appropriately, why not?

I steeled myself for the scene I knew, from reading about it, would be coming next—my mother, my hysterical, wailing mother, falling apart on Christmas Eve. She was sobbing as she crumpled in front of a life-size nativity scene, alone in a Sunday school room at her family's old church. Jesse—my dad—had been watching, filming, without her knowing. He'd recorded the image of this sad pregnant girl, transformed into an utterly unforgettable symbol because of her backdrop here—the Virgin Mary and baby Jesus, made out of construction paper and bits of real straw, their smiling crayon faces.

Seeing her, seeing Mary . . . it was too much. I snapped my laptop shut and curled into a tight ball under my blankets. Another knock pounded on the door, and I pulled my comforter up higher, wrapping it around my ears to muffle the noise.

At some point, the knocks faded away and I managed to drift off, lost somewhere in that hazy in-between state of consciousness. Suddenly I was younger, much younger, my body smaller and less sure of itself as I walked the halls of my old middle school. The specifics of the scene were achingly familiar: the smell of burned pizza crust and too-sweet sauce emanating from the cafeteria, the squeak of my new green sneakers against the shiny tile floors, the sound of my sixth grade social studies teacher droning on about the Battle of Gettysburg from an open classroom door. Something was about to happen. My skin prickled with the knowledge of it, the memory that was still snagged in a shadow, just outside my reach.

But then—the voices. Laughing, howling, the distinct crackling of boys who might be turning into men physically, but mentally and emotionally still had light-years to go.

I remembered those voices, that feeling, that day.

It was the moment I met Ethan.

I followed the sounds now as I had six years ago, drawn by some strong, innate sense that I was needed. That somebody needed me. I turned a corner and faced a boys' bathroom. The laughter was louder now, clearer, but beneath the glee and the pride, I heard another, softer sound, a sob, a plea. "No," a voice said, shaky and desperate, "please, no!"

"Shut up, you fat dweeb. You love math so much, start counting the seconds you can go without needing any air. Entertain yourself at least."

"God, he's so fucking heavy," another voice complained. "My arms are getting tired."

"Pussy."

"I'm not a pussy! He's the pussy."

"Agreed." Another round of laughter, the sound of slapping palms.

I didn't think—I didn't consider the fact that this was a boys' bathroom, that I was a girl stepping into out-of-bounds territory—I just put my hands on the door and shoved my way in.

"Stop." Even I was surprised by how calm I sounded, how strong and confident. "Stop. Now." I was staring at three hulking eighth graders, boys I recognized as some of the popular kids who hung around the gym entrance at the end of the day.

Dangling in the air between two of them was a fourth boy, upside down, unrecognizable because his face was hidden in the water of the toilet bowl below him.

The three boys stared at me, their mouths hanging open, first in amusement but soon morphing into what seemed to be more like wide-eyed shock.

And then, as if I had physically walked over, yanking down their arms, they let him go. Pulled his head back into the fresh air, placed him down—gently—onto his own two feet. They nodded at me, cheeks red, eyes turned down to the floor. The three of them shuffled toward the door, and one of them—the leader perhaps, as he'd been observing the other two while they did the dirty work, arms folded across his bulky chest—even mumbled what sounded like "sorry" as they disappeared into the hallway.

The bathroom was quiet, silent except for the slow sniffle of the lone boy who still stood in front of me, water dripping from his dark black hair, broken glasses dangling around his ears. We'd never met, but I'd seen him in the music room before, playing his clarinet.

"Thank you," he said, not able to meet my eyes.

I walked over and hugged him, not caring that I could feel drops of toilet water splashing down onto my shoulders.

"I'm Iris," I said, still holding him tight. I didn't know why I cared so much exactly, so deep down inside of me, but I did.

"Ethan."

The scene seemed to pause there—a fuzzy, glowing freeze-frame as we hugged—when my mom called through the door again, louder and more distraught this time, jerking me awake.

"Iris, *please*, open the door so we can talk about this. You wouldn't have to go forever, but just for now. Just until we figure out what to do in the long run. Let's get you out tomorrow. We can go wherever you want, honey, I don't care how expensive the flight is . . ."

She wanted me to fly out the next day. *The next day.*

No. I wouldn't do it. I didn't know what I would do

instead, but I could figure that out later. For now, I needed peace and quiet away from my mom's relentless pleading. I needed to be somewhere no one could find me, not my family, not Kyle Bennett.

Without making any kind of plan beyond that, I pulled my jacket on and grabbed my cell phone and purse. And then quietly—as quietly as I possibly could—I slid my window up and stepped onto the fire escape. I pushed the rusty ladder down slowly until it hovered just above the ground. Luckily my parents had insisted on fire drills every year when I was little, just in case. I knew how to work the ladder on my own, to make my getaway if necessary.

My feet hit the cement ground by the side entrance to the basement, and I wiped my dirty palms against my jeans. I started down our block, yanking the hood of my jacket up to cover my face. It was still light out. I would walk to the park first, and then decide where next. Walking was good. Walking gave me time to slow my thoughts, to take a deep breath with each step forward. Walking reminded me that I was just like everyone else, two feet on the ground, arms swinging, heart pumping in my chest. I was human. I was zero percent divine, one hundred percent mortal. I didn't need any fancy DNA tests to prove that.

I tried to clear my mind, to push all of it away, but I kept going back to the dream, the memory that it had brought back to me. Why *had* it been so easy to save Ethan?

Why hadn't the boys laughed me off, dared me to do something to stop them? Why had they looked at me like that, listened to me, *apologized*? Just like in the cafeteria earlier—Bryce and Noah, the way my stare shut them up so instantly . . .

No. Not now. There was too much else that needed to be worked out first.

I picked up my pace and was almost at the end of the block when I saw him, popping out from behind a black pickup truck.

Kyle Bennett.

Looking much bigger, much more imposing, now that I wasn't staring down on him from two floors up. He stopped just a few feet in front of me, blocking my path.

"I won't touch you," he said, his hands held high up above his head. But I had already jumped back, my legs banging heavily against my neighbor's iron gate. "I swear, I won't lay a hand on you."

"What do you want?" I asked, the words scratching up along my throat. My heart was pounding hard, racing faster than I would have thought possible without first exploding from my chest. "I can't help you. Whatever you may think, I can't help you."

"Well, I'm not so sure of that. And while I've had some conversations with your mom about all of this—about my sweet little girl—I wanted to give you the chance to answer on your own first. To make the right decision. *Please.* I'm begging you."

He turned away for a beat, lowering his arm a few inches so that he could wipe a stray tear with the sleeve of his leather jacket. His face looked so sad, so achingly pathetic, that I almost couldn't be afraid of him. There was hardly room for anything but pity.

But that didn't change the situation. The answer was the same.

"I'm sorry, but . . . I can't help you. Even if I wanted to. I can't." I thought about my idea from earlier—going to Green Hill to disprove him, to disprove everyone. But what if my parents were right? What if that only made everything worse, made people even more fanatical? I couldn't do it. I couldn't take the risk. "I can't," I repeated, louder this time.

Kyle shook his head and spat on the sidewalk. "Fine. *Fine.* I tried my goddamned best." Any trace of sadness was gone from his face now—there was only fury, red and raw and burning hot. He flung open the front door of the truck and jumped inside. "I'm done with being nice, but don't think you've seen the last of me," he said, his lips curling up in a terrifying snarl. "This was just the first round." He slammed the door shut, the engine roaring to life. I stood paralyzed, watching as he drove off down the street. My eyes lingered even after he disappeared around the corner. Back to Green Hill and Ella.

I probably should have turned right around, run straight up my front steps, but—no. This was even more cause to sort everything out—to make sure that things like this wouldn't keep happening. I needed to keep Kyle away for good, to end this ridiculous misunderstanding once and for all.

And so I kept walking, one foot in front of the other, away from Kyle, away from home.

I passed through Grand Army Plaza, feeling dwarfed as always by the grandness of the Soldiers' and Sailors' Arch, the towering, majestic Brooklyn Public Library, and the wide pillared park entrance just in front of me. I walked until I came to my bench, then immediately regretted that I hadn't thought to bring my violin. My shaking fingers ached for the bow, distraction.

I stared off into space, my thoughts whirring in an endless vortex, an ominous black tunnel leading nowhere I could see. *Where should I go? What should I do?*

One of my friends' houses, maybe? They were acting so weird, though, and I was too tired to play normal. Besides, if their parents got a whiff of anything odd, I'd be sent straight back home anyway.

I glanced up, my eyes catching on some movement across the meadow—a woman sitting down near a small flock of pigeons.

Mikki? I squinted.

It *was* Mikki, tearing off tiny chunks of bread, tossing the bits into the circle. It was a relief to see her, to see anyone familiar. I didn't want to be alone right now—even if Kyle was probably already a bridge away from me, I couldn't shake his words, that look in his eyes.

I stood from the bench and made my way over to Mikki. She was so enthralled by the pigeons that she didn't notice me, not even when I paused just a few feet away. I was mesmerized by how attentive she was, cooing along with them, the sound she made so authentic that I could hardly separate her voice from those of the birds themselves. I watched as she reached out to stroke an unusually pretty pigeon, its feathers looking almost metallic in the early evening sun.

"Mikki?" I said quietly.

She jerked up, slipping from her crouch to topple onto her backside.

"Iris!" She looked up at me, chuckling. "Goodness, girl, don't scare an old lady like that."

"I'm sorry, you looked so . . . so peaceful here, but I wanted to say hi."

"Sure, sure," she said, patting the grass next to her. "Glad you did."

I sat down, hugging my knees in to stay warm. The wind was picking up, bringing in much cooler air as the day began to fade. Mikki finished off the loaf of bread and we sat in silence for a few moments, watching the pigeons as one by one they flew away, bored with us now that the food was gone.

I felt her turn to me then, sensed that mesmerizing green gaze on my face without having to actually see it. "Something wrong?" she asked.

"Things at home are just . . . they're a little bit complicated right now," I said slowly. "So I'm looking for somewhere else to go. Just to get away and think a little."

She looked up toward the sky, and then back at me. "We got some time yet before it's dark. So tell me. Tell me about complicated."

"Do you . . ." I started, taking a deep breath. "Do you remember how I asked you about miracles? About believing that something miraculous could actually happen?"

Mikki nodded.

"Well, my family . . . This is crazy, Mikki, but my family, they believe. They believe a miracle happened."

She stared at me, waiting for more. "So? Go on. What was it? The miracle?"

I turned away, not able to look her in the eyes. "Me, Mikki. *Me.* My family thinks that *I'm* a miracle, and they think that that means I can help other people. Make other miracles happen, maybe. Make the world a better place. And they're not the only people who believe it—there are desperate people out there, people who think I can help them. One of them has been watching our home, watching me. He just confronted me on my way here, begging me to do something. But I can't. I can't actually *do* anything. Even if something kind of miraculous did happen, a long time ago."

I exhaled, waiting for her to respond. Mikki was silent, though, dead still. Everything I'd just said must have sounded like entirely nonsensical babbling to her, I realized, without more context. She'd think I was insane, probably. That was what I would think, if the situation were reversed.

After a minute with no response, I glanced back up at her, dreading the expression I would see on her face. She was still watching me, but I couldn't read the look in her eyes.

"Okay," she said finally, shrugging her shoulders. "So what now? Where will you go?"

"I don't know." I sighed, tugging at a few stray blades of grass. "My mom wants me to leave the city. Go somewhere different and hide away. For now, she says. But my life is here. And sure, I'll go away to college next year, but I'd still have my identity. This would still be home. I don't know what the answer is, but I can't believe it's just to run off somewhere."

"But you said there's someone outside your home giving you trouble? Sounds dangerous to me. Maybe your mama has a point."

Maybe that much was true—it *was* dangerous. There was no denying that. I'd read all about the dangers in my mom's book. Dangers from those who didn't believe her, people who called her a heretic, who wanted her to suffer for her lies. Threatening calls from strangers, nasty messages shoved in her locker and plastered on a website dedicated to Virgin Mina haters. And the worst of it, the mob that had rushed her house in the end—the mob that was so rowdy, so determined, they'd ended up knocking my mom unconscious.

There were dangers, too, from those who *did* believe—those who believed too much, expected too many things from her. From her baby.

But who was to say they wouldn't find me again? Kyle had tracked us down here, hadn't he? Maybe people could track us down anywhere. And when they did . . . when they did, they'd be even angrier.

A cold gust of wind pushed against us, snapping me back into my body. I pulled my jacket around me more tightly, yanking the zipper up to the bottom of my chin.

"Mikki . . . does it seem like it's getting dark too early? Or darker than usual maybe?" Something about the air around us definitely felt off. Like the sun was running off before it should, ending the day with one sharp pull of the curtain.

Mikki scrunched her nose and squinted up into the sky. "Hm," she grunted, spinning her fingers through the air like gnarled weather vanes. "I think we're in for some rain."

"I usually check the weather first thing every morning, but I guess I've been a little distracted." I looked up, really seeing the park for the first time since I'd sat down with Mikki. I realized with a start that suddenly there was no one else in the meadow or on the surrounding loop, that the entire park was oddly empty and still.

"When did everyone else leave?" I asked, the tiny hairs at the back of my neck prickling, making the decision for the rest of my body that it was time to be anxious. "It's not that late. People should still be out."

"They must know more about the weather than we do. I guess they remembered to check their fancy phones today," she said, winking at me. It would have felt like a joke, but the worried creases around her eyes said otherwise. Mikki knew better than I did what it meant to have a storm sweeping toward us. I was always comfortably inside when the rain hit, or at least dashing around with an umbrella for a few unpleasant minutes if absolutely necessary.

Just as I grabbed for my purse to check my phone, the rain began. A few drops to start, heavy and solid against the top of my head. As I scrambled to push myself up to stand, it rapidly turned into a steady downpour.

"What should we do?" I asked, grabbing for Mikki's hand.

"I don't think that's the question," she said, shaking her head at me. "Question is what *you* do, and what *I* do. You . . . I think you best be heading home. And me, I'll figure it out, find somewhere to hide away. Just got to get there fast enough now."

"No," I said, more forcefully than I'd intended. "No. I'm not letting you just run off. It's almost dark, Mikki, and it's cold. The wind is already bad and it's just starting up." I pulled her along as I started running toward the edge of the meadow. Mikki dragged behind me, not able to move as quickly as I could. I slowed my pace, my mind racing, trying to decide next steps.

"Mikki," I said, loudly enough to carry over the ominous whirling of rain and wind. "I want you to come home with me." The words were out before I'd really thought them through, but what else was there? I couldn't leave her out here alone. My parents—they couldn't say no. Especially not after everything they'd said earlier. They thought I was special? Well then, they'd let me protect Mikki, wouldn't they?

I choked down a laugh—or maybe it was a sob; I couldn't quite tell.

"No, no," Mikki said. "You're being silly. You go on home. I'll take care of me."

"Mikki," I said, clasping her hand even more tightly in mine. "Please. Just until the storm's over. My parents won't care, I promise. We have a spare bedroom in our basement. And you don't even have to stay the whole night if the rain stops before then, okay?"

She jerked to a stop so suddenly, our hands fell apart and I just barely saved myself from slipping backward into the wet grass. I turned back to face her, pleading; her green eyes were still so clear and sharp, even in the torrents of rain that were now lashing against us from all sides. Those usually perfect braids were falling around her neck, swinging wildly in the wind. She looked more myth than human to me, like a warrior from an epic battle, standing strong against whatever tests nature threw her way.

"Okay," she said. "Just this once. Just until the storm stops."

I smiled, relief washing through me as heavy as the rain.

We didn't speak as we started off toward my parents' house. Every step seemed to take twice as long as usual, walking straight against the combined force of wind and rain. At first I kept my eyes sharp, scanning frantically for a cab to hail. But the handful I saw were all taken, everyone else clearly as eager as we were to be out of the rain.

I gave up after a few minutes and splurged on a flimsy bodega umbrella instead, though it was hardly enough to keep both Mikki and me shielded. By the time we turned onto our street, my clothes were entirely soaked through, plastered thick and cold against my shivering limbs.

"We're almost there," I said, looking up toward my house and our distinct gold front door. But as my eyes focused through the sheets of rain, I froze.

"No," I gasped. *"No."*

"What is it?" Mikki asked, bumping up against my back.

I didn't—couldn't—say anything. I pointed instead, my eyes locked on the scene ahead.

Because outside of my house—my *home*—there were three brightly lit-up news vans. The reporters themselves were nowhere to be seen, likely hunkered inside the vans until any real action started happening. But still, they were there. Surrounding our front gate.

Waiting.

Kyle Bennett had wasted no time—he must have made the call the second he drove away from me. I had ignored his threat. And this . . . this was the consequence.

I yanked Mikki through the gate just beside us, pulling her under the tiny roof that covered our neighbor's basement entrance. It didn't completely protect us from the rain, but it was better than the umbrella at least, making it safe enough for me to check my phone.

There was a long list of missed calls and texts. Most of them from my mom. First to yell at me for leaving, after she must have pried open my lock to find that I'd disappeared. THE FIRE ESCAPE, IRIS? REALLY? COME HOME IMMEDIATELY. PLEASE. But then—Forget what I said. Reporters are here now. Stay away tonight, go to a friend's until we can sort this out. Call me when you're there and please stay safe. They say this storm will be a big one, so please let me know all is okay and you're warm and dry. And another, soon after: I'm sorry, Iris. I'm so sorry this is happening. I love you so much and we're going to figure this out together. We're going to find somewhere safe for us to go as soon as we can get a flight. Please just tell me you're okay.

There were texts, too, from my friends. Ari was the first to chime in: I have reporters calling me nonstop. They're at your house?!! This shit is nuts. Your mom told me the plan. She's right, get out of town. Come here, she'll get you early AM and you can leave.

There were similar messages from Delia and Ethan. I should listen to my parents and leave town, hide away somewhere until the story died down. Come over. They'd help me with my getaway.

How could they be so certain that my mom was right? They hadn't asked anything at all these past few days about what I was really feeling. Besides Ethan gushing about my

dad's video, they'd avoided the topic altogether. Pretended to go on like everything was okay, even as it so obviously wasn't.

Maybe they thought it would be easier if I did go away for a while. Easier for them.

A new text came in, interrupting that dark, terrible thought. It was Aunt Hannah now, with the name of a hotel she'd meet me at tonight. She'd no doubt turn me straight over to my mom, probably even hire a private plane to fly us somewhere far, far away.

A surge of fury flooded through me, warming me up even against the cool gusts of rain.

No. I wouldn't go to that hotel. I wouldn't listen to any of them.

Not Aunt Hannah or my friends, who were all blindly following my mom's orders without asking me how I felt, what I wanted.

And especially not my parents—not after they'd lied to me for seventeen years, controlled my entire life for me without giving me a chance to make my own decisions. I couldn't trust them to tell me everything, not now. They fed me bits and pieces of the truth when it was convenient for them—when it fit with their plans for me.

But this would be my choice. My good or bad decision to make.

I didn't have to check my wallet to know that a hotel

room was out of the question, even for the grimiest, most roach and rodent infested of dives. My only credit card—linked to my parents' account for emergencies—had expired the previous month. I'd asked my mom about a new one, but the topic had gotten lost with everything else going on. Regardless, I didn't want their help right now. I needed to figure this out on my own.

"I'm not going home," I said, leaning into Mikki to steady myself. My entire body trembled with anger as I stared down the street toward the vans. "Where else can we go?"

Mikki pursed her lips, her face crinkling in concentration.

"Well," she said slowly, "there is one place. Where I go when the weather's real bad. An emergency shelter only, so you don't have to apply and all that, like you do for a more permanent bed. They don't ask a lot of questions. Not *too* far from here, but still a walk in this rain, even if we use the subway. United City Mission, it's called."

United City Mission. It sounded familiar to me. Where . . . ?

Zoey. Zane Davis's little sister, that day at the soup kitchen. She'd said it was nice, that she'd liked it there.

"Come with me," Mikki said. The words sounded so simple. I didn't have to decide anything else right now; I just had to follow. Mikki had no other expectations of me.

And who would think to look for me there? No one. Ever. I almost laughed out loud, it sounded so perfect and so preposterous at the same time.

"Yes," I said, already nodding on instinct. I didn't think about it—I didn't let myself. I had to believe that it was a sign that I'd overheard Zoey mention United City Mission. It had to mean something, didn't it?

Mikki looked at me, her eyes wary even as her lips tried to smile. "It's not what someone like you is used to. It's not a motel or anything fancy like that. But it's just for a night, and I don't feel right sending you off alone right now, you looking so shook up and scared. So if you can't go home, come with me."

"I trust you," I said. Maybe I was crazy for believing in Mikki, but I did. And she was right—it was only for one night. "I have . . . I have friends who stay at that shelter, too." Maybe not quite *friends*, but Mikki didn't have to know that. "My mom texted me, told me herself to stay away tonight. So that's what I'm doing. I'll let her know I'm safe."

Mikki blinked away the rain from her eyes. And then she gripped my hand tighter and pulled me away from the basement roof, back into the storm.

"Okay, then," she said. "Let's go."

Chapter Nine

WE RODE THE SUBWAY for a half hour, shivering in our dripping wet clothes. Finally we climbed back into the rain above, Mikki steering me through the now darkened streets, streets that I soon began to lose track of—streets that I barely recognized or had never seen at all. She was taking me into a new Brooklyn, a Brooklyn very much outside of my world of brownstones and bicycles and farmers' markets, organic food, organic cotton, organic soap, organic everything.

I hadn't thought the storm could get worse than it already was—but I was wrong. The cold sheets of rain were slicing into us harder and more aggressively as we plunged forward, numbing me to the point where I could almost pretend that I wasn't hurting. Almost.

"Are we close?" I asked. My throat constricted around the words. I was lost and scared, so far from everything and everyone I knew, everyone but Mikki, and I'd met her, what—three times? I had the urge to go back on everything, tell her that no, I couldn't possibly stay at a shelter with her. I would go meet Aunt Hannah and I would fly away with my mom in the morning, just like everyone was telling me to do.

No. I needed time away from my parents, from everyone who *loved* me right now. I could do this. I'd befriended homeless people my whole life, hadn't I? I'd helped at the soup kitchen, too. This night would be new for me, but it wasn't so far-fetched, was it?

"There," Mikki said, pointing straight ahead. I squinted through the rain, following the direction of her finger to see a brick church at the end of the block. It looked dark at first glance, the big white entrance doors bolted shut. I started to panic, wondering if Mikki had gotten the streets confused and dragged us to the wrong church, but then I noticed light spilling out from the side of the building. An old gate hung open over the sidewalk, leading into a narrow alcove with two glowing streetlamps mounted alongside a small door.

"So that's where we . . ." Mikki tugged at my arm, guiding me through the gate. I sucked in my breath, steeling myself for whatever came next. For the people, the conditions, the beds—if we were lucky enough—that would be nothing like my bed at home, nothing like any hotel bed I'd ever slept in or the mounds of blankets and pillows I'd used for sleepovers.

Mikki pressed a buzzer on the door, and after a few seconds of stillness I heard a clicking from inside.

The door swung open. A tall, husky man stood in the brightly lit entrance, waving us in. "Come in, come in. It really started coming down out there fast," he said. His voice was loud, heavy, but warm and smooth still, too, like it filled up his entire throat before it burst out into sound. The room we stepped into was small and spare, but tidy. I saw a teetering wooden desk covered in stacks of papers and a computer that looked older than me, a clump of plastic chairs, and a potted tree that I didn't need to inspect up close to see was fake, the plastic flowers more vibrant than anything I'd ever seen in nature.

"Oh, Mikki, right?" the man asked, his somber face breaking out into a wide smile. He leaned in closer, patting her on the shoulder. "Didn't recognize you at first, it's gotten so dark out there already. You came in this summer? That big thunderstorm at the end of August?"

"Sure did." She nodded. "You got a good memory."

"Have you heard the reports about this storm? A real doozy. The weather folks thought it would break up off the coast, but now we're right in the center of it. They're calling the storm Severus. Sounds mighty scary to me with a name like that. Not a night to be out and about, so I'm glad you made it here."

He turned to me for the first time, peering down from his vantage point of what seemed to be nearly two feet above me. I shrunk at least another few inches under his gaze, scared that he'd somehow sense I was counterfeit, faking my desperation. But I wasn't—that was one thing I wasn't faking. I *was* desperate.

"And what's your name, then?" he asked.

I opened my lips, *Iris* about to slip out, when I caught myself.

"Clemence," I said instead. My mom's pseudonym, the first spare name that popped into my mind. If she used it as a mask, so could I.

"Clemence," he said contemplatively, like he could learn all there was to know about me just by the inflection of those two syllables. "I'm Benjamin. And how old are you, Clemence?"

I wasn't sure of the best answer here—minor, not a minor?

I hedged my bets. "Eighteen." Nearly enough. Older seemed safer, like I had more right to be on my own, no parents or guardians other than Mikki to claim me.

He looked over at Mikki, paused for a beat, then turned back to me.

"Okay. Well, we're in luck. The men's room is filled

up, but we have a few beds left in the women's quarters for the night. So we're happy to take you in."

I nodded, my head spinning with relief. We wouldn't have to go back out there. It was warm and dry in here. This man was kind to Mikki, which made him good in my book.

Benjamin handed me a clipboard with some paperwork to be signed—which I filled in as Clemence Verity, because I was too shaken up still to come up with anything more creative. Benjamin didn't ask for any identification, which surprised me—but who was I to argue? I handed him back the pen and papers and looked everywhere but directly into his eyes.

"Well then, let me show you around, Clemence. We already served a warm dinner for the night, but we have some leftovers in the kitchen that I'm happy to bring out. There are three other staff members here with me tonight. We were expecting a crowd once word of the storm hit. They say it could last through most of tomorrow, with severe flooding and power outages and the like. I'm afraid we'll have to start turning people away soon enough." He sighed, staring at the closed door behind us.

I wanted to reach out and hug him, but I fought the urge. I wasn't sure of the etiquette there. He had patted Mikki's shoulder. So contact was okay? Were there rules and codes about these sorts of things?

"So the tour," he said again, beckoning us to follow him down a short hallway leading out of the central entrance and office area.

There wasn't much—a kitchen and dining area where I met another staff member, Mariela, who was finishing the post-dinner cleanup. It was much smaller and less impressive than the kitchen at Blessed Mercy, the counters and cabinets all looking older, more tired, but it still felt familiar to me. It had the same smell: a mix of coffee grounds and fake orange cheese from the box, with an edge of lemony bleach. I fought the urge to start wiping down the counters. I wasn't the volunteer tonight.

Mariela wasn't as immediately warm as Benjamin, but was still friendly enough. She wore her tiredness less subtly, her movements blunt and exaggerated as she started to unpack the dinner items she'd just finished putting away. I couldn't blame her, though, for any edge—I could see the purple rimming her lower lids, the tiny red veins that made her eyes look dull against her dark, olive-toned skin. The only bright thing about her was her shirt, an oversized pink T-shirt with a big winking Minnie Mouse face.

I cringed, looking away.

"No, I don't need anything, really," I said, perhaps a bit too forcefully. I hadn't eaten since a few bites of lunch in the cafeteria—which seemed like weeks ago, not hours—

but I would be okay. Taking a bed made me feel guilty enough.

"I'm fine, fine," Mikki said, waving Mariela off. "Well. Maybe that lemon granola bar there, that would be nice. But a bed out of that crazy rain is all we need tonight."

Benjamin nodded, turning as he started toward the front office. He stepped back, though, blocked by someone or something else in the hallway.

"Sorry there, Z. Didn't mean to bump you," Benjamin said, shifting so that I saw who he was talking to.

Z—Zane. Zane Davis. He was there again.

And he was staring straight at me, cool but curious, his deep amber eyes puzzling to fit me into these surroundings.

I stared back at him, refusing to break eye contact first.

"No worries," Zane said, glancing away, turning back to Benjamin. "I was just going to ask you if I could say good night to my little sister. And say thanks for having the staff look in on her again tonight, like last time . . . it's tough being separated. For both of us. But like I said before, we should have a new place soon." Zane looked down as he said this, his eyes focused on his boots. "My family . . . this is just temporary. They know we're here."

"Of course," Benjamin said. "I understand. I only wish

we were bigger, so that we could have a room just for kids and families. But I'm heading to the ladies' bedroom now, giving Clemence here the tour. I'll grab Zoey for you."

Zane's eyebrows twitched at *Clemence*. He flicked his gaze back to me, looking even more intrigued.

I smiled before I could catch myself. We both had secrets.

Benjamin and Mikki moved into the hallway, and I ducked my head and followed, feeling Zane's eyes following me as I walked away. We stopped at a closed door just beyond the reception area.

"Nothing fancy," Benjamin was saying, as he yanked a key from his front pocket and turned it in the knob. He glanced back at me, his hand paused on the door. "I don't know what you're used to, Clemence, being new to us and all. We're a small facility, all volunteers from our congregation. Good people who take it upon themselves to cover the shifts. We know how overcrowded the city-run facilities get, especially on nights like these. It's small, but we want to do our part in any way we can. We owe at least that much to our community."

I nodded, overcome with gratitude—gratitude and guilt and shame, because did I deserve to be there? Really?

Benjamin opened the door, stepping inside to make room for us. It was a small space, but every last inch of it was utilized. A dozen single beds, cots, set up in two tight rows of six. Every mattress was covered in jumbled patterns of blankets and pillows, plaids and florals and stripes, and above each one there was a small shelf for personal items. It was clean but chaotic, so much stuff and life packed into one tiny room. I took it all in: the beds, the shelves with their meager piles of belongings, the bright strip of fluorescent lights on the ceiling. The only art on the wall was an ancient-looking Jesus portrait, the paint dull, flecking off the canvas. He was smiling down at a group of ratty-looking children, his arms wide and welcoming, like he wanted to hug each and every one of them simultaneously, assure them that everything would be okay.

I yanked my eyes away. I refused to look at it again—to think about it. *Him.*

And then I was forced to see the one thing in the room I hadn't studied yet, the hardest part of all. The people. The other women—the old, young, big, little, tired bodies sprawled out on the beds, some already asleep, others sitting up, awake, staring right at me. There was a steady buzz of voices, women talking to each other or to themselves.

I swallowed and bit down on my bottom lip, hard enough that I tasted a drop of blood on my tongue. Something rustled against my fingertips—Mikki's hand. She wove her fingers around mine, squeezing my palm against hers.

". . . and then the bathroom is back through the hall-way," Benjamin was saying, but I'd missed the rest of his instructions.

Nine, I counted, which meant one bed left now that Mikki and I were there. From the women I could see, the ones not hidden away under mounds of blankets, everyone looked to be older than me, everyone but one—Zoey.

She was at the end of the row closest to the door, with a small, flimsy folding screen set up between her bed and the next. It made her sleeping area at least a little more private. But she still had full view of the front, and she turned to watch us, her eyes sharp and attentive, sizing me up. Did she remember me? Had she thought I was eaves-dropping, too, that day at the soup kitchen?

"Zoey," Benjamin said. She peeled her gaze away from me, glancing over at Benjamin with the tiny beginnings of a smile. People liked Benjamin, I could tell. Even tough-as-nails people like Zane and Zoey. "Your brother wants to say good night. He's in the hallway."

She nodded and slipped out of bed, looking even smaller than I'd expected, now that she was standing so close to me. I noticed, too, those music note tattoos again. Seeing them there, so permanent on her skinny neck, I thought of Caleb. I missed him with a breathless pang. I tried to imagine him with tattoos, him doing anything so mature or edgy. I wanted to hug him—and I wanted to lock him away somehow, keep him young and innocent forever. I caught myself staring and looked away as she brushed past me, my skin prickling with the uneasiness of a memory, a memory circling closer and closer.

The rumor—the story that Zane had tried to kill someone who'd somehow wronged his little sister. The scissors. Was it true? Had someone done something to Zoey? The thought made my stomach turn. She looked so little and fragile in her massive T-shirt, probably another hand-me-down from Zane.

"So that's the tour, Clemence," Benjamin said, yanking my focus back to the rest of the room. "Any questions?"

I shook my head.

"I'll leave you to it, then," he said, starting for the door. "There is staff at the desk around the clock if something comes up. And we check in on the sleeping quarters throughout the night, too, so don't be alarmed when you hear some coming and going."

"Thank you," I said, the words more of a whisper.

Benjamin closed the door behind him, leaving a silent void in his place. There was a moment with no movement, no sound, just me and Mikki standing in the middle of the room, a dozen eyes slanted in our direction. My direction, more specifically. The one who didn't belong.

"I'll be right across the room, so you wake me if you need anything at all, you hear?" Mikki dropped my hand

and shuffled over to one of the spare beds. Both cots next to hers were already occupied. There was an open bed next to Zoey's, and another at the farthest corner of the room. I claimed the one by Zoey, kicked off my old green-and-white Converse sneakers, lining them up neatly under the bed, and peeled back a thick pile of blankets. I tried not to wonder when they were last cleaned, tried not to think about how likely it was that lice or bedbugs were lying there in wait, hiding out before launching a sneak attack on their next victim. My skin crawled. I clenched my teeth and fought the urge to claw myself. It was in my head. It was all in my head.

There were a few dark stains on the bottom white sheet, dark stains that I couldn't think about, couldn't wonder why they were there, who they had come from. I pulled a yellow thermal blanket back up to the pillow, lay down on top of that instead.

Angry or not, I needed to at least text my parents for now. Otherwise, it would be a matter of time before they had the police on my trail, which would only make the whole situation infinitely worse. I pulled my phone from my purse and scanned through the most recent messages from my mom—each one increasingly anxious about my whereabouts.

I started typing: I saw the vans. And your messages. I'm safe now, staying with friends from school. A brother and sister. You don't know them, but it's fine. There are adults, don't worry. I pressed send. There *were* adults, so it wasn't a total lie. Mikki for one. Benjamin and Mariela. And the other strangers sleeping all around me.

She tried calling, but I let it ring. There was no privacy. And besides that, I wasn't ready to talk. Not yet. Another text came through almost instantly. I don't love that you're with people I don't know, not now. You can stay put for tonight because of the weather, but tomorrow I'm going to meet you at a hotel. I'll send details ASAP. Will book our flight then.

My response flew from my fingers. I'm not going. I don't know what the solution is. But I'm not just going to hide away. I'll call you in the morning. Going to bed now. I paused for a minute, debating, and then added, Love you. I loved them so much, even if I was angry. But it only made their betrayal that much worse.

I set my phone to silent and shoved it back in my purse, checking my wallet then to see exactly how much cash I had with me. Buried under a few receipts was a crumpled twenty-dollar bill. My stomach twisted into sharp knots. Twenty dollars. I regretted that terrible ten-dollar umbrella even more. I jammed the wallet back in my purse and pushed all of it under my pillow. I doubted anyone would try to steal it in my sleep, but still . . . just to be safe.

I peeled off my wet jacket and sweatshirt, hanging

them from hooks on the shelf above my head. There was still the issue of my T-shirt and my sopping, heavy jeans, but I couldn't bring myself to strip down any further. It would all just have to dry while I slept. I let my head fall against the big, lumpy pillow and pinched my eyes shut. The fluorescent lights above still flooded in, a blazing yellow and orange spiral swirling around the deep purple of my closed eyelids. I tried to move the spiral, control it, spin it in and out of focus. Anything to distract myself, to be less in this moment, less aware of the fear pulsing through my veins.

This is okay. I am okay. This will all be okay. It would only be for tonight, and tomorrow I'd figure out the next piece of the plan.

I wished that Mikki were closer. I wished that I could crawl in bed next to her, curl myself up so that she could rock me to sleep.

The bedroom door opened and closed, and I listened as Zoey walked up next to me, just inches away, the squeak of her bed as she settled back in under her blankets. I kept my eyes closed tight, my arms pinned to my sides, one long, rigid line of tension from my toes to the top of my head. I took a deep breath, regretted it. The scent in the room, musty and stale, a fusion of sweat and grime and desperation, did little to calm my heightened senses. My ears suddenly seemed to have superhuman strength, every rustling blanket, every inhale and exhale, every shift on the mattress sounding exaggerated and amplified, too close, too urgent. There was still a hum of voices, indecipherable murmurs mostly, but one woman was much louder, ranting about her deadbeat ex, her kids who weren't there. I couldn't imagine actually falling asleep like this. Would they turn the lights off at some point? Or was that too dangerous?

I heard the door open a second time, and Benjamin's subdued voice as he covered the basics about the sleeping quarters. It must be a new woman. The last bed. Had there been any others with her, others Benjamin had been forced to turn away? And if not—what if they came later in the night? Pounding on the door, drenched to the bone, forced to find shelter somewhere on the streets.

Because of me.

I shook the thought off, flipping myself over and burrowing my face into the pillow. Soon after the final woman settled in, the lights went down, a shudder and a blink. There was a hazy orange night-light by the door, casting off just enough glow that I could still make out each bed, each woman's silhouette. The chattering became more mellow.

A wave of exhaustion washed over me with the darkness. The adrenaline that had pushed me through the day was entirely gone now, leaving me so bone-achingly tired that sleep did seem possible after all.

I started slipping, swaying, falling. I saw my mom's

face, my dad's, Caleb's. I was reaching my arms out toward them, hoping they would pull me back in. And then, just as they were getting closer, just as I could practically feel Caleb's fingertips brushing against my own, a sound jolted me wide-awake.

A broken sob followed by sniffles and the rhythmic, rolling tremble of mattress springs. The sounds were close, very close. Zoey.

I sat up and crawled along my bed, peering around the edge of the screen. The blanket was pulled over Zoey's head, her body tucked into a tiny lump at the end of the bed, as close to the door as possible.

I didn't think first. I just reacted. I reached out—our beds were so close, I barely had to stretch—and rested my hand on her trembling back. I felt her muscles tense and stiffen below me. I sucked in my breath, waiting.

She didn't pull away, or jump up, rip my hand off, and scream at me to leave her alone. Instead, after a few moments passed, she let herself cry again, softer this time, more even and controlled.

We stayed like that, my palm rubbing circles on her back, slower and slower until finally she fell asleep, her breathing deep and calm. I frowned into the darkness, wondering what had happened in her life to bring her to this night, this place. And then, gradually, hand still resting on her back, I drifted off to sleep.

Chapter Ten

I WOKE UP the next morning with my arm dangling over the side of my bed and my feet resting on my pillow. Zoey was gone, her blanket smooth and tucked around the edges of the mattress, though a faded pink duffel bag still sat on her shelf. She hadn't left yet, not for good.

Did they kick us out at a certain time? And if so . . . then what?

I just wanted to be plain old boring Iris Spero again, playing my violin at the park, drinking bubble tea with my friends, watching old movies on the couch with my family, our Sunday night takeout special.

But I didn't know how that could ever happen now.

I was too anxious to just lie there, pretending to sleep. I needed to use the bathroom anyway, and then I'd stretch my legs, see if the storm had passed. And after that, I'd call my parents. I was afraid to look at my phone—at the slew of texts that had no doubt followed my abrupt sign-off the night before.

I glanced over at Mikki, but she was still curled up under the blanket, sleeping. I counted—ten women in their beds, meaning only Zoey and I were awake. There was no clock, though, no window to gauge the natural light. I got out of bed anyway and slipped on my shoes and my still slightly damp sweatshirt, smoothed down the knots of hair spilling from my ponytail. I gave up, though—there was no mirror, and I hadn't thought to pack a brush. What did it matter, anyway?

The door was locked on the outside for those in the hallway, but from the inside I was free to leave. I gently closed it again behind me, waiting to hear the soft click of the lock falling back into place. I turned toward the restroom, but my path was blocked—I couldn't move another step without bumping straight into Zane, hovering in the hallway, arms folded across his chest and a soggy, graying newspaper in his hand.

"God, are you always just lurking around in hallways?" I asked, the question sounding meaner than I'd intended. He'd knocked me off balance, again.

"My sister's using the ladies' room. I was waiting for her. Is that a problem?"

"I'm sorry," I started, my face reddening—a fact that

I'm certain he took note of, given the slight smirk pulling at the corners of his mouth. "It's just been . . . a long night. A long day. A long few weeks, really."

"A long few weeks," he said, staring down at me, tapping the newspaper against his chest. He sighed. "I know what that's like. A long few years, really. Or just a long fucking life."

"I really am sorry," I said, easing back so that I could pass around him and head for the door, soak up some fresh air while Zoey used the restroom. "But I have to—"

"Wait," he said, reaching out with his free hand to grab me around the wrist. I jumped back, shocked by the contact. His hands were rough, strong, too tight around my arm. He must have sensed my unease, because he loosened his grip, though he didn't let go altogether. "I need to show you something first. Somewhere quiet." He jerked his head back toward the desk, where I saw two staff members pretending not to watch us. "It's still pouring out. Pretty bad, actually—they said they'll even let people stay during the day so no one has to go back out there right now. Power lines down, flooding all over the streets. A fucking mess. They usually kick people out, night shift only, but not today."

I nodded, not sure why he was telling me any of this— why he was talking to me at all, given our past encounters.

"We can step outside, though. There's a roof over

some of the courtyard. Just a few minutes, okay?"

"Why?" I asked, still acutely, wholly aware of the fact that his hot palm was pressed along the inside of my wrist.

"I need to tell you something. Private."

"I really can't imagine there's something you can't just say . . ."

Zoey stepped out of the bathroom door next to us, and I paused. She didn't look at me.

"Hey, Zo," Zane said, hunching down so that he was closer to her level. "I need to talk to this girl for a few minutes outside." Zoey glanced over at me now, tilted her head curiously, as if she was trying to figure out what kind of business could possibly be going on between her big brother and this stranger.

"Okay," she said, nodding. "I'm still tired, anyway. If they're not booting us, maybe I'll just go back to sleep for a little."

Zane kissed the top of her head and then stood up straight, catching my eye as he motioned toward the door. I followed him, because—I don't know why, exactly, other than because he obviously had some sort of reason, and what was five minutes of my day? It wasn't like I had any actual *plans*. While Zoey asked at the front desk to be let back into the bedroom, I stepped outside behind Zane.

It was pouring even harder than I'd expected, sheets of icy water blasting sideways through the courtyard. Rain thudded against the roof above us, spilling from an over-hanging drainpipe in one massive torrent, a waterfall cascading into a colossal dark and muddy puddle just a few inches away from my feet. I had left my jacket in the bedroom, which I regretted now as I pulled the hood of my sweatshirt up tighter around my head.

"Okay, so . . . ?" I almost couldn't hear myself over the pounding rain, the wind that was rushing around us in circles, a wild vortex in our little courtyard.

"So," he said, flipping open the newspaper that had been rolled up in his hands. A tabloid, with big, bright letters and a big, bright photo smeared across the front. "So *this*."

My heart pounded, burst, a catastrophic explosion in my chest that sent tiny black stars spiraling through every last bit of me. I reached out to grip the wall so I wouldn't crash onto the slick cement beneath me. Zane grabbed my shoulders, anchored me to the ground.

"I thought you needed to see this," he said, the words quiet, so much quieter than the rain, so much quieter than the thrumming that was still tearing through my body.

I had known this would happen, hadn't I? Those reporters, after all, they'd been outside my house for a reason. But still . . . knowing and seeing, they were two very different things.

Because right there in Zane's hands, it was my face—it was *my face* on the front page of the newspaper.

My face, and three words.

The Missing Messiah?

"I came out earlier and found this here, wrapped up in plastic. No one else in there would have seen it," Zane said, tilting his head toward the door, the front desk. "And they probably won't go out in the rain for another one. I won't tell anyone. Not my story."

I nodded slowly, in a daze. I had grabbed the paper from his hand, and now I sank down to the filthy wet cement and stared unblinking at the front page while the storm hammered down all around me. I couldn't feel the rain, though, couldn't feel the cold or the wind or Zane's eyes, watching me while I read. Nothing mattered but this paper in my hand.

Reporters weren't prowling just on the streets of Brooklyn, apparently. They had also gone straight to Green Hill, the place where all of this had begun.

Reporters had knocked on doors, and people had talked. From the perspective of the article, they were all *concerned*. Someone must have leaked that I'd left home the day before. Where had I gone? Was I safe? Would I ever come back, or was I running like my mom had done almost eighteen years ago? They were concerned for me—but they were also concerned for themselves. They talked about the old story of Virgin Mina—of the joyous discovery that her baby had *lived!*—and how special I could be. How maybe I was the answer so many people were searching for. Especially now. After Disney.

Kyle Bennett, of course, was at the head of the pack. *"I saw her up in Brooklyn after I first found out Mina's baby was alive. Just for a minute, looking down at me from her window. I knew right away it was her. I felt it. You don't need to even talk to her to know how special she is. It's like it radiates out of her eyes in waves, this kind of peace and calm. I saw her and I knew that everything would be okay. That she was here now. Please, Iris. Please help us."*

I read his words again, that last line. *Please help.* He made no mention in the article of our conversation—because he hadn't given up, not at all. He was just changing tactics. I had said no to him once, but could I keep saying no? No to him, and now to everyone else, too.

I started dry heaving, sweat dripping down the back of my neck, my forehead, despite the wind whipping through the thin sleeves of my sweatshirt. There was nothing to throw up—my lunch the day before a long-distant memory—and I was too tired, too empty, to do anything but collapse against the dirty cement.

"Iri—Clemence," Zane said, stooping down to the ground next to me. I felt his hand on my back, patting me, a stiff, clumsy thudding against my shoulders. "You need to get back inside right now. It's cold and you're soaking wet. You're going to get sick. Okay? Let's go."

"I can't," I whispered. My throat burned, raw from the heaving. "I can't go in there. I can't go home. I can't go anywhere."

"Well," he said, his hand slowing, stopping, but still resting on my shoulder. "You can't just go nowhere either. That's not an option. Trust me."

"Did you read the article?" I asked, whipping my head up, catching him off guard. He jerked his hand back, braced his fingertips against the ground to keep himself from toppling over.

"Yes," he said, hooking me with his sharp eyes. "So people think you're pretty special, huh?"

I tensed, waiting for him to laugh. But he didn't.

"Yeah, whatever this shit is, it seems pretty fucking scary. I give you that. I heard about your mom before, you know. I heard about some girl that people thought might be carrying the next Jesus or whatever."

Even Zane had heard about Virgin Mina. A secret about *me*, and somehow I was still the last to know.

"My grandma always used to talk about it when I was little. Told me that we live in a fucking terrible world these days, because people can't even believe that God might still try to come down and do a little good for us shitheads once in a while. That we don't deserve to be helped if we screwed over the one person who might have been able to do something." He laughed then, but it wasn't at me or about me. "If only she'd known I'd end up here, with that girl she thought was dead. That you were here in Brooklyn all along, that whole time she was talking about you, wishing those people hadn't mobbed your mom. I don't believe in heaven or God or any of that shit, but still. I hope she's looking down right now smiling."

The idea that he knew me, that his own grandmother had believed in my mom, made me want to bolt out of that courtyard, to run through the rain, to go anyplace where not a single person knew my name. But it also made me awestruck, that his grandmother, a woman who'd never met my mom, had held so much faith. Enough so that years after the baby had been "lost," she'd still sat there in Brooklyn talking about it with her grandson.

Mina had meant something. *My mom* had meant something. And I did, too. I could. If I chose to, maybe.

But no. I cut myself down. *No,* I couldn't mean something, not if people really knew me. Then they'd see that I was just like them, that I couldn't help even if I wanted to. And of course I did, I'd want to help people if I could, if I had the power. But I didn't. So I couldn't.

I didn't know what had happened to my mom, why that old lady Iris had come to her, made her pregnant—but that didn't make me a savior. Maybe the whole point had been that miracles *could* happen, right here, right now, to the most normal of people in the most normal of everyday places. A random, small-town girl and a random, small-town pizza place. If we believed that my mom became pregnant just like *that*—snap!—through some sort of flick of the spiritual wand, we could believe in anything, really. We could believe that there was something, someone looking over us.

Maybe the pregnancy had been the whole reason and the whole lesson. I was just the inevitable by-product. A baby. Nothing more, nothing less.

"Zane," I said, even just that one word shaky on my lips. "Zane, maybe what happened to my mom is really true. It sounds crazy, but I just—I don't know, I don't think my mom's lying, not about this. But it ends there. I'm not special. I'm not some kind of Messiah."

"I wasn't saying that you are." He paused, his lips twisting up into an almost smile. "*Clem.* I just said it's what my grandmother used to say, and I guess it's what some of these crazy-ass people in Pennsylvania believe, too. But me?" He folded his arms across his chest, drilled into me even deeper with those cool, stony eyes. "I haven't seen proof of anything magic from you. No wings. No fucking beams of light." He waved a hand around my head as if to prove there was nothing there. "You seem like a pretty normal girl to me. No offense."

"None taken." I laughed, then immediately choked it back down my throat. "Trust me, I wish everyone else felt the same way. And they would, if they met me. I wanted to go down to Green Hill and prove it, prove that I'm normal, but my family . . . well, my family didn't think that was such a good idea."

"So what *are* you doing, then? Why are you here?" Zane asked.

"I don't know." I looked away, blinked my eyes, and squeezed to hold back the flow of tears threatening to spill out. Crying wouldn't help right now. And I especially didn't want to cry in front of Zane, even if he was being friendly, treating me like another human being and not just some speck of litter to crush under his heavy brown boots.

"I saw reporters outside my house last night and freaked. My mom is determined to send me away somewhere, force me into hiding until this all blows over." The words were coming out faster now, all of my reasons flooding back in. "But I don't want to just run away, because who knows when and *if* it will blow over . . . I want to be here. I don't want to change my name and make up a whole new life. Like she did. Even if everything does kind of suck right now. My old life, it's gone—maybe for good—and I have no clue what is supposed to happen next."

"Well," he said, leaning up against the rough brick wall behind us, "I certainly don't have any grand solutions for you. All I can say is, maybe stay here until tomorrow. Tell your parents you're riding out the storm. Take it one day at a time. That's the best you can do sometimes."

With those last words, I could practically see his face close off, the shifting and rearranging that locked down his tongue, pulled a glossy veil down over his eyes. I wanted to ask more, ask where *he* was going tomorrow. But I didn't—I didn't think he'd have an answer. It seemed like "one day at a time" was probably what had brought him and Zoey to this place, too.

"Okay," I said, instead of all the questions I'd rather have been asking. I tried my best at a smile. "I'll stay, then." I appreciated his advice, more than he knew, probably. I hadn't expected it, not from him. I never would have expected anything at all from Zane Davis.

He didn't smile back, though, just turned away as he pushed himself up off the wall.

"Until tomorrow."

Chapter Eleven

THE OFFICE WAS bustling when we stepped back inside. Everyone, it seemed, had decided to wait out the storm and stay at the shelter for the day. The front desk had an activities bin that held one deck of cards—minus two Kings and a Joker, according to the cranky old man in a faded Michael Jackson concert T-shirt who, regardless, still grabbed them; Monopoly and Life; some torn-up-looking comic books; a few old crossword puzzle books with nearly every page partially filled in, only the most impossible answers still blank; and a jigsaw puzzle of some ancient-looking English castle at sunset.

I found Mikki in the kitchen picking at cereal and asked if she wanted any comics or puzzles, but she shook me off as we started back toward the bedroom. I grabbed a banana on my way out—my hungry eyes wanted to take more, but my guilt was stronger. "I got thousands of minutes of sleep to catch up on, girl," Mikki said, hopping into bed and yanking the blanket back over her head.

The bedroom was cleared out otherwise while the rest of the women ate breakfast and milled around the games. I'd call home now—I'd reassure them that I was fine, make sure that they were safe in the storm, too. And I'd stand my ground.

I reached for my cell, but even after a few frantic jabs at the power button, the screen stayed ominously black. *Shit.* A whole string of curses spilled out, until Mikki grunted angrily from her bed, silencing me. I should have turned it off while I slept to conserve energy—because of course I hadn't thought to pack a charger before I'd stormed out of the house. I could ask at the desk about borrowing a spare charger, or if that wasn't an option, using their office phone. They might say no, but I had to at least try. I had told my parents that I'd call today. To push them more than I already had . . . well, that wasn't an option.

Once the office had quieted down, everyone else either in the kitchen or back in the bedrooms, I picked up the puzzle box, the only sad-looking item still remaining, and hovered by the desk.

"Hello," I said quietly, peering down at the older man who now sat there. He was as different from Benjamin as could be, pale and gray haired and petite. He glanced up at me, but he didn't smile. There was a sense of tension around him, a negativity that seemed to infuse the air around us. Maybe because it was a last-minute, unexpected shift. A whole day of sitting around the shelter, crossing his fingers that nothing dramatic would happen, no fights erupting between roommates, no illicit drug activity or wandering drunks or schizophrenic breaks. Maybe he'd rather be safe and warm and alone in the quiet of his apartment all day, drinking coffee and watching the news from his sofa, nothing to worry about except what he and his wife would make for dinner. But he was here instead, with the sad smells, the sad sounds, the sad sights, a cloud of sad that you couldn't pull your head out of.

"Yes?"

"I was wondering if maybe there was a spare iPhone charger I could use?"

"Nope," he said, pursing his lips.

"Okay . . . maybe there's an office phone I could use? Just for a few minutes. It's pretty important. Please?"

He squinted up at me, and for a second, an instant, I wondered if he knew. If he'd seen the newspaper after all, seen the photo of me taken from the latest school yearbook. But no, he was just squinting because he didn't trust me—he knew nothing about me, nothing about the article, but he didn't trust me just because I was there. I was one of *them*. I wondered why he volunteered to begin with—a sense of obligation maybe, Christian duty. People did "good" for all different reasons.

"I'm afraid that's not part of our policy."

"Please, sir, I really, really have to make this call. I hate to ask you if I can be an exception, because I'm sure everyone would want to use the phone if they could, but . . . Five minutes, tops. *Please.*"

The furrowed lines along his forehead eased, his skin looking instantly younger and smoother. He sighed, glancing at the watch on his wrist.

"Listen. I don't know why exactly I'm doing this, but . . . I'm going to step outside for a very quick smoke. Five minutes. I shouldn't be leaving the desk empty right now, but Shari and David are both in the kitchen cleaning up . . . should anything urgent happen. But otherwise, no one would know if someone just happened to use the phone. Right there, on that shelf."

He stood up, digging around in his pockets before fishing out a lighter and a box of Marlboros. "So just to make it clear. When I come back in, no one will be on the phone. Got it?"

"Got it," I said, trying not to give away my shock that he'd decided to help after all. My heart was thudding, panicked suddenly by the idea of talking to my parents. I could be strong. I had to be. I'd let them know that I was safe—that there was absolutely no reason to alert the police—but that I wasn't budging.

"Thanks again, Mr. . . ." I said to his back, as he was

already halfway through the room. He turned around, just for a beat, before unbolting and opening the door.

"Jackson," he said.

"Thank you, Mr. Jackson."

"Don't thank me. I didn't give you permission, after all." The door shut behind him.

I lurched for the phone, my three hundred seconds already ticking away. I dialed once, fumbling the numbers in my nervousness, and then tried again, remembering to press star-six-seven this time to at least superficially block the ID. I was pretty sure they wouldn't be pleased if they traced the call to a homeless shelter. Half a ring in, and my dad was there, on the other end.

"Hello?"

"Dad." I exhaled, finally.

"Iris, sweetie, thank God," he gasped into the phone. "Noel, it's her!" I heard exclaiming, activity buzzing around him.

A click, and then, "*Iris*," my mom chimed in from the other line. "We've been trying to call your cell all morning, but it's going straight to voice mail."

"Hi, guys," I said, the feeling of homesickness already gnawing at my stomach just from hearing their voices— and it had only been a day. Less than a day. "I forgot to bring my charger, and my friends have different phones. I'm . . . I'm using their house line now."

"Where are you?" my dad asked, hand probably already on the front doorknob. "Where do these friends live? I'm coming to get you. Right now. We need to resolve this, sweetie, and you being . . . you being wherever the hell you've been hiding out, it's not going to fix anything. We have to sort this all out together, okay? I know you don't want to leave Brooklyn, but it's the best option we have. The only one we have, really, that I can see."

"I saw the newspaper today," I said.

They were silent.

"I read the article. 'The Missing Messiah.' I'm not. I can't be."

"I know you must be scared, honey." My mom sighed, her words so quiet now that I had to press my ear closer to the handset to make sense of them. "I'm scared, too; we all are. Which is exactly why we have to send you away right now. I was looking into Southern California, maybe. Your dad has a lot of friends out there from work, and Izzy would be close by. Somewhere outside the city, more hidden away, where people won't think to look . . ."

"I know you chose to leave, Mom. You ran away from Green Hill. And maybe that was best for you. Maybe that was the right decision at the time. But right now . . . right now I need to figure out what's best for me. I need a way to end it somehow, once and for all."

"Oh, Iris," my mom said. There was an edge to her

voice, a panic that I'd never heard before. "I just don't think it's that easy . . ."

"I saw Kyle—right when I left the house, he confronted me." Both parents gasped on the other end of the line. "He didn't hurt me. He just said he wanted to give me a chance to answer for myself. To make my own choice about whether or not to help. I said no, and he must have made the calls right after. But the point is . . . he found us once. He'll find us again, even if we run. And if it's not him, it'll just be someone else, right? Someone will always find us. Running to California isn't a permanent solution. My photo is *everywhere*. Even if I go three thousand miles away, people will recognize me."

There was a pause before my mom spoke again. "I get your point. I do. But there's too much going on right now, sweetie. These reporters, they're calling us nonstop and knocking on the door for interviews, and . . . and what if Kyle comes back? What if he . . . *followed* you?"

"He didn't," I said, the terror in her voice stabbing through the phone. *No.* I'd seen him drive away. For the time being.

"Please," my mom said. "Please just let us pick you up. We'll go someplace private to talk about it all face-to-face."

"No," I said, gritting my teeth to keep my voice steady. "I want to take it one day at a time. Today, I need this. I need time off, away from everything. Tomorrow . . . I don't know about tomorrow quite yet. I won't know until it gets here."

"I've never heard you talk like this before," my dad said. The words didn't sound critical or judgmental—just surprised. I was usually so easygoing, so ready to do whatever made my parents happy. But that was because we usually agreed, at least on the important things. I hadn't had to compromise myself in the process—until now.

"Well, I've never felt anything like this before. I always knew who I was before this."

"We still know who you are, Iris. And deep down, you know it, too. This doesn't have to change everything."

"But it does, doesn't it? It changed Mom's life entirely. It changed yours. It changed everyone's life that I care about. And it will again. It already has."

They didn't answer that. They knew it was true. Too true.

"I'll call you again . . . soon." I didn't want to be more specific than that. I couldn't be.

There was a pause.

"We love you," my dad said. "We love you and Cal more than anything in this world."

"I love you, too," I whispered.

I kissed my fingers, tapped them against the phone. And then I hung up.

I needed a distraction.

I shook out the puzzle pieces on the floor between my bed and Zoey's. She had gone back to sleep after breakfast, or was hidden away under the blankets at least. I was hoping she wouldn't be annoyed at me for tampering with her territory, but the room was too cramped to piece it together anywhere else. Though the puzzle itself was probably a lost cause from the start—it certainly didn't look like there were a full one thousand pieces in the pile. The colors were faded, the scraps of a larger picture torn and peeling around some of the jagged edges.

Someday soon I would buy the shelter a new puzzle. I would buy ten puzzles. I would drop them off for Benjamin with a thank-you card and a tin full of Ethan's mom's salted caramel pretzel brownies.

I started organizing. Blue sky pieces here, green and flowery grass there, gray bricks of castle walls and turrets in the middle. I let my mind drift as I sorted, relieved for now to have nothing to focus on but shapes and shades and shadows. Like meditation, almost. There was no tabloid article, no Green Hill, no desperate parents in a brownstone only a few miles away. Just me, turning a heap of mismatching pieces into something ordered and beautiful. Something that made sense.

I was so busy fitting blue into other blue, squinting at the possible cloud formations, that I didn't notice when

Zoey pushed away the blanket and sat up to observe.

"That's not the right piece," she said, startling me. I blinked up at her, then back down at the pieces in my hand. She was right. I was forcing two parts together that weren't made to fit.

"Good eye," I said, smiling up at her. "Want to help? I have a feeling all the pieces aren't here, but maybe we can find some paper up at the desk and make our own if we have to. I'm determined to leave no space empty."

She cocked her head, her lips pursed together in a tight line. I could feel the *no* before she said it, braced myself for the rejection.

"Okay. I guess."

I tried to hide my surprise, afraid to make her second-guess the decision. Instead I just nodded and shifted over, making room for her.

"Can you hand me the box lid?" she asked, crouching down so close to me that our shoulders were pressed up tightly against one another.

I reached behind me for the lid, which I'd barely been looking at so far. It was more about the initial clues right now, sky versus ground versus building. I held the castle out in front of us, and for the first time, my breath hitched. My stomach swooped and twisted. A classic, crumbling castle—in England, maybe, but still. A few months back, it would have meant nothing to me, but now . . . now I couldn't see any castle without thinking about Disney, about Cinderella's castle, about all those kids and families.

And from the way Zoey froze next to me, the way her breathing cut off with a gasp, she couldn't look at a castle anymore either, not without seeing the same terrible images playing out like a terrible flipbook.

"Sorry," I said, dropping the lid onto the floor. "It was the only puzzle. Do you still . . . ?"

The question faded from my lips, though, when I saw the single tear slowly rolling down her cheek. Her eyes were glassy, unreadable, as she kept staring down at that castle. One tear turned into two, three, four—a steady, silent stream.

"Zoey," I started, my voice low. There were a handful of other women in the room, most curled up in bed, sleeping, or staring off into space, but from what I could tell, none of them cared about us enough to pay much attention to our conversation. Not even Mikki, who hadn't moved from bed since breakfast. "Zoey," I said again, willing myself to ask, "do you want to talk about anything? If you do, I'm here. If you don't, that's okay, too. Up to you."

She didn't answer right away. I assumed that she wasn't going to, that we would just sit there instead, her crying, me wanting to do something to make it better but not being able to. Not being able to do a single damn thing to help her out, because I was just *me*, just Iris, because our lives were too separate, because she couldn't trust a stranger, and because I couldn't even touch the surface of understanding what made a little girl like her so broken and beaten down.

"My cousin, Brinley . . ." she said, the words so quiet I had to lean in even closer to hear, so close that her lips were practically grazing my cheek. "She was at Disney with her choir. Some big contest. She had the prettiest voice I ever heard. She used to sing to me, every night before bed. And every morning, too, while we got ready for school. She didn't care that she had to share her room with me. And her bed and her clothes and her toys. Everything. She told me I was her sister, and Zane was her big brother. We lived with them for so long, and my real mom and dad had been gone for so long that . . . that I sometimes even forgot. I forgot she wasn't just my real big sister." Her whole face seemed to collapse then—eyes, nose, mouth folding in on themselves, dissolving in her heavy tears and the quiet, racking sobs that shook her tiny body.

I wanted to respond, to reassure her somehow, but I couldn't speak. I knew what she was saying, of course, without her actually saying the words out loud.

Brinley had been at Disney World in August.

Brinley had been killed.

Brinley no longer sang her to sleep every night, no longer started her day with a song.

"She was there," Zoey whispered through the tears. She was hugging herself, squeezing her palms against her stomach, as if her insides were imploding and she was trying her best to hold it all together. "When it happened. When the bombs went off and killed so many people. She was there. She got hit and she . . ." I closed my eyes and listened to her inhale, exhale. "Died. She died right then. That's what some of her friends said, friends that were there with her. Some of her friends got to be okay. They got to come back home. But Brinley . . ." She reached up and grabbed for her blanket, balling it up and shoving it between her teeth. I saw her temples clench as her jaw tightened, as she funneled all the hurt and the rage into that bite, teeth on teeth, cutting through the thin material.

I put my arm around her, bracing myself against her trembling shoulders.

Her face was flushed, shiny now with sweat and with tears, but after a few minutes the shaking slowed. I felt her muscles, slowly, one at a time, release. The blanket fell from her lips onto the floor, covering the piles of colors, the lid, the castle.

"Why did Brinley have to be one of the ones who died? Why did her friends get to live and she didn't?"

I shook my head, pulling her in closer. "There aren't

answers for things like that, Zoey. It's not fair. None of it's fair."

"I don't get how people can be so bad. How they can just kill people they don't even know. Why would anybody do that?"

"I don't know either." I sighed, smoothing my hand against her dark braids. I realized now, close up, how neat and precise they were. Did she braid them herself? Did Zane?

"I don't think anyone understands something like this, really," I went on. "I think that these people who did it—I think bad things have happened to them, too. I think they've been hurt. And they were angry. And that kind of hurt and anger made them do something awful that didn't actually help them, or help anyone at all. It was wrong. It was a terrible, terrible mistake."

I wanted to ask her more. I wanted to ask why losing Brinley also meant losing her aunt and uncle, losing the only home she had, the only guardians other than Zane, who was potentially still a minor—and a minor with a record, no less.

"I don't even know your name," she said. She pulled back, just a little, not so much that my arm slipped away from her shoulders. Just enough that she could tilt her face up and look at me with her red, swollen eyes. "I've been crying to you all about my family, and I still don't know your name." She laughed, and for a second—just a second—I saw a spark in her eyes, a light that hadn't been there before.

"I'm Iris," I said. "I go to school with your brother, Zane." As soon as the words were out, I realized my mistake. I wasn't Iris here. I was Clemence. But it was too late to take it back, and besides that, how could I lie to her? How could I lie to this little girl who had just told me so many sad, deep-down scary things about her life?

Everyone in this room was probably running from something or someone, just like I was. My secret wouldn't matter to them.

Unless they believed, like Zane's grandmother. Believed that Virgin Mina's baby was destined to help people, people just like them.

But Zoey hadn't read the article. Zoey wouldn't put it all together.

"That's a pretty name," she said, very matter-of-factly. There was no hint of anything else, no sense of recognition.

I took a deep breath and let it fill me up, slow my racing pulse.

"Should I clean up the puzzle?" I asked, my free hand already reaching out to scatter the neat piles.

"No," she said, batting at my arm. "No. Let's do the puzzle."

"Are you sure?"

She nodded. "It's okay. It's just an old castle, right? I don't want to be scared anymore."

The rain finally stopped as the sun went down, but by then the power had gone out. A flicker, a burst, and then nothing. There was a generator for the church's heating system, and a few electric lamps scattered around the rooms, but it was dim. Too dim to do anything but go to bed right after dinner—cold cheese sandwiches, fruit, and canned tomato soup. There were granola bars, too, and I stowed two in my pocket for later, just in case. My stomach had been growling loudly all day, and I was desperate to make it stop. I could leave and go to a bodega, buy a few granola bars for myself and not worry about taking them from the homeless shelter, the people who really needed them—but I only had that twenty-dollar bill. I wasn't sure just how long I needed to make it stretch.

Mikki had gotten up to eat with the rest of us, but we didn't have the chance to talk much before she smiled at me, tapped my shoulder, and scurried back to her bed. And Zane—he had left to "attend to business" elsewhere, asking if I'd keep an eye on Zoey until he returned, some-time before bedtime, he promised. Zoey had been mostly silent after that, but she'd stuck close to my side. I was glad. I felt safer with her next to me, less like the outsider. I needed her as much as she seemed to need me.

Benjamin, back again for the second night, knocked on the door soon after dinner, asking if Zane could say good night to Zoey. She soared out of her bed at the news that her big brother was here, her eyes so bright and ex-cited, I could almost believe that there was a regular little girl in there somewhere. A little girl waiting for the world to prove her wrong.

She was back a few minutes later, still beaming as she climbed onto her bed.

"He asked if he could talk to you for a minute, too." She squinted her eyes at me, a curious-looking smile on her lips.

I turned away before she could see my frown. I was nervous to see him—nervous about what he might have to say to me after a day out in the real world beyond the shelter.

"Hey," I said quietly, closing the bedroom door be-hind me. "How was your day?" I considered asking more about Zane's "business," but I doubted he'd tell me, and I wasn't sure I'd really want to know.

He didn't bother to respond, just cocked his head toward the front door and started down the hallway, assuming without glancing back that I would be following him.

I was.

Benjamin waved at us from his post at the desk as we passed by. I tried to smile back, but I couldn't. I was shaking now, a tremor that kept my fingers in constant motion, my hands clenching and unclenching. The dread was sinking back in again—deep in—after a day of avoiding thinking much about myself at all. I'd been too busy thinking about Zoey, but now it was all me again. All Mina and Iris and what would come next.

"What's happening, Zane?" As soon as we were out the door, I lodged myself right in front of him, staring up into his eyes. "Say something."

He looked away, kicked at a filthy dented-up can on the ground, one of the many disgusting pieces of debris that had flooded into the courtyard.

"It's not just that one paper. It's all of them. And on the news, too, and I even saw some posters up in the subway station."

"Shit." I rocked back, almost slipping on the muddy cement. "How do people care this much? *Why?*"

"Disney fucked people's minds up," he said simply. "People need something to make it better. Anything. Even something as crazy as all of this. Your mom's old supporters are all over the story. And even people who didn't believe before seem to be reconsidering. I don't know . . . You can't see thousands of kids blown up and not question the world a little."

We were both silent after that, staring out over the dimly light courtyard.

"What do you think I should do?" I asked finally, turning to face him. He was already watching me, though, his eyebrows raised as if he was surprised that I was so desperate for his opinion.

"Well, you'll have to leave here in the morning. You could try to find another shelter, I guess, but other places are crowded. It takes time. And they'll ask a shit ton of questions that I doubt you're prepared to answer. With all these pictures of you floating around, someone's going to recognize you. It'll just be a matter of time."

I nodded, my harsh reality sinking in. I was at the end of the line. I had to move on, even if I had no idea where or what or how that would be.

"Go to bed," he said, his face taking on an expression that looked strangely like pity. "Think fresh on it tomorrow. Maybe something will come up."

"Is that what you do?" I asked. "You and Zoey. One day at a time?"

"It's different."

"How? Do you have a plan? Is it true what you told Benjamin, that this is only temporary?"

He looked away, shaking his head. The connection—whatever fragile connection we'd somehow been forming—was already caving in. I could feel him backing away before he even took a single step.

"Don't you worry about us, okay? My life is my problem to figure out."

"Listen, I care about what happens to Zoey," I said, taking a step closer to him, refusing to let him brush me off so easily. "She told me today . . . she told me about Brinley. About how you used to live with your aunt and uncle but now you don't anymore. What happened?"

"And that is *definitely* none of your damn business," he said, his lips drawing into an angry, ugly scowl. His nose flared, his eyes widened—everything about his face was suddenly five times bigger, stronger, scarier.

"She shouldn't have said anything to you. And you shouldn't have been poking around asking questions that you had no right to be asking. You don't know her. You don't know me."

"I *didn't* ask," I bit back. Hot, thick anger swept past the worry and the fear and the weakness I'd been feeling only the minute before. Anger was better right now. Anger was a distraction. "She told me. On her own. She started sobbing, looking at a stupid castle puzzle, and told me the whole thing. She was sobbing last night, too, while I was trying to sleep. Did you know that? Did you know that she cries herself to sleep at night?"

Zane's head reared back hard, like he'd been back-handed across the face.

"I'm sorry," I said, my stomach already twisting with regret. Just that fast, the anger had faded, left me feeling nothing but small and helpless. "I don't blame you. I'm just saying, Zoey needed to talk, even if I am a stranger. She's clearly got a lot on her mind, and I just wanted to help, even if all I could do was sit there and listen. I know it doesn't make much difference. But I couldn't walk away."

Zane was quiet. His eyes were closed now, squeezed tightly shut, and I could see the steady rise and fall of his chest, hear the deep breaths in and out.

"I don't want this life for her," he said, his eyes snapping open. "I don't want any of this. I don't want our shitty past, our shitty future. But it's fucking hard to do a single thing about it. Because every time I try, every time I think maybe I've got it figured out, I just get beat down all over again. If it wasn't for her—if it wasn't for Zoey—I would have stopped trying years ago."

He turned back for the door. I tried to yell out to him, tried to follow, but I was stuck, weighted down by everything he'd said to me, by everything wrong with my life, and now everything that was wrong with his life, too, and with Zoey's. You couldn't see that little girl, too skinny for her age, too hollow and too tough with those tattoos and that jaded slant to her eyes, and not want to help. And you couldn't see Zane, either, with his pain that he wore like full metal body armor, and not want to do something—*anything*—to make both of their lives just a little bit easier.

But I didn't know how. Not with my own tomorrow a big, gaping black hole looming just inches in front of my feet.

I didn't know what any of us would do tomorrow. Not me, not Zane and Zoey.

I didn't know anything at all. Not anymore.

Chapter Twelve

I WOKE UP early the next morning, or maybe I'd never really slept at all. Most of the night felt like an endless loop of tossing and turning, the sheets damp from my hot, sticky sweat. The room was too poorly ventilated for restful sleep, too dense with the scent of the other women—the women here now, with me, and the women who had come before us. The women who were next, too, the ones who would fill this bed after me.

The room was still and dark, the only sound the heavy, rhythmic breathing coming from the other beds. I tried to lie there just a little longer, to close my eyes and visualize what now, what next, but I was too jittery to stay in bed. I needed coffee and fresh air and to move my legs, to walk somewhere, anywhere. Maybe if I started taking steps, I'd magically end up where I was supposed to be. *Maybe.*

I had to wake Mikki up first, though, before making any decisions about the day. We hadn't talked about it at dinner, in front of everyone else, but I didn't want to leave without her. We'd come together. I assumed we'd leave to-gether, too. I was surprised she hadn't asked more about the news vans at my house and why exactly we'd run—but then again, we'd had no real private time since we got here.

My bed creaked as I started to slide out of it, and I froze, scared to wake Zoey up. I didn't want to explain to her why I was leaving or where I was going. I would see her again, somehow. I would check up on her—and on Zane—when I had better figured out my own situation. I couldn't help her until I'd helped myself first. Slowly, one tiny movement at a time, I managed to climb out of bed without making any noise. I grabbed my purse and jacket from the shelf and tiptoed over to where Mikki slept.

Only she wasn't in her bed when I got there. The blan-kets were smooth, tucked tight under the pillow. There was nothing on the shelf, not a single trace of Mikki. She'd been there that night, though, hadn't she? When the lights went out? I was sure of it. She'd gone straight to her bed af-ter dinner, and when I'd left to talk to Zane, she'd already been asleep.

But why would she leave so early?

How could she go without even saying good-bye?

My legs were stiff, suddenly ten times their usual weight, but I forced myself to start moving toward the hall-way. We'd only met a few times, after all. I guess I'd been silly to think that had meant we were *friends*. Why should she have stuck around for me?

Tomorrow, today, this morning, had already seemed petrifying enough when I thought she'd be with me. But now—now the idea of leaving the shelter, of walking out the door and down this street heading nowhere at all, seemed impossible.

I had to go, though, if for no other reason than that they'd be kicking us out, anyway, in just a matter of time. The sun was up; the storm was over.

Mr. Jackson was at the desk again, leaning back in the chair with his eyes closed, his head propped up against the wall behind him. Better this way, that I didn't have to say bye to him either. I didn't have to say bye to anyone. I would just disappear.

I slipped out into the courtyard, inhaling the after-rain smell, the damp brick, the still-wet cement beneath me. My feet turned toward the front gate. I glanced back once as I walked, and I blew a tiny kiss, a thank-you to Benjamin, to Zane and Zoey, and to all the other men and women whose names I would never know.

The traces of the storm were everywhere around me, at odds with the bright shininess of the now-blue sky— garbage and tree limbs and leaves were scattered along the sidewalks, and the street itself was strangely quiet, people still wary, maybe, hiding out. A street sign just above me dangled precariously from its pole: DUMONT AVE. I was probably only a handful of subway stops from home, but I might as well have been on another island altogether. North, south, east, west? Not a clue. Some of my friends seemed to have a built-in compass—they emerged from any subway stop and knew exactly what direction to walk in. I was a born-and-raised city kid, but I still needed a map or smartphone if I ventured beyond my everyday territory.

And this—this was definitely beyond. Yes, I was used to being in the minority in New York City. But I'd never been so obviously the odd one out before, the glaring inconsistency. I was *other* in this neighborhood. I was the lost-looking white girl, in my expensive organic denim jeans and a vintage bomber jacket that my dad had probably bought for me at twenty times the original price. At the shelter, I'd at least had Mikki, and then Zoey and Zane, to make me feel less conspicuous. No one had questioned me there, at least not out loud. Even if I looked different, I still looked just as desperate. Hopefully that desperation would help me again now.

I kept my head down, walking as quickly as I could without looking like I was running—without looking like I was scared. I had a vague idea of where Mikki and I had surfaced from the subway. I'd find the train first.

"You got beautiful eyes, sweetie," a voice called out from my right. I didn't shift my gaze, not wanting to give him any attention. But I could still see his bright white sneakers from the corner of my eye as they moved in closer. "Didn't you hear me?" he asked. "You got beautiful eyes. You should say thank you when somebody compliments you."

I glanced up, shaking, and forced a smile. It hurt to tug my lips so tight, to fight their every instinct.

"Whew," he whistled. "Beautiful smile, too."

Before I could stop him, he grabbed at my hand. I seized, panicking, too afraid to tear it away and provoke him even further. He pulled it to his lips, gave it a quick, dry peck. I lurched backward, but he grabbed my hand even tighter, his smile twisting into an ugly sneer.

"What is it, princess? You think you're too good for a kiss from me? Is that it?"

"No, n-n-no, that's not—no," I said, stumbling over the words. My blood, hot and pulsing, raced through my limbs, my head, my heart.

"What are you doing around here anyway? You lost?" The grin was back. "Maybe I should just show you around a little, then, huh?" He tugged hard on my hand, and I stumbled closer to him.

I opened my mouth, to answer or to scream, I wasn't sure.

"Hey!" a loud, rumbling voice called out from behind me. "Get your hands off her!"

Zane.

I spun around, jerking my hand free as Zane pounded up the sidewalk toward us, his face blazing with anger. He shoved his way between us, becoming my shield.

"Aw, man, relax, I was just paying her a compliment," the guy said, his hands up in surrender as he took a few steps back. "You can have her. She ain't my type, anyway." He spat on the cement, his squinting eyes focused on me, before he backed up and started walking away.

Zane watched, arms and legs tensed and ready, until the man disappeared around the corner. He turned toward me then, his entire face softening. "Shit, I'm sorry, Iris. I saw you heading out of the shelter and, I don't know, I was curious. I wanted to make sure you were okay . . ."

I nodded, numb, as I rubbed the wrist that the man had touched, frantic to wipe away the traces.

"He probably was just messing with you, but I still want to pound his face in for it. I don't do that shit anymore, though. Try not to, anyway." He cracked a weak half smile. "But what are you doing out here? Do you have any clue where you're going?"

"No, I . . . I don't know." I fought the urge to step closer to him, to feel even more protected from the rest of the world. "My friend"—I tripped over the word, but kept going—"my *friend* Mikki's gone, left me all alone without even saying bye, so now I have no clue where I'm going. It's tomorrow, here and now, so I'm just doing what you said. One step at a time. I still just don't know where any of the steps are actually going to take me."

Zane stared at me, his lips pursed. He ran his fingers along his jaw, over the ridges of that jagged dark scar.

"Well, I don't think you should be out here alone. You don't know your way around, clearly. So would you want to . . . ?" Zane's eyebrows knotted above those dark honey eyes. But then he shook his head and closed his mouth, looked at the sky, away from me.

"Would I want to . . . ?"

"I can't even believe I'm saying this," he said, laughing. "I can't even fucking believe I'm saying this out loud right now."

"Saying what?" My hand reached out before I could stop myself, latched on to his warm, solid wrist.

He stared down at my hand, but I kept it there, my palm against his skin.

"Come with me and Zoey," he said, his face tilting back up to meet my gaze. "If you want. No pressure. I just thought maybe you'd be safer for now, and . . ."

"Yes." I took my first real breath since the stranger had approached me, the fresh air making me almost woozy with relief. "Of course I'll go with you guys."

A look of surprise flashed across his face. "You're sure?"

"Of course I'm sure. You did just save me, after all. And as shocking as it might sound to you, Zane Davis, I trust you. I think you're a decent guy, no matter how tough you might act." I blushed, embarrassed by the over-the-top honesty of the admission, but I kept my eyes on his. It was true, after all. I *did* trust him. He knew my secret, and he was keeping it for me.

"But you haven't even asked where we're going."

I shrugged. "Anywhere with you and Zoey seems better than going nowhere by myself."

"I'm not sure that's true," he said, his voice more subdued. "But it's your decision. And it seems to me like you've already made it. So let's go wake up Zoey, and we'll head out. I already trashed the newspaper again today. I got your back. Okay?"

"Okay." I nodded. "Thanks."

Zane turned back toward the shelter, and I followed. We walked more slowly this time, now that neither of us had anyone to run from or after.

"So where *are* we going?" I asked. "Not that the answer will change my mind."

He glanced over at me, and I could swear there was a smile in his eyes—or at least the usual frown was lifted, even if only a tiny bit.

"Nothing definite, but there's a distant relative—or maybe he's just an old family friend, no one's really sure of the connection anymore. Anyway, he's usually willing to let us crash for a few days if we need it. It's where we went right after . . ." He coughed, and the words trailed off.

"And you think he'll let me crash, too?" I asked.

"No guarantees, but . . . he's not a terrible guy. More decent than most people I know, anyway. Not that that's saying a whole lot. He's not around most of the time anyway, so he usually doesn't give a shit, as long as we're not permanent fixtures. I'm not too worried."

"It seems like you never get too worried," I said, realizing just then, somehow, that my hand was still wrapped tight around his wrist, our arms dangling in between us as we walked. I dropped it, embarrassed that I'd been clinging for that long. But if he'd noticed, he hadn't stopped me. He hadn't pulled away.

"Why would you say that?" he asked, looking straight ahead, not acknowledging either way what he'd thought of my hand finally letting go.

"Because you just seem so sure you'll work things out, one way or another. Every day."

"Well, I do . . ." He sighed, shaking his head. "I do worry. All the damn time. I just got real good at hiding it. Mainly for Zoey. I worry for her, anyway. Not me. Never for me."

After we picked up Zoey, we rode the subway for a few stops and then walked for what felt like hours, but I couldn't be sure how much time had really passed. I saw an old, run-down phone booth at one point along the trek and considered calling my parents, but what more did I have to say? I wished I could talk to Caleb, though—Caleb, who probably felt abandoned, terrified that he'd lost his big sister for good. Or . . . maybe he was glad to have some time away from me.

Maybe they all were relieved—not just Cal, but Ari and Ethan and Delia, too. Had they been trying to reach me? I'd left them stranded after their initial texts—hopefully my parents had at least given updates. But even if my phone hadn't died, I wasn't sure I could handle their questions. Their judgment.

"We're here," Zane announced. I pushed my thoughts—their faces—far away.

I glanced around, trying not to stare as we stood waiting in front of a rusty metal door with shattered glass panels. There was a tiny hole in the center, cracks radiating out in all directions like icy white veins. An angry rap song blared from a passing car. Suddenly it was like everything was magnified, the volume on life jolted up with so many overlapping noises—a baby crying, a woman yelling, a siren blaring in the distance. I smelled spicy, fried food and pot and garbage and something else, something sweet and doughy and amazing, reminding my stomach that I hadn't eaten anything that morning before leaving the shelter.

I forced myself to look away from the splintered glass and focus on Zane instead. "So should I just wait out on the steps, then?" I asked, determined not to let my fear show. Different didn't have to be bad. Different could be just that—different.

"Yeah," he said, his hand already pressing down on a button marked 5B. "Zoey, you stay down here, too, okay? I want to talk to Uncle Anthony first, make sure it's cool that we're here."

"What if he's not home?" I asked, just as a screeching buzzer went off and the lock thudded in the door.

"He's usually home this early still. Or more likely, his night just ended a little bit ago." Without more explanation, Zane pushed through the door and disappeared into a dimly lit hallway, cracked yellow tiles leading to a narrow stairwell. A stale, sour odor hovered in the air, lingering even after the door shut and locked again.

I looked over at Zoey and forced a smile, grabbing her hand on instinct. She sat on the stoop, pulling me down next to her. I tried not to grimace as I settled against the cement, the ambiguous smears of dirt and caked chunks of something that I hoped was old food, rather than vomit, if I had to choose. But it wasn't as if I was pristine at that point either, now that it had been over two full days without a shower or a change of clothes.

"So what's your uncle Anthony like?" I asked, trying to keep my voice casual, not too anxious or inquisitive.

She crinkled her nose, her lips puckering. "Eh. He's okay. I guess."

"So he's a nice guy?"

"He's better than nothing. And nothing's what we usually got now."

I was about to ask where exactly in Brooklyn we were, when a new question occurred to me.

"Zoey," I started, hesitating, "when you're moving around like this, how do you go to school? It's Sunday, so tomorrow . . . tomorrow will you go to school?"

"Maybe," she said quietly, not meeting my eyes. "I mostly do."

"Mostly?"

"I go when I can," she said, sounding frustrated now, more defensive. "Zane walks me there in the mornings as long as it's not too far from where we're staying. He misses school sometimes but that's just because he's too busy walking to drop me off and pick me up and figuring out how to make money and where we'll go next."

I nodded. "I know," I said. "I can tell how much he

loves you. I'm sure he knows how important it is that you go to school. He doesn't want either of you to get in any trouble."

"Well, he gets in trouble all the time. But I don't. He said if I don't go enough, the school might find out he's taking care of me and he's only seventeen. So they'd take me away 'cause he's not old enough to do that alone. But no way is anyone stealing me from Z." Her sharp eyes were staring right at me, daring me to challenge her somehow. But I wouldn't. Because she was right—she should stay with Zane. He would fight for his sister.

Fight to the death, I thought, and immediately shuddered. Those rumors, the scissors and the time locked away. I didn't want to think about what could have caused it, if any part of it was true—what someone had done to Zoey to deserve such extreme retaliation.

"Do you go to school usually when you're at Uncle Anthony's?" I asked instead. "Or is it too far? I can always help walk you there."

"Don't you have to go to school, too? With Z?"

Now it was my turn to look away. I'd barely thought about school. I'd go back, though. Soon. I had to, right? "Yes, but I'm . . . I'm taking a little break. Just for a little."

"Why?" Her dark eyebrows pulled together, nearly a perfect V on her furrowed forehead. "You can't just 'take a break.' It's *school*. You have to go."

"It's a long story." I sighed. "Just trust me. I can't go back there right now." A series of terrible scenes flashed across my mind: the sneers and the rolling eyes, the conversations my classmates would no doubt be having about me first thing the next morning. They all would have heard the news, of course. They all would know. And they would laugh, I was sure of it. They'd be laughing so hard that anyone could think I was some kind of *savior*. I was the weird girl, the girl who made friends with the homeless, the girl who played her violin for strangers at the park.

"We got time," Zoey said, jutting her pointy little elbow into my side. "What else we got to do right now but talk?"

"I just got in some weird, mixed-up trouble, that's all," I said, staring up at the clear blue sky. Not at her. It was risk enough already that she might overhear kids talking at school about me, put the pieces together for herself. But maybe not—kids probably had far more interesting things to be discussing. "I'm still sorting it out. When I do . . . maybe we can talk about it then."

"That's not fair," she said, her voice so low I almost missed it in all the other sounds around us, the cars driving, honking, pulsing with music. She pulled her hand from mine and pushed herself a few inches down the stoop, putting more distance between us. "I told you all about me. About *Brinley*. About how Z and me got no parents, no aunt and uncle now either. And you won't tell me anything. Why don't you have a home right now? Hm?"

"Zoey," I said, desperate to have her understand that this wasn't personal, that I didn't want to tell *anybody* else about my secret. "You have to believe me that . . ."

But before I could try to explain, the door behind us yanked open. I looked up, hoping to see Zane, but instead there was a tall white-haired man, wearing a faded black tank top that stretched tight over his round belly. I felt cold just looking at his bare skin.

"You that girl Zane wants to have stay for a few days?"

Zane, thankfully, appeared behind the man then, putting one hand on his shoulder to make room on the stoop next to him.

"Yes, Uncle Anthony," he said, his voice sounding purposely steady, calm. "This is Clemence."

"Clem—?" Zoey asked, looking from her brother to me, but she closed her mouth, frowning as she bit down on the question.

"You got yourself into any trouble that's gonna get me in trouble to keep you here?" he asked, flecks of spit flying from his lips. A drop hit my cheek, but I kept my face straight.

"Not at all, sir," I said, standing up to bring myself closer to his level, though he still towered over me by a good foot. "I just had a fight with my family and we all need some time to cool off. I . . . I have a little money. Not much, but a little. If that helps."

"Well, I won't be feeding you," he said, squinting down at me.

"Of course not. I just . . . just need a floor to sleep on, if that's okay. I'm not any trouble, I promise. You won't even notice I'm here."

"Hmph," he huffed, his hands rubbing up and down his belly. I gritted my teeth, willing him to agree. *Please. Please say yes.*

I stared into his eyes, made myself smile in a way that I hoped looked reassuring, hopeful but not too expectant.

"Ah, okay," he muttered, throwing his hands up. "Why the hell not? What's one more, right?" He slapped Zane on the back and headed inside, not saying another word as he started trudging up the steps.

"I wasn't sure it'd be a go," Zane said, watching me. "I thought he was coming down just to say no to your face."

"Well, he didn't, did he?" I smiled, ignoring any doubts, any questions about why Anthony had changed his mind. Instead, I let the relief unwind through my tense muscles. "Today at least is figured out."

"Yeah, I'm so glad you're safe, *Clemence*," Zoey hissed, jumping up off the stoop. "You know, don't you?" she asked, turning to glare at Zane, too. "You know whatever secret she won't tell me, right? Why else would you call her

Clemence if her name's Iris? Or, no . . . which is the lie?"

Zane shrugged, looked off toward the street.

"Fine. No one tell me anything. I'm just a kid, right?" She looked back at me, her eyes boiling with what looked like just as much hurt as anger. "I'll just have to figure it out on my own, then."

Zoey turned away and started toward the stairwell. But then she halted, spinning back around.

"I might be a kid still, but you know what I already learned so far? Secrets don't stay secrets. *Ever.*"

Chapter Thirteen

UNCLE ANTHONY'S APARTMENT was a strange mix of spare and cluttered; he didn't seem to own much, but what he did have was thrown into haphazard heaps across the sticky, stained wooden floors. Besides an over-sized, scuffed leather couch in the living room—Zoey's and my "bed," according to Zane—most of the furniture was a random assortment of recycled goods. Plastic crates stacked as shelves for books and DVDs and old records, a few pieces of wood balanced over cardboard boxes for a coffee table, a TV propped on cement blocks. It wasn't much, but it was functional, more or less.

Anthony disappeared back into his bedroom, and Zane left soon after we'd settled in—he had work to do, he said, but wouldn't look me in the eye when I pressed for more details. I couldn't help but think that, whatever his "job" was, it wasn't aboveboard. Drugs? Some kind of stolen goods?

I shook the thoughts off. It wasn't my business. He wasn't prying into my life, and I shouldn't pry into his. And besides, he did what he had to for Zoey—I didn't doubt he'd do whatever necessary, no matter how many laws he had to break.

With Zane gone, that left just me and Zoey, who refused to acknowledge my existence, and an entire day together. She plunked down on the sofa with a handful of Oreos and some cheese crackers from Anthony's shelves, flipping through the channels. I found the two granola bars from the shelter at the bottom of my purse, now only slightly smashed, and allowed myself to eat one. I'd have to look for a deli at some point to pick up more food, but I didn't want to leave Zoey all alone—even if she would have clearly preferred that I did.

She looked mesmerized by the TV. Even commercials had her transfixed, wide-eyed and motionless. I settled in at the opposite end of the sofa, leaving as much distance between us as I possibly could. I didn't know Zoey all that well, but I could already tell that trying to change her mind would have the opposite effect; she'd have to forgive me on her own terms.

A few episodes deep into some painfully sweet and unfunny kids' sitcom—unfunny to me, at least, but Zoey couldn't stop giggling—I started dozing. My eyes shuttered, the lids suddenly too heavy to force open, and I burrowed more deeply against the soft, worn leather of the sofa. Zoey's happy laughter lulled me. I slipped away to the sound of it, eased into a deep sleep with the peace that Zoey was still capable of being a kid, at least sometimes.

The laughter seemed to twirl through my mind, shimmering, sparking in the darkness as it reached out and made contact with another laugh, another cheerful sound. But it was as if this one laugh multiplied, like a happy virus spiraling out of control—because it was a whole chorus of laughing now, breathy giggles and gigantic, ringing laughs, so lovely, so perfect. A light went on, but I still couldn't see clearly. There was some sort of veil pulled down in front of my face—white light and fuzzy shapes and the sense of movement and activity all around me. I clawed at the veil, laughing, too, laughing because the sound was so contagious. I wanted to see them, wanted to be a part of the group in front of me. But I couldn't seem to tear the veil away, couldn't remove that lingering wall between me and everybody else.

Who were these laughing people? Did I know them? Did they know me?

"*Hello*," I called, "can anybody help me?" Nothing, just more laughter. "Hello?"

I reached again for the silky gauze, clenching my jaw as I slashed at it with my front teeth. A tiny hole! I bit down and yanked, the gap stretching, light streaming in. *Yes!* I was closer now, so close to seeing . . .

But then—a bang, a horrific popping sound that seemed to shake the air around, above, under me. Because what was I standing on? Nothing? Clouds? Light? The sound gained momentum, rolling and tumbling, like a thunderstorm and fireworks and a car crash, all on top of the other, noise clashing with more noise.

The bright light flickered and went out; the air shook and I shook along with it, as if I were suspended by a string, my limbs flapping, snapping in all directions.

And then, just as suddenly as it had begun, it stopped. I waited a few moments before I allowed myself to breathe in, out. The noise, whatever it was, had passed, and I was still there.

But then I realized—there was no more laughter. I tore at the veil, and this time it fell away. I was surrounded by darkness, hollow, empty darkness, except—except for a pinprick of light, a flame in the distance. There was a hushed sound then, too. It was somebody . . . somebody crying?

"Hello?" I said, the question coming out as a whisper. I coughed, clearing my throat, and wiped my sweaty palms against my face to prove that I was real, that I existed. "Hello?" again, shaky still, but louder this time.

The sound stopped; the light wavered. My whole body

tensed, and I leaned forward, waiting, tilting my head so that I could better listen for a response.

"It's you," a soft, far-off voice said. A little girl, I think.

"I'm Iris," I said, clarifying.

"I know." A pause, a moment with no breath. "You're here. You're finally here."

"Stop! Stop screaming."

Everything was still dark, all dark, but there were hands on me, warm hands pressing down against my cheeks.

"You're okay. You're *okay*. It was just a dream."

My eyes snapped open to see Zoey hovering over me, kneeling on the couch with her arms out to steady me.

"I'm awake," I told her.

She took her hands away from me, but she stayed just as close. "I thought you would never stop screaming. You were twitching, too, like you were fighting the air. It was scary."

I blinked, remembering what had happened—the laughter, the light, the explosion, and then nothing, nothing except for that one quiet voice. *You're finally here.* I shuddered, terrified, somehow, by that little girl's voice, that proclamation. She had sounded so *certain*.

"You're still shaking," Zoey said, frowning. She pulled

a faded Star Wars comforter down from the back of the sofa and shook it open over me, tucking the edges in around my legs.

"Thank you," I said. *It was only a dream*, I reminded myself. *All of it.* I was here, on this sofa, with Zoey.

"You really can tell me, you know," she said, the words quiet, tentative. "What I said earlier—about secrets. I was just mad. I didn't mean it. But after I told you about Brinley . . . I felt better. It made missing her hurt a little less. Not much. But a little."

"I want to, but . . ." I just couldn't. I needed to know more about what people were saying, beyond that one tabloid Zane had shown me. I needed to read the articles for myself, be up-to-date on exactly what was being said. There didn't seem to be any newspapers, though, in the rubble piles scattered around the room, and there certainly wasn't a computer in there for me to prowl for online articles. I could scan through papers at a deli later, but otherwise the TV was my only hope. And I could only do that if Zoey was sleeping—still risky, since she'd be on the sofa.

But I wanted to know *now*, immediately, this very second.

Zoey's usually strong, brave little face was crumbling as she watched me. "What could you have done that is so bad you can't tell me?"

"It's not that it's so *bad*"—I sighed—"or at least nothing I did. It's just that people have made a big mistake about me, and my mom wants to send me away. I'm not ready to do that, so I just . . . I just need to clear my head a little. Figure out what next."

"Can you tell me at least if you're Iris or if you're Clemence? I hate not even knowing what name is real. If either of them even *is* real."

"Hey. It's Iris," I said, placing my hand on her chin and tilting her face upward so I could look her in the eyes. "I never lied to you, Zoey. Clemence was . . . Clemence was for everyone else at the shelter. Not for you and Zane."

She didn't smile, but she did nod before turning her attention back to the TV screen. I didn't fall asleep again, as numbing as the long string of shows became. I was too freaked out by the dream, too desperate for some other connection with the outside world. I almost suggested turning the TV off and going for a walk—doing anything other than just sitting around on Anthony's couch—but I didn't know this neighborhood at all. And I had no working phone if we got lost or found ourselves in any kind of trouble. Leaving with just Zoey felt too risky. So I sat, feet tapping, picking at my cuticles, staring blankly at the screen. My fingers twitched for the violin, so much so that they almost ached with the need. I couldn't remember the last time I'd gone this long without playing; maybe never, not since my first lesson. I was six when I started, just out of kindergarten.

When the door finally opened and Zane stepped in, I flew off the sofa to greet him.

"Hey!" I said, waving and grinning as I nearly slid across the floor in my overenthusiasm.

Zane raised his eyebrows, squinted at me. "You okay?"

"Sure! Fine. We've had a good day here," I said, my cheeks burning now at my total lack of cool. "I'm just happy to have you back here with us." Even more burning.

Zane laughed, shaking his head as he started toward the kitchen. "Whatever, crazy girl. I brought dinner, too, so that might just push you over the edge of happy."

I noticed now the plastic bags he was dropping onto the kitchen counter, my stomach seizing at the delicious, greasy smell of fried rice, egg rolls, and what I hoped was chicken and broccoli drenched in brown sauce. As I stood drooling, Zane picked Zoey up from the sofa like she was nothing but a feather, hoisting her above his head and spinning her around in the air. She reached her hands out like she was flying, a superhero, all smiles and giggles.

"You were already on my good side," I said, practically running over to the kitchen counter. "But now you might just be my very favorite person on the planet."

All thoughts of scavenging for papers, watching the news, getting out of this apartment for some fresh air—

none of that mattered, not with the way my stomach was somersaulting in anticipation of the feasting ahead.

Zane plopped Zoey down on top of the counter, giving her a quick peck on the forehead.

"How much was it?" I asked, remembering to have at least some manners as I savagely unwrapped and bit into a perfectly crisp, juicy egg roll.

"Nah," Zane said, waving his hand at me as he scooped a big heap of fried rice onto a paper plate. "Don't worry about it. I got it tonight."

I opened my mouth to insist, but Zane looked over at me, an exaggerated scowl on his face. "You're not paying. So just enjoy that goddamn egg roll." He broke out in a full-on grin then, his white teeth igniting the rest of his face.

I had never seen him smile, not like that, not at me. He was so beautiful when he smiled—so beautiful that I almost told him that out loud, that he could light up a room, that he should do it more often. But then I stopped myself. Because there were reasons he didn't smile more. Couldn't smile more, probably, without it being entirely fake. This smile, though—this smile was definitely genuine.

I smiled back before popping the rest of the roll into my mouth in one gigantic bite. We stayed like that, smiling, our eyes locked, until Zoey squeezed in between us and started riffling through the pile of take-out containers.

We took our plates into the living room and sat in a little circle on the floor, silent for the first ten minutes while we devoured our food. Then, once we were all a little less ravenous, Zoey started telling us about the time Brinley spilled an entire plate of egg foo young on her pristine white choir uniform, and how she'd read somewhere that only holy wine would be able to clean the stain. The story was funny and sad and ridiculous all at once—I couldn't always tell if their eyes were misty from crying or from laughing so hard—and from there, Zoey kept telling us more memories of Brinley. Silly ones and sweet ones, every kind of Brinley story there was, with Zane chiming in with his own anecdotes that usually had me cracking up, almost as if I'd known her, too. I felt like I did, listening to them talk about her like this. I could feel her there, in the room, almost as clearly as I felt Zoey and Zane.

She was still real. She always would be, in that way. In memories.

For the first time since Disney, I didn't feel guilty that I hadn't lost someone that day.

Because now, hearing about Brinley, I had.

After Zoey dozed off on the sofa, deep inside a food coma, I tapped Zane on the shoulder. I tilted my head, motioning for him to follow me toward the kitchen.

"Is there somewhere we can talk?" I whispered. "Somewhere"—I shot a glance over at the sofa—"she won't hear?"

He squinted, puckering his bottom lip, silent for a moment. And then a flash in his eyes, and his fingers were around my wrist, pulling me along. We tiptoed past Zoey, toward the door. Zane eased the lock open and we quietly stepped out. When were both safely in the hallway, he grinned at me.

"The roof," he said.

"The roof?"

"We're on the top floor, right, but here's this middle door," he said, pointing to an unmarked black door opposite Anthony's. "I never tried it before, but it's gotta go somewhere."

"What if Zoey wakes up?"

"Shit. Good point. Hold up." He put a finger to his lips and disappeared back inside the apartment. I grew more anxious as I waited, counting the cracked linoleum floor tiles to calm myself while I walked a slow, straight line down the hall.

"All good," Zane said from behind, knocking me off my track. "Left her a note. Just said we ran out on errands, not to worry. But I doubt she'll wake up. She looks pretty knocked out."

I spun around, facing him and the black door.

"So we're trying this?" I asked. Heights didn't usually freak me out, but there was something about being out on a roof, in this strange new apartment and this strange new neighborhood—with Zane—that made my heart pound and my blood rush. But that wasn't necessarily a bad thing. I felt alive, real, *human*.

He just smiled back, reaching his hand for the door. He jiggled the knob a few times, left, right. "Damn. Locked. But . . ." he said, reaching into his back pocket. "Looks like an easy one, so just give me a sec." He withdrew a plastic card from his wallet with a flourish and started poking at the lock. Within seconds, Zane pushed the door open, revealing a dark ascending stairwell.

"Seriously," he said. "Too easy. I was hoping for at least a little bit of a challenge." He waved me forward, but then stopped, moving so that he stood in front of me, blocking the stairs. "Let me check it out first. Make sure it's not totally nasty and dangerous up there. I don't want it on my hands if . . ." He stopped, his eyes widening before he turned away, suddenly intent on studying those same linoleum tiles.

"If what?" I asked, the question burning in my already queasy, full stomach. "What were you going to say, Zane?"

"Nothing," he said, shaking his head. "It was just a joke. But a shitty joke."

"If it's just a joke, then say it anyway." I folded my arms

against my chest, trying to look far cooler and far stronger than I actually felt.

"I was going to say that . . . Shit, Iris," he said, running his hands over his close-cropped black hair. He still couldn't look at me. "I'm sorry. I was going to say that I don't want it on my hands if I kill the next Jesus, or, you know. Whatever people out there are saying."

"You're right," I said, almost a whisper now. "That was a shitty joke."

I stepped forward and nudged Zane aside, taking the stairs two at a time. I needed to be away from him, those words. That name. *Jesus.* I needed to be free. There was another door at the top—unlocked, fortunately—and I yanked it open, walking out onto the roof before he could stop me.

"Iris," he called out, but I ignored him, stepped farther out into the dark night sky. This building wasn't particularly high, but I could still see the streets stretching out in a grid, the people, tiny as dolls, walking beneath the halos of streetlamps. Rooftops always felt magical to me, like I was floating on clouds hovering just above New York City—its rivers and bridges and bright flashing lights, the skyline that people traveled from all over the globe to see. Everything was brighter, neater, better somehow, from up above. The world made more sense when you saw it from a distance; you became one tiny part of a much bigger, grander machine. You were somehow more alone and less alone, emptier and fuller, all at the same time.

"Iris, c'mon." Zane brushed up against my shoulder. "I'm sorry, okay?"

I couldn't acknowledge him, just kept staring out at the lights, the blur of movement happening for miles into the horizon. So many lives packed into these buildings all around me, so many lives and so many people, going about their nights, laughing, crying, eating, studying, fighting, breathing, dying.

I was just one. Just one piece.

"Seriously," Zane said, grabbing my wrist and spinning me around to face him, his broad chest and piercing eyes replacing the skyline, the stars. "You have got a serious temper. Didn't see that coming."

"I do *not* have a temper," I said, frowning as I pulled away from his grasp. "I just thought that you were a . . . a friend, I guess, as silly as that sounds. I thought you understood me. But I'm clearly just a joke to you. This whole thing—my whole *life*—is just a joke to you. Are you helping me out because it's fun? Is this entertainment? Please tell me, Zane, what the hell is in any of this for you? Because I'm just confused." The questions, the doubts—they'd been there waiting, lurking somewhere deep down since that moment he'd pulled me out to the courtyard and told me that he *knew*. Everything. But I hadn't let myself listen, because I couldn't. I needed Zane. And so I'd let myself play dumb.

"You're not a joke to me," he said, his eyes still fixed on mine. I held my breath, balled my clammy hands into fists at my sides. "Honestly, I don't know why exactly I'm helping you. I just know that I have to. No"—he shook his head—"that's not right. I *want* to help. There's . . . there's, God, I sound crazy, but there's just something about you. Something special, I guess."

"Don't," I said, stepping backward. My voice shook; my whole body shook. "Don't you dare say that. Don't you try to tell me that there's anything special . . ."

My foot hit something solid behind me and I stumbled, my standing leg wobbling as my weight shifted back. I threw my hands out to find balance, desperate to throw myself forward toward the roof, solid ground. My entire body was screaming—stomach, heart, lungs pounding with alarm. My mouth, though, was oddly silent. Wide open, lips cracking, but no sound was coming out. I had no air left to give.

My eyes locked with Zane's for a second—his horror, my horror—before he lurched forward. He grabbed at me, pushing me to the floor of the roof. It wasn't until we came to a stop, our arms and legs all knotted up together, that I looked back toward the edge. There was just a short ledge there, a ledge that my knees would have buckled over, a ledge that would have done nothing to stop me from hurtling over the side of the building.

"Shit, Iris," he said, the words muffled by my sweatshirt. His head was pressed hard up against my collarbone, his body bracing over mine as if I could still teeter, still roll away, if he let me go. "Do you know how fucking scary that was? I thought"—he lifted his head up, our eyes meeting, just inches apart—"I thought it would be too late to save you. That I wouldn't be fast enough. I thought you were going to die."

The words ripped me open and poured inside, like icy, stinging water flooding through every gash. *I almost died.*

I didn't think, couldn't think. I freed my arms from under Zane and grabbed at his face, pulling it closer to mine. I pushed myself up and pressed my lips against his. I had never kissed a boy before—never *been* kissed by anyone but my family, a peck on the cheek or forehead—and I'd always worried, wondered what that first time would be like, the awkward fumbling and the bumping around. But it was entirely natural and instinctual now, no how-to manual required. In the moment before I closed my eyes and let the kiss take over everything else, I saw the flash of confusion in Zane's eyes. But, my lips on his, his lips on mine, I didn't *feel* the confusion.

I felt nothing but right, solid and safe and warm. I

felt okay again, better than okay, like I was higher than this roof, higher than any roof, like I really *was* on the clouds, above everything happening below. I was above the news stories and the speculation, above my family and my friends, above everything that had gone so wrong with my life.

Our lips moved faster, his palms on my face, my hands wrapped around his neck, pulling him in deeper.

"Iris," Zane whispered, lifting up so that his lips were just barely above mine. "Iris, you don't really want this. You don't really want me, I mean."

"Yes, I do." I was sure of that—I hadn't realized it before that moment, maybe, but that didn't matter. I knew it now. I had thought I wanted Gabe Goodman, all summer long, agonizing over what I could say or do to make something happen. To make *us* happen. The way I felt now, with Zane, was so much different. So much better. I pictured the two of them side by side: quiet, angelic Gabe with his shy smiles, sweetly playing his violin; and Zane, so tall and commanding, his strength rolling in waves off his words, his stance, his every movement. I bit down on my lip to hold back a laugh, the contrast of the two so absurdly amusing. I'd thought I knew what I was looking for. I was wrong.

"You don't know anything about me," Zane said, pulling me back to the roof—the image of Gabe slipping from my mind for good. "And I wouldn't want you to, either, because I'm not a good person. I'm not like you."

"I know plenty of things about you," I said, my lips brushing against his. "I know that you're not just a big brother to Zoey. You're practically a dad to her, and she adores you. Worships you, really. I know that you've probably dealt with more shit in your life than I can even begin to understand. And I know that no matter what mistakes you've maybe made, you do what you have to do to survive, to keep Zoey safe. You're angry, maybe, and you act tough, but I know the Zane that Zoey sees is the real Zane. The Zane I've seen, too. The one who is helping me for no good reason at all, even if he thinks I'm probably a little crazy and stupid for running. The Zane that just saved me a few minutes ago, in case you already forgot. And earlier today, too, from that terrible guy on the street. Twice in one day . . . pretty impressive, I'd say."

"So you know a few things, maybe."

"A few pretty important things," I corrected.

"What about you?" he asked. "I don't know much of anything about you, except for the fact that people think your mom was, like, a modern-day Virgin Mary."

"Trust me, nothing else is quite that exciting."

"Tell me anyway," he said, sitting up to look at me.

"Okay," I said, pulling myself up next to him, close enough that our shoulders and knees still touched. "Well, my parents are great, or at least were until I found out they'd been keeping this huge secret from me. That my *dad* isn't technically my dad, that no one is." The thought stung all over again. But even still, I missed my dad as much as I missed my mom and Cal. "And I have a younger brother, Caleb, too. He's right around Zoey's age, actually, and he's already wiser than I am. It's a shame *he* wasn't my mom's firstborn." I forced a laugh, and Zane wrapped his arm tight around my back. "But he's been pretty freaked out about everything. Understandably. Part of me wonders if it's easier for him with me gone."

"I seriously doubt that's true," he said quietly. "What else?"

"Let's see . . . I've played the violin for over a decade. It's my baby, really. And I miss playing it right now almost as much as I miss my family. And my bed."

"I played guitar a little, mostly when I was younger," Zane said. "My dad had one, and he left it behind with the rest of us. But I sold it a little while back, needed the cash. I sucked anyway. It was just something to do. It stopped my brain from thinking too much when I played. Made me calm down."

"If you ever get a new one, we'll have to play together. I bet you're not as bad as you think."

Zane snorted. "I am. Trust me. It's not happening."

I closed my eyes and smiled, letting the image of the

two of us making music at the park together play through my mind. Zane was right. The scene was hard to actually imagine.

"Iris . . ." Zane paused. "Why do you keep running? I mean, really? It seems like you have a good family who cares about you. A home. And friends, too. I've seen you at school before, the little clique you go around in. You guys always seemed a little weird together—that punk girl who's always growling, the nerdy, chubby guy with the gigantic glasses. The other girl, the quiet one. She was in my art class once. Super fucking talented, didn't say a single word. Just painted her mad crazy, brilliant strokes. And then you. I never knew what the hell to make of you."

"I'm surprised you noticed. We usually seem to slip under the radar."

"Yeah, well. I'm alone most of the time. Lurking in hallways, as you put it. You notice a lot then."

I was quiet for a moment, my eyes lost in the endless black sky above. "I'm running because I don't know what else to do. I thought some time away would help. That then I'd be able to stand up to my mom and make her understand that I'm not going to leave town like she wants. And somehow figure out how I can stay here and be safe still. Figure out what the rest of my life is going to be like, now that so much has changed."

"How's that plan coming along, then?"

"Ha." I swatted at him, my hand lightly tapping his cheek. "It hasn't been a total failure so far. I somehow convinced this random stranger to take me in. I'm pretty sure no reporters and no parents will think to find me here."

"What would they say if they did? Find you with me, that is. I'm not any parent's dream, that's for damn sure. You'd probably be grounded for the rest of your high school life, anyway, so you wouldn't have to worry about facing the public."

"They know I'm with a guy. And his sister. I told them that much to keep them calm. *Relatively* calm."

"You know what I mean."

"My parents wouldn't judge you. Or at least, not you specifically. I've just . . . I've never dated or anything like that before." My cheeks burned hot at my use of *dated*—it's not as if *we* were dating after one strange, spontaneous kiss on a roof. "The only guy they've ever met is my friend Ethan, the one with the gigantic glasses, as you put it. So yeah, they'd maybe be worried thinking that I'd run off and started some wild fling with you. But you can't take that personally. Any strange guy would make them worry that way."

He paused for a beat. "Well, they don't have to worry. About that, I mean."

"I know."

"I mean it. First off, I don't *date*. My life's complicated enough already. I don't have time for all that drama and shit. Second, you . . . you're too good for any of the asses in our school, trust me. And my name is definitely on that list."

"Oh, please. You're not nearly as bad as you want everyone to think you are."

He smiled at that, and I leaned in closer, feeling brave. I could see the smile in his eyes, too, so close to mine now that they were just a blur of colors, gold and black and glowing. He kissed me again, softer this time. I closed my eyes, sunk into the feeling of it, the warmth of his body, the cool night breeze. I was convinced that I was glowing under him, shining brighter than any of the dim city stars dotting the sky. I was alive there; I was bright and radiant and infinite. I *was* special, in that moment. Up there on that roof. With him. He had said so. And somehow from him, from Zane, I couldn't not believe it was true.

But that thought, that word, *special*—it reminded me with a jolt why I had asked him where we could be alone in the first place. The questions I had for him, all the things I needed to hear about the world beyond this apartment building. I had thought I couldn't wait, but I was wrong. In the morning he would take Zoey to school, and I could go out and buy a stack of newspapers, keep the TV on all day. Tomorrow.

Tonight was for this.

Zane. Me.

The sky.

We lay out there, tangled up, sometimes kissing, sometimes not, until I dozed off and woke up to Zane carrying me down the stairs and back into the apartment. I groggily smiled up at him before closing my eyes again, letting my head fall against his chest.

But then—*"Zoey?"*

The word jerked me awake. Zane set me down on my feet, so quickly I barely had time to steady myself, and he bolted toward the TV. My eyes followed his, saw what he saw—my face, consuming everything else on the screen. Everything else in the room. There were words, too, big and white beneath the picture of me, and a voice speaking in the background—but I couldn't make sense of any of it, couldn't see anything but my face, couldn't hear anything but Zane's voice, saying, "Zoey! Turn it off! *Now!*"

I ripped my eyes from the screen and toward the sofa, though I already knew what I would see. Zoey, wide-awake and perched on the edge of the seat. Her eyes were round, unblinking, like she hadn't noticed that Zane was yelling at her, hadn't noticed that we were even in the room at all.

Zane turned back toward the TV, reached out and pressed at all the buttons until the screen finally flashed to black.

"You were supposed to be sleeping," he said, storming across the room. He crouched down, stared her in the eye. "What you just saw—that's Iris's personal business. No one—not you, not those news people—has a right to be talking about her."

She was silent in response, eerily still. I held my breath, waiting. I started to feel light, dizzy, but then she opened her mouth.

"You're wrong, Z," she said, calmly, matter-of-factly. "Because we *should* know. We should all know."

Her head slowly turned, her eyes meeting mine.

"It's you," she said, the words clear, chiming like bells. "You're *finally* here."

Chapter Fourteen

YOU'RE FINALLY HERE. The words from my dream. Here, now, coming out of Zoey's mouth, they were infinitely more horrifying. My knees collapsed, my back slamming against the wall behind me as I slid down to the floor.

Zane jerked up and ran toward me, but his eyes were on his little sister. "She's *finally here*? What kind of bullshit is that?"

"Like Grammy used to tell us," she said, still staring at me as I shivered and shook on the floor. I wanted to look away from Zoey, to make her—all of this—disappear, but I couldn't. She was so sure. So hopeful. "She used to talk about it all the time, especially in the end, when we'd visit her at that crappy old-people home. Grammy always hoped she was still alive, and she is, Zane. She *is* alive, and we found her."

Zane knelt down next to me, wrapped an arm around

my trembling shoulders. "We didn't *find* her, and even if she's here now, that doesn't mean anything, Zo. What Gram thought—Iris is just a regular person, okay? She's just like us."

Zoey shook her head, scrunching her lips into a little frown. "That's not true, Zane," she said, her voice quieter now. "And you know it, too; you just won't say it."

There's just something about you, Zane had said, up on the roof. But didn't all guys say that to a girl if they wanted to kiss her? Everyone was *special* in his or her own way. I was special, but so was Zoey, so was Zane.

I could feel him next to me, could feel the heat radiating from his body, but I didn't turn my face to see his expression. I didn't want to know. He was silent, not denying Zoey, and that already said too much.

"Iris," she said, her eyes even rounder, more pleading, "I know Brinley's already gone. But maybe there are other people you could help. Why are you just hiding?"

"Because," I said, the word breaking apart on my lips. Zane gripped my shoulder, pulled me closer against his side. I took a deep breath, tried again. "Because you're wrong, Zoey. They all are. Even if I wish you were right. I can't help anyone. I'm just a normal person. I'm just as likely to walk into a hospital room and save someone as you are."

"Have you tried?" she asked. Three words, so simple.

"No," I answered, blinking.

"Then how can you be so sure?" She folded her arms across her chest, those bright eyes now squinting, challenging me.

"I just know, Zo," I said, though I was suddenly just a little less sure of myself. "How do *you* know that you can't save people?"

"Trust me," she snorted. "My dad definitely wasn't *God*."

God. My *dad*. It was a thought, a connection, a rationale I had tried to avoid in the past few weeks. It was enough just to acknowledge that the dad who'd raised me wasn't biologically responsible for me.

Yes, my mom had been a pregnant virgin.

But maybe I was all made up of *her*. All one person, one genetic code. Maybe there was nothing else; maybe she had been enough. Maybe *she* was the special one. Without actually testing, we'd never know for sure. But this is what I would choose to believe, what I *had* to believe, to stay sane: if I were studied, I would look the same as everyone else, deep down on the most fundamental level of what makes us all human. I was my mom, all the way through. And I was okay with that.

"So what would be so bad about trying?" Zoey asked, yanking me back to our conversation. "I think I'm right, but . . . even if I'm not, won't you be showing everyone else that you're just regular, too? Isn't that what you want?"

What she said—it made sense. It was like what I'd said to my family, that I'd go to Green Hill and somehow prove everyone wrong.

But maybe first I had to prove it to myself. Just to be certain. Just to be one thousand percent, without a doubt, absolutely sure. I'd ripped a cuticle for Caleb, showed him that I bled, just like he did. But that wasn't enough.

"Even if I wanted to," I started, wiping my sweaty hands along the tops of my legs, "I wouldn't know where to go, *who* to go see. I didn't know anyone personally." I still felt ashamed to admit it, especially after hearing all about Brinley.

"I know someone," Zane said. His voice was quiet, so quiet that I wasn't sure I would have heard him if I wasn't pressed against him, my head tucked under his chin, vibrating with the deep buzz of his throat. "If you want to meet someone—if you want to make sure—I know someone who was at Disney."

"Who?" I asked, the question out of my mouth before I even thought about asking. Before I thought about *why* I was asking. Because did it matter? Did the *who* matter? I wouldn't go no matter what. I couldn't.

Could I?

Zoey stood up from the couch and slowly made her way over to us. She crouched on the floor at my side. I looked from Zoey to Zane, at their identical somber expressions.

"Who is it?" I asked again, my face tilted up toward Zane, my eyes just inches away from that angry scar and that dark tattoo, a pointy vine that snaked along his jaw. He was right—there was still so much about him that I didn't know. But I wanted to, if he'd let me.

"She was one of Brinley's best friends," he said, not looking at me as he spoke. "Abigail. She was at their house almost as much as we were. She was in choir with Brin, so they were together when it happened. Brinley . . . she was gone right away, but Abby was lucky. Or maybe not so lucky; depends on how you look at it. She lived, but she'll never be the same. Blind in both eyes, burns all down her body . . ." He trailed off, shaking his head. "It's so fucked up what they did there. It's so beyond fucked up. Abby was a beautiful girl, so happy and sweet and jumping up and down all the time, and now she's been living on a hospital bed. She's never going to see again. She's never going to see her parents' faces, or her bedroom, or her damn dog she loves so much. She'll never see Brinley either; no one will. She probably wouldn't even want to see a world with no Brinley in it anymore. The two of them were inseparable. Sisters."

"I was their sister, too," Zoey whispered.

"Yeah, you were, Zo," Zane said, reaching across my lap to grab her hand. "They loved you as much as you loved them. And Abby still loves you."

"But she doesn't want me to visit. I send her cards and never get anything back. She stopped loving me, now that Brinley's not my cousin anymore." Zoey's voice was so little, so sad, I wanted to wrap myself around her and never let go. I wanted to make sure that the world would never hurt her again.

Zane stiffened next to me. "Brinley will *always* be your cousin. Always."

"But you don't believe in heaven, Z. So doesn't that mean there's no more Brinley?"

"I don't know what I believe."

"How about you, Iris?" Zoey asked. "What do *you* believe?"

I felt the blood rush to my face, my cheeks, the tips of my ears burning hot. I didn't really believe in God, or in heaven, or in any kind of structured, orderly religion. Did I believe that Brinley was gone forever? That she was nothing but dust and decay?

No. But I didn't believe she was looking down on us from the clouds either, the only answer Zoey probably wanted to hear.

"I think we have souls," I said, slowly and carefully, the weight of each word heavy on my lips. I shut my eyes, but I could still sense Zoey's stare cutting through me, two beams of white-hot light. "I think somehow, somewhere, a little piece of us always lives on. The piece of us that makes us who we are. We can't see it with microscopes; we can't weigh it or study it in a lab. We just have to believe that it's there. That no matter what happens, a tiny piece of us will always keep going. We'll keep *being*."

Was it true? Did I mean that? I wanted it to be true, I really did. I wanted to believe it, for Zoey's sake, for Zane's, for my own.

My eyes were still closed, but I could feel Zoey fall into me, feel her skinny arms squeeze around me so tight that I lost my breath.

"My tattoo," she said, her words muffled against my shoulder. She pulled back from me, and I opened my eyes as she tilted her head, showing me her jaw up close, that swirl of dark black notes. "Zane let me get this for Brinley. So it would help me to always remember her. Remember how much she loved to sing. She even wrote her own songs . . ." Zoey's voice faltered.

"I'll go," I said, the words tumbling out before I could stop them. "If Abigail lets me, I'll go to visit her."

Zoey turned back to face me, grinning despite the tears still rolling down her cheeks. The edges of her lips curled higher and wider—dangerously high, dangerously wide.

"I can't promise anything at all," I said, my heart pounding, racing from the electric shock of her hope. "I'll go, but I won't be able to do anything, really. Maybe I can just . . . I don't know, cheer her up a little?" The idea sounded flimsy to me, entirely without basis. And if she wouldn't even let Zoey visit, why would she let me? I would try, though. I would try for Zoey and Zane. Maybe even a little for myself.

"Thank you." Zoey sniffed, still smiling at me like I was her favorite person in the whole wide world. Her superwoman. Zane didn't say anything, but he leaned in, giving me a quick peck on the top of my head.

The kiss only made Zoey's grin grow bigger.

"So what's the plan?" I smiled back, my heartbeat soaring way beyond its normal rhythm. "Where do I go?"

Abigail's parents agreed immediately.

They'd let Abigail turn Zoey away, maybe, but they wouldn't allow that to happen for me. They wouldn't refuse *Mina's daughter.*

"So they know who I am, then?" I asked Zane, after he'd walked back inside from his phone call on the rooftop. He hadn't even needed to say anything. I could see it in the cautious way he stepped into the living room, the tiny smile that even a tough guy like Zane couldn't hide.

It was late morning on Monday, which meant Zoey was back in school. Anthony was nowhere to be seen—typical, according to Zane—so it was just the two of us. Zane hadn't mentioned going to class, and I hadn't either. School was part of my old life. I wasn't ready to somehow fit it into the new.

Zane looked at me and nodded. "Yeah. The basics at least. But they've seen the news. They know who your mom is. And they know it's all top secret, you being here with us—that it's all off if it's leaked. They want you to come, Iris. They really want you to come."

"And you trust them?"

"I don't know them all that well," he said, his gaze steady, fixed on me. My stomach swirled with the knowledge that this was real now, that I would actually be doing this—this silly, pointless, nonsensical thing. "But I know them well enough to be sure that they won't go running off and telling everyone. The most important thing to them is Abby. And if there's any chance that . . . well, that you can help her in even a little way, that's all that matters to them. They're not going to do anything to risk that."

"But you know that I probably can't, right? Definitely can't," I said, correcting myself.

"I don't know what you can do. And I don't think that you can really know that either."

"That's not true," I said, suddenly feeling indignant.

Who were all these people to think they knew what I was capable of better than I did? I knew what I could—and couldn't—do. I knew, and *only* I knew. "I can't heal anything, Zane. I can't, for example, touch that scar on your face and make it better. I can't make it go away."

As soon as the words were out, I wanted to claw them back in. "I—I didn't mean that," I sputtered, looking away, unable to meet his intense gaze. "Well, I did mean that I can't help you, or anyone, but . . ."

"It's okay," he said.

"No, it's not, it's none of my business, that scar, and I had no right to bring it up."

"Iris. Seriously, it's okay. Look at me." He touched a finger lightly to my chin, tilted my face until I was looking up straight into his eyes. His usual guard, that icy veneer of his, was nowhere to be seen. Instead of the anger, there was hurt. Sadness. The reflection of things that he'd seen and would never un-see.

I reached out and touched the scar, my fingers tracing lightly over the cool ridges along his jaw. He didn't pull away or stop me. Our eyes still locked, my fingers reached the tip of the scar, the point closest to his lips.

Zane sighed, reaching up to catch my hand, pressing his hot palm against mine. He let them linger there for a moment, resting against his scar. Then he eased our hands away slowly, though he didn't let go.

"You really want to know?"

I nodded, squeezing his hand more tightly. "But only if you want to tell me."

"I don't want to scare you away. I don't want . . ." He paused, his whole face tensing as he sucked in a deep, shuddering breath. "I don't want my life to be too much for you, Iris. Too complicated. I don't want you to feel like I'm nothing but baggage. Because I am, that's probably true, but . . . but I'm trying to make it better. For Zo. She deserves a better life than the one we've been stuck with so far. And you—you have enough to worry about already without adding in all of my issues."

"You're not baggage, Zane," I said, leaning in closer, my knee pressing up against his. "I want to know *you*. The good and the bad."

Zane laughed at that, but it was an empty laugh. His eyes still looked just as sad, no hint of a smile. "Trust me, there's a lot more bad than good. The good I could probably catch you up on in sixty seconds or less."

The room was quiet for a moment, nothing but the sound of our breathing and the dim rumble of traffic from the city outside those walls.

"You've probably guessed this much," he said, breaking the silence, "but our mom and dad were total fuckups at the whole parenting thing. My dad stopped by here and there in the early years, but we were just one of a handful of families to him. Not that any of his families mattered. He had his boys. Still does, I guess, but I wouldn't know for sure since it's been about five years since we heard anything at all. He never grew up, never became a real man. If he's still alive right now, he's probably passed out on someone's couch—he'll wake up at three in the afternoon, sell a few scammed phones, make just enough cash to get his next high. Pass out, do it all over again tomorrow."

He paused, shaking his head slowly. I could feel the rage, the resentment, reaching out from him, its own living, breathing thing—like a limb that I couldn't see but knew was still there, just as much a piece of him as his arms, his legs.

His words, though, they made me think about my dad—about how devoted and loyal he'd been to me my whole life. Being a father, I realized . . . it was about so much more than just shared blood.

"And my mom . . ." he started again, "my mom tried. She did what she could. But it was too much, and one day a while back, she took us over to have dinner at my aunt and uncle's and then she . . . she took off. No one knows where, or if they do, no one tells us. She calls once in a while, says she'll be back for us someday. Her brother, though, my uncle Leo, Brinley's dad—he made something of himself, unlike the rest of the family. He trained to be a mechanic and he worked his ass off to provide for my aunt and Brin. He was a good man. Still is, maybe, somewhere deep down, at least. We came and went from their place at first, stayed with other friends sometimes, but in the end we were pretty much living there full-time."

He stopped, staring off at the ceiling. I waited, holding my breath, for him to continue. But seconds passed, minutes, and still nothing.

"Zane . . ."

He glanced back down at me, and I saw the tears pooling in his eyes. That tough facade was crumbling, disappearing. His face looked years younger.

Zane was a boy. He was just a boy who had lived too much too soon.

"Everything was good," he said, each word shaking and unsteady, an obvious effort. "Great, actually, the best it had ever been for the two of us. Leo and his wife, Monica, were solid people. We had three meals every day, and I never had to worry at the end of each month that we'd have to pack up and move. Monica was so sweet to Zoey, treated her the same way she treated Brinley. She was furious at my mom, hated her for leaving us like she did, but she never said a bad word in front of Zoey. But after Disney . . ." He flinched at the word. "After Disney, it all changed. Everything. It changed so fast, I can barely even explain how it all happened."

He cocked his head, squinting at me. I shifted, crossed

and uncrossed my legs, even more anxious now.

"Sorry," he said, blinking at me, as if he'd just realized that he'd stopped talking. "I was just thinking that I've never said any of this out loud before. I never talked about what happened to anyone. Only Zoey knows, but she was there; she saw what went on for herself. You . . . you're the first person I'm telling. It's crazy, you know, since I've only really known you for a few days now. It just—I don't know, it feels like more than that, I guess. It feels like you get me already, and I didn't even have to try."

"I know exactly what you mean," I said, bumping him with my shoulder. We were silent for a moment, the confession sinking in.

"When they found out about Brinley," Zane finally said, "they kept it together, Leo and Monica, for a few days, up until the funeral was done. They were both hysterical—but only behind closed doors. Zo and I heard them crying all night, and she'd be crying all night, too. It was like we were living with a ghost. Brin was still there. She was everywhere. After the funeral, after Leo had to go back to work, it got real fast. Leo and Monica stopped knowing how to function. They stopped eating, stopped cleaning. If they couldn't be taking care of her, they couldn't be taking care of anyone. Not themselves, not Zoey or me."

He paused, the sickening weight of the story seeming to press every last bit of air from the room.

"So we came home from school one day, not even a week after the funeral, to find my aunt had thrown out every single thing in Brinley's room, even all the clothes and the toys that Zoey could have used, too. She was drunk, maybe even high, I don't know—she might have been desperate enough by then to be taking something to numb it all. Anyway, she was raging, but I was upset that she hadn't stopped to think about Zoey before throwing it all out. So I dragged Zoey to the bedroom and went to confront Monica. She started screaming, spitting at me—she was acting insane, like a crazy lady out on the street. When I looked in her eyes, I saw a stranger. It was like everything, all the pieces that made Monica *Monica*, had died with Brinley."

He shuddered, as if the memory, even now, made him go cold. "I hadn't realized at first, but Leo was home the whole time, too, even more messed up than Monica was. When he heard her screaming at me, he came out raging. He kept shouting that we needed to get out, that we had no right to keep bothering his family. I said some things back, I don't even remember. Before I knew it, he had an old kitchen knife jammed up against my throat. Gave me a warning cut, the scar I have now. And then he told me that I had five minutes to disappear for good before he got rid of me himself. He said . . ."

Zane squeezed his eyes shut, and I felt his entire body

tense next to mine. I tensed, too, terrified for what was to come.

"He said that if Brinley couldn't be alive, Zoey and I didn't deserve to keep breathing either. I grabbed Zoey and ran like hell. Haven't spoken a word to either of them since. They might regret it. They probably do. They were good people, before those fucking lunatics took their daughter from them. But I never want to see their faces again after that bullshit. Ever."

I wanted to hug him, but I wasn't sure I could even move. I wasn't sure I could even breathe.

"Right after that," he continued, pulling me back to him, "I got my tattoo from one of my buddies. Zoey begged and begged to get one, too, and I finally let her do it. For Brin. Probably proves I'm not the best guardian, but it was important to her." He pulled his T-shirt back to show me the tattoo more fully—thick, jagged lines curling from the top of his neck down to his collarbone, and extending beyond that to skin I still couldn't see.

"It's a vine with thorns surrounding the letter *Z. Z* for Zoey, not for Zane. It was a reminder to myself that I'd protect her always, no matter what. And it was also to prove that not only the scar from Leo would mark me. I can mark myself, too."

"That scar," I said, my words fragile, almost too quiet to be heard, "that scar makes you infinitely more amazing to me. That scar makes you the strongest person I know."

Zane opened his mouth as if he was about to refute me, deny that he could ever be amazing or strong, but I reached out and put my fingers to his lips.

"I know you don't believe it yet, but you deserve good things, Zane. You deserve to be happy." I leaned in closer, my lips landing softly on the scar. "You deserve to be loved."

Chapter Fifteen

"WHAT DID YOU just say?" Zane asked, pulling away. His eyes were squinted at me like I'd just made some kind of awful accusation—I might as well have said he was repulsive and I hated him, from the way he was looking at me now.

"That you deserve happiness," I said, the words shakier this time, less certain. "And love, you deserve love."

"Don't say that." He cut me off, turning his face so that I could no longer see his eyes. "Please, don't say that, Iris. You don't mean it."

"What . . . ? Oh no, I didn't mean it like *that*," I said, my heart pounding as I pieced together just how exactly he'd interpreted my words. "I didn't mean it as in *I love you*, that's not what I was trying to say, it's just . . ."

"Well, whatever—however you meant it, it's not what I do. I told you that last night—I don't have time for that bullshit. I love Zoey, and that's it. I don't love, and I don't get loved either. There's too much hate to have room for anything else. Better you know that now. Okay?"

I nodded, too numb to say anything else.

"I need to head out now," he said, prying his fingers from mine as he pushed off the couch. "I have some work to do before I pick Zoey up from school."

"What kind of work do you do, anyway?" The words slipped out before I could stop myself. As much as I didn't want to care, I did.

His scowl deepened. "That's my business. Don't you worry about it."

"Fine," I said, already regretting that I'd asked. I'd known that would be the answer, hadn't I? Especially now, when he was already so on the defensive. "But what about Abigail?" I was desperate to bring him back, to remind him of what really mattered. "When will we go?"

"We can go whenever we want," he said, shoulders hunched as he jammed his hands in his pockets. He glanced at me for a second before turning back to face the door. "As soon as tonight, I guess. It's your decision, if you're ready or not. She's home now, back at their apartment in Crown Heights."

"Okay," I said, trying to keep my voice steady. Where had the real Zane gone? The Zane who talked about his family, the Zane who cried if he needed to cry. "Let's go tonight, then."

I would focus on this. I would focus on proving that I was right, that I was as ordinary as I said I was. After I proved it—to myself, once and for all, and to Zane and Zoey—then maybe I could prove it, somehow, to my family next, my friends. Keep on proving it until everyone else believed me, too.

Zane gave a brisk nod. "Okay. Tonight, then. I'll pick Zoey up and we'll meet you back here. We'll all head out together."

I nodded, even though he couldn't see me. He didn't look back once as he walked out of the room.

"See?" I said out loud, to no one at all. "I touched your scar, and I didn't come anywhere close to healing *you*. Not anywhere close."

Soon after Zane had left me in the empty apartment, the entire colossal reality of my promise hit—the hopes that Abigail's parents were pinning on our meeting. To me, this was just a doomed experiment. But to them . . . to them it meant everything.

A wave of nausea swept over me and I jumped from the sofa, racing to the bathroom. I just barely made it there in time, hands and knees pressed to the cracked tile floor, my face hanging over a toilet that likely hadn't been cleaned in years. I shook as I purged everything out, every muscle pulsing, pounding as my stomach emptied.

"What the hell is going on here?"

I jerked myself up, spit and tears running down my face.

"Jesus, you're a sorry sight."

"Oh my god, I'm s-so sorry," I stuttered, wiping at my mouth with my sleeve. Anthony was frozen in the doorway, his face an angry grimace as he stared down at me.

"I didn't know you were home, I thought you were out, I . . ."

He waved me away in disgust, turning so that he didn't have to look at me. "I was sound asleep in my room. Woke up to some nasty howling and didn't know what the hell was going on. Thought some strays musta crawled in the window and were going at it, from those awful sounds I was hearing."

"I'm sorry I woke you," I said, trying to push myself up, hands gripping the grimy toilet rim for support. But I was too shaky and weak still. "I wasn't feeling well. But I'm okay now. I'll clean everything up, don't worry. I just need a few minutes and then I'll . . ."

But Anthony didn't seem to be listening. He had spun back toward me, his brow scrunched, eyes squinting in concentration. "Why do you look so damn familiar?" he asked, taking a step closer as he studied me. "They never brought you around here before; I'd have remembered that. No, you've never been here, but . . ."

"You must be thinking of someone else," I said, my fingers curling even more tightly around the edge of the porcelain. I looked away, desperate to break the connection, to be out from under his scrutinizing glare. "We've definitely never met, but I get that a lot. I have one of those faces, I guess." I was rambling now. "Anyway, I'm going to clean up, so you can just head back to bed. I won't be disturbing you again."

He continued to stare, unblinking, as I tried for a second time to push myself up off the floor. I was successful this time, standing on my wobbly but upright legs. But we were too close now, our eyes level, aligned across the all-too-limited space between us.

"I'm going to clean up," I repeated, hoping this time the words would stick.

Anthony shook his head, grunted. The moment seemed to have passed, for now. "Fine. But don't do it again, you hear? Next time you get sick, use the sidewalk and let me sleep."

He turned away, leaving me alone in the bathroom. I wanted to feel relieved, but I couldn't, not really—that had been too close. Maybe Anthony hadn't put the pieces together yet, but he still could. He could turn on the news at any minute now, or pick up a paper with my smiling face below the headline.

The truth hit me all over again, just as I'd said it to my parents. There was no point in running. I couldn't stay hidden forever, not from my family and friends, not from the rest of the world, either. I was buying time, nothing more.

Time to prove that I wasn't what or who people thought I was. Hopefully.

The rest of the afternoon was an agonizing sludge of time, too many hours of lying on the sofa, nothing to do but stare at the ceiling and think about what I would say, do, feel when I sat down next to Abigail's bed.

I must have dozed off at some point, because one minute I was alone, wondering what Abigail would look like, what she would say to me, and the next I was opening my eyes to Anthony once again leaning over me. I jerked up, instantly tensed and wide-awake.

"You're her," he said, simply. His voice was quiet but confident—no hint of a question this time. "The girl on the TV and in the papers. Christ, *everyone* seems to be talking about you. Talking about whether or not you're some kind of miracle child."

I sat up and swung my legs around to brace my feet against the floor. There was no point in denying it now. "I just needed some time on my own to figure things out . . .

starting with how to handle all these reporters."

He scratched his neck slowly, considering. "Seems like a whole lot of people are looking for you, not just the reporters. And you're *here*." He chuckled.

The laugh wasn't intentionally sinister, maybe, but it still made my skin crawl. I hugged myself, smoothing my hands against the prickle of goose bumps tracing up my wrists. My eyes caught the clock above the stove. School had ended an hour before, which meant Zane and Zoey would be back soon. I hoped. As long as they were coming straight here . . .

"I bet some reporters would be *real* happy if I could give 'em a good scoop. Rumor is you're on the run and your parents won't say where you went."

I didn't respond. The room was silent, other than a car alarm blaring outside on the street. I could feel Anthony staring at me, his cool eyes assessing, but I refused to look up, to give away my fear. If he knew how scared I was, he'd also know just how much power he held over me.

"What's Zane playing at with a girl like you, anyway?"

"He's just my friend," I said, the words sounding weak even to me. "He just wanted to help me out."

"Zane doesn't just *help* anyone." Anthony laughed again. "Zoey maybe. But that's out of obligation. Zane does what Zane wants. For himself. Don't you forget that."

I shook my head, anger welling up alongside the fear.

"So why do *you* help?" I asked, trying to redirect the conversation. He didn't exactly reek of compassion and moral obligation, after all. Why let them intrude on his sad little bachelor pad?

"Hmph," he grunted, scowling at me. "That's got nothing to do with you."

"Well," I said, forcing my voice to sound much tougher than I actually felt, "you know all my personal business now, don't you? So it only seems fair."

"It doesn't really matter anyway, okay? I knew their dad when we were kids. Their mom, too. I feel bad for them, that's all. I don't do much. Give them a place to stay sometimes, just to get them off the streets. Zane, he was friends with my son, too. Before."

"Before what?" I asked, my curiosity making me bolder.

"Before. That's all you're getting. This ain't about me anyway. It's about you. About what I'm supposed to do with some crazy runaway girl on my couch. A crazy runaway girl that everyone seems to be looking for right now. Maybe I could even get some sweet reward out of the deal." His eyes lit up at this, making my stomach dip.

"I'll leave. I'll stay somewhere else. And we can both pretend this never happened."

"And leave me out of the fun?"

"It's not *fun*. And it's not your business."

"I want to talk to Zane," Anthony said.

"We both already know what Zane will say. We'll leave if you try to call any reporters about this. There's nothing in it for you."

"Well then, good thing Zane's not here just yet, isn't it? Only you and me. And I'm willing to bet not a single other person knows where you are right now?" He paused, his grin growing wider at my silence. "I figured. So you're my little secret right now . . ."

He sat down next to me on the sofa, much closer than necessary. His cool, gleaming eyes were studying me, evaluating my worth, like a pawnshop dealer trying to pin down his price tag. I wanted to leave, run away, far away from this apartment, but I couldn't, not without Zane. Not without meeting Abigail. I had promised him and Zoey.

Anthony pulled out his phone.

"No, don't call anyone, please . . ."

A flash went off in my face. *Click, click.* A second flash, a third.

"Wanna smile, look pretty for the camera? No? Well, no matter, I have proof at least. Can't no one accuse me of lying when I—"

I grabbed at the phone and missed, Anthony's much longer arm holding it high above my reach.

"Nice try. Now, where do I send it off to first, hm . . . ?"

Just as I coiled and prepared for a second lunge, the lock clicked and the door flew open.

"We're going to Abby's!" Zoey yelled, flinging herself across the room and onto my lap. "You're really going to Abby's! We all are." Her cheeks were flushed, eyes shining with giddiness.

"What's going on in here?" Zane asked, his gaze shifting from me to Anthony. I was gasping for air, my heart still racing, not ready yet to believe I was safe, even with the two of them there. Zane frowned as he stepped closer to Anthony.

"Calm down, Z," Anthony said, waving Zane off. "Your friend and I were just having a little talk, that's all. Right, *Iris*?" He grinned at me, all his yellowed, crooked teeth on display—all the teeth he still had, that is, as quite a few seemed to be missing, making his smile even more broken and unsettling.

"He knows, Zane," I said, tearing my eyes away from Anthony. Zoey was subdued now, wrapping her arms around my neck as she pulled herself closer against me. "He's convinced there's something in it for him. Some kind of reward if he gets an exclusive. He just took a few pictures of me with his phone, and . . ."

Before I could finish, Zane dove forward and ripped the phone from Anthony's hand. "You have *nothing* to do with this," Zane said. He shook his head, his scowl so deep I almost didn't recognize him. "We're leaving. I'm deleting the photos right now, and you aren't going to say anything about this to anyone. What Iris wants to do next is her own damn business." He tossed the phone back to Anthony, catching him off guard as it slammed against his chest. "You're a sad old man and I'm sick of you. I'm done. I don't need this charity."

"You're not really done with me. After all, I know where Zoey goes to school," Anthony said, smiling. "If I can find her, I think I can find you."

"Fuck you," Zane said, his eyes burning with fury. He took a step closer to Anthony. I squeezed Zoey tight, wondering if we should run. But I couldn't move.

"Do I have to remind you why you owe me?" Zane asked, towering over the sofa.

"Now, I don't think we have to get into that right here," Anthony said, his voice suddenly sounding much less confident.

"I think now is the perfect time. Because let me remind you that if you make me angry—if you do anything to upset Iris—I have a whole lot more serious damage I can do."

"That's *our* business, Zane," Anthony said, standing up. "We had a deal. You kept it all under wraps, and I'd help you and your sister when you needed me."

"Well, guess what?" Zane laughed then, the sound so frigid, so raw, I felt myself edging farther away. "I don't want your help. Ever again." Even with Anthony standing, too, Zane seemed to dwarf everything else in the room. "I'd rather be on the street than have a thug like you providing another damn thing for me. I have too much pride for that."

"Stop, Z, just stop right there," Anthony said, putting his hands up as he took a step back. "It doesn't have to come to this. I won't say anything about the girl, okay? Photos are deleted, done. Let's just pretend none of this ever happened. Our secret."

"I can't trust that. I can't trust you," Zane said, sneering down at him, shaking his head. Zane turned then, those flaming eyes directed straight at me.

"Iris, I'm telling you this so that you know. Just in case Anthony should decide to change his mind and do anything to out you, or try to make it look like he has some role in all this."

"Zane, no—"

Zane put a hand up, silencing him. Anthony turned to face the wall, his shoulders sagging with defeat. "Zoey," Zane said, turning to his sister, "go to the bathroom and close the door."

She didn't fight it—I don't think anyone would have disobeyed Zane in that moment. She scrambled to the bathroom, shutting the door quickly behind her.

Satisfied, Zane turned back to me. "Uncle Anthony's son used to be my best friend. Tony. We grew up together.

He was older, like a big brother to me and Zoey. A few years back, though, Tony and I were hours late to pick up Zoey after school. It was getting dark, and she was outside of the school the whole time waiting for my stupid ass to get there. And there was a guy . . ." Zane paused, his shaking hands balling into fists at his sides. "There was a guy there, hassling Zoey. Had his arm around her, was talking in her ear. Tony and I . . . we lost it. Beat him up bad. Really bad."

This was the story I'd been so scared to hear. The start of the rumor.

"I caught myself, remembered that my little sister was there, screaming and crying for us to stop. So I went to her, but Tony . . . he kept pounding on the guy. We heard a siren then, and Tony took off. But I couldn't run, not with Zoey. So I took the rap. The cops had some security footage, saw I wasn't alone. But it was dark—they couldn't ID him. And I wouldn't give a name. That guy, he lived, but he's out of it . . . can't even speak anymore, just sits in a chair all day. I went to juvie for a while, but Tony, he was eighteen, so he wouldn't have got off so easy. I paid the time, but I will never forgive myself for letting her see me go off like that. And if I hadn't been late, none of it would have happened. That's why now . . ." He bowed his head, lifted his hands to cover his face. "That's why now I just try to be the best big brother I can be," he said, the words muffled behind his hands. "That's why I don't deserve any-thing, not even Zoey."

"Where's Tony now?" I asked. It was the only question I could process.

"He went to live with his mom in Atlanta after that," Zane said, his face still hidden behind his palms. "Never saw him again. He never said anything to me, no apology for letting me be the only one to go down for what we did. He was defending my sister, yeah, but still—he took it too far. We both took it way too far."

"He was a good kid, Zane," Anthony said, turning back to us. He sounded so broken, I almost pitied him. Al-most. "You know he was. It was just a mistake, that's all . . ."

"Zoey," I said, the word breaking my heart as I said it aloud. To have seen that, and when she was so young—I couldn't imagine, I just couldn't.

I stood up and walked to the bathroom, opened the door. I pulled Zoey in and hugged her more tightly than I'd ever hugged anyone in my life. And then I grabbed her hand, leading her back to the living room.

"We're leaving," I said. I couldn't look at Anthony. I couldn't look at Zane either. "It's time to go see Abby. It's time to *do something.*"

Chapter Sixteen

ZANE'S KNUCKLES TAPPED against the door marked 3B and I steeled myself, squeezing my sweaty hands into tight balls.

This was happening.

The door swung open almost instantly. A short but sturdy, powerful-looking man stared at us from just behind it, his dark brown eyes scanning from Zane to Zoey. To me. They stayed on me, penetrating with an intensity that made hairs prickle along the back of my neck.

After a long pause he blinked and stepped back, motioning us inside. He remembered to smile then, though his eyes stayed just as focused on my face. My cheeks burned under his scrutiny.

"I'm Iris," I said, though it was clear I needed no introduction. He nodded slowly, a few seconds passing before he remembered to reciprocate. "I'm Sam Henry," he said, his voice booming, a shock in contrast to his initial silence.

At that he finally broke his gaze, turning to look back over at Zane and Zoey. "It's good to see you kids again. It's been . . . it's been a long time. Too long."

Zane put out his arm, and Sam latched on, shaking his hand. They nodded at one another, unspoken words seeming to pass between them. Zoey reached out, too, after the men broke apart, wrapping her arms around Sam's waist.

"I miss Abby so much," she said, the words muffled against Sam's striped button-up, the shirt faded but still crisp and fastened at the wrists.

"We all do," Sam responded quietly. He closed his eyes for a moment, patting Zoey's shoulder.

"You're here," a woman's voice said from behind us. I turned to see her rushing toward me—a blur of blue cotton and gold earrings and curly black hair, the deep brown of her arms as they reached out and pulled me tight against her chest. "I am so glad you came. Praise Jesus for bringing you here to us. To our Abigail."

Hearing that word again—hearing *Jesus*—made every last drop of my blood go cold. I had nothing to do with Jesus. Jesus had nothing to do with me. How could I be letting this woman, this family, believe that for even a second?

"I'm not . . ." I started, but the words got choked off against the thick, perfumed curls that crushed against my face. Our bodies were pressed together so close I could feel her trembling against me, feel the rapid beating of her heart.

I couldn't finish that sentence.

She pulled back, beaming at me. "I'm Janelle," she said. "And it is a grand honor indeed to meet you, Iris Spero." She clasped her fingers firmly around my palm. "I told Abigail you were coming earlier, and it was the first time I've seen her smile in . . . first time in weeks! First time since all of this began, maybe. I've been telling her about you ever since I first saw you on the news. First heard about who you are. Now, I'd heard a little about your mom back then, everybody did, but I was a stupid teenager, didn't pay it any attention. I've been reading up about her now."

I nodded, my panic swallowing me up entirely. Before I could say or do anything to halt the momentum, Janelle was pulling me along behind her, glancing back with those eager eyes, that hopeful smile. All I could do was walk, one step at a time.

And then we stopped, Janelle and me—the rest of them somewhere behind us, I supposed, or nowhere at all, because it didn't matter, nothing else mattered—in front of a closed door. The door was blank, solid white, except for one little glittery purple *A* sticker placed right in the center.

Janelle squeezed my hand, so warm and alive against my rigid, icy fingers—and then she let go. She reached for the knob, twisted, pushed. Every gesture, every movement forward, was like a crashing cymbal, each louder, more shocking than the last.

The door opened and Janelle put her hand on my back, nudging me inside. "We're here, sweetie. Iris and me."

I took a few steps, eyes still on the old parquet floors, before I looked up—before I looked at the bed. At Abigail.

The second I saw her, the tiny, broken girl propped up against a mountain of pillows, my heart shattered—thousands of tiny, jagged pieces, all ripping and tearing through the rest of me, slicing open every organ, every vein in their path.

I stood like that, bleeding on the inside, staring. Staring at the white bandaging wrapped around the top of her head, ending just below her eyes; and the lower half of her face that was uncovered, but still red and rippled with burns. Her mouth, though, her pink lips, seemed to somehow have gone entirely untouched. And on those lips, despite the bandages, the burns, the eyes that would never see again, even if they were uncovered—there was a smile.

She was smiling because I, Iris Spero, was now in the room with her.

"I'll leave you two alone," Janelle said softly. I heard the click of the door behind me.

A moment passed in silence before I could force my mouth to speak. "Hi, Abigail," I said, the words so soft I worried that she wouldn't be able to hear, not under the gauze that partially covered her ears. I felt relieved, suddenly, that she couldn't see my face, couldn't see the fear and the heartbreak—and then, just as instantly, I felt utterly guilty for having had that thought at all, even for a second.

This was a little girl who would never see again.

I walked, crossing over the rest of the space between us. "Hi, Abigail," I said again, louder this time, as I sank onto the old wooden chair set right next to her bed. The chair where, I had no doubt, her parents had taken constant shifts since Abigail had come home from the hospital. "I'm Iris."

"I know," she said, her voice fuller, more animated than I would have expected. It was hard to imagine anything lively at all emerging from such a frail, damaged-looking body. "My mama told me all about you. Even before she knew that you were with . . ." *Zoey and Zane*, it seemed like she was about to say, but she trailed off. The names were still too hard, maybe, too much a reminder of the past. Of Brinley. "You can call me Abby, though."

I nodded for a moment before realizing that she couldn't see me.

What was I supposed to say next? What was I supposed to do?

Nothing—there was nothing to say, nothing to do. I was stupid to have come there at all, to have pretended that there was any real purpose besides my selfish motive to prove myself right. To prove that I was no one special.

"I'm really sorry," I said. She'd probably heard those words too many times already, more times than she needed for the rest of her lifetime. But still, I *was* sorry. I was so much more than sorry. "Do you want to . . . to talk about anything?"

She was silent—considering, I thought, based on the way she pressed her lips together. It was hard to know, I realized, without seeing her eyes, what she was really thinking in response, how she was really feeling. I was so used to having eyes tell me what I needed to know about a person—whether their smile was real, whether they were bored or angry or tired or distracted. Without eyes, I felt stranded.

"Have you talked to Brinley?" she asked, the words floating out from those soft, miraculously untouched lips.

"Have I . . . have I what?" I asked, confused.

"Brinley. Have you talked to her since . . . since it happened?"

Abby knew, didn't she, that her best friend had died? She must have—that was why she had refused to let Zoey visit, after all, wasn't it? "I never met Brinley," I started. "I didn't know Zane and Zoey until just—"

I gasped, choking around my own words as the real meaning of her question crashed down on top of me.

She was asking if I'd talked to Brinley *after* she died.

She was asking if I'd talked to her dead best friend. In heaven, probably, because that was where she thought I was from, where I *belonged*.

"No, I . . . I . . ." I couldn't speak. I could barely breathe.

"Darn," she said, her lips turning into a tiny frown. "But I guess you're here on earth right now instead of being up there."

Up there.

"You're here helping *us*." She paused, sucking in a tiny breath of air. "Right?"

"I'm not . . . I'm not exactly sure what I'm doing right now," I said, the only answer that I could possibly give. "I'm kind of new at this whole thing."

"Oh." Those perfect lips turned down in disappointment. She was silent as her little chin began to quiver. Were there tears under those bandages?

Could she even still cry? Through the wounds, the scars around her eyes?

To not be able to *cry* . . .

"Abby," I started, gripping my quaking hands against the sides of the chair. "There is nothing more in the world that I would rather do than help you get better right now. To help everyone who was hurt at Disney be completely better again. But I don't think . . . I don't think it works that way."

"Then why are you here?" she asked quietly.

I opened my mouth, about to say again that I didn't know, that I didn't have a single clue about how to be the person that she needed me to be. But I couldn't, I couldn't say it again—not without at least *trying* first. Not without making some kind of effort to prove the words true, doing rather than saying.

Before I could stop myself, I uncurled my fingers from around the seat of my chair and reached out toward her. I laid one hand, then both, along the sides of her face— half of each palm resting along the rippled burns of her exposed skin, the other placed lightly on top of the gauze covering her eyes.

We sat like that, perfectly still, for our own private eternity. I was waiting for—I don't know what I was waiting for, because nothing could possibly happen. The burns wouldn't magically wiggle and stretch and smooth them- selves beneath my fingers, new skin washing over the old, as perfect and pristine as the day she was born. She wouldn't suddenly start tearing off the bandages, proclaiming that her eyes had opened and she could *see*!

But I couldn't bring myself to pull away, couldn't bear facing Abby's realization that I was completely useless. I was a *fraud*. And so I kept my hands pressed against her, waiting for something, anything else to interrupt and put an end to our misery.

Finally, Abby spoke.

"I'm not . . . I'm not sure if I feel anything." Her mouth was pursed in concentration, the just barely exposed tip of her nose scrunching beneath the bandages. "But I don't know. Your hands are so soft. And so cold. They feel so nice against my face. I don't feel different, though, really. But do I look different to you?"

Even now, even after my pathetic hands had proven themselves completely powerless . . . she still had hope. I could hear it there, fighting on regardless of the total lack of proof or cause.

"No," I whispered. "You look the same to me."

"Maybe it takes time," she said. "Maybe it's not something that happens right away."

Stop! I wanted to shout. *Stop trying to find truth in this! Stop believing in the impossible—stop believing in* me.

"Maybe," I said back.

Coward's words. I hated myself for saying it, but I couldn't stand to watch her crumble right in front of my eyes. I wanted to run away and never have to see her again—never have to witness up close the total loss of her faith in me, in *miracles*, in good things still existing in this sad, empty world the Judges had left behind.

She smiled. Abby smiled, because of a single word—

because of my false promise. She looked amazingly peaceful and content, despite everything.

My deceitful skin crawled in agony, waves of heat scorching me from the inside. I couldn't stay in this room. I needed to go.

Before I lifted my hands—before I severed myself from Abby entirely—I prayed. I didn't pray to God, to any god, because I had never believed in one and I still didn't now. But I prayed in the way my mom had prayed all those years ago—the way she and my dad still prayed today, their whispered appeals behind closed doors.

I prayed to Iris. The *real* Iris. The first Iris, and the Iris who really mattered.

Please, I screamed on the inside, that one word rattling through my head like a deafening clap of thunder. But how—I cut myself off—how could a *thought*, a silent, invisible spark of the brain, go anywhere at all?

It didn't matter, though, not now. I had to try. For Abby, I had to try.

Please, Iris. Please talk to me. Please let me know what my purpose is here. Because if I can't help this girl, if I can't help anyone, why was I even born? Why am I here at all?

I wanted it to work, I realized. The desperation coursed through my veins, my heart thudding faster, louder with every beat.

I want to be the person Abby needs me to be.

I want *to be special.*

"You're crying," Abby said, the prayer, my own shocking words, dissolving around me like the final notes of a beautiful, tragic song.

I *was* crying, slow, heavy tears dripping onto Abby's cheeks below. I had stood up at some point, too, without realizing, and was standing directly over her now, my hands attached more firmly to the sides of her face.

"I'm sorry," I said, my voice thick and husky.

"Don't be. Your tears feel nice."

I squeezed my eyes shut, and this time I pulled my hands back for real. I had done all that I could do—and I still had failed.

But if I had failed, Iris had failed, too. Iris had failed in the moment I needed her most.

She had come to my mom—so why not me? Why not come to me?

You're so important, so valuable to us. Keeping you and the child safe is all that matters now.

That was what Iris had said to my mom, that night at the restaurant. But if we were so important, so valuable, why wasn't she there with me now? She had told my mom that we'd know—we'd know the reason for all of this eventually, someday. *The time will come,* she'd said. *You'll know when it does.* If this wasn't the time—right here, right now—what other time could there possibly be? The idea of a worse time, a darker time, was inconceivable.

"I need to go now," I said quietly, already backing away.

"When will you come again?"

"I—I don't know," I stuttered, my hand clenched around the doorknob. "I'm not sure yet."

"I guess there are a lot of other kids like me you have to visit, too, huh?"

I wouldn't be visiting other kids like Abby—there was no point. But I couldn't say that, not to her.

"Bye, Abby." I pushed the door open, relieved that I was mere inches from my escape. "It was so great to meet you."

"It was nice to meet you, too," she said, and I glanced back at her one last time, the image of this precious little girl searing into the deepest corners of my mind.

I was burned now, too, even if my mark was invisible from the surface.

I was burned from the inside out.

Chapter Seventeen

I DIDN'T SAY good-bye to Sam or Janelle on my way out of the apartment—I didn't even acknowledge Zane or Zoey. Instead I steamrolled right through the living room and down the two flights of stairs to the front entrance, where I finally crumpled on the stoop, wheezing and gasping to fill my lungs.

The front door flew open.

"What's wrong?" Zoey asked. She crouched on the step in front of me, forcing me to meet her eyes. "What did she say to you?"

"She thanked me," I said, swallowing a sob. "She was glad I came."

"So then . . . why are you crying?" Zoey frowned.

"Because," I sputtered, clawing through the air. "Because it's a lie. I didn't actually *do* anything. She has hope now, but it's all wrong. She shouldn't, not because of me."

"Let's get off this stoop," Zane said, gripping my

shoulders. He pulled me to my feet, my legs trembling as I leaned against him.

Before I even realized what was happening, Zane had settled me into a cab, squeezed between the two of them on the backseat. I kept my eyes shut for the whole ride, opening them only when we stopped in front of a gray and battered-looking old motel.

I didn't have nearly enough cash to cover a night there, and Zane shouldn't be paying for it either—but I didn't say that. I didn't stop him. He practically emptied out the vending machine, too, on our way to the room, buying chips and pretzels and candies for dinner. I wasn't hungry, though I hadn't eaten at all since our Chinese feast the night before. Zane insisted I eat something, shoving a king-sized Butterfinger into my hands.

Our room smelled sour and damp, the walls, the blankets, the towels all so faded and tired looking, saturated with too many sad lives. I quickly inhaled the Butterfinger, and then threw my jacket on the first bed and headed straight for the bathroom, locking the door behind me. I stripped off my filthy clothes and turned the shower on, blasting myself with steaming hot water. I hadn't showered since I'd left home, three days before. Had it only been three days? Mikki, the shelter, Zoey and Zane and Uncle Anthony, Abby . . . I washed all of that off me, scrubbing at my skin until it was pink and raw.

I climbed back into my dirty clothes and stared at myself in the mirror—at my tired, red-rimmed eyes and knotted, dripping hair. I looked pale and sickly and utterly helpless. I was no one's salvation, not even my own. I recognized now for the first time the irony of the shirt I'd been wearing all along—an old yoga T-shirt that had *Namaste* in gold, sparkling letters. Namaste, a Hindu greeting. *I bow to the divine in you.* The divine in all of us.

Where was my divinity now?

I opened the bathroom door and climbed into bed next to Zoey, who was already sound asleep, a pile of empty candy wrappers scattered all around her. Zane, though, was sitting awake and upright on the bed next to us. Even without glancing over, I could feel his sharp eyes cutting through me, all the questions that he wanted to ask about what had happened in Abby's bedroom. I ignored him, yanking the scratchy motel comforter over my head. I should call my parents—the motel room phone was right next to me, after all—but I couldn't, even though I knew they were probably panicking. I'd made no guarantees about when I'd call next. Soon. I would call soon.

I didn't know what I would do in the morning, where we would go next or if there would still even be a *we* at all—but then, I hadn't known what the next day would bring since I'd first climbed down the fire escape and away from home. Three days, and I wasn't any closer to figuring out a way to improve my messy, upside-down life.

I had tried to prove to Abby that I was worthlessly human, not a shred of anything bigger or better. Yet she had still believed, as much as or maybe even more than ever.

What else could I do?

Iris, I prayed again, squeezing my palms together against my chest, just above my racing heart. *Iris, please.*

Help me.

I woke up the next morning to Zoey's frantic tugging, her crouched knees bumping into me as she grabbed at my shoulders, shaking me hard against the pillow.

"It worked, Iris! It worked! It really, really worked!" she shouted, her words giving way to a burst of squealing, ear-splitting laughter.

"What are you talking about, Zoey?" I asked, rubbing at my dazed, sleep-heavy eyes. I tried to sit up despite her jittery hands bumping me around, but it required too much energy that I didn't have to spare.

"Abby! It worked!"

This time, the words jolted me upright. The room around me was suddenly perfectly crisp, too crisp, the edges and the colors sharp and fierce and penetrating.

"What do you mean 'it worked'?"

"It worked! You fixed Abby!" She sat back, letting go

as she threw herself against the pillows next to me, panting for air. "I mean," she said, her breathing slower now, steadier, "not completely. Not yet. She's still blind, and she still has scars. But her parents called Zane this morning and said that she's out of bed for the first time since it happened. She asked her mom if she could walk her all around the apartment so she could start finding things and doing things on her own. And it's because of *you*, Iris. Don't you see? It's all because of *you*. I knew that you were special. I just knew it!"

Her words were a chaotic swirl in my mind, nothing but nonsense. Of course I hadn't done anything. Of course I hadn't made Abby better.

She was improving because she *believed*. She believed that I'd made a difference—and so I had made a difference, indirectly at least. A self-fulfilling prophecy.

I had given her hope, and somehow, that hope had its own kind of power.

Maybe hope isn't always about the perfect ending. Hope is making the journey easier.

My mom had written those words in her book; the full line came to me now in a flash. Mina's words. Words that hadn't jumped out when I first read her story, though they'd obviously climbed deep inside my mind and latched on tight.

But just because I'd given Abby the hope she needed

to get out of bed—to slowly, one day at a time, move on with her life—it didn't mean that I'd worked a miracle. It could have been anyone who'd walked into that room and placed their palms against her burned face.

No.

It couldn't have been just anyone, I realized. Because there was no one else who could have given Abby that sense of unlimited possibility—the irrational but persuasive belief that miracles could actually happen.

I had happened, after all. It was just like Mikki had said to me, when I'd asked her about miracles. If there was one miracle, there could be more.

And I—I was the most likely source.

The weight and the gravity of it all, it was too much; it changed everything. It made every doubt and every hesitation I'd held since Kyle Bennett had knocked on our door simultaneously less true and truer at the same time. I wasn't divine, but that didn't mean I was powerless.

On the contrary, I had too much power, whether I wanted it or not.

Zoey reached out and grabbed my hand, curling her fingers tightly around mine. "What are you thinking about, Iris? Say something."

Her big round eyes were glossy, stains of tears still running down her cheeks. Zane was right there, too, perched behind her on the side of the bed. His gaze was drilling into me, and I stared back, unblinking. I tried to read his thoughts, but whatever he was feeling now was too well masked.

I sighed, turning back to Zoey. "I'm thinking . . . I'm thinking that she's only better, sweetie, because I gave her hope. She believed I could make her feel better, so this morning . . . she *felt* better. I don't think that I actually healed her—I *know* that I didn't—not in any medical sense. I just gave her the courage she needed to get out of bed. To start accepting the fact that her life will always be different—but she's *alive*. Good things can and will still happen."

"But you still did that," Zoey said, her eyes watching me in a way that seemed frighteningly like *awe*. "So you still fixed her in a way. Right?"

"Well . . ." I trailed off as I shifted in the bed, kicking the twisted sheets and comforter off my legs. I was suddenly way too hot to be covered in blankets, sweat beading along the back of my neck. "I guess I helped her a little bit, yeah," I admitted, the heat rising to my cheeks. I tilted my head and stared up at the chipped white ceiling, the brownish-yellow flowering stains that someone had unsuccessfully tried to cover with a thin coat of new paint. "But that doesn't mean that I'm really special, Zoey; you have to understand that. Abby just *believes* that I am, and that's why my being there worked at all. That's why I was able to cheer her up a little."

"But even if that's the reason," Zane interrupted, jerking my eyes back to his scarred, beautiful face, "does it matter? You being there was better than you not being there. So what about all the other victims like Abby? All the other kids? If they believed in you, too, and you visited them, touched their wounds or whatever the hell it takes to make them feel even just a little bit cured . . . shouldn't you do it? Don't you owe that?"

"*Owe?*" The word burned its way up my throat. "Owe *who*? Why do I owe anything to anyone?" I felt selfish saying it, but I was enraged by Zane's idea—this idea that everyone's happiness was my responsibility somehow. My *duty*, as Kyle Bennett had called it. Visiting these kids would be deceitful. I'd make them temporarily happier, maybe, but what next? When their burns didn't fade, their missing limbs didn't grow back, their eyes still couldn't see . . .

"Yeah, *owe*," Zane said. "If you're the only one who can make people feel that kind of crazy hope, don't you think you should at least try?"

"That's not fair," I snapped. "You make it sound so simple."

"So tell me, then . . . if your parents want to hide you away somewhere safe, probably put you up in some fancy hotel a hundred times nicer than this shithole, why are you running? Why didn't you just let them protect you from the nasty outside world? Why are you *here*?"

"Stop it," I said, fighting hard to keep my voice steady. "Just *stop*. I didn't ask for any of this."

"Yeah, well, neither did Brinley. Neither did Abby. A lot of people have to deal with a life filled with crap that they didn't ask for. You think I love what I got? Do you, Iris?"

Zane was right—I knew that he was, even if I wasn't ready to admit it out loud. I'd had everything up until now, my entire life one long string of blessings. But now—now I had more than everything. More than any one person could ask for.

I had so much that it terrified me.

"I don't think I'm strong enough to be this person— this person that people need me to be," I whispered. "I want to be her, I really do. I realized that yesterday with Abby, that I *want* to help. I want to make people better, even if it's just deep down, not on the surface. But I don't know if I can. I don't know why *me*."

Zane stood, pacing around the edge of the bed. "Iris. If you weren't asking *why me*, that would be even crazier. I mean, seriously, think about it: some people could have totally abused this kind of power. And you wouldn't. You would never do that."

I shook my head, blinking back tears.

Zane stopped midstep and turned back to face me.

"So maybe . . . maybe that's why you."

Sam and Janelle had passed on a phone number to Zane.

A phone number for Angelica Byrne, the leader of a network of families who had been at Disney on August twenty-fourth. Families who had lost one or more of their members, and families who had made it through alive, but with scars on the outside, the inside—or, in most cases, both.

Disney's Children, it was called. It was just one of a handful of national organizations, according to Sam and Janelle, but this group in particular had a strong presence across several children's hospitals in the New York City area.

"What do they expect me to do with it?" I asked. I knew the answer, though. Of course I did.

Zane raised his eyebrows and gave me an incredulous-looking smirk.

I could hear Zoey singing from the bathroom, where she was taking a bath overflowing with a bottle of bubbles that Zane had bought at the front desk. She sounded so happy. Too happy, given the cause. The singing was proba-bly at least somewhat due to the fact that Zane had agreed school was too far to bother trying for this morning, but I had a sinking feeling that it was more about Abigail. More about me.

"I have no clue what the right decision is here. That's the answer, Zane. If I go, if I actually meet any of these families, then I'm outing myself completely. It's me proclaiming to the country—to the *world* even—that I *am* special. That I am some kind of miracle—and that because of it I have some kind of power that other people don't have."

I laid my head down on the pillow, my face turned toward the wall, so that Zane's stare felt at least slightly less piercing. "If I do this, if I start making these kinds of visits, there's no going back. It would change *everything.* For good."

"I hate to be the one to say this," he said. "But your life is already going to be different, no matter what you do right now. You can't hide forever; you know that. And if you decide to do nothing, to walk away—people might not be so happy. They might . . . I don't know, they might be pretty angry. Angry that you ignored them when they needed you."

I heard the sound of paper, rustling pages, and jerked my head up. Zane had thrown a newspaper between us on the bed. I didn't want to look, not right now. But . . .

Curiosity won. I grabbed at the newspaper and stared. My body processed instantly—pounding heart, twisting stomach, sweat tingling along my spine—but my mind . . . my mind took longer.

There was a nearly full-page photograph of our brownstone—at least, I assumed it was our brownstone. I could see our sunny gold front door. But it was hard to be completely certain at first because of the massive signs posted along the sidewalk, the flowers and the photos hanging from the wrought-iron front gate, the messy, colorful lines of graffiti scrawled across the beautiful stone walls: IRIS SPERO IS OUR SAVIOR. SAVE OUR CHILDREN. SAVE US ALL.

The biggest, grandest display was a banner being held high by strangers, two middle-aged women I'd never seen before in my life, standing just in front of our gate. The banner was me—a larger-than-life *me*, my yearbook photo blown up to showcase every last minuscule detail of my face. If you stood close enough, you could probably count each freckle and each pore. There was more, too: gems and glitter and streamers covering every square inch around my face, shining and glimmering in the sunlight beaming down on our house.

My house had become a memorial.

My house had become a *shrine*.

"Okay." I tossed the paper down, letting the pages scatter to the floor. Zane looked at me, eyebrows raised, as I pushed myself up from the bed to stand. "I'll go.

It's completely, mind-blowingly insane, but I'll go. I'll meet with this group. Even if I have no clue what I'm doing right now, doing anything at all seems better than doing nothing. If I fail . . . then at least I tried."

"You'll go," he repeated, staring at me with a dazed look that I couldn't entirely read, surprise and fear and doubt and maybe some admiration, too. I wanted him to admire me, more than I'd ever needed to be admired before, maybe—but not for this. Not for a cause that I didn't at all deserve. Heat flared through my cheeks and I looked away.

"Yes," I said, "I'll go."

Zane didn't say anything in response. Instead he walked over and pulled me into his arms. But his embrace felt too light, loose and cautious, so I pressed my face hard against his chest, burrowing in deep. I needed him close, needed his solid, sturdy weight anchoring me to the dingy motel room floor.

"I don't get you two. At *all*. But I still kind of like it."

I jumped back from Zane's arms and turned to see Zoey, standing just outside the bathroom door. Hands on her hips, head cocked to the side, a twisty, mischievous grin on her lips.

"There's nothing to get," Zane said from behind me, his tone too brisk and clipped. The words sliced through me, deeper than I would have liked, but I kept my face straight, my eyes on Zoey. I moved closer to her, breathing in the strong scent of fruity pink soap that wafted from her coils of dark wet braids, filling up the entire bedroom. It smelled like childhood and happiness, cherry ChapStick and Froot Loops and berry Pop-Tarts. It smelled like easier and simpler times.

It made me realize exactly what we had to do next. *We.*

I took another slow breath and steeled myself. "I decided to go visit some of the other kids," I said to Zoey. "Some of the other families who were down at Disney."

She smiled up at me, and if I still had my doubts, in that instant they fell away.

"But before I do any of that, we have something else to do first. Somewhere else to go."

"Where?" Zane asked, eyebrow cocked.

"Home," I said. "We're going *home.*"

Chapter Eighteen

ZANE TOOK MORE convincing than Zoey.

"I'm not leaving Iris," she insisted, locking her hand around mine.

"I can't keep running," I said. "You're right, Zane. It's pointless. Running away hasn't made anything better. And I need my family, I do. My parents lied to me, yeah, but . . . I can't hold a grudge forever. They don't deserve that. I just have to convince them to let me stay here, in Brooklyn, while we sort out the rest. But I'm not leaving you guys to stay with another Anthony. We have a spare room in our basement you can use. Give yourself some time to figure it out. Okay?"

"Please, Z?" Zoey begged, her big eyes pleading.

"Fine. Just for a few nights, tops. I'll find something else by then, okay?"

That was the easy part.

I considered calling my parents first, warning them.

But I didn't want to give them a chance to refuse Zane and Zoey. My hope was that they'd be so relieved to see me, they wouldn't even think to turn them away.

Our cab ride home felt painfully long. Zoey held my hand, asking about my parents, my brother. I tried to give her the basics, but I couldn't keep my eyes off Zane—his rigid profile as he stared unblinking out the window, a tiny muscle flexing along the side of his scarred jaw.

I could see the shrine as soon as we pulled onto Park Place. It was every bit as big and bright and ridiculous as it had looked in the photo. No, more so, now that I was seeing it up close. Twenty people? Thirty? My stomach burned, but I swallowed back the fear. So yes, they would know I was there, in my home. But wasn't it better than people thinking I was on the run?

"You can stop here," I said, a few brownstones ahead of my own. I grabbed my keys, squeezed them tight in my palm, and shoved my twenty-dollar bill into the cabdriver's waiting hand. We lingered for a moment in the backseat, looking up through the small crowd toward our golden door.

"So this is home," I said, suddenly embarrassed by the grandness of our three-story brownstone. "Let's just run through the people waiting out there, okay? Ignore them. Don't say anything."

Zoey nodded, her already round eyes even wider than usual. "Which floor are you?"

"All of them," I said quietly.

Zane stepped outside first, circling around the cab to open Zoey's door. "Hold my hand, Zo."

She latched on to him and pulled me outside along with her, the three of us moving forward in one solid chain. With Zane at the lead, people didn't pay attention to us until we were through the gates, nearly at the bottom of the stoop.

"Iris!" a voice shouted. "Iris! Iris!" Others joined in.

"Keep moving," Zane said, but I couldn't help turning back toward them, the blur of faces yelling my name.

There was only one thing I could see, one sign. One message.

Big, bright red caps: PROVE YOURSELF NOW, OR WE'LL BRING BACK THE CRUCIFIX.

Zane tugged at my hand and I stumbled up the last step. There was a sign posted on our front door, very large and official looking, warning people that they were forbidden from crossing the gate. Any trespassers would be prosecuted. A sticker just below that advertised a brand-new state-of-the-art security system. I jammed my keys in the door and swung it open, the three of us nearly toppling to the foyer floor. I kicked the door shut behind us.

"I'm home!" I yelled, but my voice sounded tiny. "Mom? Dad?"

An alarm was wailing from somewhere in the kitchen,

and I could hear the sound of fumbling feet and shifting furniture in the living room.

My mom and Aunt Hannah appeared side by side in the entryway to the foyer, their faces drawn and pale but still so wonderfully familiar. The alarm shut off. And then from behind them—"Aunt Izzy!" I squealed, shocked to see her there, in Brooklyn, especially since Aunt Hannah had said she was overwhelmed with work during football season. I was so happy she was there, I almost forgot about everything else, the sign, the people, my last few days on the run. Always solid, reliable Aunt Izzy, with her pin-straight dark hair pulled back in a tight ponytail, and a baggy San Francisco 49ers sweatshirt hanging down over black spandex leggings. So strong and so gorgeous, de-spite not having even a touch of mascara on her face.

This happy relief at seeing her, though, was immedi-ately flooded over by a crushing wave of guilt—because clearly she hadn't come from across the country for a good, positive reason. She was here for my mom, to be a rock through all the torment my parents were going through. Torment I'd made infinitely worse by running away.

But then I was swallowed up by six arms, dragged into a blur of cheeks and hair and tears—my tears, their tears, all one messy, beautiful puddle. "I'm sorry for not coming home sooner, I'm so sorry," I choked out, over and over again, my mom hushing me, a hand patting my hair, tucking the tear-damp strands behind my ears.

I slowly pulled myself back. "I'm so glad to be home," I said, smiling at my mom. She smiled back, a genuine smile that made her eyes shine, like sunlight hitting ocean.

"And what about us?" Aunt Izzy asked, clapping a hand down over my shoulder. "I come all the way to New York City for you, you silly girl, and I don't even get a big 'so glad to see my favorite aunt in the whole wide world' when I get here? Ungrateful little brat!"

"Favorite my ass," Aunt Hannah said, swatting at Aunt Izzy's arm. I laughed as they pretended to glare at each other. But watching the two of them with my mother made me miss Ari and Ethan and Delia so much that my heart seemed to physically burn in my chest.

"And you are . . . ?" my mom asked. I followed her gaze, shaken with the realization that Zane and Zoey were still there, too—had been there in the background watching our over-the-top emotional display the entire time. I felt a stab of sadness for them, sadness that no one missed them like this. No one felt like their whole world was totally upside down without the two of them there to keep it steady and grounded.

"Zane Davis," he responded, edging up to stand next to me, so close our shoulders brushed. "I go to school with your daughter, ma'am. And I've been with her these last few days—with my little sister, Zoey, too," he quickly interjected, motioning for Zoey to join us.

"Mom," I started, willing myself to say the words before I could lose my nerve. "Zane and Zoey . . . I told them they can use the room in the basement for a little while. Okay?"

Her eyebrows shot up as she turned from Zane back to me.

"Stay here? Sweetie, there's so much going on right now, so much to sort—"

"That's part of it," I said, taking a step closer to her. "They've actually helped me start figuring some of this out. Yesterday I . . . yesterday I went to see a little girl, Abigail, who'd been hurt at Disney. Zane and Zoey know her, and they thought that it might help her—might help *me*—to see her. To at least try. I had my doubts going in, and I still have my doubts, but they were right. It did help. A little. I felt like I was doing something. And right now, something feels a lot less scary than nothing."

PROVE YOURSELF NOW, OR . . .

I looked down at my beat-up old Converse sneakers to avoid their eyes, to avoid showing them my panic.

"You should be proud of what your daughter's done," Zane said, his calm voice digging deep into my tangled nerves. "What she's going to be doing with other kids like

Abby. I don't know how or why I got pulled into this, but—but I'm glad I did."

I'd never heard Zane sound so formal before, so polite and respectful. It was a new side to him—one of many sides, it seemed.

"My grandmother," he continued, "she was a big believer in you. She always told me and Zoey that it was a shame how people treated you. That they should have just accepted that maybe something good had actually happened. She's not with us anymore, but . . . I know she'd be happy right now, if she knew."

I looked up as my mom stepped toward him, wrapping her arms around his shoulders. "Thank you," she said quietly. "For taking care of my baby. For everything you just said to me. Thank you."

She pulled away from him, turning all her attention back to me. "You have a lot to catch me up on, it seems. But for now, Zane and Zoey are welcome to stay. Izzy and Hannah, why don't you show them downstairs?"

"All right," Aunt Izzy said, winking at me. "Will do. Because that's about all the lovely emotion I can handle in one sitting, anyway." She rested her hands on both Zane's and Zoey's shoulders, steering them toward the basement steps. Zane glanced over at me before disappearing, and that moment, our silent exchange, gave me a new burst of courage.

"She's home." I turned back to my mom, now with her cell phone clamped tight to her ear. She moved toward the living room, and I followed close behind. "Honey, Iris is home. She's safe." She paused, and I could hear my dad exclaiming at the other end. "We'll talk when you guys get here. Okay? I love you."

She dropped the phone onto the coffee table and collapsed on the sofa. "Sit," she said, patting the cushion next to her. I obeyed, settling in close at her side.

"Where were you, Iris? Where were you *really*?"

"At a shelter," I said softly, my eyes fixed on my knees, my dirty jeans that were greatly in need of changing. My mom gasped, but I kept talking. "For two nights, anyway. I went with a friend . . . a friend from the park. But I knew Zane and his sister went there sometimes—I'd overheard them saying it at the soup kitchen the other week."

"I take it they weren't volunteering there, too?"

"No," I said, too exhausted to explain the finer details. "But I had to go, Mom—everything here, it was all just too much. I was angry and I was hurt. Scared. Nothing felt normal anymore. Nothing felt right. And I certainly wasn't ready to deal with the reporters. I'm still not ready for them. And Kyle Bennett . . ." I trailed off, the familiar fear swallowing me whole.

"I know, sweetie." She sighed. "I get it. I don't like that you ran, but I get it. Of course I do. And I shouldn't have tried to make you leave against your will. I still think it's the right thing, but—but it's not just my decision. It's yours, too."

She paused. I felt her cool, smooth fingers on my chin, tilting my face until our eyes met.

"Is it true, then?" she asked. "What Zane said? About you visiting a little girl from Disney . . . ?"

I nodded. I could feel my chin trembling, my lips, but I bit down hard, refusing to cry. "It was terrifying. Abby, she's blind now, and has all kinds of burns . . . I didn't think I did anything, just said a few stupid clichés and cried with her for a little while, but I guess today she was doing a little better. Not physically, or anything. But she got out of bed. She wanted to be up and moving around at least."

"I see," my mom said. Now it was her turn to look away.

"Sweetie," she started, her voice breaking. She took a deep breath and tried again. "Do you remember, in my book, how I described my dreams the night after Iris came?"

There had been so many facts, so many details. I spilled them all out in my mind, searching for the right answer. "Colors," I said, the image flashing back to me. "You saw lots of amazing colors."

"That was part of it," she said, "but it was more specific than that. I wrote: 'That night I dreamed in bursts of light and explosions of colors like magical fireworks that would put even Disney World's most spectacular displays to complete shame.' That was the exact line. That was my dream."

"What are you . . . ?" The question fell away. Colors. Fireworks. *Disney.*

She'd written those words seventeen years ago.

Seventeen years before the Judges had come.

"Maybe you're right," my mom said. "Maybe you shouldn't run. Because maybe . . ." Her breath hitched, her entire body shuddering against mine. She paused for a moment as she turned to face me. "Maybe *this* . . . this is exactly why you're here."

Before I had time to dwell on my mom's terrifying premonition, the front door banged open and my dad and Caleb came running into the living room.

"Iris!" my dad called out, his gap-toothed grin like a flashlight blazing through a pitch-black room. "I am so glad you're back. *So* glad."

He leaned in to wrap me in his arms, squeezing so tight I had to fight for breath.

"I'm glad, too," I said, the words coming out in a wheeze. I *was* glad—glad to see my dad, glad to see all of them. We weren't perfect, but we were family.

My dad let go, smiling and misty-eyed as he perched on the sofa arm next to my mom. She leaned back against him, closing her eyes as his arms circled her thin shoulders. I looked over at Caleb, who was standing a few feet off still, watching us.

"Come here, silly," I said, opening my arms wide. He took a step toward me, close enough that I could pull him in for a hug.

"You scared us," he said quietly, his voice shaky. He was letting me hug him, but he wasn't hugging back. "I thought you were really gone. For good."

"Never. I would never do that, Cal. I just needed a little time."

"You're not going anywhere else, right?" He wiggled out of my hold and sat down on the floor, staring up at us.

My dad's smile tightened as he glanced down at my mom. Her eyes flickered open, meeting mine with silent approval.

"No," she said, reaching down to pat Caleb's arm. "She's going to stay here. With us."

A tapping sound at the doorway made us all jump. I turned to see Zane, with one cautious foot stepping into the room, and Zoey peeking out from behind him.

"Actually, it's not just me staying here," I said, standing up from the sofa. "These are my friends, and they'll be here with us for a little, too. Zane, from my school, and his sister, Zoey."

I watched as Caleb's eyes shifted from Zane to Zoey,

a slight blush dotting his cheeks. I bit down on a smile. Caleb was too young for crushes. Or was he?

My dad, on the other hand, looked entirely baffled. I watched him turn to my mom, saw her subtle, single nod in answer to his questions. He paused, just a fraction of a second. And then he stood and walked over to Zane, extending his hand.

"Welcome to our house, then," he said. "You can call me Jesse."

Jesse. My dad was Jesse again.

And just like that, with one little word, it was as if the last seventeen years of lies fell away.

Later that evening we all ate dinner together, my parents and Aunt Izzy and Aunt Hannah sticking to the safest questions possible—basic details about the shelter, where Zoey went to school, whether Zane and I had ever shared any classes. I mentioned that Zane had been in an art class with Delia, and as soon as I heard her name on my lips, I felt the immediate need to speak to her, speak to all my friends.

I waited, though, until after Hannah and Izzy had said their good-byes, and after Zane and Zoey had settled downstairs for the night. My dad, it was decided, would drop Zoey off at her school in the morning when he took

Caleb to his. Zane said he would walk himself, though, from the way he avoided my parents' eyes when he said it, I wasn't so sure *school* was actually where he'd be headed.

I didn't say anything about whether I'd be going or not. Nobody asked.

Back in my room I plugged in my phone. Messages lit up the screen, most of them from my friends. They *had* been trying to reach me—nonstop. I skimmed it all and called Delia first, on instinct. Maybe because she'd be the easiest, the most understanding.

"Are you okay?" she said breathlessly into the phone after barely half a ring.

"I'm fine. I'm home. And I want to tell you everything. In person, though. Tomorrow?"

There was a pause, a rustling on her end of the line.

"Why the hell did she get the first call?" Ari demanded. "Because I'm looking at my phone as we speak and I don't seem to have any missed messages from you. What about you, Ethan?" she called out. I heard Ethan mumble in the background, something that caused Ari to grunt with at least some renewed confidence. "I'm glad it's not just me you bypassed."

"I called Delia because I trusted her to be the nicest to me about it. I'm a coward, what can I say?"

"Where have you been, Iris? Your mom said something about you staying with some brother and sister from school? Who the hell are you talking about?"

"You're not going to believe this, but . . . I've actually been with Zane Davis. And his little sister, Zoey. We were at a shelter for the first two nights, and then—"

She screamed, a string of illicit words tumbling out at full volume. I yanked the phone back from my ear, wincing.

"At a *homeless* shelter? With the crazy guy who stabbed someone with scissors? What in God's name were you doing with him?"

"Ari . . . it's not like that. *He's* not like that."

"Are you kidding me, Iris Spero? He's *exactly* like that. You can just tell."

"I'm tired, Ari. Let's all talk about this tomorrow, okay? Come over after school."

"So does that mean you won't be back, then? No more school?"

I was suddenly exhausted, the last four nights of running crashing down all at once. "I have a few other things I need to do. Things that I'll tell you about tomorrow. When we talk civilly and calmly face-to-face, okay?"

"Fine." She huffed. And then she sighed. "I love you, Iris. You're insane but I love you. We all do." I heard a clicking that must have been her tapping speakerphone, because then: "Good night, Iris!" "We love you!" Ari, then Ethan and Delia.

I smiled. "I love you, too."

I hung up and started peeling back my blankets, my eucalyptus-scented, puffy white cloud of a comforter, when my eye snagged on the violin case across the room.

I dropped the blankets.

My hands trembled as I settled onto the blue wing chair and unclasped the case.

The bow. *My* bow.

It felt like weeks since I'd played, not days. I had butterflies. It was like I was going on a first date—or how I imagined I'd feel going on a first date, since I technically never had. The rooftop with Zane, whatever that was, was clearly *not* a date.

I lifted the violin up, tucked it tightly under my chin.

And then I played.

Chapter Nineteen

I WOKE UP the next morning to a gentle knocking on my door. My eyelids were still heavy with sleepiness. It had been after two when I'd finally put down the violin. My fingers ached now, but it was a good ache; they were meant to play, meant to burn.

"Come in," I called out, expecting to see my mom.

But no, when the door opened, it was Zane looking in. I sat up quickly, smoothing down the wild strands of my matted hair.

"Hey," he said, smiling—a smug-looking smile, damn him—at my futile attempts to make myself more presentable. "Sorry to wake you. But your dad just took Zoey and Caleb to school, and I wanted to see if you were going to meet up with Angelica today. The Disney's Children lady."

"I think so. I think I need to do it fast before I chicken out. Where does this Angelica live? You said Brooklyn?"

"Yeah, Fort Greene, so it's close enough. I just called

her to check in, and she said she's free all day. I can go with you. If you want."

"You want to go?" I asked, surprised. "But I thought you were busy today. School or . . . whatever your personal business is that you do." I turned away, unable to look him in the eye to see how he responded to that. It was his business, but I didn't have to like it. Zane was too good to be doing anything illegal. He had too much to lose.

"If you want me to go with you, I'll be there," he said, his voice husky, gruff almost. "I feel like I'm partly responsible for getting you into all this. And I'm not just going to leave you hanging now. If you need me, that is."

I nodded. "I'd like that. I want you there, if that's okay with you."

Zane left me to get showered and ready, which took much longer than it should have. How did someone dress for something like this? I settled on tights and a vintage green dress covered in bright yellow daisies and sunflowers. It was my happy dress, for big exams or auditions, days that needed to start out bright and cheery. Today certainly qualified.

My mom was waiting for me at the kitchen table when I came downstairs.

"Where are you going?" she asked, eyeing the purse and jacket slung over my wrist.

"I'm meeting with the founder of Disney's Children,

the support group I'm going to maybe get more involved with. Angelica Byrne; she just lives in Fort Greene. I won't be gone long, I promise."

"I don't want you going alone. I'm coming, too."

"No, it's okay. I won't be alone. Zane offered to come."

"Doesn't Zane have school?"

"Mom . . . please. I think I need to do this on my own. Zane will just stand in the background in case I really need him. Which I won't. It'll be fine. Okay?"

"This isn't a good idea. It's not just the mobs outside. I haven't heard from Kyle Bennett since you left and that scares me. I'm not buying that he's satisfied just because he broke the news to everyone. I don't like his silence. I don't know what it means, but I don't like it."

"That's why I have Zane. People don't mess with him. Trust me. Kids at school avoid even passing him in the hallway if they can help it."

"And *that's* supposed to make your mother feel better?"

"He's a good guy," I said. I could feel every muscle reflexively tightening, my back straightening in defense. "He's just misunderstood."

She shook her head, sighing. Any relief she'd felt at my return seemed to have already passed. Her skin was pasty, her eyes rimmed with dark purple circles. From the looks of it, she'd gotten less sleep than I had in the past few days, even though she'd been in her own bed.

"Today, Iris. Let me just come today, okay? Please do that much for my sanity right now. I want to get a feel for this Angelica lady, and the group, and what exactly the next steps would be. And if afterward we both agree it feels right, I'll let you have more freedom. You can go with Zane from here on out. Can we agree to that?"

I nodded. I couldn't be totally unreasonable, not after everything I'd already put them through in the last few days. And this was still *my* decision, after all, my plan of action. I had control over my own life again. I could compromise.

"Thank you," she said, giving me a weak smile. "We'll go out the kitchen door. We can use the gate in the backyard, cross through the McAllisters' property, and then have a cab waiting for us right on the other side. I don't want any of those fanatics on our trail."

"Okay," I said. "Sounds like a plan." I walked over and wrapped my arms around her, tucking her head beneath my chin. Her already petite frame felt thinner to me. Fragile. "I'm going to be fine, Mom. But you said it yourself yesterday. That dream . . ." I trailed off. I closed my eyes and squeezed them tight, trying to see what she'd seen, those outrageously astonishing colors. It didn't work, though. All I saw was black.

"You have to do this, don't you?"

"I think I do." I breathed out, her wavy hair tickling my lips.

"I always knew there was a reason—that you were born to do *something*. And as much as it scares me to say it . . . I think this is it. I think it might be your time, my baby girl."

I lifted my head, meeting her eyes.

"Let's go, Iris. Your crazy, beautiful destiny awaits."

"I'm so honored to have you both here," Angelica said, her gray eyes bright as she grinned at me and then my mom, leaning in closer from across her kitchen table. "I speak for everyone in Disney's Children when I say that I am grateful beyond words that you've decided to meet with us. I've been following the news, of course, with everything people have been saying about you, and with everything that's happening at your home right now . . ."

She reached over the table and squeezed my hand. I itched to glance back at Zane, to remind myself that he was still here with us, too. But he had pulled his chair farther away from the table, leaving Angelica, my mom, and me in our own more intimate bubble.

I forced myself to smile, and Angelica continued. "I'm just relieved to know that you're safe. There were some who've been speculating that you were missing because the wrong people got ahold of you. People who didn't buy into the whole miracle-baby thing. They're out there, of course, but from what I've been reading and hearing, it seems like there are a good amount of people who believe in you." She dropped my hand and turned her gaze to my mom, her grin growing even wider. "Personally, I believed you when I was a teen, just about your age at the time it all happened. I was fascinated by the whole story, just fascinated. And that video that your friend Jesse made, your husband now, I believe . . . ?" Angelica raised her hand to her heart and fluttered her fingers, beaming at my mom. "Hit me right here. That's when I knew you were telling the truth. I was heartsick for months when I thought you'd lost the baby. It just wasn't right. It wasn't right how people treated you, no matter what they did or didn't believe."

"Thank you," my mom said quietly. "That means a lot."

Angelica looked back at me then, and I nodded, too emphatically. But I didn't know what to say, really. Her tone, the look in her eyes—I felt like we were *celebrities* to her, humbly accepting her reverence and adoration. Was this how it would be from now on? How did actual celebrities handle this every day of their lives? I was already overwhelmed, and it had been less than five minutes. I had a newfound respect for my mother, her strength and her patience. I reached down and found her hand under the table, interlacing my fingers tightly with hers.

"I called Sam and Janelle after I heard from Zane, and they couldn't stop raving about the wonders you worked on little Abigail. And now to think that you'll meet so many other kids . . ." Her eyes glossed over with tears, and she paused for a moment, swiping at her wet cheeks. "I was at Disney that day with my husband and our two kids, and our best friends and their kids, and . . . well, the four of us were lucky enough to make it out with just a few scratches from all the flying debris. But my best friend, Claire . . ." She squeezed her eyes shut as the words trailed off.

Angelica looked ashy, suddenly, in the white sunlight spilling through the kitchen's lacy red curtains. She opened her eyes, staring at me as she continued on. "Claire survived. But she lost her husband and two of her kids . . . They were right at the castle when it happened, while Claire and her youngest daughter, Lula, were making a run to the restroom. It could have been all of them, Iris. Thank God, because it could have been *all of them*."

Angelica frowned, slowly shaking her head as she studied me. *Me*, I realized with a start. She was glad to have my mom there, too, but *I* was the focus. The answer.

To her, my mom's story was in the past.

Mine was the present. The future.

"Even still," she continued, bringing me back, "we have to remember what we have. Honor those we lost, but recognize that those who survived have to find a way to keep on living. That's why I wanted to start Disney's Children. I thought that if all of us banded together, we could help one another heal. Help in any way we can. Donations and hot meals, driving families to and from the hospital for visits or treatments . . . or even something just as simple as a hug and shoulder to cry on. But it's hard. The people who have it the worst—they can't think about anything but their own families right now. I figured I had a lot to give, since I was one of the lucky ones, so . . . so starting something like this was the least I could do."

"Can I meet Lula?" I asked, the question catching even me off guard. My mom squeezed my hand harder.

"Of course," Angelica said, her frown instantly lifting into a smile. "I was already hoping you would be willing to meet her, since she was my inspiration for all of this."

"How is she doing? What . . . what were her injuries like?" I braced myself, waiting to hear the worst.

"She's better off than most. A few burns and cuts on her legs, but other than that, most of the healing she has to do is on the inside. I can't imagine a seven-year-old girl like her having to mourn one member of her family, let alone three. And Claire . . . Claire's trying her best to keep up a front, but she's devastated, of course. Just devastated." Her voice broke and she blinked, turning away from us.

"Take me to them," I said, sounding so drastically more confident than I felt. Inside I was dizzy and nauseated and unstable, my heart racing and my palms coated in a slippery layer of cool sweat. But there was no going back. I had to do this.

Or no, it was more than that.

I *wanted* to do this.

Claire opened the door to her ornately decorated brownstone with a weak smile, her arms briefly reaching out, hesitating, before she turned away.

She had probably been an uncommonly gorgeous woman before, all porcelain skin and high, sharp cheekbones, towering over me by a good six inches. But she looked to me like a sad flicker of beauty now, her red-rimmed eyes lined with dark circles, greasy hair in a sloppy bun, bones that seemed just a little too pronounced, too severe. I swallowed my tears and looked away, the weight of her grief a tangible, breath-sucking creature.

"She refuses to go back to school," Claire said, shutting the door as Angelica, Zane, and my mom stepped into the foyer behind me. I forced my eyes back to her, watching as she gave Angelica a brief, one-armed hug and nodded in acknowledgment toward Zane and my mom. "She refuses to leave her room except for when I make her come to the table for meals. I don't know what she does all day in there, really. Whenever I knock, whenever I try to interest her in doing anything at all, she just sits there staring. She's a ghost, my baby girl. She's a ghost, and she's all I have left in this world."

The rest of us were silent. There were no words to bridge that void. Claire walked over to me, lightly taking my hand as she led me toward Lula's bedroom. "She barely says a word to me lately, but maybe she'll open up more if it's just you in the room. I'll wait right outside. Just in case you need anything." She knocked twice, opening the door though Lula hadn't responded, and then she nudged me into the room. The door closed behind me, though not all the way. There was a thin sliver of air, just enough space for our words to carry.

I couldn't think about Claire listening, judging. It would only terrify me more.

In this room, it was just us. Me and Lula. Me standing frozen in front of her doorway, Lula sitting in a heap of blankets on the bed, curled into a tiny ball as she hugged her knees in tight. She was as beautiful as her mom, a miniature version of her with thick, wavy black hair and pale skin, dark eyelashes framing stunning sapphire-blue eyes.

"Hi," I started, taking a few small steps closer to her.

"Hi," she said back, her voice barely above a whisper.

"Do you mind if I sit on your bed?" I asked.

She shook her head, squirming over a few inches to make room for me.

"I know you're probably sick of hearing this," I said, easing onto the edge of the mattress next to her. "But I am so incredibly sorry to hear about everything you've gone through. My heart is broken for you and your mom. For everyone that you lost."

She nodded, her wide, solemn eyes staring up at me.

"I don't know . . . I don't know what your mom's told you already. But my name is Iris. And I just wanted to meet you. To tell you that I'm here if you want to talk."

"I know. My mom told me about you," she said, her voice a little louder now, loud enough that I could hear the deep-down trembling behind it.

I nodded, unsure of what should be said next. I tried to relax the muscles of my face, somehow conceal the anxiousness with at least some semblance of calm. Because as tough as it had been to meet Abby, it was infinitely harder now. Lula *saw* me. She saw all of me—every frown, every shudder, every tear.

"Will my mom and I ever be happy again?" she asked, the words pouring out in a rush—as if they'd been hovering on her lips for days, waiting for their chance. "Because right now I'm so sad. I'm so sad that sometimes . . . sometimes I wish I wasn't here. I wish I was with my dad and my big brother and sister."

Those words, those terrible words, hit me like a punch straight through the stomach.

"Lula, yes," I said, reaching out to clasp her small hand. "You will absolutely be happy again. You'll miss them always, every day, I'm sure. It's okay to cry and to feel sad. But they're still here with you—always. They're a part of you. And they'd want you to keep on living, to be as happy as you can possibly be. Because you deserve that. You and your mom—you both deserve happiness. It just takes time."

She studied me, unblinking as she bit down on her lower lip with two adorably crooked front teeth. "Do you know these things because you're special? That's what my mom told me. That you're special and not like everyone else."

"I'm . . . I'm just me," I said, my heart pounding harder. "I'm just Iris. All I know for sure is that I want you to feel better, and that I am wishing for that so hard." I squeezed her hand as I said it, shutting my eyes to fight back the dizzy feeling washing over me, the hazy black dots spiraling through my vision. "I believe that you *will* feel better, Lula. Slowly maybe, but you'll feel better again soon. Trust me. Please just trust me," I whispered, struggling to still the tremors that swept over me, my hand shaking around hers.

"Okay."

I opened my eyes and we watched each other, silent for a few endless, stretching moments. And then she smiled.

I exhaled, pushing out all the breath I hadn't realized I'd been holding in.

I smiled back.

Chapter Twenty

"WELCOME HOME, YOU terrible little shithead of a friend," Ari said, though the cool, cutting words couldn't mask the quake in her voice as she pulled me in close for a hug. "Don't you ever, *ever* do anything like this again, Iris Spero. Do you hear me? This was so not okay. I thought you were gone. For *good*." She broke on that last word, her body trembling against me.

A pang of guilt seized my stomach. I hadn't meant to cause her that kind of fear, not after she'd gone through it all before, everything with her father . . . "I'm so sorry, Ari, really, I just—"

She sniffled, burying her face deeper in my sweatshirt to hide any tears. "You're lucky nothing happened to you, Iris, that's all. A homeless shelter? There are enough crazies in this city as it is, and there's a very specific breed of crazy that's obsessing over you at the moment, in case you hadn't noticed."

"Seriously, Iris, we're just relieved you're back," Ethan said, giving me a massive bear hug after Ari finally released me. "I can't even believe the ridiculous crowd we had to shove through to get inside the house. Were you able to get any sleep last night after you got home? Do they leave at night at least?"

"Some of them stuck around, I think, but . . . I slept okay," I said. "I played the violin until I pretty much collapsed. It was cathartic."

He stepped back, allowing Delia to take her turn. But instead of hugging me, she reached into her paint-splattered tote bag and pulled out a small square canvas.

"I painted this after you left. I've been painting non-stop, actually—it's the only thing that could calm me down. So in a way, you were a great inspiration. But don't run away again. Once was enough, okay?" She flashed a tiny smile, handing the painting to me.

I looked down at the dark sweeping lines, blacks and blues and deep purples, the angry swirls of the storm, spilling from all four corners of the canvas. In the center, though, there was a hazy golden bubble, safe and untouched. And right in the middle of all that light, there was a miniature me—on my bench at the park, violin held tight, eyes closed as I drifted off into the music.

"This is how I thought about you, whenever I got scared. I pictured you in your happy place."

I put the painting down on the nightstand and threw myself into her arms. "You're so damn amazing, you know that, right?" She latched on tight in response.

We let go after a long minute of squeezing, and I settled down on the wing chair by the window. Ethan and Delia curled up on my bed, and Ari perched on the arm next to me, scowling as she observed the crowds outside.

"Some of those posters," Ari started, not taking her eyes off the window, "they're pretty threatening, and I don't like it at all. It looks all *rah-rah, go, Iris* at first glance, but . . . but it's scary. 'Crucify the Spero.' I mean . . . what the fuck?" She shook her head, squinting as she edged closer to the window. "Equally terrifying, the ladies right behind him, waving around a big yellow banner that says, 'You must save us all.' I don't know which is worse. I mean, what good do they think standing out there is going to do? What is the end goal here, people?"

"Maybe your mom wasn't wrong about hiding for now," Ethan said, frowning so deep his eyeglasses slid a few inches down his nose. "I mean, I don't want you to leave us. But it's completely horrifying that all these desperate extremists are right outside your front door. This doesn't feel remotely safe."

"No," I said, so loudly that even Ari flinched, nearly slipping from her precarious perch on the chair's arm. "No. That's part of what I wanted to tell you guys today. I know it's crazy, but I think I have to deal with this. I think it's . . . it's what I'm supposed to do."

"You don't have to do anything, Iris," Ari said. "All these signs, it's nonsense. All of it."

"That's the thing. I'm not so sure it is."

She turned away from the window to face me. "So you're saying that you don't believe just the part about your mom being a virgin. You believe *all* of it. You believe that you're . . . you're *destined* for something?"

"Maybe. Maybe I do. I don't know . . ." I took a deep inhale, gripping the chair cushion for support. "What I do know is that I've visited two kids in the past two days, two kids who were victims of Disney. And for whatever reason, my being there seemed to help. Maybe in just a small way, but still. It helped. And I don't think I can just walk away from that, silly as that might sound."

"That doesn't sound silly at all, Iris," Delia said quietly. "If they want to believe and it helps, where's the harm?"

"Thanks, Delia," I started. "I just—"

"The harm is when they realize she can't actually *do* anything," Ari cut in, throwing her hands up in the air. "Seriously, Iris, where did you even get this idea in your head?"

"I'm not claiming to be healing them. I'm just visiting them and sort of boosting morale. And I told you last night, I've been staying with Zane Davis, and it turns out that—"

"Yes, the crazy gangster thug who went to jail before for stabbing someone with scissors. I heard you last night, but I still don't get it," Ari said, her brow furrowing deeply. "How in the world did he come into any of this?"

"He's not crazy and there were no *scissors*," I said, my face burning with irritation. I balled my fists even tighter around the cushion, trying to contain all of the many hot, angry words threatening to spill out. After all, hadn't I thought the same things just the week before? "He's not a thug, either. Or a criminal in some gang." Well, technically he *had* been in juvie. And maybe he still did do illegal things—but if he did, it was only to keep him and Zoey afloat. I hoped. I'd forgotten about the gang rumor, but . . . no, he couldn't be. I'd be able to tell, wouldn't I? I'd have seen more hints?

Ari tilted her head, studying me with her squinted purple eyes.

"What's going on with you and Zane? What other hidden life are you keeping from us? Quite a leap from that sweet blondie-boy Gabe you obsessed over all summer, isn't he?"

"What? No. It's not like that. It's nothing. And anyway," I said, the words too fast and clipped, suspicious even to my own ears, "this is more about his little sister, Zoey. I happened to connect with them the day after I ran away, and we ended up kind of banding together.

Helping each other out. They lost a cousin at Disney."

"God, that's terrible." Ethan sighed. "I can't imagine."

"Right. She—their cousin, Brinley—was down there for a chorus trip at the time. She died instantly, but her best friend, Abby, lived, and Zoey asked me to meet her. So I did. And it seemed to get her out of bed at least, if nothing else."

"Well, I think it's cool, what you're doing," Delia said, looking pointedly at Ari.

"So do I," Ethan chimed in. "I mean seriously, I told you, after watching your dad's video—"

A knock made Ethan halt in midsentence. The door was already partway open, and Zane stood in the hallway, peering in. He lingered there, looking strangely uncertain with three strangers—relatively speaking—staring him down. We all went to school together, yes, but even in the same hallways, we'd been walking through two very different worlds.

"Hey, Zane," I practically squealed, cringing at the sound. "Meet my friends. Ari, Delia, Ethan. Guys, this is Zane Davis. You know him from school," I said, plastering a grin on my face as I bobbled my head back and forth between them. "Delia, I think you guys had art together, right?"

"Yep, last year." She gave a little half wave.

"Hey," Zane said, nodding his head in general acknowledgment of the group. But he kept his gaze on me.

"I was just filling them in on everything. Disney's Children. Abby."

He looked away, his eyes moving down to my shiny wooden floor.

"Yeah, about that. It's why I came up. Her parents just called me. They said she won't stop talking about you and asking when she gets to see you again. I know you have a lot of people to see, but . . . you know. She's special, Abby. To me, at least."

It took a lot for him, I was sure, to be that open—especially in front of strangers.

"Sure. Of course, I'll go back." I didn't know what else I could say to her, but I would go back. For Zane. Just as I was about to say that, my eyes shifted to the violin case propped up against my chair.

I grinned.

"I have an idea." Maybe my words had been enough for Abby and Lula the first time—had lulled them into some temporary kind of calm—but for a second time, a third time? What more could I possibly say? If there was anything I knew for sure, it was that sometimes, the most important things weren't said with words.

They were said with music.

"Do you want to come, too?" I asked Zane, as soon as I'd told the four of them what I wanted to do. I would play the violin for Abby, for any of the other kids whose families wanted me to visit. "And can you call her parents back and see if later today's okay for them?"

"What about us?" Ari asked, loudly and pointedly kicking up off the arm of the chair to stand. She landed right in front of me, arms crossed, blocking me from getting up. "Why him?" She gave a quick sideways glance to Zane before pinning those sharp purple eyes back on me. "Don't you want *us* to be helping? We are all musicians, you know. We could play, too."

"Zane knows Abby," I said softly, afraid to hurt her more than I probably already had. "It's because of him that I went to her in the first place. That I'm doing anything at all right now except sitting here feeling scared and useless. I don't want to overwhelm her, but . . . maybe another time?" The words sounded halfhearted, even to my own ears. Why *did* I want only Zane there, and not one of my best friends?

Maybe . . . because Zane knew only this new me. The old Iris—her normal life, her normal problems—she didn't exist for him. We'd both been running when we met.

But we had stopped now. Together.

"You could have talked to us about it," Ari said. "We

could have helped you brainstorm, figure something out if that was what you wanted to do. You dropped a bomb on us and then ran away while you tried to figure it out. Without us."

She was right. Maybe I hadn't given them enough of a chance. But still—I couldn't regret those days away. Those days had changed everything.

"Ari," I said, desperate for her to understand, "I didn't know what I wanted to do, either, or if I even wanted to do anything at all. Until Zane and his little sister convinced me to try it, for Abby's sake."

"Fine," Ari said, backing up so quickly she bumped up hard against the window. She blinked a few times, her dark eyelashes glistening, before turning away from me. Ari crying, twice in one day. It was unheard of. And it was because of me.

"I'll need you guys, trust me," I said, wrapping my arms around her from behind, nudging my chin against her shoulder. "I have no clue what's next. All I know is that right now, tonight, I want to play the violin for Abby. That's all."

"I get it, but . . . just know that we do want to help," Delia said. Next to her, Ethan enthusiastically bobbed his head up and down in agreement. "It feels strange to see all this happening to you, and not actually be doing anything to make it better."

"I know, it's just that . . . I'm not sure I know quite what *better* is yet," I said, giving Ari's shoulders one last squeeze before letting go. "But when I figure it out, you guys will be the first to know."

"I'll go call Janelle," Zane said, his feet already moving toward the door, "let her know we'll head over soon. It was, uh, nice to meet you guys. See you around." He flashed a tight, unconvincing smile as he stepped out, boots clomping quickly down the hall.

"I want to like him, Iris," Ethan said quietly. "For your sake. I do. The rumors are so ridiculous and I hate myself for believing them. It's just hard—it's hard to let go."

"Thank you." I smiled. I'd needed to hear that more than I'd realized. "There's a lot I don't know about Zane yet, true. But everything that I do know . . . He's a good guy. I have faith in his motives here."

"No offense, but you trust a lot of people who seem questionable to me," Ari said, still not turning back to face me. "You're lucky with all the random people you've talked to on the streets that you've never gotten yourself into any worse situations. Not everyone is good, Iris. Not everyone has your best interests at heart."

The words stung. She was right; not everyone was safe, and the crowd outside proved that more than ever. But I had to stand by my instinct.

"If you can't trust Zane, Ari, then please—trust me."

Ari was silent at that, her shoulders rigid as she stared out the window.

"I think it's maybe more than luck, though," Delia said, her already quiet voice almost a whisper now.

"What do you mean?" I asked, my whole body stiffening.

"I just mean that . . . people seem to listen to you, Iris. Even if it feels totally random and against their own inclination sometimes. Like at school, with people like Bryce and Noah, and Carolina . . . when you put them in their place, give them a look . . . I don't know, they just get it. They stop. You just have that effect on people."

"Huh," Ethan said, shaking his head. "Never thought about it, but you have a point. Sounds crazy, but . . . what the hell, this whole thing is crazy, right?"

"Stop," I said. *"Stop."* But my head was already spiraling through other moments: the first day I'd met Ethan, at the shelter with Mr. Jackson . . . "I'm just friendly. People respond to friendly. I smile a lot. That's all there is to it." I was right. I had to be right.

All three of them stared at me, silent.

I pulled on my jacket to signal the end of the conversation, and the rest of them followed my lead. I grabbed my purse and the violin case and was the first out the door.

Worries about Ari, Ethan's doubts, my own doubts even, Delia's absurd comment about *luck*—I had to push it all away. The music, that was what mattered. Just me and my violin, and Abby of course, too, listening and hopefully finding some small kind of comfort, some kind of release. Music was always my cure, better than sleep or Advil or steaming chicken noodle soup.

Zane was waiting for us down in the kitchen. My parents, Caleb, and Zoey, thankfully, were nowhere to be found. My mom had mentioned a quick shopping trip with Zoey after school—basic supplies and a few new clothes, maybe. I couldn't believe they'd leave me alone for long, even with my friends and Zane there. I called a cab and then jotted off a quick text saying where I'd be, and that, *yes*, not to worry, I was definitely using the back door. We headed out through the yard and across our neighbor's property, the five of us parting ways as my taxi pulled up along the sidewalk.

Ethan and Delia both pulled me in for a hug. And then suddenly Ari was there, too, squeezing me so tight from behind that I swore I could feel her heart thudding against my back.

The four of us, all stitched up together tight, just like it was supposed to be.

Zane was already in the cab when I finally pulled away.

"I know it felt a little tense," I said, breaking the silence as the car started down the street, "but they don't hate you or anything. They just don't know you. And they're always wary of strangers. Instinct, I guess. We were all kind of on the outside, until we found each other."

"It's fine," he said, eyes locked on the view outside his window. "It's not like I care. Everyone thinks what they want about me, anyway. I gave up trying to change any-one's mind a long time ago."

"You might say that," I said, my voice barely a breath, "but I'm not sure it's really true." The words were so quiet, I wasn't sure he'd heard. He didn't answer, at least, and I didn't repeat myself.

We didn't speak as we pulled up to Abby's apart-ment building, as we climbed the two flights of stairs and once again found ourselves swept into Sam and Janelle's cramped but cozy apartment.

If Janelle had been excited before, she was nearly bouncing through her skin now.

"I'm glad you're back so soon!" she gushed, clapping her hands as she did a little dance around me, circling like a bee over a juicy new flower. "Abby's been so much more active and engaged since she met you. She came out to the kitchen for tea with her grandmother today! We even got her to laugh a few times. It might sound like so little to you, but it's not, Iris. Trust me, it's not. Not after how it's been." She slowed for a beat at that, like the dark had suddenly seized her again, dragging her back through all of the worst memories from the past weeks.

"I'm glad I'm here again, too," I said. But the familiar gnawing burn of anxiety was back in a sudden rush. I'd reacted so quickly, got in that cab so fast, I hadn't had time to worry. It hit me now, all at once.

I lifted my violin case up in front of me, hugging it close to my chest. "I had the idea that maybe Abby would like me to play some songs for her." It sounded silly and inadequate to me now. Why would a few songs on the violin make a difference? I was good, sure, but I was still only learning. And it was just music, after all.

Just music.

No. Music was special. I believed that. I'd always believed that.

Janelle nodded, already fluttering again, the darkness dispelled. "Abby loves music, you know. It's why she was down at Disney to begin with . . ."

We both froze.

"I don't want to upset her more, if . . ."

"No," Janelle said. "*No.* It's not music we should blame. Go on. Go play for her."

I nodded and started for the room, my hands sweating as they clamped tightly around the case, my shield. The door with the sparkly *A* was open this time. Even though Abby had likely heard me out with her parents, I still cleared my throat, letting her know I was there now.

"Hi, Abby," I said, leaving the door open behind me

this time. Sam and Janelle could listen, too, if they wanted. Why not? Playing music for people—it was what I did, who I *was.*

"Hi," she said, squirming to pull herself into a more upright position. "I didn't think you'd be back so soon."

I set the case on the floor as I let myself fall into the chair by her bed. "I thought you might like it if I played a little music for you. I heard you like to sing. And I love music, too. I love the violin. So if it's okay, I thought maybe I could play for you?"

"Sure," she said, her smile drooping just a little. She was disappointed, maybe—she'd hoped I was there to do something bigger—or, as it was for her mom, the music was a reminder. Music had become too linked to Disney in her mind.

But Janelle was right. The music wasn't to blame.

I pulled the violin out, precisely and slowly, buying more time as I considered what to play first. My chin was on the rest, the bow in my hand. The moment hung there, suspended, as Abby waited.

And then I heard the opening notes. I'd already started playing.

"Defying Gravity," from *Wicked.* I'd figured out the notes for myself after seeing it on Broadway, giving it my own twists and turns.

For the first minute, Abby's lips were tensed, a tight,

straight line that seemed to cut entirely through the small portion of her face that I could see.

I kept playing, though. I kept trying.

Her shoulders twitched. Was she upset? Angry? But after a second twitch, a third, I realized that no—she wasn't upset or angry, she was *swaying*, rocking back and forth in sync with the music. Her hand, too, resting on top of the blanket, the tips of her fingers tapping out a soft beat against the puff of her comforter. The movements, no matter how subtle, filled me up, golden liquid sunshine spilling through my fingertips. I sat up straighter, played louder, deeper.

As I came to the end, the final chorus, her lips slowly turned up.

"Play more," she said, as soon as my bow came to a halt. "Please, please keep playing."

So I did. I kept playing. I knew other Broadway tunes, music she might recognize.

And a few songs in, Abby started singing along.

It didn't necessarily get *easier* after that.

First there was Charlotte, an adorably redheaded and freckled eight-year-old girl who'd lost her right arm in the bombing—Charlotte, who asked me to watch *The Little Mermaid* with her; by the end, we were both singing and dancing while we twirled around the room, me with my violin, her swinging around her favorite doll. Then there were two five-year-old twins, Andrea and Andrew; Andrea didn't have a scratch on her, but Andrew had burns all across his face, chest, and upper arms. Andrea cried through most of my visit, but Andrew—Andrew was calm, soft-spoken. When his sister left the room for a snack, he asked me to especially try to help her. He told me that he would be okay, as long as she could feel okay, too. They curled up on Andrea's bed together as I played for them, humming and then making up silly new words as they pretended to sing along.

Tommy, Alexa, Tyler, Jia, Ruby. For three days, I made back-to-back visits to kids in all different states of recovery, most at home, but some still in the hospital—and always with Zane and the violin at my side. Angelica had asked the parents not to tell others about my visits, and everyone was quick to agree—they'd do anything, try anything, if it meant they could have even a tiny shred of hope. My mom stood by her word, letting me and Zane go on our own, but she or Dad still called me every half hour, just to check in. They were terrified, but they weren't telling me to stop. Our neighbors across the yard had started letting me and Zane in through their back door, allowing us to wait in their foyer until a cab arrived. We'd run down their stoop then, our hoodies pulled up tight.

I felt just as scared each time, just as helpless when I walked into the room with an anxious new face studying me. But my violin—it gave me confidence. It spoke when I couldn't. And each time, I felt more sure when I left— more sure that, no matter what the cause, there had been a small shift for the better. A tiny glimpse of happiness, a smile, a song, a laugh—something, no matter how minute or subtle, that hadn't existed when I first arrived. Because, for better or for worse, my reputation was more power- ful than I could have realized. My presence, my music, my hand in theirs—it was all together a magic pill that every- one was only too eager to swallow.

But then I met Maddie Rae Stevens.

Maddie was a beautiful five-year-old who had been in a coma since that day at Disney World, and she'd been showing increasingly alarming signs of physical deterio- ration. I held her hand more tightly than I'd ever held anything in my life, but I felt nothing there. She was like a doll, a fragile, breakable doll that had no chance of ever coming to life. Her dad, Owen, stayed in the room with us the entire time, his red, sleepless eyes carving through me with their vicious desperation.

"Save my little girl," he begged after I'd said my good- byes. He continued yelling down the hallway as Zane led me past nurses and doctors who followed us too closely with their eyes. "God damn it, save her! You're supposed to be some kind of savior, aren't you? Why aren't you saving *her*?"

But I'd known from the first second I walked into that room with Maddie Rae. And Owen knew, too, as much as he didn't want to accept it. I couldn't—no matter how hard I tried, no matter how fiercely I played my music or pleaded with the other Iris to help me—change a single thing.

No one could save her, no matter how much anyone *believed*.

Because sometimes, not even hope was enough.

Zane and I were silent on our ride back home from meeting Maddie Rae. But as the cab started to turn down the street just before mine, I slammed my hand against the plastic window behind the driver. "No!" I yelled, shocking all three of us.

The cab lurched.

"No," I said more quietly, gritting my teeth. "Park Place. Drive to Park Place. Drop us off just past Underhill Ave. Please."

"Iris?" Zane asked, his hand landing on my knee. "What are you . . . ?"

"What's the point in trying to hide what I'm doing? Won't it be better if they know I'm trying at least? The way people were watching us at the hospital today, I doubt my little visits are a secret anymore, anyway."

I felt desperate, doubtful, but I was still hurtling forward.

"I don't know. I think we should talk to your parents first . . ."

"They'll tell me no," I said, just as the cab stopped in front of our house. I shoved some bills in the driver's hand and threw open the door before Zane could try to stop me.

I held my head up as I marched toward the clusters of people standing between me and my front gate. I'd noticed from my bedroom window the day before that there were ribbons—cloths of all colors and sizes—tied along the iron posts. Now, up close, I watched as a woman tied a red string, double knotting it, her eyes closed as her lips moved silently up and down. Praying.

People were stopping by to leave their prayers for me, their wishes.

Their demands.

"Excuse me," I said, nudging two women who were holding up a large neon-yellow banner. I blinked as I stepped past them and Zane was suddenly right in front of me, his hand wrapping around mine.

"*Iris!*" One person whispered it, and then another. "Iris! Iris!" My name spread through the lips of everyone around me, a crowd of maybe twenty or so people. It sounded like hundreds, though, my name hissing like a sticky breeze all around me.

As soon as we'd passed the gate, Zane locked it behind us. It was a joke of a barrier, more ornamental than anything, three feet high and easily surmountable for anyone who wanted to try.

But it stopped them—for now. I stood on one side, and they stayed on the other.

An older man in a faded army jacket and fuzzy black cap leaned in, his arms nearly brushing against me. "Iris, we need you to—"

I stepped back and held my hands up, motioning for silence.

It was only then that I noticed the news van, the camera angled straight at my face. But I kept going.

"Please. Please listen. I'm trying; I am. I'm visiting people who need . . ." *Me*, I almost said. But that word, that idea, still caught in my throat. "People who need help. I'm not ignoring you. I see you out here every day, and I'm listening. But standing with signs in front of my home isn't doing any good. I need my privacy. Please go back to your lives, and let me live mine. I'll do my best, but that's all I can promise. Okay?"

Instead of nodding and waving good-bye, as I'd maybe naively hoped, they responded with a chorus of eager questions, more frantic even than before, pressing in tighter, closer to the gate. The voices, the words, all melded into one long, terrible string as I leaned back against Zane's chest for balance.

Who are you helping? Tell us more! Can you help me? My mom? My sister? Who do you think you are? Liar! Healer! Touch my hand! Damn you! Help me! Burn in hell! Sign my Bible! Iris! Iris! Please!

I saw the two women with the banner I'd first passed on the sidewalk, both in their seventies, I'd guess, with graying hair and glasses, colorful scarves, and knit beanies. They reminded me of Nanny. But then my eyes landed on that neon yellow. YOU MUST SAVE US ALL. The poster Ari had seen the other day.

"I'm doing all I can do," I said, though my own frail voice was nothing against the crowd. "You have to believe me."

"Let's go," Zane said, tugging me up the steps. "You did what you wanted to do." I let him pull me along, turning away from the crowd.

Ari had been right.

The old ladies' poster was just as scary as the CRUCIFY THE SPERO banner she'd seen out there, too. Because it was still a threat. What if I *didn't* save everyone? And I couldn't. Maddie Rae was proof of that. So what then?

What would be my punishment?

Chapter Twenty-One

I DIDN'T IMMEDIATELY tell my parents about my public announcement, but I hadn't needed to. My face was all over the news, my grand proclamation about helping people, my assurance that I was doing the best I could do.

"Oh, Iris," my dad said with a sigh, hugging me as we all sat in the living room, staring at the TV screen. Cal was perched on a chair by the window, peeping through the curtain every few minutes, his pale face disturbingly blank. "I know you probably thought you were helping, but . . ."

My dad didn't need to finish the sentence. The crowd had more than doubled after my little display. Now that people knew I was definitely here, that I was definitely helping, they were only more determined to beg me or condemn me. Apparently the "please go away" bit of my speech was the least memorable.

Cops had tried to break the crowd apart, at least temporarily. And my dad had disappeared for a while and come back with a gigantic pit bull—Marvin, my dad's friend's dog, whom I'd already met a handful of times. Friendly enough but fiercely loyal, and entirely intimidating looking with his massive, slobbery jowls. He'd be sleeping by the front door all night, watching over the stoop. Marvin made me feel safer than the security system, but still . . .

After dinner I peeked out from the front window, and at least a few people were back, lingering along the sidewalk. I pulled the curtain shut and collapsed on the couch, every last inch of me drained. Even my skin somehow felt tired, my hair, my fingernails.

How long could I do this? How many days, how many kids?

"Hey," Zane said, dropping down on the floor in front of me, Zoey and Caleb just behind him. Zoey hopped onto the sofa and I shifted my legs, letting her curl up along my side. I patted the other open cushion, motioning to a hesitant-looking Caleb. But he shook his head and crouched down next to Zane on the floor. He'd still barely spoken to me since we'd all come back together. I needed Cal time, I realized. One-on-one, just the two of us. This weirdness, it had to end.

But right now . . . right now I just wanted to lie there.

"You don't look so good." Zane brushed a stray hair

from my face, tucking it behind my ear. My cheeks warmed at the touch.

One good thing about being so busy, so tired, so scared and confused—I didn't have time to analyze what was going on between me and Zane. How much time we were spending together, how he was still sticking around. How glad it made me that he was.

"I'm just worn out," I said. I took a deep breath, letting it out slowly as my thoughts settled in, heavier and more solid. Every doubt and every fear that I'd ignored—had to ignore, if I was going to do this at all—started creeping back in. I was too weak to hold it back. "I don't know how long I can keep this up, how long I can keep giving people hope before they realize I'm just a disappointment, that I can't *actually* heal them . . . And there's school to consider, too. Orchestra, my training, auditions. The rest of my life. I mean, really, what *am* I doing?"

"Firstly, you're not a disappointment, Iris," Zane said, frowning at me. "You're not claiming to be working any crazy magic on these kids. You're just making them feel like they still have good and happy things to live for. Sure, some people are still going to get angry if you don't solve things for them. Like that ass today at the hospital, who had no right to take anything out on you." His hands balled into fists at his sides, and he jammed them hard in his pockets, sighing. "But, Iris . . . you'll never make everyone happy. It's not possible. So you have to do what makes *you* most happy."

I nodded, his words spilling through my cluttered brain like cool water.

"And maybe you don't see it," he said more quietly, his intense gaze searing into me, "but you've changed in these last few days. There's something in your eyes that wasn't there before. A fire. Like you want to be doing this. You *need* to be doing this. It's who you are."

I wasn't sure he was right about that. But I wasn't sure that he was totally wrong, either.

"All I know," I said, "is that what I'm doing now—it feels too small for how exhausting it is. If I'm going to do anything at all, putting myself out there like I am . . . then I want to be doing so much more than this. It feels so insignificant when I think about how many kids are still out there, like I'm barely scratching at the surface."

"What are your options, though," Zane asked, "besides getting every kid in one room?"

Every kid in one room. Impossible, obviously, but still— there was something to that, the idea of bringing these kids all together in some way. Kids who were mostly going through so much of this recovery alone, in their own isolated family units.

"What if . . ." I started, trailing off as a zillion tiny fragments of an idea began colliding in my mind.

"What if what?" Zoey asked, batting at my leg to get my attention.

"I don't know, I'm just thinking, but . . . what if we could somehow get a group of these kids together? Kids who are in this general area, at least."

"And what, just hang out?" Zane asked, his brow furrowing. "A lot of these families are struggling to get by, with all the medical bills. Parents needing to quit jobs to take care of their kids, or getting fired because they're too deep in grief to work. Janelle and Sam didn't talk about it—they're too proud for that shit—but I know things are hard right now."

"So you think we should help with some kind of fund-raiser, maybe?" I asked, though the question immediately felt so obvious. The kids could come together, and they could help raise money at the same time—much-needed money for their families, and for other families who couldn't actually be there.

"Maybe," Zane said. "But what would the kids actually *do*? Not to be a downer or anything, but most of the more injured ones can't do much of anything right now. And even the kids who *can* don't want to. So what would you have them all do, just wave and fake smile for a camera to get money?"

"I don't know," I said, raking my fingers through one particularly knotted strand of hair. The idea was there but not—I could just barely see A and C, and B was missing altogether. I squeezed my eyes shut and thought about these kids, these strong, resilient, awe-inspiring kids I'd met in the last three days. Zane was right—they certainly weren't up for any dance marathons or charity sporting events, but that didn't mean they had to just sit around in their chairs.

"I have an idea," Zoey said slowly, "though it's probably nothing. It's probably dumb."

"I'm sure it's not dumb," I said, pushing myself up so that I was sitting, facing her. "I want to hear anything you have, trust me."

"Well, I told you how Brinley was super into music. She used to write some of her own songs. They were really, really good. Weren't they, Zane?" She glanced over at him and I followed, watched him nod in agreement. "Some of them were funny; some were really serious. She was so good at it, she would have been . . ." Her voice caught, but she shook it off, straightened her shoulders, and looked at me straight on. "She would have been famous someday, I bet, if she hadn't died. She would have been a superstar."

"I'm sure she would have been," I said, overcome again with the deep, persistent ache that had clung to me those past few days. Every family, every child I'd met—when I left them, it was as if I physically carried a piece of their heartbreak with me. Like a bag of jagged rocks, no two the same, rattling and scraping against me everywhere I went, every hour of the day. But I couldn't toss them out, couldn't scatter them behind me, no matter how painful they became. I needed to carry them. I needed the constant presence, the weight, the reminder.

Brinley's music. My music, too. Slowly, creakily, as if an old rusty knob was twisting in my mind, a door opened and there it was . . .

"Music," I said, the realization dropping on me all at once, so heavy, so certain, that I wasn't sure how I'd been oblivious to it before then. "That's one thing that all the kids I've met have in common. They can make or at least appreciate music—whether it's them singing or humming or tapping, or even just swaying their shoulders and listening. Music makes people feel better. And music," I said, grabbing for Zoey's hands, "is something that Brinley can help us with, too. Do you think we could look through some of her songs, Zoey?"

As soon as I'd said the words, I realized my mistake. Of course we couldn't get to Brinley's music. Not without talking to her parents, Zane and Zoey's aunt and uncle.

But it was too late to backstep. I could see it in Zoey's eyes, all of her ordinary defenses gone as she smiled at me, those warm golden brown eyes so alive and so radiant.

"I'll ask them," Zane said, his voice steady and even.

Like it was that simple. My jaw gaped open as I turned to face him. He would go back there—he would see Monica and Leo again? For *this*?

"I think it's a good idea," he continued, his lips pulled tight into a straight line as he returned my stare. His eyes were dark and glassy, unreadable. He must be scared— how could he not be?—but he was too proud to let Zoey see. To let *me* see. "Zoey's right, Brinley's songs were great. I always told her she had the mind of an old lady trapped in a little kid's body, the things she used to think and say. These songs . . . her songs were pretty deep. They were *real*. Brin would like this idea, I think, getting these kids together to do her songs."

"And maybe they could write some of their own songs, too," Caleb chimed in softly. It was the first time he'd spoken since we'd sat down, and the sound of it—his voice, the hope—made me warm with happiness. "They could sing some of Brinley's stuff to start—but they could maybe be writing new songs, too. Songs about what happened. About their lives now." He paused, sucking his lips in as he waited to hear our response.

"That's perfect, Cal," I said, grabbing his hand before he could stop me, the excitement buzzing through me louder now, more urgent. "And maybe . . . maybe it doesn't have to be just a one-day, onetime thing."

I stopped myself there, the idea whirling and building

to epic proportions in my mind. Too grand to say out loud, maybe. Too big to take back.

"What do you mean?" Caleb asked. He pulled his hand away.

"I'm not exactly sure, but . . . maybe some of these kids can keep singing and writing songs—maybe they can travel to other places, around the country, around the *world* even, so they can spread the message beyond New York City. Then it's not just this one place. It's everywhere."

I could go, too, I realized, the words jolting every other thought to a standstill. *I could go with them.* Play my violin. Play my music, too.

I could travel—the country, the world—meeting hundreds of thousands of people along the way. People who I had no doubt would come out to see these kids. People, too, who would come out to see *me*.

I'd be putting auditions and college on hold for a little while—but I wasn't giving up on my dream, was I? All I'd ever wanted was to play music. This wasn't school orchestra, but I had a feeling it would be even better. Much better.

Zane had said that I needed to do what made *me* happy. But I also knew I wasn't off the hook—and I never would be, not for the rest of my life. Because I needed to do what made *other* people happy, too. Maybe this way, though . . . I could do both.

This idea was insane. It was big, too big probably. But I wanted it.

Zane shook his head, a loud, unfamiliar belly laugh spilling from his lips.

"You're even crazier than I thought. But you're going to do this, aren't you?"

I couldn't sleep that night. Instead of fighting it, I did what I'd been simultaneously desperate to do and desperate to avoid ever since I'd been back home with my laptop, the sleeping screen a black, unblinking eye staring at me from my desk.

"Iris Spero," I typed in the search bar.

I shouldn't have been surprised by the number of results. Not after I'd seen the thousands of pages that had been dedicated to my mom. But still, seeing my name, over and over, a long list of news articles, blogs, social media sites—it was a lot to take in. *Virgin Mina. Messiah. Second Coming. Heaven, Hell. To believe or not to believe. Heretic. Crucify. Damnation.*

The keywords blazed from the screen, the black ink of the text seeming to spill out from the monitor.

I clicked a new page open, logging in to my e-mail.

There were 21,057 unread e-mails.

I had checked the previous week, just before I ran off.

I'd gotten 21,057 new messages in one week.

PLEASE SAVE MY DAUGHTER said the top subject line, an e-mail that had come in two minutes before. I opened it.

> Dearest Iris,
>
> My little girl Brianna Lynn has stage-four leukemia. She is seven years old. We have tried everything and now we need you. I was a little girl when I heard about your mom, and I believed her, I did. And now I believe you. Please prove that I am right. Please save my little Brianna. E-mail me back ASAP and we'll meet you anywhere.

I clicked the arrow at the top of the screen, to the next message.

> *BURN IN HELL!!!!*
>
> Iris, I sent you three e-mails in the last week after my boyfriend got in the car crash and was in a coma. Three e-mails and you ignored me. And guess what? He fucking died. He fucking died this morning. I needed you and you did nothing. I wasn't sure I believed in you anyway, but now I just believe that

*you're a damn useless liar and you'll rot in hell. Thank
you for nothing. Fuck you and I hope you're happy now
because my life is ruined forever.*

One more, I clicked over one more time. I couldn't
help it.

It was just a subject line, though. A subject line and a
glaring white message box.

DO YOU WANT TO BE CRUCIFIED?

I slammed my laptop shut. My entire body shook
against the chair, a tremor that started from the deepest,
darkest core of me, radiating out until my teeth chattered
and my fingers tapped against the wooden desk.

I crawled into my bed and pulled the blankets over
my head. Marvin barked once, twice, and then fell silent
again. Every tiny sound in our old, creaky brownstone suddenly seemed too loud, too suspicious. A clinking pipe, or
the click of the front doorknob? A breeze on the window,
or footsteps on the first flight, the second?

The police had been paying special attention to our
house over the past week—circling our block throughout
the night, their bright lights flashing over our stoop—but
surely that wouldn't stop someone. If the person was desperate enough, angry enough? I'd seen their faces today,

heard their excitement, their rage. I couldn't erase any of it: the crowd, the prayer ribbons, the long list of e-mails. It was all too real.

I threw the blankets off and left my room, tiptoeing down the stairs. I knocked once at my parents' door, gently, and then opened it a crack.

"Mom," I whispered.

The springs squeaked, a silhouette emerging from the bed, black against the moonlight spilling in from behind their curtains.

"What is it?" she asked quietly, shuffling into the hallway, hand on my back as we moved into her office. "Is everything okay?"

I nodded. And then I shook my head, tears pooling on my eyelashes.

"I feel like I made everything worse today, and all I wanted was to make it better. I just checked my e-mail, and I have over twenty thousand new messages, Mom. Twenty *thousand*."

Her face tightened, all points and angles as she pursed her lips. "I'm sorry, Iris. We should be doing a better job of protecting you from things like that."

"No. I asked for this," I said, covering my face with my hands. "I just—I felt like I was doing something good the last few days. Helpful even. But now I see how angry people are, too, and it's so scary. I feel like there are risks either way—like maybe there is no right decision."

"Maybe there's not," my mother said, cradling me like a little girl as we settled onto her love seat. "Maybe there's never really a *right* decision. Maybe I shouldn't have run all those years ago, but I did. Right, wrong, I don't know. But I don't regret it."

"But it was easier for you. Because you had Iris. The *real* Iris. She was helping you."

"Sweetie, half of the time I thought I was crazy for even seeing her at all. Trust me, that didn't make anything easier. It wasn't until after that big protest—when I almost lost you, and somehow I ended up with Iris, in our old tree house—that I was entirely sure I hadn't made her up . . . Do you remember that part from my story?"

I nodded. Of course I did. The tree house was in the woods behind my mom's childhood home, a little kingdom where she, Hannah, and Izzy had often played. And later, it was where she'd taken the pregnancy tests. Where she'd first found out it was real. *I* was real. After she'd been knocked down at that final protest, when she was unconscious, in the car on the way to her doctor's office—she was there in the tree house again, too. With Iris. A warm, golden, sunny day, where Iris told her that everything would really be okay.

A dream, but not a dream, because afterward, my mom had a bright green leaf in her hand to prove it. A leaf that Iris had left with her. A leaf that shouldn't have existed at all, not in the bitter cold of February, when leaves were long dead and crumbled into dust on the ground. A vision, maybe. A visit to another dimension. Magic.

"Where's the leaf now, Mom?" I asked, shocked I hadn't thought to ask before.

"That leaf," she said as she smiled at me, her eyes clearer than I'd seen in weeks, "is still pressed between the pages of my old copy of *Anne of Green Gables*. Right where I put it all those years ago." She nodded her head toward the overflowing bookshelves just a few feet in front of us. "Go get it. You can have it, if you want."

I sprang up from the seat, out of her arms, already knowing exactly where the book was on her shelves. Other books came and went, but never *Anne*. The pages fanned apart in my hands, the spine cracking open to the exact page.

The leaf. The leaf was still green, a fresh summer green. I blinked, looked again. Brown now, crinkled around the deep veins spreading out from the blackened, shriveled stem.

Of course it wasn't green. It was an old leaf, about to fall to pieces.

"It's not mine." I shut the book, the fear and the doubt creeping back in. "Iris gave it to you. Not me. She seems to be ignoring me." I sounded petty, but it was true, wasn't it?

She'd been there for my mom, not once but a handful of times. Why not me?

"She gave you something very special," my mom said quietly, standing from the sofa and reaching out to brush her warm palm against my cheek. "More special than a leaf. Those green eyes, Iris . . . those are *her* green eyes. I've never seen anything else like them—the intensity of that color, the ring of gold that shimmers along the edges. Like sparkling emeralds. They're amazing, sweetie. Those eyes were her gift to you. They mark you. Those eyes are how you see the world. How you see all the people in it, every single person you meet."

My green eyes. They were more distinctive than most, I supposed. But I'd seen this color on other people. Mikki— Mikki's eyes were just as pure green, gold accents framing the irises and making her already catlike eyes seem deeper, wiser.

Mikki.

The world seemed to topple from beneath me, as if the floors of our house had crumbled under my feet and I was somehow just floating now, surrounded by nothing but leaves and light and air. I squeezed my eyes shut and fought off the dizzy sensation, my up and down melding together.

All I could see was Mikki's face seared across the backs of my eyelids, those green eyes staring back at me.

Mikki.

Mikki, who had only just appeared at the park at the end of the summer, so soon after Disney had been bombed. Mikki, who had always seemed to be there, right by that very same bench, whenever I came, whenever I hoped that I would find her. Mikki, who had listened to me that first day I'd heard about Virgin Mina, who had shown up just before the storm, gone with me to the shelter, and then suddenly, with no warning, disappeared, leaving me alone with Zane and Zoey. I had barely thought of her since, with everything else going on.

But now these facts settled in one at a time, like drops of water all running together into the same clear, glittering pool.

I opened my eyes, my feet landing back onto the sturdy planks of wood beneath me.

"Mom," I said, a smile breaking out across my face, "I was wrong—the truth was staring me right in the face, but I missed it until now. She's been with me all along. I just didn't know how to recognize her."

My mom cocked her head, her eyebrows raised in confusion. "What do you . . . ?"

"Iris," I said. "I've met *Iris.*"

Chapter Twenty-Two

I SLEPT UNTIL almost noon the next day. The sky had been brightening with the first smudges of oranges and pinks when my mom and I finally went to bed. I'd told her about Mikki, her green eyes and our conversations, about Abby and all the other kids, about my idea. My wild, beyond ambitious plan.

My mom hadn't told me I was crazy, though. Not even close.

"If you want to do it, then I support you. I believe in you, Iris," she'd said, sighing into my messy, tangled hair. "I believe in you more than I've ever believed in anything."

I'd fallen asleep easily after that. There were still those 21,057 e-mails. Or thousands more, now that another twelve hours had passed. There were still the signs outside, the ribbons.

But I believed in my plan. I believed in music. And my mom—my mom believed, too.

I pulled out my yoga mat for the first time in weeks, it felt like, and stretched and flowed for almost an hour. I was sweating at the end, my arms shaking as I kicked down from the final headstand. My head spun, dizzy with the rush of blood, and I bowed down on the mat until I regained my center.

Iris, I remembered again, the idea still so new. *I met Iris.* I smiled, soaking up the sun that spilled in through my curtains.

After a long shower, I braided my wet hair, a thin band that ran across the top of my head like a crown, and pulled on a vintage checkered green dress that I loved. I was ready.

Zane was at the table when I walked into the kitchen, fiddling with his phone and plowing through a shockingly massive stack of toast smeared thick with chunky peanut butter.

I wanted to ask Zane about Mikki—what he remembered, what he had thought of her at the time. Because I hadn't made her up. It wasn't possible. Benjamin had known her, after all. She must have been there, as real and as visible to everyone else. That didn't mean that she wasn't *Iris*—my aunt Gracie had seen Iris, and so had my dad, back when it all started.

But I didn't ask, because I also wanted her to be my own for a little while longer. I needed to go to the park again, to see if she would still be there.

"You *better* not have gone through the entire jar," I said, hands on my hips as I glared from the doorway. "I can't start my day properly without peanut butter."

"Whose fault is it that you're starting the day at one in the afternoon?" he asked, not looking up from his phone as he dangled a piece of toast in my direction.

I lunged and grabbed it from his hand before he could take back the offer.

"Jesus, you're like a wild dog," he said, dropping his phone to the table as he finally stared up at me, wide-eyed with surprise. "You really are serious about that peanut butter."

"Mm-hm." I grinned as I took a huge first bite. "Peanut butter, yoga, the violin. And I guess my family and friends, they make the list, too. It doesn't take much to keep me happy."

"I think my list is even simpler," he said, pausing as he shoveled half a slice in his mouth at once. "Peanut butter. Zoey. Enough money for a bed somewhere and more peanut butter. Maybe some pizza, too. Not with the peanut butter, though. Never with." He smiled at me, the first easy smile I'd seen from him since that night up on the roof.

We still hadn't talked about it, not a word.

But he was here, wasn't he, staying at my house? Skipping school, going with me on every visit? He had been out again the last two evenings, though, doing some "business"—and I still hadn't asked where, why, not after my first failed attempt. But I'd overheard him on the phone as he'd left the night before—I was halfway down the stairs, but he was too angry, in too much of a rush to see me. I heard "cops" and "stash" and "don't do anything until I get there." I held my breath, waiting for the door to slam behind him.

I knew he had to be making some money, of course, one way or another. He had a cell phone to pay for, if nothing else. It was easier not to ask for details, though, just like it was easier not to talk about what was going on or *not* going on between the two of us.

Him just being there seemed like enough. More than enough, at least until everything else became more settled.

And then . . .

I blushed, realizing how intently I was staring into Zane's eyes. He broke contact first, suddenly focused on ripping the last piece of toast into a handful of tiny squares.

"I've been thinking a lot," I started, sitting down across from Zane, forcing my brain back to the important things to be discussed. The here and now. "About what we talked about yesterday. About those lyrics . . ."

"Don't worry about me," Zane said, shaking his head. "I can handle seeing them again. I already called my aunt this morning. Apparently during her manic binge-cleaning fit, the song notebook was the only thing she couldn't bring herself to throw away. Lucky for us. When Zoey mentioned it last night, I hadn't even considered that the notebook might have been trashed. But they feel sorry for how everything went down. I knew they would. I just didn't want to give them the satisfaction of ever being able to apologize. But getting these songs—getting these songs is worth it. I can suck up my pride. I'm going to head over there now, okay?"

I nodded, faint almost, as the reality set in. With Brinley's songs nearly in Zane's grasp, we were that much closer to bringing Zoey's vision to life. I hadn't told Angelica or anyone else at Disney's Children yet, but I knew without question that she'd be ecstatic. She'd be ecstatic about anything that involved me being even more active with the Disney's Children community.

"Should I come with—" I started, but the words were cut off by the buzz of the front doorbell. Marvin started barking, loud, threatening growls.

I reached up for the buzzer on the wall. "Hello?" Static. "Anyone?"

We waited, watching each other. After a minute without a second alarm, I sat back. Marvin was still barking, but it had slowed to a more level snarl. Had one of the fanatics finally gotten bolder? The gate—the warning sign and the security cameras—had been enough to keep them at a distance, but that was yesterday. Things had changed since I'd announced myself out there on the stoop for the entire world to see.

Zane moved toward the foyer, disappearing from my sight. I held my breath. But after a few seconds he was back, shaking his head. "Whoever it was is gone. Marvin is back to chewing on some nasty old bone. There are some people on the sidewalk still—a few of them near the gate doing that weird thing with the ribbons. So I guess it could have been any of them. But maybe it was just some poor delivery guy who landed at the wrong door."

I don't think either of us believed that.

"Maybe I shouldn't head over there now . . ." Zane hesitated.

"No, you go. My dad's been working half days, so he'll be home soon. And my mom's upstairs in her office if I need her. She's just oblivious to the buzzing and the barking, which isn't surprising. Or . . . or I'm happy to come with. If you want."

"No," Zane said, shaking his head as he grabbed both of our plates from the table and headed toward the sink. He was quiet as he poured the soap and scrubbed. It struck me now how entirely bizarre and surreal this moment would have seemed a few weeks back. Zane Davis, in my kitchen, washing dishes. The most bizarre part, though, was how normal it felt.

"I need to do this on my own. I don't expect them to be crazy again, but . . . just in case."

"Sure. I get it. My friends are coming over soon anyway, after school. I wanted to tell them about the new idea. Make them, you know, feel more a part of everything. They all play instruments, too, so it's perfect."

"Yeah," he said, not quite meeting my eye. "So I'll catch you later, then. Don't worry about me, okay? And call me if you need anything."

I nodded, clumsily kicking the chair back as I stood to face him.

He waited a beat, then stepped toward me, closing the gap between us. He pulled me into his arms, leaning down to lightly peck my forehead.

I tilted my head up, closed my eyes, waiting. My stomach leapt, spun.

Zane pulled away. He was through the living room, into the foyer, without a single glance back.

The door closed loudly and I collapsed back in the chair.

But then, the door opened again.

"Zane?" I called out, an uneasiness prickling along my skin.

He stepped into the living room, a single sheet of paper in his hand.

"This was on the doorstep. I think whoever buzzed . . . they must have left it."

"Wh-what is it?"

"It's a funeral announcement, Iris. A funeral announcement for Ella Bennett."

Zane left, but only after my mom had come down from her office and assured him that she'd stay there with me. She'd called my dad, too, who said he'd be personally stopping by the police station on his way home. But what could they do? It was only a funeral notice, after all. We didn't even know if it was Kyle Bennett himself who had been there.

And really, it didn't matter if it was Kyle, or a friend of his, a stranger. The message was the same. If someone was determined enough to get to me, they would. Waving a banner, watching for me, leaving a prayer ribbon—it might not be enough for everyone. The gate and the security cameras, Marvin, police circling the block . . . none of it was foolproof. This was the first real breach, but would it be the last?

I couldn't stop staring at the announcement. Ella's face at the top, all wide hazel eyes and smooth ivory skin. She was like a pretty little doll, with her shiny brown curls and rosy red cheeks, grinning mischievously up at the camera.

She was eight years old when she died. The funeral had been held the previous day, in Green Hill.

What if I had gone, weeks back?

What if I'd answered Kyle's desperate plea and seen Ella before she passed away?

It wouldn't have changed a damn thing.

I knew that. Deep down, I did. But the question was still there, a thick knot tugging deep inside my stomach.

"You're sure, Iris?" my mom asked for the third or fourth time since she'd seen the announcement. I was lying in my bed, Ella staring down at me from the nightstand. "You're sure you want to go through with this idea? Because if you do—if you keep doing this—Kyle won't be the last devastated parent."

"I know," I whispered. I cleared my throat and tried again, more confidently this time. "I know. But I did nothing, Mom, and he was just as angry. I'd rather do something than nothing."

Before I could take it back, I called Angelica and told her the plan. And she loved it; of course she did. She said we couldn't start working on it soon enough, and that she'd start making calls today to get the ball rolling. *Today.*

I hung up just as Ari's name lit up my cell.

"We're here, waiting on your back deck. I didn't want to start banging on the glass doors and give you a heart attack."

"Good thinking. That probably would have pissed Marvin off, too."

"Marvin?"

"Oh, right. I'll introduce you."

My mom gave my hand one last squeeze before we headed downstairs to greet them. I let Marvin sniff around them for a few minutes so he'd remember that they were the good guys, and then we settled in the living room. As soon as we'd all curled up together on the sofa, I held the funeral announcement out for them to see, my own eyes still transfixed by that dazzling little girl, her heartbreaking smile. "That guy from Green Hill who started all of this? It was his daughter. She was the reason he came looking for me at all."

Ari grabbed the paper from my hand and studied it. Her eyes drifted to me, back to the picture, to me again. "*Shit*. I'm sorry, Iris. You know you can't feel guilty about this, right? Tell me you know that."

"I don't know what I feel. Except it makes me even more sure that I need to do something."

"You already are doing something," Ethan said. "You've visited so many kids already."

"It's not enough, though," I said, fighting to keep my voice steady. "It would take too much time to see everyone who wants to meet me."

"So what *do* you want to do, then?" Delia asked.

"Right, well, I had this idea last night with Zane and Zoey . . ." I started, not sure where to look, with all three of them scrutinizing me so closely. I chose Ari first. Winning Ari over was the test. If she approved, you knew she meant it—that was one of the things I loved about her most.

"I talked to the Disney's Children founder about a big fund-raiser I thought the group could do. I was thinking maybe in a month or two, but she wants to strike now while the story's on everyone's mind, so she's thinking as soon as next week. For the first fund-raiser, at least, since it might end up moving around to different venues. I had the idea that all these kids could get together and sing or make music in some way—which I guess sounds a little trivial, but it was something that I thought all of them could actually do. Even the kids with the most serious injuries, as long as they aren't stuck in hospital beds still."

"What would they be singing?" Ethan asked.

"Well, that's partly how Zane and Zoey figured in . . . I told you how they lost a cousin at Disney, Brinley—she was down there for a chorus trip. Apparently she was an amazing singer. Only a kid, but she wrote her own songs. I haven't read them yet—Zane's supposed to be back with them any time now. But I thought we could work with that to start. We'd have a rehearsal with the kids leading up, and then they'd sing a few songs at the fund-raiser. Some of them might have instruments they want to play, too.

And we're going to have music stations for the kids to write their own songs. Angelica thought we could find some local musicians to volunteer . . ."

"And the donations are going to what?" Ari asked, squinting up at the ceiling.

"For now, we're thinking it'll go to families who need support, like medical expenses, or covering the loss of income if they've had to leave their jobs. But then we're hoping the kids can do more performances, write more songs. Different kids, too, depending on where we're performing, or how long they can be on the road. A rotation, maybe. I don't know." I sighed. As much as I wanted to do this, I was already exhausted by the sheer enormity of it all. It felt impossible that I was actually leading something this momentous, when a few weeks back I'd been just another seventeen-year-old girl in New York City.

"That's all sounding really cool, Iris," Ethan said quietly, "but would you be traveling, too? What about . . . what about school? It's senior year. You should be applying to colleges. And not to be an ass, but . . . didn't you freak out when your mom wanted you to leave Brooklyn? Weren't you fighting to stay *here*?"

"Yes," I said, shaking my head. "But that was different. If I'd jumped on a plane then, I would have been hiding. I would have been running away, pretending to be anyone but Iris Spero, and that just felt entirely wrong. This is getting on a plane, yeah . . . but to face it all head-on. I'd be leaving Brooklyn, maybe—temporarily—but it's not about running from a place. It's about *not* running from who I am."

"It's the exact opposite of what your mom did," Delia said. "She left Green Hill to disappear. You're leaving Brooklyn to be out in the world, all loud and proud."

"Exactly." My lips twitched, caught somewhere between a smile and a frown. "I'll miss you guys while I'm gone, and I'll miss my family and Brooklyn. Because if the first fund-raiser here goes well and these Disney's Children performances work out—then yes, I want to travel with them. I can probably do work on the road and still graduate on time. But music was always the dream, right? And that's what I'd be doing now. Making music. Sharing it with other people. I can still go to college later, and I will. I'll figure it out. But I need—"

"We know," Ari cut in, raising her hands in surrender. "You need time to figure it out. I get that, as long as you don't erase us from your life altogether. Okay? We need you. You're the glue. And you need us, too. We're your people."

"My *best* people." I grinned at her, and she grinned back, as sincere and unguarded a smile as I'd ever seen on Ari's face.

"And as for school, I think you need to do what you

need to do. College will always be there. This idea sounds pretty damn awesome, way cooler than our lame school orchestra. You'd probably regret it for the rest of your life if you didn't follow through."

Hearing those words, an enthusiastic seal of approval from Ari of all people—it was everything I'd needed to move ahead. I exhaled, my whole body instantly feeling a hundred pounds lighter.

"Oh, and of course I forgot to mention one of the most important parts," I said, clapping my hands on my knees. "I need the three of you up on stage for the New York show. I have a feeling none of the kids will bang on the drums quite like you do, Ari. And Ethan and Delia, you two are totally going to rock the woodwinds. Seriously. Please. Music has always been our thing. It wouldn't feel right without you guys at my side."

"You didn't even have to ask, Iris." Ari snaked her arm around my back and I leaned into her shoulder. "I would have been offended if you *hadn't*."

"Seconded," Ethan said.

"Thirded," Delia chimed in. "If that's a word. But yes, I'd be honored."

"Thank you, seriously, you don't know how much—"

The front door opened and all of us turned, staring as Zane walked into the living room.

"I have them," he said, pulling a notebook out from

the pocket of his hoodie. "All the songs. They're amazing, Iris—even better than I remembered. Broke my damn heart all over again that this little girl won't ever sing or write another word. She had a gift. A serious gift." He looked up then, frowning slightly, as if he'd just realized that we weren't alone in the room—my friends had also witnessed this uncharacteristic moment of vulnerability. They needed to see this Zane, though. The Zane I knew. The Zane I cared so much about.

"Can I see?" I asked quietly, reaching my hand out.

He nodded, dropping the little book onto my open palm. I looked down, my hands shaking as I slowly flipped to the first page.

"This first one is called 'Hear Me,'" I said. I took a deep breath and then I began, reading the words out loud.

Here I am, so hear me now
Here I am, so hear my song
These words are mine, these words are yours
They're from my head, they're from my heart
If you hear me now, hear my song
You'll see just how alike we are
That deep down where it matters most
We love, we cry, we hurt, we laugh
We fight, we learn, we hide, we dance
We live our lives, we dream our dreams

The differences, they're there, they are
But we are human, we are the same
And maybe someday, someday soon
We'll be friends, you and I
We'll sing together, you and I.

The room was silent when I finished. Tears poured from my eyes, the words in front of me swimming as drops fell heavily onto the pages. To think of Brinley, the beautiful mind that had written these words—to think of her dead, cold and lifeless and below the ground, was like a razor-sharp claw raking jagged slashes across my heart.

"These are," I started, choking down a massive sob, "perfect. This song . . . how did this song come from a little girl? It's so real. It's so *true.*"

"I know," Zane said quietly. He stared out the window, his wide shoulders tensed as he clenched his knuckles around the lower ledge. "They're all like that. I remember most of the basic tunes, the rhythms, and I know Zoey does, too, so we can teach you. I used to hear her singing them all the time, but I never paid enough attention to the words. I never told her how much of a genius she was when I had the chance."

"Maybe you didn't ever tell her," I said, gently putting the notebook down as I stood from the sofa and moved toward Zane. I rested one hand lightly, tentatively, on his shoulder. He didn't flinch or brush me off, so I kept it there. "But you're honoring her now. Nothing is as good as having her back, but maybe this is the next best thing."

I felt his strong shoulders tremble beneath my hand. He ducked his head down, fighting back tears that I wished he'd let himself cry.

"Well then," Ari said from behind me. I jumped at the sound, pulled away from my private moment with Zane. "That was definitely spectacular, and I'm definitely on board. So . . . what next?"

Chapter Twenty-Three

THE FUND-RAISER came on bigger and faster than I could have ever imagined.

In less than a week, we'd had several hundred families sign up to attend the first event in New York City, and thousands more had requested to be involved in future countrywide programs. Nearly two hundred kids were participating this first time around, which included the event itself plus a few rehearsals to learn the ten songs we'd chosen from Brinley's notebook. We had an impressively accomplished staff of volunteer musicians on hand, too— Angelica said they had all begged her to be involved. The grander and more impressive the plans became, the harder it was for me to believe that without my nudge, none of this would have happened.

But I couldn't deny how many people had joined Disney's Children because of me, because of *who I was*. I couldn't deny how excited volunteers got at just the sight of me—it was almost a physical, quantifiable thing, the increase in energy and enthusiasm that swelled when I stepped into a room. People smiled wider, moved faster, accomplished more, and brainstormed bigger, better ideas. It was almost as if they fed off me somehow, and all it took was the simple fact of me being there, with a smile or a few encouraging words.

It was bizarre—bizarre and unsettling and absurd. But it worked. It had made this event possible. I told myself, over and over again, that I was just doing my part, playing my role.

I was Iris Spero, daughter of Mina. This was my duty.

The big night had arrived, hanging over the ledge just in front of me. I had only blinked, it seemed, and there I was, sweating profusely, my heart banging around under the weight of my ornately beaded dress—a vivid green the exact shade of my eyes, shimmering with tiny gold accents. The dress had been made specifically for me, a gift from a designer who I'd never heard of before. It had showed up at my doorstep with a note pleading with me to wear it for this first performance. She had worked on it day and night, she'd said, since she'd heard about what I was doing for these children. Children like the daughter she'd lost, the daughter she'd give anything to have back.

Even if it hadn't been the most beautiful dress I'd ever

seen—which it absolutely was—I wouldn't have been able to say no, not after reading her letter.

But the dress wasn't the only thing we'd discovered on our doorstep.

In the days since Ella Bennett's funeral notice had appeared, there'd been other "gifts" left on our stoop: a picture of Ella and Kyle and a little boy who must have been Parker, standing in front of Cinderella Castle—*before*—its sweeping stone turrets and shiny blue spires still intact; an article from Green Hill's local paper about the Bennett family and a fund-raiser that had been helping with Ella's hospital bills; a worn-looking old doll, with scraggly blonde curls and a chipped smile and beady glass eyes that didn't stop staring; a photograph of my mom as a teenager, her belly round and pronounced as she leaned against the lockers in her old high school hallway.

There was never any note. But words weren't necessary.

I won't forget.

I breathed in deep and brought myself back to here. Now. All the people I *could* still help.

Zoey held my hand, Caleb, my parents, and Zane hovering close behind. My aunt Gracie was there with us, too, her arm locked around my mom's waist. She'd flown in on a red-eye from Texas that morning to surprise us. "The second your mom told me she was pregnant with you, I believed," she'd said to me at breakfast. "That's the power of family. I wouldn't have missed this day for anything." Aunt Gracie was only twenty-five now, closer to my age than my mom's, but she was usually so cool, so unflappable and composed, that I forgot there were only eight years between us. She looked giddy and nervous now, though, twirling the tulle skirt of her bright pink dress as we waited.

We stood in front of the grand, arching doors of the auditorium at Carnegie Hall, which had lent us the space free of charge for the night's event. Apparently someone high on the board there had lost a sister and a nephew of his own at Disney and considered it the least he could do in their memory. The hall looked spectacular and surreal, with glittering, glowing stars lining the way into the main event space, each one marked with the name of a victim.

Angelica had refused my offer to come earlier that day for setup. She'd insisted that I arrive once everyone else had settled into place—that I had already done more than enough. But I wasn't naive. She wanted a grand entrance.

All eyes on me.

I nodded back at my family and then at the two black-suited men standing at either side of the entrance. They pulled open the doors at my signal, beaming at me as I stepped forward.

Cameras flashed and people cheered, whooping and whistling and clapping their hands. Those who were able stood as I made my way down the plush crimson-red aisle, waving and smiling and fighting back the overwhelming urge to run—to hide in the bathroom, purge every last bite of my dinner into the toilet. Spots swam across my vision and I clenched my fingers more tightly around Zoey's palm, reaching for Cal with my free hand. He waited for just a second, then latched on tight. The sounds hushed around me, my dress felt lighter, the lights above me dimmed. I was floating, falling, flying . . .

But then my eyes refocused and I saw my grandparents and Aunt Hannah—and Aunt Izzy and Ellen and baby Micah, visiting from California, just to see me—all of them grinning and wildly clapping. And I saw the rows of chairs at the front of the room, up on the stage. Ari and Ethan and Delia. The children. *My* children. Some in wheelchairs or leaning against walkers, some in bandages and casts. Some were held in their parents' arms; others were standing on their own, healthy and untouched, at least on the outside. They were big and little, boy and girl, dark, light, skinny, chubby, pale, freckled, tan, braided, and buzzed. All were in matching green and gold T-shirts. And they were smiling. They were all smiling.

I surged forward, running those last steps, Zoey and Caleb dragging behind me, until I reached the stage.

"I'm here," I said, reaching my hands out toward every last one of them. "I'm here."

Everything had been perfect so far.

I collapsed against the black leather chair in my private dressing room offstage, sighing in relief. I had fifteen minutes to myself for the intermission. The kids had already performed eight of Brinley's songs without a hitch— some sang and some played instruments: drums and triangles, flutes, trumpets, guitars. I played my violin for parts of each. It was a patchwork of noise, raw and beautiful. At the start of the second half, we'd have stations where groups of kids would work with the professional musicians on writing their own songs. After thirty minutes, we'd ask for a few of the groups to perform what they'd written so far, and then, finally, we'd close with two more of Brinley's songs, with "Hear Me" to be the very last.

I could see it all playing out now, my eyes closed as I burrowed farther into the soft leather. There was so much energy and life out in that room. Besides my family and friends, there were a handful of familiar faces: Sam and Janelle; Claire; Abby and Lula, both up on stage, Abby singing, Lula swinging a tambourine; some of my teachers and a few *incredibly* unexpected classmates, such as Carolina Matthews and Noah Kennedy, cheering along with everybody else; even Monica and Leo, who Zoey had pointed out to me from the stage—Zane had allowed them this small pass for Brinley's sake, though he'd made it clear it was too soon for anything more.

And about halfway through the first set, my eyes had landed on Benjamin, standing and clapping and swaying so eagerly that my already overwhelmed heart nearly combusted in my chest. I'd mailed him a personalized invitation, along with puzzles and caramel brownies—and a brief thank-you note explaining my stay at the shelter. But he'd never responded, and I'd assumed that he wouldn't come, that he'd felt deceived or betrayed by "Clemence." But from the way he grinned at me up there on the stage, I don't think he was disappointed. Not in the least.

Mikki—or Iris, whatever I was supposed to call her— she wasn't there. I'd tried to invite her, stopping by the park a handful of times in the past week during our planning breaks. I'd brought the violin, too, hoping that the playing would magically lure her in. But she hadn't come.

I jumped at the sound of a knock on the door, my eyes snapping open. I had left my family and friends out front by the stage, saying that I needed just a few minutes to myself to prep for the rest of the event.

It's okay, I told myself, pushing up from the seat. *I'm ready. I can do this.*

"Come in," I called out. "It's not locked."

I expected to see my mom, or Angelica or Zane, maybe. But instead it was a tall, broad-shouldered girl I'd never seen before—just about my age, I'd guess—with freckles all across her pale, pinkish skin and bright red hair pulled into a long, thick braid. She wore a simple faded blue dress, a few sizes too big and hanging over a pair of old lace-up brown boots.

"Hello?" I said, trying to mask my rattled nerves. There were plenty of people here tonight from Disney's Children who I hadn't had the chance to meet yet. Still, it was unsettling that she'd pushed past everyone else to see me privately. It felt wrong to me, off. But I had a role to play, even now. I forced my lips up, tried to smile. "Can I help you?"

"Yes, please," she mumbled, her gray eyes jumping from me to the ceiling to the floor. She stepped into the room, shutting the door behind her.

Alarm seeped in, a cold shudder that sent the hair along my neck and my arms on end. Was I safe? Should I run? She was intimidating physically, towering above me—but she looked tired, too, weak, with her drawn face and that pale skin.

Not just tired. She looked sad, I realized. Deeply, painfully sad.

"I'm Iris," I said, extending my hand, though I had a feeling the introduction wasn't necessary. She looked down at it for a beat before reaching out, clasping her fingers around mine, cool and scratchy at the touch.

She shook a few times before saying, "I'm Elisabeth McDan—" She cut herself off, pulling her hand out of my grasp as she took a few steps back. "You can just call me Elisabeth."

"Okay," I said, "Elisabeth. It's nice to meet you. I only have a few minutes before I have to be back out there, but . . . is there anything in particular you wanted first?"

She bit down on her lip, her entire face scrunching inward. "Yes," she said, "there is." She faced me straight on, but her eyes were fixed just above mine, somewhere along my forehead. "Can we sit down? Just for a minute. I know you're busy, but I came all the way up here from Oklahoma and I . . . I just have some words I need to say. While I have the nerve."

I nodded, easing myself back down onto my seat as she settled in the chair opposite mine.

"My dad, Iris, he . . ." Her voice broke, and she closed her eyes for a moment, her chest rising and falling heavily beneath the tattered collar of her dress. My mind raced to fill in the gaps—her dad, he had died at Disney, hadn't he? Or maybe she'd lost a sibling that day, a little brother or sister, and what had he done in his grief? Run off, maybe? Or worse—was it too much to bear, had he . . . had he taken his own life? I gripped my clammy hands around the arms of the chair, steeling myself for those terrible words to spill out of her mouth.

"My dad," she started again, this time her large gray eyes staring directly into mine. Her pupils were wide and penetrating, a dark abyss that threatened to yank me into the spiral of her agony. "He was part of the Judges. He was part of the group that bombed Disney."

I gasped.

The Judges.

In all the moments of the past weeks, all the moments since I'd run away, distracted by my own life—I hadn't stopped much to think about the people who had caused this. Even as I'd looked into the faces of these children, hugged their broken bodies—I hadn't thought about the people who were actually behind the tragedy. I hadn't thought about what they were doing right then, how they were coping or not coping, scheming or not scheming. They had seemed peripheral to the devastation, somehow. Peripheral to the reality of these kids and their everyday lives, their futures.

But now, Elisabeth here in front of me, I realized how strange it was that I'd forgotten—I'd forgotten that this hadn't all happened by chance or by some terrible misfortune. This wasn't an earthquake or a twister or a superstorm. This was human will. This was a *choice.* Anger seethed through my bones, a blistering, quick-burning fire. I thought of my classmates' rage, how much I'd resented it. They had taken it too far, but still—I understood the very core of it. I felt it deep down inside of me.

"Why?" I asked. It took every shred of willpower to push out this one word.

"I don't know," she whispered, shaking her head. "I don't know. He's not an evil man, though I know that's probably impossible for you to believe, and I can't expect you to take my word for it. There's a lot of good about him. There is. He loves his family more than anything, always took care of us. He'd work double shifts, getting home from one job at ten o'clock at night and up at three in the morning for the next. And he didn't complain much—I could tell that he was tired and overworked. Frustrated. Angry that he did so much and got so little. No matter how many hours he worked, he could still never do all the things for our family that he wanted. He couldn't buy us new clothes or take us out to nice dinners. He could never afford trips or vacations. We'd never even left the state. He certainly could never have afforded . . . *Disney*."

Her cheeks flared with color at the word, pink blooms spreading to the tips of her ears and down along the exposed white of her neck.

"I didn't know, Iris. I swear I didn't, and neither did my mom. I didn't know just how far the anger was taking him. He met some people who felt the same way he did

while he was out at the bar one night after a shift at the fac-
tory, and . . . it sucked him in. Plain and simple, it sucked
him in, changed him. The promise of revenge, I think.
Justice, in his mind. I don't think that his intentions were
pure evil—he wanted the world to be more equal. More
fair. But the way he went about that, the way they all went
about that—I can never forgive him. I love him, I always
will, but I can't forgive what he did, killing so many people
and trying to play God. I wanted you to know how sorry I
am. But I also wanted to let you know that my dad, he may
have done an evil thing—as evil as it gets—but I still don't
consider him an evil man, not all the way through. And I
think—I think I need your forgiveness for that, too. If you
can understand. But I get it if that's impossible. I just had
to ask. I had to try."

She shuddered and collapsed back against the chair,
her entire body deflating now that the words were out—
these words that had been filling her, taking her over so
completely. The flush had left her cheeks, and now her
face looked alarmingly white, gray almost, under the cool
light of the ceiling lamp.

"What is your dad . . . Where is he now?" I asked. Our
eyes were locked, both of us barely blinking, barely breathing. I couldn't look away. I saw so much, too much. Fear
and fury. Love.

"In jail, waiting for trial. My mom is pretending he's

dead. I spoke to him only once, right after it happened. I said, 'Daddy, tell me that they have it wrong. Tell me that you had no part in this. That you didn't know what was happening.' You know what he said back? He said, 'I knew exactly what I was doing. God help me, I knew.' He'll regret it, if he doesn't already. He'll wish he were dead, so he doesn't have to deal with the memory of his decision. But I hope he lives a long, long life thinking over every last piece of what he did—looking at pictures of every little face lost because of him—and I don't care if that makes me sound terrible for saying so."

"I forgive you," I said. The words slipped out before I had a chance to think about them. Because what did it actually mean, *my* forgiveness? It wouldn't change anything, not really. No more than if anyone else had said it. But the words made Elisabeth feel better. And besides that, they were true. The anger . . . it was fading. I felt strangely calm in the wake of her confession, like the storm had passed—black skies, winds gusting and rain thrashing, branches spiraling through the air—and we were left now in a sort of hushed aftershock.

I stood up and walked across the room, crouched next to her chair so that we were eye level. "Not that you even need forgiveness. He's your *dad*. He's a part of you. Even with the bad, you can't forget all the good. And I don't think you should feel guilty about that." I thought about my dad, and all the good *he'd* done—how much it outweighed the lies. If there'd been any resentment left before Elisabeth had walked into this room, it was gone now. Because he was my dad. No matter what, he was still my dad, in every way that mattered.

I made myself focus back on Elisabeth, this moment. The second half of the show would be starting soon. "I hate what your dad did, and I believe he deserves punishment. But I don't hate *him*."

She squeezed her eyes shut, tears pooling down her cheeks. "Thank you, Iris. You don't know what that means to me."

I reached out, wrapping my fingers around her fists.

After a pause she blinked and opened her eyes, her brow crinkling for a moment as she seemed to study my face up close. "Do you think maybe you could talk to my dad, too? I don't expect you to forgive him, or to absolve him or anything like that. But I think it would be good for him. And good for me, too, maybe."

Talking to her dad, to one of the Judges—it was too much to think about, especially tonight, surrounded by these recovering, surviving kids.

But someday?

"Maybe," I said, squeezing her hand. "Let's see how it goes."

She smiled, a fresh wave of tears glossing over her eyes.

The look she was giving me . . . it was a little *too* appreciative. It felt different with the kids—it was easy for them to idolize people older than them, no matter the reason. But from someone my own age? It made me feel too important. Too powerful.

"I should get back out there," I said, letting go of her hands as I stood up, "but . . . you can come. If you want. You don't have to tell anyone about your dad."

"Are you sure?" she asked, gaping up at me. "You're sure that's okay?"

I nodded. "Yeah. Maybe celebrating these kids will help you feel better."

She stood up next to me, swiping at her tear-stained cheeks with the sleeve of her dress.

"You're right," she said quietly. "Let's go."

She followed a few cautious steps behind as we made our way out to the main stage. I saw Zane standing with Caleb and Zoey by Abby's wheelchair, Zoey saying something that had the others spellbound. Caleb seemed oblivious to everything else in the room but her, his bright eyes and bright smile radiating from across the stage. I would have been alarmed if he'd looked that adoringly at any other girl his age—but Zoey was Zoey. It was impossible not to adore her once she let you in.

Still, I couldn't help but wish he'd smile at me again with even half that amount of enthusiasm. Cal was here, supporting my big day, but he hadn't opened back up to me yet—not all the way.

Zane noticed me and Elisabeth, eyebrow raised as he made his way toward us, cutting through the crowd of kids and volunteers.

"Zane," I said, "this is Elisabeth. Elisabeth, Zane. Zane's been helping me with Disney's Children. And Elisabeth..." I glanced over at her, struggling to think of any appropriate way to introduce her. She reddened, looking away as her tall frame curled and shrank in around itself, scared prey retreating back inside the shell. "Elisabeth lost someone close to her because of the attacks. So she came all the way from Oklahoma to be here tonight. To be with all of us."

"I'm sorry to hear that," Zane said, nodding at Elisabeth. "Glad you could make it." He still looked on alert, though, his shoulders rigid as he stepped closer to me. "Are you ready to start up again, Iris?" He tilted his head toward the rows of cameras behind us, capturing the performance for TV news outlets across the country. A bright digital ticker hung above them, calculating the fund-raising totals as donations were called in and made online. Just barely under one million dollars, and we were only halfway through the night.

"I'm ready," I said, grinning up at him. But then—"I almost forgot! I didn't want you to feel left out during the music stations."

"What do you mean?"

I peered out over the stage, scanning until my eyes found Ari. She was sitting by her drums with Ethan and Delia, laughing and clapping her hands as she watched two adorable little boys try out her beloved cymbals.

"Ari!" I yelled, waving her over. She winked and jumped up, disappearing behind the thick curtains.

"I have a surprise for you," I said to Zane, my palms suddenly slick with sweat, my heart racing.

"I don't do surprises." Zane grimaced, shaking his head. "They tend to be the bad kind."

"Not this one, I swear."

Ari broke through the crowd around us, a big black case cradled in her arms.

"Open it," I said, nudging Zane forward with my elbow.

He stood frozen for a beat, his eyes deeper and darker than ever as they drank me in.

"What did you go and do?" he asked softly, but he was smiling as he moved toward Ari. He popped the metal clasps and slowly opened the lid.

A guitar, the fresh glossy wood impossibly shiny under the blinding stage lights.

"It's my thank-you for everything," I said. I took a deep breath. "And I figured that since you're a part of this . . . then it's about time you start making music again, too."

Chapter Twenty-Four

"THIS IS REALLY happening tomorrow, right?" I asked Zane, bypassing the hello as soon as he'd answered his phone. I'd been waiting all day for him to be out of class, his final day at school before the trip. He'd gone back for the last few weeks, but I—I'd been keeping up on my own time, with both of my parents' help. It was easier that way. My orchestra instructor, Mr. Keeny, had even volunteered to come over for lessons, walking me through our performance songs. The best part of school had come to me.

"This is *really* happening," Zane said, laughing. I grinned, plunking down on my window ledge and leaning my cheek against the frosty pane.

"I know. Tomorrow. We're getting on a plane *tomorrow*." I sighed, the words still so shocking to hear out loud. "How was Zoey this morning? My mom said the meeting went well."

It had been her and my dad's idea entirely—arranging to become authorized foster parents for Zoey, with both of her biological parents off the grid for now. "I can't help but feel like you met those two for a reason," she'd said the day after the fund-raiser. "But I don't think Zane should be going at this alone. And I just wouldn't feel right sending her to a stranger."

Zane had taken a few days to agree. But he'd come around.

He'd gone with Zoey and my parents this morning to meet with the Office of Children and Family Services. The process had officially begun.

"Oh, she was bouncing around when we dropped her off at school afterward. Let's face it, I'm a decent enough big brother, maybe, on a good day anyway, but she needs more than that right now. Oh . . . and that reminds me." He paused, quiet for a moment. "My aunt and uncle called again today, begging for a second chance to take her in, but . . . no way. Maybe someday they can be in her life again, but one step at a time, you know? They need to prove they deserve it. Letting them come to the event was enough for right now."

"Completely," I said, my head thudding against the window as I nodded. "I'm just glad Zoey and Caleb will have each other while we're gone. I feel less like I'm abandoning him."

"Yeah, for real. They're a bizarre pair of friends. But I guess you and I are pretty bizarre, too. Never would have seen it coming."

Friends. We'd spent a lot of time together planning in the past few weeks—Zane and me, along with Ethan and Ari and Delia, who, not surprisingly, hadn't taken long to warm up to him once he let the real Zane show. And so far, friends was all we seemed to be. That kiss, that moment on the roof—it almost seemed like I'd dreamed it now. Zane was soft around me, sweet, but like a big brother. A big brother who would do anything to keep *both* of his little sisters safe.

"I'll see you tonight, then," he said. "I have some business I have to finish up now."

Business. The word crawled its way into the pit of my stomach. But whatever he was doing, it would end now, right? He'd be with me on the trip. Whatever associations he had here . . . they'd have to end. And maybe things would be different by the time he got back.

We hung up, and I rested the phone on the window ledge, staring out. The crowd gathered around the sidewalk was as big as ever today. Flowers and farewell banners and that same enormous glittering portrait. The prayer ribbons had now completely overtaken the gate—the iron covered in a rainbow of strings and cloth. People came from all over to tie them there; they'd come by to pray, reflect for a bit, and then move on, go about the rest of their days. There were flags now, too, emerald green with *Spero* written out in yellow swirly letters. Someone had started selling them after the fund-raiser, and I'd seen them out there fluttering every day since. I'd noticed a fair share of less-than-adoring signs, too—signs declaring that I was an impostor, that I had no right to be pretending I was any kind of miracle worker.

Overall, though, the more public I became, the more praise I received.

The Disney's Children event had been a huge success— and it wasn't even about the money, really, though we had made over four times what Angelica had projected. The real success, for me at least, was the *feeling.* The silence in the room at the last note of "Hear Me" . . . it was the loudest, fullest silence I'd ever heard in my life.

In the last two weeks since the fund-raiser, planning had been in full swing—the Disney's Children tour was happening. It was on. And I would be going along for the ride . . . with Zane. As soon as I'd mentioned that I was going on the trip, that it was really happening—and that there was more than enough money for a guest to join me—he'd insisted before I had a chance to ask. Zane was probably better off studying on the road with me anyway, and he had no parents or guardians to hold him back.

My mom would be coming, too, at least for the first few

stops, until we took a break for the holidays; we'd discuss the rest from there. My dad and my grandparents would stay at our house, taking care of Cal and Zoey.

Some of the kids from New York would be going on the first leg, joining up with kids in other cities—singing and playing Brinley's songs, and gradually adding in the new ones, too, the songs that had come out of the first fund-raiser. Songs that these kids would hopefully keep on writing. Only, I had convinced Angelica to change the name, convinced her that to move on, we had to let go a little first.

The Doves. We were the Doves now.

Doves, because the birds made such beautiful, haunting sounds. But more than that, because doves meant peace. And peace . . . peace was what we all needed.

As for the first stop of our tour, we were going back to the beginning, to where a number of the most critical victims and their families were still staying.

Orlando, Florida.

The realization flared through me again now, hot and blinding. I'd be seeing the ruins of Disney for myself.

I pushed the fear away as I stood. There was too much else to get done before I left.

I was tempted—as I was most days now—to run down and check the front stoop, to see if there'd been any other photos or clippings left behind. It had been a few days now. Better not to look, though, so I could still cling to my hope. Maybe we were all moving on. Slowly.

I took a deep breath and stared at my disheveled, upside-down room, the scattered piles of clothes thrown on top of my bed, wishing that I really *was* magical—that I could wave my arms and have everything neatly tucked and ready in my bag. But no, no such luck. No magic. Despite all of this, the fund-raiser's success, the good things still to come—I still knew that deep down I was just Iris Spero, plain and simple.

An ordinary girl, with an extraordinary beginning.

I was glad, though. I was glad it had been me.

A knock rattled the door, and I sighed, relieved to be able to put off packing a little longer.

"Hey, sweetie," my mom said, poking in her head. "Can I come in?"

"Yeah, of course," I said, sweeping clothes aside to make room for us on the bed.

She settled next to me, and I realized then that she was holding a book in her hands. I tilted my head to read the spine. *Immaculate.*

"What is . . . ?" I started to ask. But then—I knew.

"I had my book bound up for you, to take on the trip. I finally named it, too, after all these years." She smiled down at it, at the cover—a painting of a pregnant girl, staring out the window into open green fields. The girl . . . she looked so much like me.

"Where did you get that?" I lifted the book out of her hands to examine it more closely. "It's not a photograph, right? It's a painting. But she's you, isn't she?"

"Your dad painted this for me. My birthday present the year it was all happening. When he gave this to me, it was the moment I knew . . . I knew he was it for me. That he saw me in a way no one else ever could."

"I didn't know Dad was this good," I said, running my fingers down the lines of my mom's wavy brown hair. "I'll have to show Delia. She'll be proud of him."

"I've had the painting tucked away in my office, with a lot of other things that I was keeping until now. Until you knew. So we took a picture and used it for the cover, because I wanted you to have all of this with you. The words, the painting. The leaf, tucked inside. In case you ever need a reminder when you're gone. A reminder of everything that happened. Everything that you are."

I nodded, already flipping through the pages. I didn't realize what I was looking for exactly, not until I found it. The night she'd met Iris, the night I had begun. Those words. *That night I dreamed in bursts of light and explosions of colors like magical fireworks that would put even Disney World's most spectacular displays to complete shame.*

"Thanks," I whispered, reaching for her hand. "I'm glad you're coming with me, at least for the first few weeks."

"I'm glad, too, sweetie. And Zane . . ." My mom paused, her lips twitching up at the edges. "I'm happy he'll be with us, too," she said, squeezing my hand. "He seems like a solid guy, and I trust your instincts. Dad and Pop and Nanny will take good care of Zoey while we're gone."

"I love you, Mom." I leaned in, resting my head against her chest and breathing in deep.

"I love you, too, Iris. And I am so proud of you. So very, very proud. I knew you were always hugely special— but *this*. Even I'm astounded by how amazing you are."

I hugged her tighter, letting the rhythm of her heart lull me as I listened to it beat softly beneath her thin sweater.

"You are my hope, Iris Spero. You are my greatest hope of all."

I needed one more trip to the park before I left—one more chance to see Mikki again. I wanted to hear her say that I was doing the right thing. I wanted confirmation. Validation. Maybe she'd find me later, appear out of no- where like she had in the past with my mom. But the park was where it had all begun, and it seemed only right to at least try to say good-bye. I would be back soon for Christmas, but would she still be there? What if her job was already done?

It was dark outside already, though it wasn't that late—only a little after eight o'clock. I had time for a quick walk, some fresh air, and could still be back with plenty of time to finish packing before bed. I walked down the steps quietly, slipping out through the back door without saying any good-byes. I wanted to do this alone.

I shivered as I passed through the park gates, pulling the hood of my thick down jacket closer around my face. As I came around the bend of the meadow, my chest ached with disappointment. The bench was empty. The park was empty, too, unnervingly so. The cold must have driven people home early. I sighed, my breath making a cloud of white in the air around me. I looked up at the moon, nearly full, so bright and so out of reach.

"I know the truth, Mikki. You were her all along, weren't you? Iris. You were here to help me, just long enough until I could sort it out on my own. You led me to Zane and Zoey, and then you disappeared."

No response. Not that I expected any, of course. All I heard instead was the wind rustling the branches above me, and cars driving along the park's western edge.

I sat down on the bench, my eyes closed as I took slow, deep breaths, letting the cool night air burn through my lungs. I loved late autumn and winter in New York—loved the electric charge of such extreme cold. It reminded me just how alive I was, my body warm and buzzing with energy.

A branch snapped behind me, pulling me out of my daze. My whole body tensed, ready to lunge into action.

Silence again.

You're fine, Iris. No one's here. It's time to go, time to get home and finish packing . . .

"I hoped I'd have time to see you again. Before your grand world tour starts." The voice hissed from the dark circle of trees behind me. I jumped from the bench, swiveling my body midair so that I was facing the shadows.

"Who-o-o's there?" I stuttered, my teeth shaking so hard I momentarily wondered if they would shatter themselves entirely.

A man emerged from the shadows, tall and hulking under his heavy parka. He took another step, crossing into the ring of light spilling out from the streetlamp above, and I knew.

Kyle Bennett. That desperate, hopeful Kyle from before was gone. This Kyle was carved out and hollow, nothing left but the rage seething out in waves across the meadow.

"Kyle," I said, fighting to take even just a tiny breath. "Did you follow me?"

"S-sure did, Iris-s," he slurred, sneering in the dim light. He was drunk, I realized, the whiff of sweet whiskey hitting me as he edged even closer. "Had to give you a proper send-off before you head to Florida. I left you some little presents at your door, too. I hope you got them all. I still just have one question I need to ask, though."

He paused, his eyes glinting as he studied me.

"What?" I asked, a whisper. "What is it?"

"Why not my daughter? Your fancy show here, your fancy trip coming up—you're just helping people left and right. People can't stop thanking you for all the good you do their kids. But why not mine? Why not my Ella? I already lost Parker . . ."

I took a few wobbly steps back, desperate for any distance I could get until I figured a way out of this—a way to talk him down somehow. "Kyle . . . I'm sorry we ignored you. I was scared when I first found out. And it was too late by the time I'd started . . . started doing anything. But I couldn't have saved her. I couldn't have done what doctors couldn't even do."

"Then what good is it that you came from some kind of pregnant virgin? Was your mom just a whore after all? Huh? Tell me that. If you can't fucking make a miracle happen, then why are you going around pretending to be some kind of god here on earth with all us lowly nobodies? You're just a big lie, Iris Spero. You're just a big nothing like the rest of us. And I'm sick of hearing people say that you're anything but what you really are. It's about time someone taught you a lesson for all these lies you're telling." He reached into his pocket, pulling out his hand to wave a bottle in the air, a clear, empty whiskey bottle glowing under the moonlight.

"No, please, no—" I had tried to run backward, afraid to turn away from him, but my ankle caught and twisted behind me. I crashed to the ground, pain throbbing up my calf.

He hovered just above, his face covered in shadows, bottle raised over his head.

I kicked my legs out in frantic circles, hoping I could knock him back just enough that I could push myself up and run. My foot landed hard against his shin, making my ankle burn even hotter. He was unfazed, though, leaning in closer.

"Help me!" I screamed. "Somebody help me!"

The glass shattered against my forehead. The moonlight above flickered, my vision bursting with bright shooting stars. The glass hit again, harder. I tensed my entire body, my nerves, my muscles crying out in pain, waiting for another blow.

But it didn't come.

"What the hell, kid?" Kyle yelled, his voice sounding anxious, much less sure of himself. "What are you doing here?"

"Get away from my sister!"

Cal.

I fought to push myself up with my elbows, but my head was throbbing and swirling, a thousand times too heavy to lift. I gave up. I could feel tears now and blood, warm and heavy, streaming down the sides of my face.

"Cal, run away!" I screamed. "Get away from him!"

"Fuck," Kyle muttered, pacing around me in circles, close enough that I could see him along the edges of my limited vision. "This isn't how it was supposed to happen. This isn't . . ."

Cal jumped between us, his back to me as he faced Kyle.

"I already called the police," he said. "They're going to be here any minute." He sounded so strong and brave, so old. My tears spilled out even faster, blurring my eyes. It hurt too much to wipe them away.

Kyle didn't respond. But I heard his footsteps, messy and frenetic, as he ran away from us, out of the meadow and onto the path that would lead him to the city streets.

"Iris!" Cal cried, finally turning to face me. He flopped himself onto the ground, his hands desperately swiping at the blood pooling around my face. "Can I call the police from your phone? I lied—they aren't coming, not yet. I saw you leaving the house and I followed. I'm sorry, I just got so scared about you being alone. But I didn't have time to grab my phone."

"My pocket," I said, wincing as I tilted my head to the left side of my pants.

I gritted my teeth as Cal made the call, determined to stay awake. It would be so easy to drift away, though, to just close my eyes for a few minutes and . . .

Cal shook me. "Don't leave me! I'm so scared, Iris, I'm so scared and I need you to stay with me, okay?" I could hear the operator, still on the line, as the phone fell to the grass.

"Okay," I said, latching on tight as his warm, sweaty hand slipped into mine. "I'm not going anywhere, buddy. And thank you. For following me. For saving me."

"You can't always be the one saving people," he said, kneeling in closer to rest his head on my chest.

Sirens wailed in the distance. Louder. Closer.

"Sometimes *you* need to be saved, too."

I was alone in the hospital room when I opened my eyes, though I could hear my parents' voices spilling in from the hallway, just beyond. A TV monitor was hanging from the ceiling in front of my bed, the news playing and a reporter—a reporter standing in front of our house. I squinted to see the screen more clearly, but the bright sterile lights sliced through my vision. I shut my eyes again, my head throbbing. I focused in on the reporter's voice, tuning out the passing murmurs from the hallway.

"We're still waiting for more details, but a source has revealed that after her little brother appeared at the scene, Iris Spero's attacker fled Prospect Park. He reportedly turned himself in to the NYPD just one hour later. It's unclear at this time how serious Spero's injuries are, but many are wondering—now that such a serious threat has been made against her life—will this change Spero's travel plans? She was set to fly out to Florida today in fact, for the next fund-raiser event with the Doves, the newly renamed Disney's Children organization, now the largest Disney survivors network in the country. Spero proved herself . . ."

The reporter continued on, but my head ached too much to take in any more details.

"Mom?" I croaked, straining to make my voice loud enough to be heard in the hallway. "Dad? Caleb?"

My dad appeared first, his face like one of those masks with two expressions at once—grinning with relief on one side, grim with terror on the other.

"Sweetie, thank God!" he exclaimed, rushing over to my bed. "You're awake. Your mom just went to grab us some coffees, but she'll be back in a few minutes. That was a nasty hit you got." He reached out, his hand stopping just short of touching my forehead, which I now realized was covered in a thick swaddling of bandages.

"Kyle Bennett, he . . . he turned himself in?" I asked, needing to be certain that the reporter had gotten that part of the story correct.

"Yes. Showed up bawling at the police station almost straight after he left the park. A drunken mess. He said he was sorry, that he hadn't meant to take it so far, but . . . but he did. He took it way too goddamn far. We're lucky you just have a concussion and some cuts. When I think about it, you at the park, him showing up like that . . ." He broke into a sob, pressing a fist tight against his mouth. We stared at each other in silence for a moment, a prickling cloud of unease seeping into the air around us. "If Caleb hadn't been following you, scaring him out of his rage . . . Jesus, Iris. I can't even think about it."

"I'm sorry," I whispered.

"You shouldn't have gone out alone. It's not safe for you right now. Too many zealots out there—on both ends of the spectrum—who would be all too happy to follow you around at night. All of this, it's making me think . . . I hate to say this, knowing how excited you are, but maybe you going out on this tour right now, maybe it's not the best idea for anyone. I know that you have people counting on you, but your safety is most important. People are bound to get angry, Iris. And it's not your fault. It's just the nature of this whole thing. People are happy when they feel like you're helping them, but as soon as it doesn't go their way . . ."

"So you think I should just cancel? Back out on all of this?" My voice sounded high-pitched and tinny, unrecognizable to my own ears.

"The kids . . . the Doves, they could go without you, no? People could still come to see them perform. It wouldn't be the same, maybe . . . but what good will you be to anyone if you get hurt? I hate to say it, but it's the truth, sweetie. All I care about right now is keeping you safe."

"I could go." I turned to see Caleb standing in the doorway, a sad, thoughtful frown on his washed-out face. "I can keep watching out for her."

"That's sweet of you, buddy, but you need to stay here with us. I'm keeping you out of this as much as possible, okay?"

"I have Mom. And Zane." I kept my lips in a careful line as I clenched my teeth, trying my hardest not to show just how much pain I was in. My head was thudding with tension, as if it was right in the middle of a heavy metal vise, some old-fashioned torture device that was proving just how much I could or couldn't take. But I couldn't let my dad know that—I couldn't add any more fuel to his argument.

"I'm glad your mom is going, but that doesn't feel like enough. And we barely even know Zane, sweetie."

"I know him, Dad. I *know* him."

"*Jesse.*"

All three of us turned to the door. My mom stood framed in the center, her cool blue eyes narrowing sharply on my father.

My dad rose from the seat, walking toward her in a straight, perfect line, as if her eyes were somehow reeling him in from across the room.

She reached out, placing her palms on his chest as she stared up at him. "This is Iris's decision to make. I love you, but I need you to understand that. We both want to keep her safe. We will both *always* want to keep her safe. But she's not meant to be hidden away. She isn't just ours anymore."

She lifted one hand, brushed it along his cheek, words and emotions and sensations I couldn't begin to touch passing between them. Their gaze burned, a heat that seemed to radiate, ignite the whole room around them. *Mina and Jesse.* I thought of them, as they'd been in my mom's pages, the powerful, natural bond that had seemed to exist from the very first moment at Frankie's—even if it had taken my mom some time to fully recognize what she'd found. Watching them now, I realized how much I wanted that someday.

My mom broke away and turned toward me.

"There will always be risks, Iris. But there will be good, too, I'm sure. It's only up to you how much you can take on. Not your father, not me. You."

Was she telling me to go? To go on with the trip, regardless of the other Kyle Bennetts I might have to face— all the many people I would inevitably disappoint along the way? And was I ready to walk back out there? The horror of the night before was still so fresh. Stumbling, crashing to the ground, Kyle leaning over me, that bottle glistening in the moonlight . . .

What if Caleb hadn't come? What if I really *had* been entirely alone?

I shuddered, closing my eyes as I rocked back and forth to the pounding inside my head.

My mom spoke again, this time her voice sounding closer, hovering near my bed.

"This is your life, Iris. It's up to you how best to live it."

Ascent

I GLANCED BACK at the car as I stepped up to the old wraparound front porch. My mom blew me a kiss, her face leaning in close against the window.

There were two cars parked in the driveway. They were home, then, probably. I took a deep breath and crossed over the faded floral welcome mat. There were flowerpots on either side, though whatever plants had grown in them had long before died. Now there was just dry, cracked soil, decayed leaves that had blown in from the yard. The pots had been forgotten.

I lifted my hand, paused for a beat, a last flash of hesitation. I'd come this far. I'd come all the way to Green Hill, where my parents had grown up. The town was exactly as my mom had described it in her book: one bustling Main Street at its center, with houses becoming sparser as we drove farther along winding green roads that cut through fields and woods. We'd made a detour first, stopping on the street outside my grandparents' old farm-house—the white plaster walls and red shutters and two matching stone chimneys, the scene that looked almost exactly as it had in the opening footage of my dad's video. We had stepped out of the car for a moment, watching the sunlight sparkle along the windows, breathing in the cool breeze that washed over us, the scents of grass and pine and dirt, a hint of wood smoke. I had closed my eyes and tried to imagine how my mom would have felt at seven-teen, with the idea of me, the reality, still so fresh and raw. I hugged her, and then we had climbed back into the car.

As glad as I was to see her old home, it wasn't the rea-son we'd come.

I steadied my breath and knocked hard against the heavy wooden door, three times.

A minute passed, and I knocked again. I could feel the steam leaking out of me. All the anxiety, the painstak-ing planning about what I would say—it had all been for nothing.

Just as I started to turn back toward the car, the door cracked open.

Kyle Bennett stepped out, dressed in a stained white T-shirt and too-baggy sweatpants. He looked much smaller than he had nearly two weeks before, that night at the park. Ten days, ten nights of dreaming about that moment, over and over again. My parents had sentenced me to bed rest to fully recover—it had left far too much time for my imagination to run wild.

Kyle's eyes widened when he realized who was on his porch, his mouth gaping open.

"What are you . . . ?"

"I came to say that I've decided I won't be pressing charges." The words were clear and firm. I was proud of myself for that.

He blinked a few times, his eyes looking dazed, as if he wasn't sure any of this was actually happening. "You're . . . you're not?"

I fought my instinct to look away, kept my gaze firmly locked on his. "No. Maybe I'm crazy for letting you go. I mean, you *did* smash a bottle over my head. I can never forget that. But . . . I also can't even begin to imagine what it must be like—what you've been going through in the past few months. It doesn't excuse what you did, but I understand why you're so angry. No one deserves what happened to you and your family."

"I still don't get it," he said, shaking his head. "Why are you really doing this?"

"Because sometimes . . . sometimes forgiving is just easier. I need to move on. My forgiveness might not mean anything to you, but that's okay. It means something to *me*."

I'd certainly thought about sending him to jail, about

punishing him for the pain—physical and emotional— he'd caused me. But I already felt sorry enough about Ella; I couldn't have saved her, but maybe I could have made things just a little easier for her, for Kyle and his wife, if I'd visited. Or maybe not. I would never know now. But either way, I wasn't sure I could live with myself if I made him suffer even more than he already had. Two kids, gone. His family broken. And I still had everything. Forgiving him was just as much for my benefit as it was for his. Maybe more so. It was time to go forward, not back. Clear conscience.

"Thank you," he said, the words hitching as his whole face collapsed. "Thank you."

His eyes looked past me, noticing the car waiting out front. Noticing my mom.

He lifted his hand slowly, waving at her. I turned to the car as she waved back.

I started down the path, walking away from Kyle Bennett for good.

"Okay," I said, pulling the car door shut as I settled into the passenger seat. "That's done. Now that I can breathe again, I'm actually kind of hungry. I was thinking . . . maybe we could go see if Frankie's still exists?"

My mom beamed at me as she turned the key in the ignition. "You got it, sweetie."

My trip with the Doves had been delayed, of course, thanks to Kyle. I'd told Angelica they could do the Orlando show without me, but she'd insisted on waiting. As soon as I had the doctor's okay—it was back on. All pieces moving ahead as planned.

We said our good-byes at the airport. They were all there, with hugs and tears and notes for me to read later, after I was up in the air. My dad and Caleb, my grandparents and Aunt Hannah, Ari, Delia, Ethan. And Zoey.

Zoey was the hardest to say good-bye to—we'd been the Musketeers, she and Zane and I, for those first few days. Those strange, terrible, magnificent days. Days that had changed everything.

"You're coming to the L.A. show next week with my dad and Cal," I reminded her, crouched down to her height, my arms hugging her skinny shoulders. "It'll go by so fast, I promise. And then it'll be Christmas soon enough." I pulled back and kissed her on the cheek, my eyes drawn toward those tiny music notes along her jaw. *Thank you, Brinley.*

I gave everybody one last hug, watching as Zane followed behind me. I couldn't help but smile when it came time for him and Ari to say good-bye. She gave him that trademark knifelike purple stare, a look that undoubtedly said, *You mess with her and I'll mess with you.* Not even the toughest boy in school was immune to Ari's wrath. She pulled him in for a hug then, gripping him as hard as she'd gripped me. He'd passed her test.

When I got to Delia, she pulled out another small painting—it was the night at Carnegie Hall, the most abstract work I'd ever seen her do. Bright, wild splashes of every color spiraled out from a sea of hazy, indistinct faces. Sprinkles of rainbow glitter and glossy black music notes overlaid the whole image, making everything pop and shine and sing. I tossed out all the magazines from my carry-on bag to make space.

My dad was last in line, and my mom and I descended on him at the same time, our arms tangling up together in a beautiful knot.

"Thank you," I said, the words muted against my dad's thick black wool sweater. He'd dug up an old green newsy cap today—a cap that, according to my mom's book, he'd insisted on wearing every day back in high school. It suited him even now, faded and slightly misshapen from years of being buried in his closet. "Thank you for believing in me. For trusting. For raising me exactly the way you did. I have a feeling that Iris— the other Iris—she'd be proud. Of both of you." I felt my dad's hand clamp even more tightly around my back.

The words stung a bit on my tongue. I meant what I'd

said, though I still couldn't help but resent the fact that Mikki had never come back. Not even at the park, with Kyle. Cal, not Mikki, had saved me.

With just one backward glance and a final wave, Mom and Zane and I started toward our gate. I was in a daze for most of the wait, the boarding, the final moments before takeoff. I thought about the life I was leaving, the life ahead—so many things that I couldn't predict or foresee. I'd known, though, from the moment my mom had given me her blessing at the hospital, I couldn't back down. This was my path. This was where I was supposed to be. On this plane, right here, right now.

It wouldn't be an easy life, but it was *my* life.

I wouldn't run again. I wouldn't hide.

"Are you okay, Iris?" Zane asked, nudging me over the armrest.

"I'm fine," I said, peeling my eyes away from the window, the view of the plane lot, and turning to face him. "It's just been a long day. I don't like good-byes."

He nodded, letting that be enough. "I've never been on a plane before," he said, smiling shyly as if he was a little ashamed to admit it. I'd guessed as much—and it was probably why my mom had insisted on Zane and me taking the two seats together, winking as she handed over the tickets. She was a few rows in front of us on the opposite side of the plane, already tapping away intently on her keyboard. "So if I get scared, I might need to . . . you know . . . hold your hand."

I grinned at that, wrapping my fingers around his. That touch, palm to palm, made me shiver. "Don't worry. I have your back."

"You know, Iris," he said quietly, leaning in so that only I could hear, "I should say a few things now, before the plane takes off. Not that I'm superstitious or anything, but still . . . better to put everything out there now, right? So, uh, firstly, when I go off during the day, doing *work* . . . I'm not out dealing or scamming or anything like that, whatever you might have thought. I . . . I work at the place I got sent after everything went down with Tony. Juvie. I'm a janitor part-time for the cash, but my main job is training to be a counselor. I talk to kids like me, little punks who are so damn angry about everything. I let them talk. I listen. It's what I want to do, after school, anyway. Work with kids like me. Help them figure out a different way. If I hadn't had Zoey to keep me straight . . ." He shook his head, wincing. "Scares the hell out of me to think about."

"Why didn't you tell me sooner?" I asked, squeezing his hand tighter.

"It's lame that I didn't just say it, I know. But I'm so used to people always expecting the worst of me . . . sometimes it's just easier to let them assume, you know? It's too much effort to always be trying to prove I'm the nice guy. Let people think what they want."

I smiled, relief swelling through me, warm and giddy and wonderful. "Don't worry, I already kind of suspected you were much sweeter and more innocent than you let on. And I think it's awesome, for the record, what you're doing. So . . . that's one confession down. What's next?"

Zane looked away, his eyes shifting to our hands clasped on the armrest. "That day . . . the day you said . . . *you* know . . . that I deserve love and all that." He coughed, and I felt the sudden heat of his palm searing through mine. "I freaked out because I knew you were wrong. I'm not sure I deserve anyone's love, besides Zoey's anyway, and only because she's my sister. She's blood. And I sure as hell don't think I deserve yours. You're way too good for me, Iris Spero. You deserve someone better . . . but even still. I want to try. I really want to try. For *you*."

"You don't have to try anymore," I said, my voice steady even as every other part of me was screaming with happiness. "You've already more than proved it. I don't care what mistakes you've made in the past. You have your scars, and I have mine." I reached up instinctively, pressing my fingers against the bandage on my forehead, the still healing cut that would probably leave a permanent mark. Zoey had drawn music notes with a Sharpie there that morning, dark black swirls that mirrored hers. "You need to forgive yourself, Zane. Because, trust me, you deserve so much good. You've earned it."

A grin broke out on his face, and I grinned back. We may have still been firmly on the ground, but I was already in the clouds, the brilliant sun shining through, beaming down on us, just us.

I leaned in closer, closer, my lips grazing his. Just as I felt him move forward, his hand brushing against the side of my face—

"Excuse me, do you both have your seat belts fastened?"

I jerked away from Zane, my eyes fluttering up to the flight attendant in the aisle next to us. She was a tired-looking gray-haired woman, snapping her gum loudly as she pointed at the seat belt light on the overhead dashboard.

I looked down, grabbing for both ends of the belt.

"Got it," I said, smiling obediently up at her.

But the gray-haired woman was gone.

Instead, there *she* was—her coppery braids pulled back in a neat bun, those bright green eyes laughing at me.

Mikki winked.

"Almost time for takeoff."

ACKNOWLEDGMENTS

Grateful.

I've always considered myself to be a grateful person, or at least I've tried to be (we all have our days!). I was aware of just how lucky I am to have my brilliant family and friends, my unfailing support system.

But writing books—first *Immaculate,* and now *Transcendent*—has made me realize just how ridiculously blessed I really am. The gratitude I know now blows me away. It humbles and inspires me daily. Every single one of you who sent me a kind note, came to a reading, posted about these books online or shared them with a friend: thank you. You are amazing, and I appreciate your effort more than I could ever put into words. You are the reason I write.

Jill Grinberg, thank you for your endless wisdom, your uncannily keen, razor-sharp insight that still leaves me in awe after more than six years of sharing an office together. Your unfailingly tough but always excellent, always necessary questions made this story infinitely better. Thank you for all that you do, and for teaching me new things—every day.

And to the entire JGLM team—I feel so beyond lucky that I get to spend forty plus hours a week in the presence of such greatness. Cheryl Pientka, your passion for books radiates, and I am so very glad to have a reader like you—a fierce warrior who spreads her love all across the globe. And Denise St. Pierre, you are truly a wonder woman, and while I wish that I could retroactively add you to the *Immaculate* acknowledgements, I'll have to just thank you doubly now. (Thank you. And really, again, thank you.)

Leila Sales, I can't even comprehend what this book would be without you. (I mean, c'mon, Iris not a musician? What?! Not possible.) You took the bare bones and blew in heart and depth and meaning. You saw the story I wanted and needed this to be before I could see any of it for myself. Thank you for believing in this book from day one, when it was just a terribly vague one-page synopsis. Your faith—it brought *Transcendent* to life.

Thank you to the entire Viking team—I appreciate all you do, always. My book would be nowhere, nothing without your support and dedication.

Pastor Kork Moyer, thank you for reading and sharing with me your vast wisdom and experience—for ensuring that this story stayed true and respectful to those who mattered most. I am in awe of the work you do, and honored to have passed the test.

To everyone in the Upper Perkiomen Valley community who has come out to readings, who has supported me in my writing, I am so appreciative, and so proud. I may live in Brooklyn these days, but my heart will always be in our lovely Valley.

And to my dear, dear friends, the loves of my life, thank you for cheering every step of the way, the good days and the less than good days. Thank you for reading early drafts, for brainstorming plot solutions and titles and covers, for letting me vent and for excusing me when I flake on plans so I can hit the next deadline. To every last one of you—thank you, always, for being there, for being you, for keeping me sane.

To my family—my wonderful extended family, old and new—thank you for the nonstop barrage of love and encouragement. Peter, you're a fabulous brother and an equally fabulous website designer; and Lauren, I will never (ever) forget our marathon phone call discussing what in the world Iris could possibly do to help the Disney kids in some way.

Danny, I remember finishing the very first draft of this a week or so after our first date. You were supportive even then, barely knowing me, texting and rallying me on to the finish line. And in the two years and three days since (happy belated anniversary!), you have continued to inspire me every single day. You make me want to write, think, be bigger and better. Always.

And lastly, Mom and Dad, thank you. Thank you for letting me grumble through my writing retreat weekends in Hoppenville, for reading every draft, for telling everyone you meet (and I do mean everyone) about my books, for loving me so unconditionally with every breath you take. I believe in myself because you believe in me. Thank you—today, always, forever.